Patricia Cornwell sold her f⬛⬛⬛⬛⬛⬛⬛⬛⬛⬛⬛⬛⬛⬛⬛
as a computer analyst at the ⬛⬛⬛⬛⬛⬛⬛⬛⬛⬛⬛⬛⬛⬛⬛
in Richmond, Virginia. It would go ⬛⬛⬛⬛⬛⬛⬛⬛⬛,
Creasey, Anthony, and Macavity awards as well as the French
Prix du Roman d'Aventure prize – the first book ever to claim
all these distinctions in a single year. To date, Cornwell's books
have sold some 100 million copies in thirty-six languages in
over 120 countries, winning Cornwell the Sherlock Award for
best detective created by an American author, the Gold Dagger
Award, the RBA Thriller Award, and the Medal of Chevalier of
the Order of Arts and Letters for her contributions to literary and
artistic development.

Though Cornwell now lives in Boston, she was born in Miami
and grew up in Montreat, North Carolina. After earning her
degree in English from Davidson College in 1979, she began
working at the *Charlotte Observer*, then moving to a job with the
Office of the Chief Medical Examiner of Virginia – a post she
would later bestow upon the fictional Kay Scarpetta.

When not writing from her Boston home, Patricia tirelessly
researches cutting-edge forensic technologies to include in her
work. Her interests span outside the literary: Patricia co-founded
of the Conservation Scientist Chair at the Harvard University
Art Museums. She appears as a forensic consultant on CNN
and serves as a member of Harvard-affiliated McLean Hospital's
National Council, where she advocates for psychiatric research.
She's helped fund the ICU at Cornell's Animal Hospital, the
scientific study of a Confederate submarine, the archaeological
excavation of Jamestown, and a variety of law enforcement
charities.

Also by Patricia Cornwell

THE SCARPETTA NOVELS

ANDY BRAZIL SERIES

WIN GARANO SERIES

NONFICTION

BIOGRAPHY

OTHER WORKS

Patricia Cornwell

All That Remains

sphere

SPHERE

First published in Great Britain in 1992 by Little Brown and Company
Paperback edition published in 1993 by Warner Books
This reissue published in 2010 by Sphere
This edition published in 2020 by Sphere

1 3 5 7 9 10 8 6 4 2

A CIP catalogue record for this book is available from the British Library.

ISBN 978-0-7515-8259-8

Printed and bound in Great Britain by Clays Ltd, Elcograf S.p.A.

Papers used by Sphere are from well-managed forests
and other responsible sources.

Sphere
An imprint of
Little, Brown Book Group
Carmelite House
50 Victoria Embankment
London EC4Y 0DZ

An Hachette UK Company
www.hachette.co.uk

www.littlebrown.co.uk

1

Saturday, the last day of August, I started work before dawn. I did not witness mist burning off the grass or the sky turning brilliant blue. Steel tables were occupied by bodies all morning, and there are no windows in the morgue. Labor Day weekend had begun with a bang of car crashes and gunfire in the city of Richmond.

It was two o'clock in the afternoon when I finally returned to my West End home and heard Bertha mopping in the kitchen. She cleaned for me every Saturday and knew from past instruction not to bother with the phone, which had just begun to ring.

"I'm not here," I said loudly as I opened the refrigerator.

Bertha stopped mopping. "It was ringing a minute ago," she said. "Rang a few minutes before that, too. Same man."

"No one's home," I repeated.

"Whatever you say, Dr. Kay." The mop moved across the floor again.

I tried to ignore the disembodied answering machine message intruding upon the sun-washed kitchen. The Hanover tomatoes I took for granted during the summer I began to hoard with the approach of fall. There were only three left. Where was the chicken salad?

A beep was followed by the familiar male voice. "Doc? It's Marino . . ."

Oh, Lord, I thought, shoving the refrigerator door shut with a hip. Richmond homicide detective Pete Marino had been on the street since midnight, and I had just seen him in the morgue as I was picking bullets out of one of his cases. He was supposed to be on his way to Lake Gaston for what was left of a weekend of fishing. I was looking forward to working in my yard.

"I've been trying to get you, am heading out. You'll have to try my pager . . ."

Marino's voice sounded urgent as I snatched up the receiver.

"I'm here."

"That you or your goddam machine?"

"Take a guess," I snapped.

"Bad news. They found another abandoned car. New Kent, the Sixty-four rest stop, westbound. Benton just got hold of me—"

"Another couple?" I interrupted, my plans for the day forgotten.

"Fred Cheney, white male, nineteen. Deborah Harvey, white female, nineteen. Last seen around eight last night

2

when they drove off from the Harveys' Richmond house, on their way to Spindrift."

"And the car's in the *westbound* lane?" I inquired, for Spindrift, North Carolina, is three and a half hours east of Richmond.

"Yo. Appears they was heading in the opposite direction, back into the city. A trooper found the car, a Jeep Cherokee, about an hour ago. No sign of the kids."

"I'm leaving now," I told him.

Bertha had not stopped mopping, but I knew she had picked up every word.

"Be on my way soon as I finish up in here," she assured me. "I'll lock up and set the alarm. Don't you worry, Dr. Kay."

Fear was running along my nerves as I grabbed my purse and hurried out to my car.

There were four couples so far. Each had disappeared, eventually to be found murdered within a fifty-mile radius of Williamsburg.

The cases, dubbed by the press as The Couple Killings, were inexplicable, and no one seemed to have a clue or credible theory, not even the FBI and its Violent Criminal Apprehension Program, or VICAP, which featured a national database run on an artificial intelligence computer capable of connecting missing persons with unidentified bodies and linking serial crimes. After the first couple's bodies were found more than two years ago, a VICAP regional team, comprising FBI Special Agent Benton Wesley and veteran Richmond homicide detective Pete

Marino, was invited by local police to assist. Another couple would disappear, then two more. In each instance, by the time VICAP could be notified, by the time the National Crime Information Center, or NCIC, could even wire descriptions to police departments across America, the missing teenagers were already dead and decomposing in woods somewhere.

Turning off the radio, I passed through a tollbooth and picked up speed on I-64 East. Images, voices suddenly came back to me. Bones and rotted clothing scattered with leaves. Attractive, smiling faces of missing teenagers printed in the newspapers, and bewildered, distraught families interviewed on television and calling me on the phone.

"I'm so sorry about your daughter."

"Please tell me how my baby died. Oh, God, did she suffer?"

"Her cause of death is undetermined, Mrs. Bennett. There's nothing else I can tell you at this time."

"What do you mean you *don't know?*"

"All that remains is his bones, Mr. Martin. When soft tissue is gone, gone with it is any possible injury . . ."

"I don't want to hear your medical bullshit! I want to know what killed my boy! The cops are asking about drugs! My boy's never been drunk in his life, much less taken drugs! You hear me, lady? He's dead, and they're making him out to be some sort of punk . . ."

"CHIEF MEDICAL EXAMINER BAFFLED: Dr. Kay Scarpetta Unable to Tell Cause of Death."

Undetermined.

Over and over again. Eight young people.

It was awful. It was, in fact, unprecedented for me.

Every forensic pathologist has undetermined cases, but I had never had so many that appeared to be related.

I opened the sunroof and my spirits were lifted somewhat by the weather. The temperature was in the low eighties, leaves would be turning soon. It was only in the fall and spring that I did not miss Miami. Richmond summers were just as hot, without benefit of ocean breezes to sweep the air clean. The humidity was horrible, and in winter I fared no better, for I do not like the cold. But spring and fall were intoxicating. I drank in the change, and it went straight to my head.

The I-64 rest stop in New Kent County was exactly thirty-one miles from my house. It could have been any rest stop in Virginia, with picnic tables, grills and wooden trash barrels, brick-enclosed bathrooms and vending machines, and newly planted trees. But there was not a traveler or a truck driver in sight, and police cars were everywhere.

A trooper, hot and unsmiling in his blue-gray uniform, walked toward me as I parked near the ladies' room.

"I'm sorry, ma'am," he said, leaning close to my open window. "This rest area's closed today. I'm going to have to ask you to drive on."

"Dr. Kay Scarpetta," I identified myself, switching off the ignition. "The police asked me to come."

"For what purpose, ma'am?"

"I'm the chief medical examiner," I replied.

As he looked me over, I could see the skeptical glint in his eyes. I supposed I did not look particularly "chiefly."

Dressed in a stone-washed denim skirt, pink oxford cloth shirt, and leather walking shoes, I was without the accouterments of authority, including my state car, which was in the state garage awaiting new tires. At a glance, I was a not-so-young yuppie running errands in her dark gray Mercedes, a distracted ash-blonde en route to the nearest shopping mall.

"I'll need some identification."

Digging inside my purse, I produced a thin black wallet and displayed my brass medical examiner's shield, then handed over my driver's license, both of which he studied for a long moment. I sensed he was embarrassed.

"Just leave your car here, Dr. Scarpetta. The folks you're looking for are in back." He pointed in the direction of the parking area for trucks and buses. "Have a nice one," he added inanely, stepping away.

I followed a brick walk. When I rounded the building and passed beneath the shade of trees, I was greeted by several more police cars, a tow truck with light bar flashing, and at least a dozen men in uniforms and plain clothes. I did not see the red Jeep Cherokee until I was almost upon it. Midway along the exit ramp, it was well off the pavement in a dip and obscured by foliage. Two-door, it was coated with a film of dust. When I looked in the driver's window I could see that the beige leather interior was very clean, the backseat neatly packed with various items of luggage, a slalom ski, a coiled yellow nylon ski rope, and a red-and-white plastic ice chest. Keys dangled from the ignition. Windows were partly rolled down. Depressed tire tracks

leading from the pavement were clearly visible in the sloping grass, the front chrome grille nudged up against a
clump of pines.

Marino was talking to a thin, blond man, someone he
introduced as Jay Morrell with the state police, whom I did
not know. He seemed to be in charge.

"Kay Scarpetta," I volunteered, since Marino identified me
only as "Doc."

Morrell fixed dark green Ray Bans on me and nodded. Out
of uniform and sporting a mustache that was little more than
teenage fuzz, he exuded the all-business bravado I associated
with investigators brand new on the job.

"Here's what we know so far." He was glancing around
nervously. "The Jeep belongs to Deborah Harvey, and she
and her boyfriend, uh, Fred Cheney, left the Harveys' residence last night at approximately eight P.M. They were
heading to Spindrift, where the Harvey family owns a beach
house."

"Was Deborah Harvey's family home when the couple left
Richmond?" I inquired.

"No, ma'am." He briefly turned his shades my way. "They
were already at Spindrift, had left earlier in the day. Deborah
and Fred wanted to go in a separate car because they planned
to return to Richmond on Monday. Both of them are soph-
omores at Carolina, and needed to come back early to get
ready to return to school."

Marino explained as he got out his cigarettes, "Right before
they left the Harvey house last night, they called up Spindrift,
told one of Deborah's brothers they was heading out and would

7

be arriving sometime between midnight and one A.M. When they didn't show up by four o'clock this morning, Pat Harvey called the police."

"*Pat Harvey!*" I looked at Marino in disbelief.

It was Officer Morrell who replied, "Oh, yeah. We got us a good one, all right. Pat Harvey's on her way here even as we speak. A chopper picked her up"——he glanced at his watch——"about a half hour ago. The father, uh, Bob Harvey, he's on the road. Was in Charlotte on business and was supposed to get to Spindrift sometime tomorrow. As far as we know, he hasn't been reached yet, doesn't know what's happened."

Pat Harvey was the National Drug Policy Director, a position the media had dubbed Drug Czar. A presidential appointee who not so long ago had been on the cover of *Time* magazine, Mrs. Harvey was one of the most powerful and admired women in America.

"What about Benton?" I asked Marino. "Is he aware Deborah Harvey is Pat Harvey's daughter?"

"He didn't say nothing about it to me. When he called, he'd just landed in Newport News—the Bureau flew him in. He was in a hurry to find a rental car. We didn't talk long."

That answered my question. Benton Wesley would not be rushing here in a Bureau plane unless he knew who Deborah Harvey was. I wondered why he had not said anything to Marino, his VICAP partner, and I tried to read Marino's broad, impassive face. His jaw muscles were flexing, the top of his balding head flushed and beaded with sweat.

"What's going on now," Morrell resumed, "is I got a lot of

men stationed around to keep out traffic. We've looked in the bathrooms, poked around a little, to make sure the kids aren't in the immediate area. Once Peninsula Search and Rescue get here, we'll start in on the woods."

Immediately north of the Jeep's front hood the well-attended landscaping of the rest stop was overcome by brush and trees that within an acre became so dense I could see nothing but sunlight caught in leaves and a hawk making circles over a distant stand of pines. Though shopping malls and housing developments continued their encroachment upon I-64, this stretch between Richmond and Tidewater so far had remained unspoiled. The scenery, which I would have found reassuring and soothing in the past, now seemed ominous to me.

"Shit," Marino complained as we left Morrell and began walking around.

"I'm sorry about your fishing trip," I said.

"Hey. Ain't it the way it always goes? Been planning this damn trip for months. Screwed again. Nothing new."

"I noticed that when you pull off the Interstate," I observed, ignoring his irritation, "the entrance ramp immediately divides into two ramps, one leading back here, the other to the front of the rest stop. In other words, the ramps are one-way. It's not possible to pull into the front area for cars, then change your mind and drive back here without going a considerable distance the wrong way on the ramp and risk hitting someone. And I would guess there was a fair amount of travelers on the road last night, since it's Labor Day weekend."

"Right. I know that. It don't take a rocket scientist to figure out that somebody intended to ditch the Jeep exactly where it is because there were probably a lot of cars parked in front last night. So he takes the ramp for trucks and buses. Probably was pretty deserted back here. Nobody sees him, and he splits."

"He may also not have wanted the Jeep found right away, explaining why it's well off the pavement," I said.

Marino stared off toward the woods and said, "I'm getting too old for this."

A perpetual complainer, Marino had a habit of arriving at a crime scene and acting as if he did not want to be there. We had worked with each other long enough for me to be used to it, but this time his attitude struck me as more than an act. His frustration went deeper than the canceled fishing trip. I wondered if he had had a fight with his wife.

"Well, well," he mumbled, looking toward the brick building. "The Lone Ranger's arrived."

I turned around as the lean, familiar figure of Benton Wesley emerged from the men's room. He barely said "hello" when he got to us, his silver hair wet at the temples, the lapels of his blue suit speckled with water as if he had just washed his face. Eyes fixed impassively on the Jeep, he slipped a pair of sunglasses from his breast pocket and put them on.

"Has Mrs. Harvey gotten here yet?" he asked.

"Nope," Marino replied.

"What about reporters?"

"Nope," Marino said.

"Good."

Wesley's mouth was firmly set, making his sharp-featured face seem harder and more unreachable than usual. I would have found him handsome were it not for his imperviousness. His thoughts and emotions were impossible to read, and of late he had become such a master at walling off his personality that I sometimes felt I did not know him.

"We want to keep this under wraps as long as possible," he went on. "The minute the word's out all hell is going to break loose."

I asked him, "What do you know about this couple, Benton?"

"Very little. After Mrs. Harvey reported them missing early this morning, she called the Director at home and then he called me. Apparently, her daughter and Fred Cheney met at Carolina and had been dating since their freshman year. Both of them supposedly good, clean-cut kids. No history of any sort of trouble that might account for them getting tangled up with the wrong type of person out here—at least according to Mrs. Harvey. One thing I did pick up on was she had some ambivalence about the relationship, thought Cheney and her daughter spent too much time alone."

"Possibly the real reason for their wanting to drive to the beach in a separate car," I said.

"Yes," Wesley replied, glancing around. "More than likely that was the real reason. I got the impression from the Director that Mrs. Harvey wasn't keen on Deborah's bringing her boyfriend to Spindrift. It was family time. Mrs. Harvey lives in D.C. during the week and hadn't seen much of her daughter and two sons all summer. Frankly, I have the feeling that Deborah and her mother may not have been getting along very well of late, and may have had an argument right before the family headed off to North Carolina yesterday morning."

"What about the chance the kids might have run off together?" Marino said. "They was smart, right? Would read the papers, watch the news, maybe saw the stuff about these couples on that TV special the other week. Point is, they probably knew about the cases around here. Who's to say they didn't pull something? A pretty slick way to stage a disappearance and punish your parents."

"It's one of many scenarios we need to consider," Wesley replied. "And it's all the more reason I hope we can keep this from the media as long as possible."

Morrell joined us as we walked along the exit ramp back toward the Jeep. A pale blue pickup truck with a camper shell pulled up, and a man and a woman in dark jumpsuits and boots got out. Opening the tailgate, they let two panting, tail-wagging bloodhounds out of their crate. They snapped long leads to rings on the leather belts around their waists and grabbed each dog by its harness.

"Salty, Neptune, heel!"

I didn't know which dog was which. Both were big and light tan with wrinkled faces and floppy ears. Morrell grinned and put out his hand.

"Howya doin', fella?"

Salty, or maybe it was Neptune, rewarded him with a wet kiss and a nuzzle to the leg.

The dog handlers were from Yorktown, their names Jeff and Gail. Gail was as tall as her partner and looked just about as strong. She reminded me of women I've seen who have spent their lives on farms, their faces lined by hard work and the sun, a stolid patience about them that comes from understanding nature and accepting its gifts and punishments. She was the search-and-rescue team captain, and I could tell from the way she was eyeing the Jeep that she was surveying it for any sign that the scene, and therefore the scents, had been disturbed.

"Nothing's been touched," Marino told her, bending over to knead one of the dogs behind the ears. "We haven't even opened the doors yet."

"Do you know if anybody else has been inside it? Maybe the person who found it?" Gail inquired.

Morrell began to explain, "The plate number went out over teletype, BOLOs, early this morning—"

"What the hell are BOLOs?" Wesley interrupted.

"Be On the Lookouts."

Wesley's face was granite as Morrell went on, tediously, "Troopers don't go through lineup, so they're not always going to see a teletype. They just get in their cars and mark on. The dispatchers started sending BOLOs over the air the minute the couple was reported missing, and around one P.M. a trucker spotted the Jeep, radioed it in. The trooper who responded said that other than looking through the windows to make sure nobody was inside, he didn't even get close."

I hoped this was true. Most police officers, even those who

know better, can't seem to resist opening doors and at least rummaging through the glove compartment in search of the owner's identification.

Taking hold of both harnesses, Jeff took the dogs off to "use the potty" while Gail asked, "You got anything the dogs can scent off of?"

"Pat Harvey was asked to bring along anything Deborah might have been wearing recently," Wesley said.

If Gail was surprised or impressed by whose daughter she was looking for, she did not show it but continued to regard Wesley expectantly.

"She's flying in by chopper," Wesley added, glancing at his watch. "Should be here any minute."

"Well, just don't be landing the big bird right here," Gail commented, approaching the Jeep. "Don't need anything stirring up the place." Peering through the driver's window, she studied the inside of the doors, the dash, taking in every inch of the interior. Then she backed away and took a long look at the black plastic door handle on the outside of the door.

"Best thing's probably going to be the seats," she decided. "We'll let Salty scent off one, Neptune off the other. But first, we got to get in without screwing up anything. Anybody got a pencil or pen?"

Snatching a ballpoint Mont Blanc pen out of the breast pocket of his shirt, Wesley presented it to her.

"Need one more," she added.

Amazingly, nobody else seemed to have a pen on his person, including me. I could have sworn I had several inside my purse.

14

"How about a folding knife?" Marino was digging in a pocket of his jeans.

"Perfect."

Pen in one hand and Swiss army knife in the other, Gail simultaneously depressed the thumb button on the outside of the driver's door and pried back the handle, then caught the door's edge with the toe of her boot to gently pull it open. All the while I heard the faint, unmistakable thud-thud of helicopter blades growing louder.

Moments later, a red-and-white Bell Jet Ranger circled the rest stop, then hovered like a dragonfly, creating a small hurricane on the ground. All sound was drowned out, trees shaking and grass rippling in the roar of its terrible wind. Eyes squeezed shut, Gail and Jeff were squatting by the dogs, holding harnesses tight.

Marino, Wesley, and I had retreated close to the buildings, and from this vantage we watched the violent descent. As the helicopter slowly nosed around in a maelstrom of straining engines and beating air, I caught a glimpse of Pat Harvey staring down at her daughter's Jeep before sunlight whited out the glass.

She stepped away from the helicopter, head bent and skirt whipping around her legs as Wesley waited a safe distance from the decelerating blades, necktie fluttering over his shoulder like an aviator's scarf.

Before Pat Harvey had been appointed the National Drug Policy Director, she had been a commonwealth's attorney in

Richmond, then a U.S. attorney for the Eastern District of Virginia. Her prosecution of high-profile drug cases in the federal system had occasionally involved victims I had autopsied. But I had never been called to testify; only my reports had been subpoenaed. Mrs. Harvey and I had never actually met.

On television and in newspaper photographs she came across as all business. She was, in the flesh, both feminine and strikingly attractive, slender, her features perfectly wrought, the sun finding hints of gold and red in her short auburn hair. Wesley made brief introductions, and Mrs. Harvey shook each of our hands with the politeness and self-assurance of a practiced politician. But she did not smile or meet anyone's eyes.

"There's a sweatshirt inside," she explained, handing a paper bag to Gail. "I found it in Debbie's bedroom at the beach. I don't know when she wore it last, but I don't think it's been recently washed."

"When's the last time your daughter was at the beach?" Gail inquired without opening the bag.

"Early July. She went there with several friends for a weekend."

"And you're sure she was the one wearing this? Possible one of her friends might have?" Gail asked casually, as though she were inquiring about the weather.

The question caught Mrs. Harvey by surprise, and for an instant doubt clouded her dark blue eyes. "I'm not sure." She cleared her throat. "I would assume Debbie was the one wearing it last, but obviously I can't swear to it. I wasn't there."

She stared past us through the Jeep's open door, her attention briefly fixed on the keys in the ignition, the silver "D" dangling from the keychain. For a long moment no one spoke, and I could see the struggle of mind against emotion as she warded off panic with denial.

Turning back to us, she said, "Debbie would have been carrying a purse. Nylon, bright red. One of those sports purses with a Velcro-lined flap. I'm wondering if you found it inside?"

"No, ma'am," Morrell replied. "At least we haven't seen anything like that yet, not from looking through the windows. But we haven't searched the interior, couldn't until the dogs got here."

"I would expect it to be on the front seat. Perhaps on the floor," she went on.

Morrell shook his head.

It was Wesley who spoke. "Mrs. Harvey, do you know if your daughter had much money with her?"

"I gave her fifty dollars for food and gas. I don't know what she might have had beyond that," she replied. "She also, of course, had charge cards. Plus her checkbook."

"You know what she had in her checking account?" Wesley asked.

"Her father gave her a check last week," she replied matter-of-factly. "For college—books, and so on. I'm fairly certain she's already deposited it. I suppose she should have at least a thousand dollars in her account."

"You might want to look into that," Wesley proposed. "Make certain the money wasn't recently withdrawn."

"I will do so immediately."

As I stood by and watched, I could sense hope blossoming in her mind. Her daughter had cash, charge cards, and access to money in a checking account. It did not appear that she had left her purse inside the Jeep, meaning she might still have it with her. Meaning she might still be alive and well and off somewhere with her boyfriend.

"Your daughter ever threaten to run away with Fred?" Marino asked her bluntly.

"No." Staring again at the Jeep, she added what she wanted to believe, "But that doesn't mean it isn't possible."

"What was her mood when you talked to her last?" Marino went on.

"We exchanged words yesterday morning before my sons and I left for the beach," she replied in a detached, flat tone. "She was upset with me."

"She know about the cases around here? The missing couples?" Marino asked.

"Yes, of course. We have discussed them, wondered about them. She knew."

Gail said to Morrell, "We ought to get started."

"Good idea."

"One last thing." Gail looked at Mrs. Harvey. "You got any idea who was driving?" .

"Fred, I suspect," she answered. "When they went places together, he usually drove."

Nodding, Gail said, "Guess I'm going to need that pocket-knife and pen again."

Collecting them from Wesley and Marino, she went around

to the passenger's side and opened the door. She grasped one of the bloodhounds' harnesses. Eagerly, he got up and moved in perfect accord with his mistress's feet, snuffling along, muscles rippling beneath his loose, glossy coat, ears dragging heavily, as if lined with lead.

"Come on, Neptune, let's put that magic nose of yours to work."

We watched in silence as she directed Neptune's nose at the bucket seat where Deborah Harvey was presumed to have been sitting yesterday. Suddenly he yelped as if he had encountered a rattlesnake, jerking back from the Jeep, practically wrenching the harness from Gail's hand. He tucked his tail between his legs and the fur literally stood up on his back as a chill ran up my spine.

"Easy, boy. Easy!"

Whimpering and quivering all over, Neptune squatted and defecated in the grass.

2

I woke up the next morning, exhausted and dreading the Sunday paper.

The headline was bold enough to be read from a block away:

DRUG CZAR'S DAUGHTER, FRIEND
MISSING—POLICE FEAR FOUL PLAY

Not only had reporters gotten hold of a photograph of Deborah Harvey, but there was a picture of her Jeep being towed from the rest stop and a file photograph, I presumed, of Bob and Pat Harvey, hand in hand, walking a deserted beach in Spindrift. As I sipped coffee and read, I could not help but think about Fred Cheney's family. He was not from a prominent family. He was just "Deborah's boyfriend." Yet he, too, was missing; he, too, was loved.

Apparently, Fred was the son of a Southside businessman, an only child whose mother had died last year when a berry aneurysm ruptured in her brain. Fred's father, the story read, was in Sarasota visiting relatives when the police finally tracked him down late last night. If there were a remote possibility that his son had "run off" with Deborah, the story read, it would have been very much out of character for Fred, who was described as "a good student at Carolina and a member of the varsity swim team." Deborah was an honor student and a gymnast gifted enough to be an Olympic hopeful. Weighing no more than a hundred pounds, she had shoulder-length dark blonde hair and her mother's handsome features. Fred was broad-shouldered and lean, with wavy black hair and hazel eyes. They were a couple described as attractive and inseparable.

"Whenever you saw one, you always saw the other," a friend was quoted as saying. "I think it had a lot to do with Fred's mother dying. Debbie met him right about that time, and I don't think he would have made it through without her."

Of course, the story went on to regurgitate the details of the other four Virginia couples missing and later found dead. My name was mentioned several times. I was described as frustrated, baffled, and avoiding comment. I wondered if it occurred to anyone that I continued to autopsy the victims of homicides, suicides, and accidents every week. I routinely talked to families, testified in court, and gave lectures to paramedics and police academies. Couples or not, life and death went on.

I had gotten up from the kitchen table, was sipping coffee and staring out at the bright morning when the telephone rang.

Expecting my mother, who often called at this hour on Sunday to inquire about my well-being and if I had been to Mass, I pulled out a nearby chair as I picked up the receiver.

"Dr. Scarpetta?"

"Speaking." The woman sounded familiar, but I could not place her.

"It's Pat Harvey. Please forgive me for bothering you at home." Behind her steady voice, I detected a note of fear.

"You certainly aren't bothering me," I replied kindly. "What can I do for you?"

"They searched all through the night and are still out there. They brought in more dogs, more police, several aircraft." She began to speak rapidly. "Nothing. No sign of them. Bob has joined the search parties. I'm home." She hesitated. "I'm wondering if you could come over? Perhaps you're free for lunch?"

After a long pause, I reluctantly agreed. As I hung up the telephone I silently berated myself, for I knew what she wanted from me. Pat Harvey would ask about the other couples. If I were her, it was exactly what I would do.

I went upstairs to my bedroom and got out of my robe. Then I took a long, hot bath and washed my hair while my answering machine began intercepting calls that I had no intention of returning unless they were emergencies. Within the hour I was dressed in a khaki skirt suit and tensely playing back messages. There were five of them, all from reporters who had learned that I had been summoned to the New Kent County rest stop, which did not bode well for the missing couple.

I reached for the phone, intending to call Pat Harvey back and cancel our lunch. But I could not forget her face when she had arrived by helicopter with her daughter's sweatshirt, I could not forget the faces of any of the parents. Hanging up the phone, I locked the house and got into my car.

People in public service can't afford the accouterments privacy demands unless they have some other means of income. Obviously, Pat Harvey's federal salary was a meager sliver of her family's worth. They lived near Windsor on the James in a palatial Jeffersonian house overlooking the river. The estate, which I guessed to be at least five acres, was surrounded by a high brick wall posted with "Private Property" signs. When I turned into a long drive shaded by trees, I was stopped by a sturdy wrought-iron gate that slid open electronically before I could roll down my window to reach for the intercom. The gate slid shut behind me as I drove through. I parked near a black Jaguar sedan before a Roman portico of unfluted columns, old red brick, and white trim.

As I was getting out of my car, the front door opened. Pat Harvey, drying her hands on a dish towel, smiled bravely at me from the top of the steps. Her face was pale, her eyes lusterless and tired.

"It's so good of you to come, Dr. Scarpetta." She motioned for me to enter. "Please come in."

The foyer was as spacious as a living room, and I followed her through a formal sitting room to the kitchen. Furniture was eighteenth century, Oriental rugs wall to wall, and there were original Impressionist paintings and a fireplace with beechwood logs artfully piled on the hearth. At least the kitchen looked functional and lived in, but I did not get the impression that anyone else was home.

"Jason and Michael are out with their father," she explained when I asked. "The boys drove in this morning."

"How old are they?" I inquired, as she opened the oven door.

"Jason is sixteen, Michael fourteen. Debbie is the oldest." Looking around for the potholders, she turned off the oven, then set a quiche on top of a burner. Her hands trembled as she got a knife and spatula from a drawer. "Would you like wine, tea, coffee? This is very light. I did throw together a fruit salad. Thought we'd sit out on the porch. I hope that will be all right."

"That would be lovely," I replied. "And coffee would be fine."

Distracted, she opened the freezer and got out a bag of Irish Creme, which she measured into the drip coffee maker. I watched her without speaking. She was desperate. Husband and sons were not home. Her daughter was missing, the house empty and silent.

She did not begin to ask questions until we were on the porch, sliding glass doors open wide, the river curving beyond us glinting in the sun.

"What the dogs did, Dr. Scarpetta," she began, picking at her salad. "Can you offer an interpretation?"

I could, but I did not want to.

"Obviously, the one dog got upset. But the other one didn't?" Her observation was posed as a question.

The other dog, Salty, had indeed reacted very differently than Neptune had. After he sniffed the driver's seat, Gail hooked the lead on his harness and commanded, "Find." The dog took off like a greyhound. He snuffled across the exit ramp and up through the picnic area. Then he tugged Gail across the parking lot toward the Interstate and would have gotten a nose full of traffic had she not yelled, "Heel!" I had watched them trot along the wooded strip separating west lanes from east, then across pavement, heading straight for the rest stop opposite the one where Deborah's Jeep had been found. The bloodhound finally lost the scent in the parking lot.

"Am I to believe," Mrs. Harvey continued, "that whoever was driving Debbie's Jeep last got out, cut through the westbound rest stop, and crossed the Interstate? Then this person most likely got into a car parked in the eastbound rest stop and drove away?"

"That is one possible interpretation," I replied, picking at my quiche.

"What other possible interpretation is there, Dr. Scarpetta?"

"The bloodhound picked up a scent. As for the scent of who or what, I don't know. It could have been Deborah's scent, Fred's scent, the scent of a third person—"

"Her Jeep was sitting out there for hours," Mrs. Harvey interrupted, staring off at the river. "I suppose anybody could have gotten in to look for money, valuables. A hitchhiker, transient, someone on foot who crossed over to the other side of the Interstate afterward."

I did not remind her of the obvious. The police had found Fred Cheney's wallet in the glove compartment, complete with credit cards and thirty-five dollars cash. It did not appear that the young couples' luggage had been gone through. As far as anyone could tell, nothing was missing from the Jeep except its occupants and Deborah's purse.

"The way the first dog acted," she went on matter-of-factly. "I assume this is unusual. Something frightened him. Upset him, at any rate. A different smell—not the same scent the other dog picked up. The seat where Debbie may have been sitting . . ." Her voice trailed off as she met my eyes.

"Yes. It appears that the two dogs picked up different scents."

"Dr. Scarpetta, I'm asking you to be direct with me." Her voice trembled. "Don't spare my feelings. Please. I know the dog wouldn't have gotten so upset unless there was a reason. Certainly, your work has exposed you to search-and-rescue efforts, to bloodhounds. Have you ever seen this before, the way the dog reacted?"

I had. Twice. Once was when a bloodhound sniffed a car trunk that, as it turned out, had been used to transport a murder victim whose body had been found inside a Dumpster. The other was when a scent led to an area along a hiking trail where a woman had been raped and shot.

What I said was, "Bloodhounds tend to have strong reactions to pheromonal scents."

"I beg your pardon?" She looked bewildered.

"Secretions. Animals, insects, secrete chemicals. Sex attractants, for example," I dispassionately explained. "You're familiar with dogs marking their territory or attacking when they smell fear?"

She just stared at me.

"When someone is sexually aroused, anxious, or afraid, there are various hormonal changes that occur in the body. It is theorized that scent-discriminating animals, such as bloodhounds, can smell the pheromones, or chemicals, that special glands in our bodies secrete—"

She cut me off. "Debbie complained of cramps shortly before Michael, Jason, and I left for the beach. She had just started her period. Could that explain . . . ? Well if she were sitting in the passenger's seat, perhaps this was the scent the dog picked up?"

I did not reply. What she was suggesting could not account for the dog's extreme distress.

"It's not enough." Pat Harvey looked away from me and twisted the linen napkin in her lap. "Not enough to explain why the dog started whining, the fur stood up on his back. Oh, dear God. It's like the other couples, isn't it?"

"I can't say that."

"But you're thinking it. The police are thinking it. If it hadn't been on everybody's mind from the start, you never would have been called yesterday. I want to know what happened to them. To those other couples."

I said nothing.

"According to what I've read," she pushed, "you were present at every scene, called there by the police."

"I was."

Reaching into a pocket of her blazer, she withdrew a folded sheet of legal paper and smoothed it open.

"Bruce Phillips and Judy Roberts," she began to brief me, as if I needed it. "High school sweethearts who disappeared two and a half years ago on June first when they drove away from a friend's house in Gloucester and never arrived at their respective homes. The next morning Bruce's Camaro was found abandoned off U.S. Seventeen, keys in the ignition, doors unlocked, and windows rolled down. Ten weeks later, you were called to a wooded area one mile east of the York River State Park, where hunters had discovered two partially skeletonized bodies face down in the leaves, approximately four miles from where Bruce's car had been found."

I recalled that it was at this time VICAP was asked by local police to assist. What Marino, Wesley, and the detective from Gloucester did not know was that a second couple had been reported missing in July, a month after Bruce and Judy had vanished.

"Next we have Jim Freeman and Bonnie Smyth," Mrs. Harvey glanced up at me. "They disappeared the last Saturday in July after a pool party at the Freemans' Providence Forge home. Late that evening Jim gave Bonnie a ride home, and the following day a Charles City police officer found Jim's Blazer abandoned some ten miles from the Freeman home. Four months after that, on November twelfth, hunters in West Point found their bodies . . ."

What I suspected she did not know, I thought, unpleasantly, was that despite my repeated requests, I was not given copies of the confidential sections of the police reports, scene photographs, or inventories of evidence. I attributed the apparent lack of cooperation to what had become a multi-jurisdictional investigation.

Mrs. Harvey continued relentlessly. In March of the following year, it happened again. Ben Anderson had driven from Arlington to meet his girlfriend, Carolyn Bennett, at her family's home in Stingray Point on the Chesapeake Bay. They pulled away from the Andersons' house shortly before seven o'clock to begin the drive back to Old Dominion University in Norfolk, where they were juniors. The next night a state trooper contacted Ben's parents and reported that their son's Dodge pickup truck had been found abandoned on the shoulder of I-64, approximately five miles east of Buckroe Beach. Keys were in the ignition, the doors unlocked, and Carolyn's pocketbook was beneath the passenger's seat. Their partially skeletonized bodies were discovered six months later during deer season in a wooded area three miles south of Route 199 in York County. This time, I did not even get a copy of the police report.

When Susan Wilcox and Mike Martin disappeared this past February, I found out about it from the morning newspaper. They were heading to Mike's house in Virginia Beach to spend spring break together when, like the couples before them, they vanished. Mike's blue van was found abandoned along the Colonial Parkway near Williamsburg, a white handkerchief tied to the antenna signaling engine trouble that did not exist when the police went over the van later. On May fifteenth a father and son out turkey hunting discovered the couples' decomposed bodies in a wooded area between Route 60 and I-64 in James City County.

I remembered, once again, packing up bones to send to the Smithsonian's forensic anthropologist for one final look. Eight young people, and despite the countless hours I had spent on each one of them, I could not determine how or why they had died.

"If, God forbid, there is a next time, don't wait until the bodies turn up," I finally had instructed Marino. "Let me know the minute the car is found."

"Yo. May as well start autopsying the cars since the bodies ain't telling us nothing," he had said, trying unsuccessfully to be funny.

"In all cases," Mrs. Harvey was saying, "doors were unlocked, keys in the ignition, there was no sign of a struggle, and it did not appear anything was stolen. The MOs were basically the same."

She folded her notes and slipped them back into a pocket.

"You're well informed," was all I said. I didn't ask, but presumed she had gotten her staff to research the previous cases.

"My point is, you've been involved since the beginning," she said. "You examined all of the bodies. And yet, as I understand it, you don't know what killed these couples."

"That's right. I don't know," I replied.

"*You don't know?* Or is it that you aren't saying, Dr. Scarpetta?"

Pat Harvey's career as a prosecutor in the federal system had earned her national respect, if not awe. She was gutsy and aggressive, and I felt as if her porch suddenly had turned into a courtroom.

"If I knew their cause of death, I would not have signed them out as undetermined," I said calmly.

"But you believe they were murdered."

"I believe that young, healthy people don't suddenly abandon their cars and die of natural causes in the woods, Mrs. Harvey."

"What about the theories? What do you have to say about those? I assume they aren't new to you."

They weren't.

Four jurisdictions and at least that many different detectives were involved, each one with numerous hypotheses. The couples, for example, were recreational drug users and had met up with a dealer selling some new and pernicious designer drug that could not be detected through routine toxicology tests. Or the occult was involved. Or the couples were all members of some secret society, their deaths actually suicide pacts.

"I don't think much of the theories I've heard," I told her.

"Why not?"

"My findings do not support them."

"What do your findings support?" she demanded. "What *findings?* Based on everything I've heard and read, you don't have any goddam findings."

A haze had dulled the sky, and a plane was a silver needle pulling a white thread beneath the sun. In silence I watched the vapor trail expand and begin to disperse. If Deborah and Fred had met up with the same fate as the others, we would not find them anytime soon.

"My Debbie has never taken drugs," she continued, blinking back tears. "She isn't into any weird religions or cults. She has a temper and sometimes gets depressed like every other normal teenager. But she wouldn't—" She suddenly stopped, struggling for control.

"You must try to deal with the here and now," I said quietly. "We don't know what has happened to your daughter. We don't know what has happened to Fred. It may be a long time before we know. Is there anything else you can tell me about her—about them? Anything at all that might help?"

"A police officer came by this morning," she replied with a deep, shaky breath. "He went inside her bedroom, took several articles of her clothing, her hairbrush. Said they were for the dogs, the clothes were, and he needed some of her hair to compare with any hairs they might find inside her Jeep. Would you like to see it? See her bedroom?"

Curious, I nodded.

I followed her up polished hardwood steps to the second floor. Deborah's bedroom was in the east wing, where she could see the sun rise and storms gather over the James. It was not the typical teenager's room. Furniture was Scandinavian, simple in design and built of gorgeous light teakwood. A comforter in shades of cool blue and green covered the queen-size bed, and beneath it was an Indian rug dominated by designs in rose and deep plum. Encyclopedias and novels filled a bookcase, and above the desk two shelves were lined with trophies and dozens of medals attached to bright cloth ribbons. On a top shelf was a large photograph of Deborah on a balance beam, back arched, hands poised like graceful birds, the expression on her face, like the details of her private sanctum, that of pure discipline and grace. I did not have to be Deborah Harvey's mother to know that this nineteen-year-old girl was special.

"Debbie picked out everything herself," Mrs. Harvey said as I looked around. "The furniture, rug, the colors. You'd never know she was in here days ago packing for school." She stared at suitcases and a trunk in a corner and cleared her throat. "She's so organized. I suppose she gets this from me." Smiling nervously, she added, "If I am nothing else, I am organized."

I remembered Deborah's Jeep. It was immaculate inside and out, luggage and other belongings arranged with deliberation.

"She takes wonderful care of her belongings," Mrs. Harvey went on, moving to the window. "I often worried that we indulged her too much. Her clothes, her car, money. Bob and I have had many discussions on the subject. It's difficult with my being in Washington. But when I was appointed last year, we decided, all of us did, that it was too much to uproot the family, and Bob's business is here. Easier if I took the apartment, came home on weekends when I could. Waited to see what would happen with the next election."

After a long pause, she went on. "I suppose what I'm trying to say is that I've never been very good at saying no to Debbie. It's difficult to be sensible when you want the best for your children. Especially when you remember your desires when you were their age, your insecurities about the way you dressed, your physical appearance. When you knew your parents couldn't afford a dermatologist, an orthodontist, a plastic surgeon. We have tried to exercise moderation." She crossed her arms at her waist. "Sometimes I'm not so sure we made the right choices. Her Jeep, for example. I was opposed to her having a car, but I didn't have the energy to argue. Typically, she was practical, wanting something safe that would get her around in any kind of weather."

Hesitantly, I inquired, "When you mention a plastic surgeon, are you referring to something specific concerning your daughter?"

"Large breasts are incompatible with gymnastics, Dr. Scarpetta," she said, not turning around. "By the time Debbie was sixteen she was overendowed. Not only was this rather embarrassing to her, but it interfered with her sport. The problem was taken care of last year."

"Then this photograph is recent," I said, for the Deborah I was looking at was an elegant sculpture of perfectly formed muscle, breasts and buttocks firm and small.

"It was taken last April in California."

When a person is missing and possibly dead, it is not uncommon for people like me to be interested in anatomical detail—whether it be a hysterectomy, a root canal, or scars from plastic surgery—that might assist in the identification of the body. They were the descriptions I reviewed in NCIC missing person forms. They were the mundane and very human features that I depended on, because jewelry and other personal effects, I had learned over the years, can't always be trusted.

"What I've just told you must never go outside this room," Mrs. Harvey said. "Debbie is very private. My family is very private."

"I understand."

"Her relationship with Fred," she continued. "It was private. Too private. As I'm sure you've noted, there are no photographs, no visible symbols of it. I have no doubt they have exchanged pictures, gifts, mementoes. But she has always been secretive about them. Her birthday was last February, for example. I noticed shortly after that she was wearing a gold ring on the pinky of her right hand. A narrow band with a floral design. She never said a word, nor did I ask. But I'm sure it was from him."

"Do you consider him a stable young man?"

Turning around, she faced me, eyes dark and distracted. "Fred is very intense, somewhat obsessive. But I can't say that he's unstable. I really can't complain about him. I simply have worried that the relationship is too serious, too . . ." She looked away, groping for the right word. "Addictive. That's what comes to mind. It's as if they are each other's drug." Shutting her eyes, she turned away again and leaned her head against the window. "Oh, God. I wish we'd never bought her that goddam Jeep."

I did not comment.

"Fred doesn't have a car. She would have had no choice . . ." Her voice trailed off.

"She would have had no choice," I said, "but to drive with you to the beach."

"And this wouldn't have happened!"

Suddenly she walked out the door to the hallway. She could not bear to be inside her daughter's bedroom one moment longer, I knew, and I followed her down the stairs and to the front door. When I reached for her hand, she turned away from me as her tears fell.

"I'm so sorry." How many times on this earth would I say that?

The front door shut quietly as I went down the steps. While driving home I prayed that if I ever encountered Pat Harvey again, it would not be in my official capacity of chief medical examiner.

3

A week passed before I heard again from anyone connected to the Harvey-Cheney case, the investigation of which had gone nowhere, as far as I knew. Monday, when I was up to my elbows in blood in the morgue, Benton Wesley called. He wanted to talk to Marino and me without delay, and suggested we come for dinner.

"I think Pat Harvey's making him nervous," Marino said that evening. Tentative drops of rain bounced off his car windshield as we headed to Wesley's house. "I personally don't give a rat's ass if she talks to a palm reader, rings up Billy Graham or the friggin' Easter Bunny."

"Hilda Ozimek is not a palm reader," I replied.

"Half those Sister Rose joints with a hand painted on the sign are just fronts for prostitution."

"I'm aware of that," I said wearily.

He opened the ashtray, reminding me what a filthy habit

smoking was. If he could cram one more butt in there, it would be a Guinness record.

"I take it you've heard of Hilda Ozimek, then," he went on.

"I really don't know much about her, except that I think she lives somewhere in the Carolinas."

"South Carolina."

"Is she staying with the Harveys?"

"Not anymore," Marino said, turning off the windshield wipers as the sun peeked out from behind clouds. "Wish the damn weather would make up its mind. She went back to South Carolina yesterday. Was flown in and out of Richmond in a private plane, if you can believe that."

"You mind telling me how anybody knows about it?" If I was surprised that Pat Harvey would resort to a psychic, I was even more surprised that she would tell anyone.

"Good question. I'm just telling you what Benton said when he called. Apparently, Broom Hilda found something in her crystal ball that got Mrs. Harvey mighty upset."

"What, exactly?"

"Beats the shit outta me. Benton didn't go into detail."

I did not inquire further, for discussing Benton Wesley and his tight-lipped ways made me ill at ease. Once he and I had enjoyed working together, our regard for each other respectful and warm. Now I found him distant, and I could not help but worry that the way Wesley acted toward me had to do with Mark. When Mark had walked away from me by taking an assignment in Colorado, he had also walked away from Quantico, where he had enjoyed the privileged role of running the FBI National Academy's Legal Training Unit. Wesley had lost his colleague and companion, and in his mind it was probably my fault. The bond between male friends can be stronger than marriage, and brothers of the badge are more loyal to each other than lovers.

A half hour later Marino turned off the highway, and soon after I lost track of the lefts and rights he took on rural routes that led us deeper into the country. Though I had met with Wesley many times in the past, it had always been at my office or his. I had never been invited to his house, located in the picturesque setting of Virginia farmland and forests, pastures surrounded by white fences, and barns and homes set back far from the roads. When we turned into his subdivision, we began to pass long driveways leading to large modern houses on generous lots, with European sedans parked before two- and three-car garages.

"I didn't realize there were Washington bedroom communities this close to Richmond," I commented.

"What? You've lived around here for four, five years and never heard of northern aggression?"

"If you were born in Miami, the Civil War isn't exactly foremost on your mind," I replied.

"I guess not. Hell, Miami ain't even in this country. Any place where they got to vote on whether English is the official language don't belong in the United States."

Marino's digs about my birthplace were nothing new.

Slowing down as he turned into a gravel drive, he said, "Not a bad crib, huh? Guess the feds pay a little better than the city."

The house was shingle style with a fieldstone foundation

and projecting bay windows. Rosebushes lined the front, east, and west wings shaded by old magnolias and oaks. As we got out, I began to look for clues that might give me more insight into Benton Wesley's private life. A basketball hoop was above the garage door, and near a woodpile covered with plastic was a red rider mower sprayed with cut grass. Beyond, I could see a spacious backyard impeccably land-scaped with flower beds, azaleas, and fruit trees. Several chairs were arranged close together near a gas grill, and I envisioned Wesley and his wife having drinks and cooking steaks on leisurely summer nights.

Marino rang the bell. It was Wesley's wife who opened the door. She introduced herself as Connie.

"Ben went upstairs for a minute," she said, smiling, as she led us into a living room with wide windows, a large fireplace, and rustic furniture. I had never heard Wesley referred to as "Ben" before. Nor had I ever met his wife. She appeared to be in her mid-forties, an attractive brunette with hazel eyes so light they were almost yellow, and sharp features very much like her husband's. There was a gentleness about her, a quiet reserve suggesting strength of character and tenderness. The guarded Benton Wesley I knew, no doubt, was a very different man at home, and I wondered how familiar Connie was with the details of his profession.

"Will you have a beer, Pete?" she asked.

He settled into a rocking chair. "Looks like I'm the desig-nated driver. Better stick to coffee."

"Kay, what may I get for you?"

"Coffee would be fine," I replied. "If it's no trouble."

"I'm so glad to finally meet you," she added sincerely. "Ben's spoken of you for years. He regards you very highly."

"Thank you." The compliment disconcerted me, and what she said next came as a shock.

"When we saw Mark last, I made him promise to bring you to dinner next time he comes to Quantico."

"That's very kind," I said, managing a smile. Clearly, Wesley did not tell her everything, and the idea that Mark might have been in Virginia recently without so much as calling me was almost more than I could bear.

When she left us for the kitchen, Marino asked, "You heard from him lately?"

"Denver's beautiful," I replied evasively.

"It's a bitch, you want my opinion. They bring him in from deep cover, hole him up in Quantico for a while. Next thing, they're sending his ass out west to work on something he can't tell nobody about. Just one more reason why you couldn't pay me enough to sign on with the Bureau."

I did not respond.

He went on, "The hell with your personal life. It's like they say, 'If Hoover wanted you to have a wife and kids, he would've issued them with your badge.'"

"Hoover was a long time ago," I said, staring out at trees churning in the wind. It looked like it was about to rain again, this time seriously.

"Maybe so. But you still ain't got a life of your own."

"I'm not sure any of us do, Marino."

"That's the damn truth," he muttered under his breath.

Footsteps sounded and then Wesley walked in, still in suit

and tie, gray trousers and starched white shirt slightly wrinkled. He seemed tired and tense as he asked if we had been offered drinks.

"Connie's taking care of us," I said.

Lowering himself into a chair, he glanced at his watch. "We'll eat in about an hour." He clasped his hands in his lap.

"Haven't heard shit from Morrell," Marino started in.

"I'm afraid there are no new developments. Nothing hopeful," Wesley replied.

"Didn't assume there was. I'm just telling you that I ain't heard from Morrell."

Marino's face was expressionless, but I could sense his resentment. Though he had yet to voice any complaints to me, I suspected that he was feeling like a quarterback sitting out the season on the bench. He had always enjoyed a good rapport with detectives from other jurisdictions, and that, frankly, had been one of the strengths of VICAP's efforts in Virginia. Then the missing couple cases had begun. Investigators were no longer talking to each other. They weren't talking to Marino, and they weren't talking to me.

"Local efforts have been halted," Wesley informed him. "We didn't get any farther than the eastbound rest stop where the dog lost the scent. Only other thing to turn up is a receipt found inside the Jeep. It appears that Deborah and Fred stopped off at a Seven-Eleven after leaving the Harvey house in Richmond. They bought a six-pack of Pepsi and a couple other items."

"Then it's been checked out," Marino said, testily.

"The clerk on duty at the time has been located. She

remembers them coming in. Apparently, this was shortly after nine P.M."

"And they was alone?" Marino inquired.

"It would seem so. No one else came in with them, and if there was someone waiting for them inside the Jeep, there was no evidence, based on their demeanor, to suggest that anything was wrong."

"Where is this Seven-Eleven located?" I asked.

"Approximately five miles west of the rest stop where the Jeep was found," Wesley replied.

"You said they bought a few other items," I said. "Can you be more specific?"

"I was getting to that," Wesley said. "Deborah Harvey bought a box of Tampax. She asked if she could use a bathroom, and was told it was against policy. The clerk said she directed them to the eastbound rest stop on Sixty-four."

"Where the dog lost the scent," Marino said, frowning as if confused. "Versus where the Jeep was found."

"That's right," Wesley replied.

"What about the Pepsi they bought?" I asked. "Did you find it?"

"Six cans of Pepsi were in the ice chest when the police went through the Jeep."

He paused as his wife appeared with our coffee and a glass of iced tea for him. She served us in gracious silence, then was gone. Connie Wesley was practiced at being unobtrusive.

"You're thinking they hit the rest stop so Deborah could take care of her problem, and that's where they met up with the squirrel who took them out," Marino interpolated.

"We don't know what happened to them," Wesley reminded us. "There are a lot of scenarios we need to consider."

"Such as?" Marino was still frowning.

"Abduction."

"As in kidnapping?" Marino was blatantly skeptical.

"You have to remember who Deborah's mother is."

"Yeah, I know. Mrs. Got-Rocks-the-Drug-Czar who got sworn in because the President wanted to give the women's movement something to chew on."

"Pete," Wesley said calmly, "I don't think it wise to dismiss her as a plutocratic figurehead or token female appointee. Though the position sounds more powerful than it really is because it was never given Cabinet status, Pat Harvey does answer directly to the President. She does, in fact, coordinate all federal agencies in the war against drug crimes."

"Not to mention her track record when she was a U.S. attorney," I added. "She was a strong supporter of the White House's efforts to make drug-related murders and attempted murders punishable by death. And she was quite vocal about it."

"Her and a hundred other politicians," Marino said. "Maybe I'd be more concerned if she was one of these liberals wanting to legalize the shit. Then I have to wonder about some right-wing Moral Majority type who thinks God's told him to snatch Pat Harvey's kid."

"She's been very aggressive," Wesley said, "succeeded in getting convictions on some of the worst in the lot, has been instrumental in getting important bills passed, has withstood death threats, and several years ago even had her car bombed—"

"Yeah, an unoccupied Jag parked at the country club. And it made her a hero," Marino interrupted.

"My point," Wesley went on patiently, "is that she's made her share of enemies, especially when it comes to the efforts she's directed at various charities."

"I've read something about that," I said, trying to recall the details.

"What the public knows at present is just a scratch on the surface," Wesley said. "Her latest efforts have been directed at ACTMAD. The American Coalition of Tough Mothers Against Drugs."

"You gotta be kidding," Marino said. "That's like saying UNICEF's dirty."

I did not volunteer that I sent money to ACTMAD every year and considered myself an enthusiastic supporter.

Wesley went on, "Mrs. Harvey has been gathering evidence to prove that ACTMAD has been serving as a front for a drug cartel and other illegal activities in Central America."

"Geez," Marino said, shaking his head. "Good thing I don't give a dime to nobody except the FOP."

"Deborah and Fred's disappearance is perplexing because it seems connected to the other four couples," Wesley said. "But this could also be deliberate, someone's attempt to make us assume there is a link, when in fact there may not be. We may be dealing with a serial killer. We may be dealing with something else. Whatever the case, we want to work this as quietly as possible."

"So I guess what you're waiting for now is a ransom note or something, huh?" Marino said. "You know, some Central

American thugs will return Deborah to her mother for a price."

"I don't think that's going to happen, Pete," Wesley replied. "It may be worse than that. Pat Harvey is due to testify in a congressional hearing early next year—and again, this all has to do with the illegitimate charities. There isn't anything much worse that could have happened right now than to have her daughter disappear."

My stomach knotted at the thought. Professionally, Pat Harvey did not seem particularly vulnerable, having enjoyed a spotless reputation throughout her career. But she was also a mother. The welfare of her children would be more precious to her than her own life. Her family was her Achilles' heel.

"We can't dismiss the possibility of political kidnapping," Wesley remarked, staring out at his yard thrashed by the wind.

Wesley had a family, too. The nightmare was that a crime family boss, a murderer, someone Wesley had been instrumental in bringing down would go after Wesley's wife or children. He had a sophisticated burglar alarm system in his house and an intercom outside the front door. He had chosen to live in the far-removed setting of the Virginia countryside, telephone number unlisted, address never given to reporters or even to most of his colleagues and acquaintances. Until today, even I had not known where he lived, but had assumed his home was closer to Quantico, perhaps in McLean or Alexandria.

Wesley said, "I'm sure Marino's mentioned to you this business about Hilda Ozimek."

I nodded. "Is she genuine?"

"The Bureau has used her on a number of occasions, though we don't like to admit it. Her gift, power, whatever you want to call it, is quite genuine. Don't ask me to explain. This sort of phenomenon goes beyond my immediate experience. I can tell you, however, that on one occasion she helped us locate a Bureau plane that had gone down in the mountains of West Virginia. She also predicted Sadat's assassination, and we might have had a little more forewarning about the attempt on Reagan had we listened to her words more carefully."

"You're not going to tell me she predicted Reagan's shooting," Marino said.

"Almost to the day. We didn't pass along what she'd said. Didn't, well, take it seriously, I suppose. That was our mistake, weird as it may seem. Ever since, whenever she says anything, the Secret Service wants to know."

"The Secret Service reading horoscopes, too?" Marino asked.

"I believe that Hilda Ozimek would consider horoscopes rather generic. And as far as I know, she doesn't read palms," Wesley said pointedly.

"How did Mrs. Harvey find out about her?" I asked.

"Possibly from someone within the Justice Department," Wesley said. "In any event, she flew the psychic to Richmond on Friday and apparently was told a number of things that have succeeded in making her . . . well, let's just say that I'm viewing Mrs. Harvey as a loose cannon. I'm concerned that her activities may prove to do a lot more harm than good."

"What exactly did this psychic tell her?" I wanted to know.

Wesley looked levelly at me and replied, "I really can't go into that. Not now."

"But she discussed it with you?" I inquired. "Pat Harvey volunteered to you that she had resorted to a psychic?"

"I'm not at liberty to discuss it, Kay," Wesley said, and the three of us were silent for a moment.

It went through my mind that Mrs. Harvey had not divulged this information to Wesley. He had found out in some other way.

"I don't know," Marino finally said. "Could be a random thing. I don't want to count that out."

"We can't count anything out," Wesley said firmly.

"It's been going on for two and a half years, Benton," I said.

"Yeah," Marino said. "A friggin' long time. Still strikes me as the work of some squirrel out there who fixes on couples, a jealousy-type thing because he's a loser, can't have relationships and hates other people who can."

"Certainly that's one strong possibility. Someone who routinely cruises around looking for young couples. He may frequent lovers' lanes, rest stops, the watering holes where kids park. He may go through a lot of dry runs before he strikes, then replay the homicides for months before the urge to kill again becomes irresistible and the perfect opportunity presents itself. It may be coincidence—Deborah Harvey and Fred Cheney may simply have been in the wrong place at the wrong time."

"I'm not aware there's evidence to suggest that any of the couples were parking, engaged in sexual activity, when they met up with an assailant," I pointed out.

Wesley did not respond.

"And other than Deborah and Fred, the couples didn't appear to have pulled off at a rest stop or any other sort of 'watering hole,' as you put it," I went on. "It appears they were en route to some destination when something happened to make them pull off the road and either let someone in their car or get into this person's vehicle."

"The killer cop theory," Marino muttered. "Don't think I haven't heard it before."

"It could be someone posing as a cop," Wesley replied. "Certainly that would account for the couples pulling over and, perhaps, getting into someone else's car for a routine license check or whatever. Anybody can walk into a uniform store and buy a bubble light, uniform, badge, you name it. Problem with that is a flashing light draws attention. Other motorists notice it, and if there is a real cop in the area, he's likely to at least slow down, perhaps even pull over to offer assistance. So far, there hasn't been a single report of anyone noticing a traffic stop that might have occurred in the area and at the time that these kids disappeared."

"You would also have to wonder why wallets and purses would be left inside their cars—with the exception of Deborah Harvey, whose purse has not been found," I said. "If the young people were told to get inside a so-called police vehicle for a routine traffic violation, then why would they leave car registrations and driver's licenses behind? These are the first items an officer asks to see, and when you get inside his car, you have these personal effects with you."

"They may not have gotten into this person's vehicle

49

willingly, Kay," Wesley said. "They think they're being stopped by a police officer, and when the guy walks up to their window, he pulls out a gun, orders them into his car."

"Risky as shit," Marino argued. "If it was me, I'd throw the damn car in gear and floorboard it the hell out of there. Always the chance someone driving by might see something, too. I mean, how do you force two people at gunpoint into your car on four, maybe five different occasions and not have anyone passing by notice a goddam thing?"

"A better question," Wesley said, looking unemphatically at me, "is how do you murder eight people without leaving any evidence, not so much as a nick on a bone or a bullet found somewhere near the bodies?"

"Strangulation, garroting, or throats cut," I said, and it was not the first time he had pressed me on this. "The bodies have all been badly decomposed, Benton. And I want to remind you that the cop theory implies the victims got inside the assailant's vehicle. Based on the scent the bloodhound followed last weekend, it seems plausible that if someone did something bad to Deborah Harvey and Fred Cheney, this individual may have driven off in Deborah's Jeep, abandoned it at the rest stop, and then taken off on foot across the Interstate."

Wesley's face was tired. Several times now he had rubbed his temples as if he had a headache. "My purpose in talking to both of you is that there may be some angles to this thing that require us to act very carefully. I'm asking for direct and open channels among the three of us. Absolute discretion is imperative. No loose talk to reporters, no divulging of information to anyone, not to close friends, relatives, other medical examiners, or cops. And no radio transmissions." He looked at both of us. "I want to be land lined immediately if and when Deborah Harvey's and Fred Cheney's bodies are found. And if Mrs. Harvey tries to get in touch with either of you, direct her to me."

"She's already been in contact," I said.

"I'm aware of that, Kay," Wesley replied without looking at me.

I did not ask him how he knew, but I was unnerved and it showed.

"Under the circumstances, I can understand your going to see her," he added. "But it's best if it doesn't happen again, better you don't discuss these cases with her further. It only causes more problems. It goes beyond her interfering with the investigation. The more she gets involved, the more she may be endangering herself."

"What? Because she turns up dead?" Marino asked skeptically.

"More likely because she ends up out of control, irrational."

Wesley's concern over Pat Harvey's psychological wellbeing may have been valid, but it seemed flimsy to me. And I could not help but worry as Marino and I were driving back to Richmond after dinner that the reason Wesley had wanted to see us had nothing to do with the welfare of the missing couple.

"I think I'm feeling handled," I finally confessed as the Richmond skyline came into view.

"Join the club," Marino said irritably.

"Do you have any idea what's really going on here?"

"Oh, yeah," he replied, punching in the cigarette lighter. "I got a suspicion, all right. I think the Friggin' Bureau of Investigation's caught a whiff of something that's going to make someone who counts look bad. I got this funny feeling someone's covering his ass, and Benton's caught in the middle."

"If he is, then so are we."

"You got it, Doc."

It had been three years since Abby Turnbull had appeared in my office doorway, arms laden with fresh-cut irises and a bottle of exceptional wine. That had been the day when she had come to say good-bye, having given the Richmond *Times* notice. She was on her way to work in Washington as a police reporter for the *Post*. We had promised to keep in touch as people always do. I was ashamed I could not remember the last time I had called or written her a note.

"Do you want me to put her through?" Rose, my secretary, was asking. "Or should I take a message?"

"I'll talk to her," I said. "Scarpetta," I announced out of habit before I could catch myself.

"You still sound so damn *chiefly*," the familiar voice said.

"Abby! I'm sorry," I laughed. "Rose told me it was you. As usual, I'm in the middle of about fifty other things, and I think I've completely lost the art of being friendly on the phone. How are you?"

"Fine. If you don't count the fact that the homicide rate in Washington has tripled since I moved up here."

"A coincidence, I hope."

"Drugs." She sounded nervous. "Cocaine, crack, and semi-automatics. I always thought a beat in Miami would be the worst. Or maybe New York. But our lovely nation's capital is the worst."

I glanced up at the clock and jotted the time on a call sheet. Habit again. I was so accustomed to filling out call sheets that I reached for the clipboard even when my hairdresser called.

"I was hoping you might be free for dinner tonight," she said.

"In Washington?" I asked, perplexed.

"Actually, I'm in Richmond."

I suggested dinner at my house, packed up my briefcase, and headed out to the grocery store. After much deliberation as I pushed the cart up and down aisles, I selected two tenderloins and the makings for salad. The afternoon was beautiful. The thought of seeing Abby was improving my mood. I decided that an evening spent with an old friend was a good excuse to brave cooking out again.

When I got home, I began to work quickly, crushing fresh garlic into a bowl of red wine and olive oil. Though my mother had always admonished me about "ruining a good steak," I was spoiled by my own culinary skills. Honestly, I made the best marinade in town, and no cut of meat could resist being improved by it. Rinsing Boston lettuce and draining it on paper towels, I sliced mushrooms, onions, and the last Hanover tomato as I fortified myself to tend to the grill. Unable to put off the task any longer, I stepped out onto the brick patio.

For a moment, I felt like a fugitive on my own property as I surveyed the flower gardens and trees of my backyard. I fetched a bottle of 409 and a sponge and began vigorously to scrub the outdoor furniture before taking a Brillo pad to the grill, which I had not used since the Saturday night in May when Mark and I last had been together. I attacked sooty grease until my elbows hurt. Images and voices invaded my mind. Arguing. Fighting. Then a retreat into angry silence that ended with making frantic love.

I almost did not recognize Abby when she arrived at my front door shortly before six-thirty. When she had worked the police beat in Richmond, her hair had been to her shoulders and streaked with gray, giving her a washed-out, gaunt appearance that made her seem older than her forty-odd years. Now the gray was gone. Her hair was cut short and smartly styled to emphasize the fine bones of her face and her eyes, which were two different shades of green, an irregularity I had always found intriguing. She wore a dark blue silk suit and ivory silk blouse, and carried a sleek black leather briefcase.

"You look very Washingtonian," I said, giving her a hug.

"It's *so good* to see you, Kay."

She remembered I liked Scotch and had brought a bottle of Glenfiddich, which we wasted no time in uncorking. Then we sipped drinks on the patio and talked nonstop as I lit the grill beneath a dusky late summer sky.

"Yes, I do miss Richmond in some ways," she was explaining. "Washington is exciting, but the pits. I indulged myself and bought a Saab, right? It's already been broken into once, had the hubcaps stolen, the hell beaten out of the doors. I pay a hundred and fifty bucks a month to park the damn thing, and we're talking four blocks from my apartment. Forget parking at the *Post. I* walk to work and use a staff car. Washington's definitely not Richmond." She added a little too resolutely, "But I don't regret leaving."

"You're still working evenings?" Steaks sizzled as I placed them on the grill.

"No. It's somebody else's turn. The young reporters race around after dark and I follow up during the day. I get called after hours only if something really big goes down."

"I've been keeping up with your byline," I told her. "They sell the *Post* in the cafeteria. I usually pick it up during lunch."

"I don't always know what you're working on," she confessed. "But I'm aware of some things."

"Explaining why you're in Richmond?" I ventured, as I brushed marinade over the meat.

"Yes. The Harvey case."

I did not reply.

"Marino hasn't changed."

"You've talked to him?" I asked, glancing up at her.

She replied with a wry smile, "Tried to. And several other investigators. And, of course, Benton Wesley. In other words, forget it."

"Well if it makes you feel any better, Abby, nobody's talking much to me, either. And that's off the record."

"This entire conversation is off the record, Kay," she said seriously. "I didn't come to see you because I wanted to pick your brain for my story." She paused. "I've been aware of what's been going on here in Virginia. I was a lot more concerned about it than my editor was until Deborah Harvey and her boyfriend disappeared. Now it's gotten hot, real hot."

"I'm not surprised."

"I'm not quite sure where to begin." She looked unsettled. "There are things I've not told anybody, Kay. But I have a sense that I'm walking on ground somebody doesn't want me on."

"I'm not sure I understand," I said, reaching for my drink.

"I'm not sure I do, either. I ask myself if I'm imagining things."

"Abby, you're being cryptic. Please explain."

Taking a deep breath as she got out a cigarette, she replied, "I've been interested in the deaths of these couples for a long time. I've been doing some investigating, and the reactions I've gotten from the beginning are odd. It's gone beyond the usual reluctance I often run into with the police. I bring up the subject and people practically hang up on me. Then this past June, the FBI came to see me."

"I beg your pardon?" I stopped basting and looked hard at her.

"You remember that triple homicide in Williamsburg? The mother, father, and son shot to death during a robbery?"

"Yes."

"I was working on a feature about it, and had to drive to Williamsburg. As you know, when you get off Sixty-four, if you turn right you head toward Colonial Williamsburg, William and Mary. But if you turn left off the exit ramp, in maybe two hundred yards you dead-end at the entrance of Camp Peary. I wasn't thinking. I took the wrong turn."

"I've done that once or twice myself," I admitted.

She went on, "I drove up to the guard booth and explained I'd taken a wrong turn. Talk about a creepy place. God. All these big warning signs saying things like 'Armed Forces Experimental Training Activity,' and 'Entering This Facility Signifies Your Consent to the Search of Your Person and Personal Property.' I was half expecting a SWAT team of Neanderthals in camouflage to bolt out of the bushes and haul me away."

"The base police are not a friendly lot," I said, somewhat amused.

"Well, I wasted no time getting the hell out of there," Abby said, "and, in truth, forgot all about it until four days later when two FBI agents appeared in the lobby of the *Post* looking for me. They wanted to know what I'd been doing in Williamsburg, why I'd driven to Camp Peary. Obviously, my plate number had been recorded on film and traced back to the newspaper. It was weird."

"Why would the FBI be interested?" I asked. "Camp Peary is CIA."

"The CIA has no enforcement powers in the United States. Maybe that's why. Maybe the jerks were really CIA agents posing as FBI. Who can say what the hell is going on when you're dealing with those spooks? Besides, the CIA has never admitted that Camp Peary is its main training facility, and the agents never mentioned the CIA when they interrogated me. But I knew what they were getting at, and they knew I knew."

"What else did they ask?"

"Basically, they wanted to know if I was writing something about Camp Peary, maybe trying to sneak in. I told them if I had intended to sneak in, I would have been a little more *covert* about it than driving straight to the guard booth, and though I wasn't currently working on anything about, and I quote, 'the CIA,' maybe now I ought to consider it."

"I'm sure that went over well," I said dryly.

"The guys didn't bat an eye. You know the way they are."

"The CIA is paranoid, Abby, especially about Camp Peary. State police and emergency medical helicopters aren't allowed to fly over it. Nobody violates that airspace or gets beyond the guard booth without being cleared by Jesus Christ."

"Yet you've made that same wrong turn before, as have hundreds of tourists," she reminded me. "The FBI's never come looking for you, have they?"

"No. But I don't work for the *Post*."

I removed the steaks from the grill and she followed me into the kitchen. As I served the salads and poured wine, she continued to talk.

"Ever since the agents came to see me, peculiar things have been happening."

"Such as?"

"I think my phones are being tapped."

"Based on what?"

"It started with my phone at home. I'd be talking to someone and hear something. This has also happened at work, especially of late. A call will be transferred, and I have this strong sense that someone else is listening in. It's hard to explain." She nervously rearranged her silverware. "A static, a noisy silence, or however you want to describe it. But it's there."

"Any other peculiar things?"

"Well, there was something several weeks ago. I was standing out in front of a People's Drug Store off Connecticut, near Dupont Circle. A source was supposed to meet me there at eight P.M., then we were going to find some place quiet to have dinner and talk. And I saw this man. Cleancut, dressed in a windbreaker and jeans, nice looking. He walked by twice during the fifteen minutes I was standing on the corner, and I caught a glimpse of him again later when my appointment and I were going into the restaurant. I know it sounds crazy, but I had the feeling I was being followed."

"Had you ever seen this man before?"

She shook her head.

"Have you seen him since?"

"No," she said. "But there's something else. My mail. I live in an apartment building. All the mailboxes are downstairs in the lobby. Sometimes I get things with postmarks that don't make sense."

"If the CIA were tampering with your mail, I can assure you that you wouldn't know about it."

"I'm not saying my mail *looks* tampered with. But in several instances, someone—my mother, my literary agent—will swear they mailed something on a certain day, and when I finally get it, the date on the postmark is inconsistent with what it should be. Late. By days, a week. I don't know." She paused. "I probably would just assume it had to do with the ineptitude of the postal service, but with everything else that's been going on, it's made me wonder."

"Why would anyone be tapping your phone, tailing you, or tampering with your mail?" I asked the critical question.

"If I knew that, maybe I could do something about it." She finally got around to eating. "This is wonderful." Despite the compliment, she didn't appear the least bit hungry.

"Any possibility," I suggested bluntly, "that your encounter with these FBI agents, the episode at Camp Peary, might have made you paranoid?"

"Obviously it's made me paranoid. But look, Kay. It's not like I'm writing another *Veil* or working on a Watergate. Washington is one shoot-out after another, the same old shit. The only big thing brewing is what's going on here. These murders, or possible murders, of these couples. I start poking around and run into trouble. What do you think?"

"I'm not sure." I uncomfortably recalled Benton Wesley's demeanor, his warnings from the night before.

"I know the business about the missing shoes," Abby said.

I did not respond or show my surprise. It was a detail that, so far, had been kept from reporters.

"It's not exactly normal for eight people to end up dead in the woods without shoes and socks turning up either at the scenes or inside the abandoned cars." She looked expectantly at me.

"Abby," I said quietly, refilling our wineglasses, "you know I can't go into detail about these cases. Not even with you."

"You're not aware of anything that might clue me in as to what I'm up against?"

"To tell you the truth, I probably know less than you do."

"That tells me something. The cases have been going on for two and a half years, and you may know less than I do."

I remembered what Marino said about somebody "covering his ass." I thought of Pat Harvey and the congressional hearing. My fear was kicking in.

Abby said, "Pat Harvey is a bright star in Washington."

"I'm aware of her importance."

"There's more to it than what you read in the papers, Kay. In Washington, what parties you get invited to mean as much as votes. Maybe more. When it comes to prominent people included on the elite guest lists, Pat Harvey is right up there with the First Lady. It's been rumored that come the next presidential election, Pat Harvey may successfully conclude what Geraldine Ferraro started."

"A vice-presidential hopeful?" I asked dubiously.

"That's the gossip. I'm skeptical, but if we have another Republican President, I personally think she's at least got a shot at a Cabinet appointment or maybe even becoming the next Attorney General. Providing she holds together."

"She's going to have to work very hard at holding herself together through all this."

"Personal problems can definitely ruin your career," Abby agreed.

"They can, if you let them. But if you survive them, they can make you stronger, more effective."

"I know," she muttered, staring at her wineglass. "I'm pretty sure I never would have left Richmond if it hadn't been for what happened to Henna."

Not long after I had taken office in Richmond, Abby's sister, Henna, was murdered. The tragedy had brought Abby and me together professionally. We had become friends. Months later she had accepted the job at the *Post*.

"It still isn't easy for me to come back here," Abby said. "In fact, this is my first time since I moved. I even drove past my old house this morning and was halfway tempted to knock on the door, see if the current owners would let me in. I don't know why. But I wanted to walk through it again, see if I could handle going upstairs to Henna's room, replace that horrible last image of her with something harmless. It didn't appear that anyone was home. And it probably was just as well. I don't think I could have brought myself to do it."

"When you're truly ready, you'll do it," I said, and I wanted to tell her about my using the patio this evening, about how I had not been able to before now. But it sounded like such a small accomplishment, and Abby did not know about Mark.

"I talked to Fred Cheney's father late this morning," Abby said. "Then I went to see the Harveys."

"When will your story run?"

"Probably not until the weekend edition. I've still got a lot of reporting to do. The paper wants a profile of Fred and Deborah and anything else I can come up with about the investigation—especially any connection to the other four couples."

"How did the Harveys seem to you when you talked to them earlier today?"

"Well, I really didn't talk to him, to Bob. As soon as I

arrived, he left with his sons. Reporters are not his favorite people, and I have a feeling being 'Pat Harvey's husband' gets to him. He never gives interviews." She pushed her half-eaten steak away and reached for her cigarettes. Her smoking was a lot worse than I remembered it. "I'm worried about Pat. She looks as if she's aged ten years in the last week. And it was strange. I couldn't shake the sensation she knows something, has already formulated her own theory about what's happened to her daughter. I guess that's what made me most curious. I'm wondering if she's gotten a threat, a note, some sort of communication from whomever's involved. And she's refusing to tell anyone, including the police."

"I can't imagine she would be that unwise."

"I can," Abby said. "I think if she thought there was any chance Deborah might return home unharmed, Pat Harvey wouldn't tell God what was going on."

I got up to clear the table.

"I think you'd better make some coffee," Abby said. "I don't want to fall asleep at the wheel."

"When do you need to head out?" I asked, loading the dishwasher.

"Soon. I've got a couple of places to go before I drive back to Washington."

I glanced over at her as I filled the coffeepot with water.

She explained, "A Seven-Eleven where Deborah and Fred stopped after they left Richmond—"

"How did you know about that?" I interrupted her.

"I managed to pry it out of the tow truck operator who hung around the rest stop, waiting to haul away the Jeep. He overheard the police discussing a receipt they found in a wadded-up paper bag. It required one hell of a lot of trouble, but I managed to figure out which Seven-Eleven and what clerk would have been working around the time Deborah and Fred would have stopped in. Someone named Ellen Jordan works the four-to-midnight shift Monday through Friday."

I was so fond of Abby, it was easy for me to forget that she had won more than her share of investigative reporting awards for a very good reason.

"What do you expect to find out from this clerk?"

"Ventures like this, Kay, are like looking for the prize inside a box of Crackerjacks. I don't know the answers in fact, I don't even know the questions—until I start digging."

"I really don't think you should wander around out there alone late at night, Abby."

"If you'd like to ride shotgun," she replied, amused, "I'd love the company."

"I don't think that's a very good idea."

"I suppose you're right," she said.

I decided to do it anyway.

4

The illuminated sign was visible half a mile before we reached the exit, a "7-Eleven" glowing in the dark. Its cryptic red-and-green message no longer meant what it said, for every 7-Eleven I knew of was open twenty-four hours a day. I could almost hear what my father would say.

"Your grandfather left Verona for *this*?"

That was his favorite remark when he would read the morning paper, shaking his head in disapproval. It was what he said when someone with a Georgia accent treated us as if we weren't "real Americans." It was what my father would mumble when he heard tales of dishonesty, "dope," and divorce. When I was a child in Miami, he owned a small neighborhood grocery and was at the dinner table every night talking about his day and asking about ours. His presence in my life was not long. He died when I was twelve. But I was certain that were he still here, he would not appreciate convenience stores. Nights, Sundays, and holidays were not to be spent working behind a counter or eating a burrito on the road. Those hours were for family.

Abby checked her mirrors again as she turned off on the exit. In less than a hundred feet, she was pulling into the 7-Eleven's parking lot, and I could tell she was relieved. Other than a Volkswagen near the double glass front doors, it seemed we were the only customers.

"Coast is clear so far," she observed, switching off the ignition. "Haven't passed a single patrol car, unmarked or otherwise, in the last twenty miles."

"At least not that you know of," I said.

The night was hazy, not a star in sight, the air warm but damp. A young man carrying a twelve-pack of beer passed by us as we went inside the air-conditioned coolness of America's favorite fixes, where video games flashed bright lights in a corner and a young woman was restocking a cigarette rack behind the counter. She didn't look a day over eighteen, her bleached blonde hair billowing out in a frizzy aura around her head, her slight figure clad in an orange-and-white-checked tunic and a pair of tight black jeans. Her fingernails were long and painted bright red, and when she turned around to see what we wanted, I was struck by the hardness of her face. It was as if she had skipped training wheels and gone straight to a Harley-Davidson.

"Ellen Jordan?" Abby inquired.

The clerk looked surprised, then wary. "Yeah? So who wants to know?"

"Abby Turnbull." Abby presented her hand in a very

businesslike fashion. Ellen Jordan shook it limply. "From Washington," Abby added. "The *Post*."

"What *Post*?"

"The *Washington Post*," Abby said.

"Oh." Instantly, she was bored. "We already carry it. Right over there." She pointed to a depleted stack near the door.

There was an awkward pause.

"I'm a *reporter* for the *Post*," Abby explained.

Ellen's eyes lit up. "No kidding?"

"No kidding. I'd like to ask you a few questions."

"You mean for a story?"

"Yes. I'm doing a story, Ellen. And I really need your help."

"What do you want to know?" She leaned against the counter, her serious expression reflecting her sudden importance.

"It's about the couple that came in here Friday night a week ago. A young man and woman. About your age. They came in shortly after nine P.M., bought a six-pack of Pepsi, several other items."

"Oh. The ones missing," she said, animated now. "You know, I shoulda never told 'em to go to that rest stop. But one of the first things they tell us when we're hired is nobody gets to use the bathroom. Personally, I wouldn't mind, especially not when the girl and boy came in. I felt so sorry for her. I mean, I sure understood."

"I'm sure you did," Abby said sympathetically.

"It was sort of embarrassing," Ellen went on. "When she bought the Tampax and asked if she could please use the bathroom, her boyfriend standing right there. Wow, I sure do wish I'd let her now."

"How did you know he was her boyfriend?" Abby asked.

For an instant, Ellen looked confused. "Well, I just assumed. They was looking around in here together, seemed to like each other a lot. You know how people act. You can tell if you're paying attention. And when I'm in here all hours by myself, I get pretty good at telling about people. Take married couples. Get 'em all the time, on a trip, kids in the car. Most of 'em come in here and I can tell they're tired and not getting along good. But the two you're talking about, they was real sweet with each other."

"Did they say anything else to you, other than needing to find a rest room?"

"We talked while I was ringing them up," Ellen replied. "Nothing special. I said the usual. 'Nice night for driving,' and, 'Where ya headin'?'"

"And did they tell you?" Abby asked, taking notes.

"Huh?"

Abby glanced up at her. "Did they tell you where they were heading?"

"They said the beach. I remember that because I told 'em they was lucky. Seems whenever everybody else's heading off to fun places, I'm always stuck right here. Plus, me and my boyfriend had just broke up. It was getting to me, you know?"

"I understand." Abby smiled kindly. "Tell me more about how they were acting, Ellen. Anything jump out at you?"

She thought about this, then said, "Uh-uh. They was real nice, but in a hurry. I guess because she wanted to find a bathroom pretty bad. Mostly I remember how polite they was. You know, people come in here all the time wanting to use the bathroom and get nasty when I tell 'em they can't."

"You mentioned you directed them to the rest stop," Abby said. "Do you remember exactly what you told them?"

"Sure. I told 'em there's one not too far from here. Just get back on Sixty-four East"—she pointed—"and they'd see it in about five, ten minutes, couldn't miss it."

"Was anybody else in here when you told them this?"

"People were in and out. Lot of folks on the road." She thought for a minute. "I know there was a kid in back playing Pac Man. Same little creep always in here."

"Anybody else who might have been near the counter when the couple was?" Abby asked.

There was this man. He came in right after the couple came in. Was looking through the magazines, ended up buying a cup of coffee."

"Was this while you were talking to the couple?" Abby relentlessly pursued the details.

"Yeah. I remember because he was real friendly and said something to the guy about the Jeep being a nice one. The couple drove up in a red Jeep. One of those fancy kinds. It was parked right in front of the doors."

"Then what happened?"

Ellen sat down on the stool in front of the cash register. "Well, that was pretty much it. Some other customers came in. The guy with the coffee left, and then maybe five minutes later, the couple left, too."

"But the man with the coffee—he was still near the counter

69

when you were directing the couple to the rest stop?" Abby wanted to know.

Ellen frowned. "It's hard to remember. But I think he was looking through the magazines when I was telling them that. Then it seems like the girl went off down one of the aisles to find what she needed, got back to the counter just as the man was paying for his coffee."

"You said the couple left maybe five minutes after the man did," Abby went on. "What were they doing?"

"Well, it took a couple minutes," she replied. "The girl set a six-pack of Coors on the counter, you know, and I had to card her, saw she was under twenty-one, so I couldn't sell her beer. She was real nice about it, sort of laughed. I mean, all of us were laughing about it. I don't take it personal. Hell, I used to try it, too. Anyway, she ended up buying a six-pack of sodas. Then they left."

"Can you describe this man, the one who bought the coffee?"

"Not real good."

"White or black?"

"White. Seems like he was dark. Black hair, maybe brown. Maybe in his late twenties, early thirties."

"Tall, short, fat, thin?"

Ellen stared off toward the back of the store. "Medium height, maybe. Sort of well built but not big, I think."

"Beard or mustache?"

"Don't think so . . . Wait a minute." Her face lit up. "His hair was short. Yeah! In fact, I remember it passed through my mind he looked military. You know, there's a lot of military types around here, come in all the time on their way to Tidewater."

"What else made you think he might be military?" Abby asked.

"I don't know. But maybe it was just his way. It's hard to explain, but when you've seen enough military guys, it gets to where you can pick 'em out. There's just something about 'em. Like tattoos, for example. A lot of 'em have tattoos."

"Did this man have a tattoo?"

Her frown turned to disappointment. "I didn't notice."

"How about the way he was dressed?"

"Uhhhh . . ."

"A suit and tie?" Abby asked.

"Well, he wasn't in a suit and tie. Nothing fancy. Maybe jeans or dark pants. He might've been wearing a zip-up jacket . . . Gee, I really can't be sure."

"Do you, by chance, remember what he was driving?"

"No," she said with certainty. "I never saw his car. He must've parked off to the side."

"Did you tell the police all this when they came to talk to you, Ellen?"

"Yeah." She was eyeing the parking lot out front. A van had just pulled up. "I told 'em pretty much the same things I told you. Except for some of the stuff I couldn't remember then."

When two teenage boys sauntered in and headed straight for the video games, Ellen returned her attention to us. I could tell she had nothing more to say and was beginning to entertain doubts about having said too much.

Apparently, Abby was getting the same message. "Thank

you, Ellen," she said, backing away from the counter. "The story will run on Saturday or Sunday. Be sure you watch for it."

Then we were out the door.

"Time to get the hell out of here before she starts screaming that everything was *off the record*."

"I doubt she'd even know what the term meant," I replied.

"What surprises me," Abby said, "is that the cops didn't tell her to keep her mouth shut."

"Maybe they did but she couldn't resist the possibility of seeing her name in print."

The I-64 East rest stop where the clerk had directed Deborah and Fred was completely deserted when we pulled in.

Abby parked in front, near a cluster of newspaper vending machines, and for several minutes we sat in silence. A small holly tree directly in front of us was silver in the car's headlights, and lamps were smudges of white in the fog. I couldn't imagine getting out to use the rest room were I alone.

"Creepy," Abby muttered under her breath. "God. I wonder if it's always this deserted on a Tuesday night, or if the news releases have scared people away."

"Possibly both," I replied. "But you can be sure it wasn't deserted the Friday night Deborah and Fred pulled in."

"They may have been parked right about where we are," she mused. "Probably people all over the place, since it was the beginning of the Labor Day weekend. If this is where they encountered someone bad, then he must be a brash son of a bitch."

"If there were people all over the place," I said, "then there would have been cars all over the place."

"Meaning?" She lit a cigarette.

"Assuming this is where Deborah and Fred encountered someone, and assuming that for some reason they let him in the Jeep, then what about his car? Did he arrive here on foot?"

"Not likely," she replied.

"If he drove in," I went on, "and left his car parked out here, that wasn't going to work very well unless there was a lot of traffic."

"I see what you're suggesting. If his was the only car in this lot, and it remained out here for hours late at night, chances are a trooper might have spotted it and called it in."

"That's a big chance to take if you're in the process of committing a crime," I added.

She thought for a moment. "You know, what bothers me is that the entire scenario is random but not random. Deborah and Fred's stopping at the rest stop was random. If they happened to encounter someone bad here—or even inside the Seven-Eleven, such as the guy buying coffee—that seems random. But there's premeditation, too. Forethought. If someone abducted them, it seems like he knew what he was doing."

I did not respond.

I was thinking about what Wesley had said. A political connection. Or an assailant who went through a lot of dry runs. Assuming that the couple had not chosen to disappear, then I did not see how the outcome could be anything but tragic.

Abby put the car in gear.

It wasn't until we were on the Interstate and she was setting the cruise control that she spoke again. "You think they're dead, don't you?"

"Are you asking for a quote?"

"No, Kay. I'm not asking for a quote. You want to know the truth? Right now I don't give a damn about this story. I just want to know what the hell's going on."

"Because you're worried about yourself."

"Wouldn't you be?"

"Yes. If I thought my phones were tapped, that I was being tailed, I would be worried, Abby. And speaking of worried, it's late. You're exhausted. It's ridiculous for you to drive back to Washington tonight."

She glanced over at me.

"I've got plenty of room. You can head out first thing in the morning."

"Only if you've got an extra toothbrush, something I can sleep in, and don't mind if I pillage your bar."

Leaning back in the seat, I shut my eyes and muttered, "You can get drunk, if you want. In fact, I might just join you."

When we walked into my house at midnight, the telephone started ringing, and I answered it before my machine could.

"Kay?"

At first, the voice did not register because I was not expecting it. Then my heart began to pound.

"Hello, Mark," I said.

"I'm sorry to call so late——"

I could not keep the tension out of my voice as I interrupted. "I have company. I'm sure you remember my mentioning my friend Abby Turnbull, with the *Post*? She's here staying the night. We've been having a wonderful time catching up."

Mark did not respond. After a pause, he said, "Maybe it would be easier for you to call me, when it suits."

When I hung up, Abby was staring at me, startled by my obvious distress.

"Who in God's name was that, Kay?"

My first months at Georgetown I was so overwhelmed by law school and feelings of alienation that I kept my own counsel and distance from others. I was already an M.D., a middle-class Italian from Miami with very little exposure to the finer things in life. Suddenly I found myself cast among the brilliant and beautiful and though I am not ashamed of my heritage, I felt socially common.

Mark James was one of the privileged, a tall, graceful figure, self-assured and self-contained. I was aware of him long before I knew his name. We first met in the law library between dimly lit shelves of books, and I will never forget his intense green eyes as we began to discuss some tort I cannot recall. We ended up drinking coffee in a bar and talking until early in the morning. After that, we saw each other almost every day.

For a year we did not sleep, it seemed, for even when we slept together our lovemaking did not permit many hours of rest. No matter how much we got of each other it was never enough, and foolishly, typically, I was convinced we would be together forever. I refused to accept the chill of disappointment that settled over the relationship during our second year. When I graduated wearing someone else's engagement ring, I had convinced myself that I had gotten over Mark, until he mysteriously reappeared not so long ago.

"Maybe Tony was a safe harbor," Abby considered, referring to my ex-husband as we drank Cognac in my kitchen.

"Tony was practical," I replied. "Or so it seemed at first."

"Makes sense. I've done it before in my own pathetic love life." She reached for her snifter. "I'll have some passionate fling, and God knows there have been few and they never last long. But when it ends, I'm like a wounded soldier limping home. I wind up in the arms of some guy with the charisma of a slug who promises to take care of me."

"That's the fairy tale."

"Right out of Grimm's," she agreed, bitterly. "They say they'll take care of you, but what they mean is they want you to be there fixing dinner and washing their shorts."

"You've just described Tony to a T," I said.

"What ever happened to him?"

"I haven't talked to him in too many years to count."

"People at least ought to be friends."

"He didn't want to be friends," I said.

"Do you still think about him?"

"You can't live six years with somebody and not think about him. That doesn't mean I want to be with Tony. But a part of me will always care about him, hope he's doing well."

"Were you in love with him when you got married?"

"I thought I was."

"Maybe so," Abby said. "But it sounds to me as if you never stopped loving Mark."

I refilled our glasses. Both of us were going to feel like hell in the morning.

"I find it incredible that you got together again after so many years," she went on. "And no matter what's happened, I suspect Mark has never stopped loving you, either."

When he came back into my life, it was as if we had lived in foreign countries during our years apart, the languages of our pasts indecipherable to each other. We communicated openly only in the dark. He did tell me he had married and his wife had been killed in an automobile accident. I later found out he had forsaken his law practice and signed on with the FBI. When we were together it was euphoric, the most wonderful days I had known since our first year at Georgetown. Of course, it did not last. History has a mean habit of repeating itself.

"I don't suppose it's his fault he was transferred to Denver," Abby was saying.

"He made a choice," I said. "And so did I."

"You didn't want to go with him?"

"I'm the reason he requested the assignment, Abby. He wanted a separation."

"So he moves across the country? That's rather extreme."

"When people are angry, their behavior can be extreme. They can make big mistakes."

"And he's probably too stubborn to admit he made a mistake," she said.

"He's stubborn, I'm stubborn. Neither of us win any prizes for our skills in compromising. I have my career and he has his. He was in Quantico and I was here—that got old fast, and I had no intention of leaving Richmond and he had no intention of moving to Richmond. Then he started contemplating going back on the street, transferring to a field office somewhere or taking a position at Headquarters in D.C. On and on it went, until it seemed that all we did was fight." I paused, groping to explain what would never be clear. "Maybe I'm just set in my ways."

"You can't be with someone and continue to live as you always did, Kay."

How many times had Mark and I said that to each other? It got to where we rarely said anything new.

"Is maintaining your autonomy worth the price you're paying, the price both of you are paying?"

There were days when I was no longer so sure, but I did not tell Abby this.

She lit a cigarette and reached for the bottle of Cognac.

"Did the two of you ever try counseling?"

"No."

What I told her was not entirely true. Mark and I had never gone to counseling, but I had gone alone and was still seeing a psychiatrist, though infrequently now.

"Does he know Benton Wesley?" Abby asked.

"Of course. Benton trained Mark in the Academy long before I came to Virginia," I replied. "They're very good friends."

"What's Mark working on in Denver?"

"I have no idea. Some special assignment."

"Is he aware of the cases here? The couples?"

"I would assume so." Pausing, I asked, "Why?"

"I don't know. But be careful what you say to Mark."

"Tonight was the first time he's called in months. Obviously, I say very little to him."

She got up and I led her to her room.

As I gave her a gown and showed her the bath, she went on, the effects of the Cognac becoming apparent, "He'll call again. Or you're going to call him. So be careful."

"I'm not planning on calling him," I said.

"You're just as bad as he is, then," she said. "Both of you hardheaded and unforgiving as hell. So there. That's my assessment of the situation, whether you like it or not."

"I have to be at the office by eight," I said. "I'll make sure you're up by seven."

She hugged me good night and kissed my cheek.

The following weekend I went out early and bought the *Post* and could not find Abby's story. It did not come out the next week or the week after that, and I thought this strange. Was Abby all right? Why had I not heard a word from her since our visit in Richmond?

In late October I called the *Post*'s newsroom.

"I'm sorry," said a man who sounded harried. "Abby's on leave. Won't be back until next August."

"Is she still in town?" I asked, stunned.

"Got no idea."

Hanging up, I flipped through my address book and tried her home number. I was answered by a machine. Abby did not return that call or any of the others I made during the next few weeks. It wasn't until shortly after Christmas that I began to realize what was going on. On Monday, January sixth, I came home to find a letter in my mailbox. There was no return address, but the handwriting was unmistakable. Opening the envelope, I discovered inside a sheet of yellow legal paper scribbled with "FYI. Mark," and a short article clipped from a recent issue of the *New York Times*. Abby Turnbull, I read with disbelief, had signed a book contract to write about the disappearance of Fred Cheney and Deborah Harvey, and the "frightening parallels" between their cases and those of four other couples in Virginia who had vanished and turned up dead.

Abby had warned me about Mark, and now he was warning me about her. Or was there some other reason for his sending me the article?

For a long interval I sat in my kitchen, tempted to leave an outraged message on Abby's machine or to call Mark. I finally decided to call Anna, my psychiatrist.

"You feel betrayed?" she asked when I got her on the phone.

"To put it mildly, Anna."

"You've known Abby is writing a newspaper story. Is writing a book so much worse?"

"She never told me she was writing a book," I said.

"Because you feel betrayed doesn't mean you truly have

been," Anna said. "This is your perception at the moment, Kay. You will have to wait and see. And as for why Mark sent you the article, you may have to wait and see about that, too. Perhaps it was his way of reaching out."

"I'm wondering if I should consult a lawyer," I said. "See if there's something I should do to protect myself. I have no idea what might end up in Abby's book."

"I think it would be wiser to take her words at face value," Anna advised. "She said your conversations were off the record. Has she ever betrayed you before?"

"No."

"Then I suggest you give her a chance. Give her an opportunity to explain. Besides," she added, "I'm not sure how much of a book she can write. There have been no arrests, and there is no resolution as to what happened to the couple. They have yet to turn up."

The bitter irony of that remark would hit me exactly two weeks later, on January twentieth, when I was on the capitol grounds waiting to see what happened when a bill authorizing the Forensic Science Bureau to create a DNA databank went before the Virginia General Assembly.

I was returning from the snack bar, cup of coffee in hand, when I spotted Pat Harvey, elegant in a navy cashmere suit, a zip-up black leather portfolio under her arm. She was talking to several delegates in the hall, and glancing my way, she immediately excused herself.

"Dr. Scarpetta," she said, offering her hand. She looked relieved to see me, but drawn and stressed.

I wondered why she wasn't in Washington, and then she

answered my unspoken question. "I was asked to lend my support to Senate Bill One-thirty," she said, smiling nervously.
"So I suppose both of us are here today for the same reason."

"Thank you. We need all the support we can get."

"I don't think you have a worry," she replied.

She was probably right. The testimony of the national drug
policy director and the publicity it would generate would put
considerable pressure on the Courts of Justice Committee.

After an awkward silence, with both of us glancing at the
people milling about, I asked her quietly, "How are you?"

For an instant her eyes teared up. Then she gave me another
quick, nervous smile and stared off down the hall. "If you'll
please excuse me, I see someone I need to have a word with."

Pat Harvey was barely out of earshot when my pager went
off.

A minute later I was on the phone.

"Marino's on his way," my secretary was explaining. "So am
I," I said. "Get my scene kit, Rose. Make sure everything's in
order. Flashlight, camera, batteries, gloves."

"Will do."

Cursing my heels and the rain, I hurried down steps and
along Governor Street, the wind tearing at my umbrella as I
envisioned Mrs. Harvey's eyes that split second when they had
revealed her pain. Thank God she had not been standing there
when my pager had sounded its dreadful alert.

5

The odor was noticeable from a distance. Heavy drops of rain smacked loudly against dead leaves, the sky as dark as dusk, winter-bare trees drifting in and out of the fog.

"Jesus," Marino muttered as he stepped over a log. "They must be ripe. No other smell like it. Always reminds me of pickled crabs."

"It gets worse," promised Jay Morrell, who was leading the way.

Black mud sucked at our feet, and every time Marino brushed against a tree I was showered with freezing water. Fortunately, I kept a hooded Gore-Tex coat and heavy rubber boots in the trunk of my state car for scenes like this one. What I had been unable to find were my thick leather gloves, and it was impossible to navigate through the woods and keep branches out of my face if my hands were in my pockets.

I had been told there were two bodies, suspected to be a male and a female. They were less than four miles from the rest stop where Deborah Harvey's Jeep had been found last fall.

You don't know that it's them, I thought to myself with every step.

But when we reached the perimeter of the scene, my heart constricted. Benton Wesley was talking to an officer working a metal detector, and Wesley would not have been summoned unless the police were sure. He stood with military erectness, exuding the quiet confidence of a man in charge. He seemed bothered neither by the weather nor by the stench of decomposing human flesh. He was not looking around and taking in the details the way Marino and I were, and I knew why. Wesley had already looked around. He had been here long before I was called.

The bodies were lying next to each other, face down in a small clearing about a quarter of a mile from the muddy logging road where we had left our cars. They were so badly decomposed they were partially skeletonized. The long bones of arms and legs protruded like dirty gray sticks from rotted clothing scattered with leaves. Skulls were detached and had been nudged or rolled, probably by small predators, a foot or two away.

"Did you find their shoes and socks?" I asked, not seeing either.

"No, ma'am. But we found a purse." Morrell pointed to the body on the right. "Forty-four dollars and twenty-six cents in it. Plus a driver's license, Deborah Harvey's driver's license."

He pointed again, adding, "We're assuming the body there on the left is Cheney."

Yellow crime scene tape glistened wetly against the dark bark of trees. Twigs snapped beneath the feet of men moving about, their voices blending into an indistinguishable babble beneath the relentless, dreary rain. Opening my medical bag, I got out a pair of surgical gloves and my camera.

For a while I did not move as I surveyed the shrunken, almost fleshless bodies before me. Determining the sex and race of skeletal remains cannot always be done at a glance. I would not swear to anything until I could look at the pelves, which were obscured by what appeared to be dark blue or black denim jeans. But based on the characteristics of the body to my right—small bones, small skull with small mastoids, nonprominent brow ridge, and strands of long blondish hair clinging to rotted fabric—I had no reason to think anything other than white female. The size of her companion, the robustness of the bones, prominent brow ridge, large skull, and flat face were good for white male.

As for what might have happened to the couple, I could not tell. There were no ligatures indicating strangulation. I saw no obvious fractures or holes that might have meant blows or bullets. Male and female were quietly together in death, the bones of her left arm slipped under his right as if she had been holding on to him in the end, empty eye sockets gaping as rain rolled over their skulls.

It wasn't until I moved in close and got down on my knees that I noticed a margin of dark soil, so narrow it was barely perceptible, on either side of the bodies. If they had died

Labor Day weekend, autumn leaves would not have fallen yet. The ground beneath them would be relatively bare. I did not like what was going through my mind. It was bad enough that the police had been tramping around out here for hours. Dammit. To move or disturb a body in any way before the medical examiner arrives is a cardinal sin, and every officer out here knew that.

"Dr. Scarpetta?" Morrell was towering over me, his breath smoking. "Was just talking to Phillips over there." He glanced in the direction of several officers searching thick underbrush about twenty feet east of us. "He found a watch and an earring, some change, all right about here where the bodies are. The interesting thing is, the metal detector kept going off. He had it right over the bodies and it was beeping. Could be from a zipper or something. Maybe a metal snap or button on their jeans. Thought you should know."

I looked up into his thin, serious face. He was shivering beneath his parka.

'Tell me what you did with the bodies in addition to running the metal detector over them, Morrell. I can see they've been moved. I need to know this is the exact position they were in when they were discovered this morning."

"I don't know about when the hunters found them, though they claim they didn't get very close," he said, eyes probing the woods. "But yes, ma'am, this is the way they looked when we got here. All we did was check for personal effects, went into their pockets and her purse."

"I assume you took photographs before you moved anything," I said evenly.

"We started taking pictures as soon as we arrived."

Getting out a small flashlight, I began the hopeless task of looking for trace evidence. After bodies have been exposed to the elements for so many months, the chance of finding significant hairs, fibers, or other debris was slim to none. Morrell watched in silence, uneasily shifting his weight from one foot to the other.

"Have you found out anything else from your investigation that might be of assistance, assuming this is Deborah Harvey and Fred Cheney?" I asked, for I had not seen Morrell or talked to him since the day Deborah's Jeep had been found.

"Nothing but a possible drug connection," he said. "We've been told Cheney's roommate at Carolina was into cocaine. Maybe Cheney fooled around with cocaine too. That's one of the things we're considering, if maybe he and the Harvey girl met up with someone who was selling drugs and came out here."

That didn't make any sense.

"Why would Cheney leave the Jeep at a rest stop and go off with a drug dealer, taking Deborah with him, and come out here?" I asked. "Why not just buy the drugs at the rest stop and be on their way?"

"They may have come out here to party."

"Who in his right mind would come out here after dark to party or do anything else? And where are their shoes, Morrell? Are you suggesting they walked through the woods barefoot?"

"We don't know what happened to their shoes," he said.

"That's very interesting. So far, five couples have been

found dead and we don't know what happened to their shoes. Not one shoe or sock has turned up. Don't you find that rather odd?"

"Oh, yes, ma'am. I think it's odd, all right," he said, hugging himself to get warm. "But right now I've got to work these two cases here without thinking about the other four couples. I've got to go with what I've got. And all I've got at the moment is a possible drug connection. I can't allow myself to get sidetracked by this serial murder business or who the girl's mother is, or I might be wrong and miss the obvious."

"I certainly wouldn't want you to miss the obvious."

He was silent.

"Did you find any drug paraphernalia inside the Jeep?"

"No. Nothing out here so far to suggest drugs, either. But we've got a lot of soil and leaves to go through—"

"The weather's awful. I'm not sure it's a good idea to begin sifting through the soil." I sounded impatient and irritable. I was put out with him. I was put out with the police. Water was trickling down the front of my coat. My knees hurt. I was losing feeling in my hands and feet. The stench was overpowering, and the loud smacking of the rain was getting on my nerves.

"We haven't started digging or using the sieves. Thought we might wait on that. It's too hard to see. The metal detector's all we've used so far, that and our eyes."

"Well, the more all of us walk around out here, the more we risk destroying the scene. Small bones, teeth, other things, get stepped on and pushed down into the mud." They had already been here for hours. It was probably too damn late to preserve the scene.

"So, you want to move them today or hold off until the weather clears?" he asked.

Under ordinary circumstances, I would have waited until the rain stopped and there was more light. When bodies have been in the woods for months, leaving them covered with plastic and in place for another day or two isn't going to make any difference. But when Marino and I had parked on the logging road, there were already several television news trucks waiting. Reporters were sitting in their cars, others braving the rain and trying to coax information out of police officers standing sentry. The circumstances were anything but ordinary. Though I had no right to tell Morrell what to do, by Code I had jurisdiction over the bodies.

"There are stretchers and body bags in the back of my car," I said, digging out my keys. "If you could have somebody get them, we'll move the bodies shortly and I'll take them on in to the morgue."

"Sure thing. I'll take care of it."

"Thanks." Then Benton Wesley was crouching next to me.

"How did you find out?" I asked. The question was ambiguous, but he knew what I meant.

"Morrell reached me in Quantico. I came right away." He studied the bodies, his angular face almost haggard in the shadow of his dripping hood. "You seeing anything that might tell us what happened?"

"All I can tell you at the moment is their skulls weren't fractured and they weren't shot in the head."

He did not respond, his silence adding to my tension.

I began unfolding sheets as Marino walked up, hands jammed into his coat pockets, shoulders hunched against the cold and rain.

"You're going to catch pneumonia," Wesley remarked, getting to his feet. "Is Richmond PD too cheap to buy you guys hats?"

"Shit," Marino said, "you're lucky they put gas in your damn car and furnish you with a gun. The squirrels in Spring Street got it better than we do."

Spring Street was the state penitentiary. It was true that it cost the state more money each year to house some inmates than a lot of police officers got paid for keeping them off the street. Marino loved to complain about it.

"I see the locals drug your ass out here from Quantico. Your lucky day," Marino said.

"They told me what they'd found. I asked if they'd called you yet."

"Yeah, well, they got around to it eventually."

"I can see that. Morrell told me he's never filled out a VICAP form. Maybe you can give him a hand."

Marino stared at the bodies, his jaw muscles flexing.

"We need to get this into the computer," Wesley went on as rain drummed the earth.

Tuning out their conversation, I arranged one of the sheets next to the female's remains and turned her on her back. She held together nicely, joints and ligaments still intact. In a climate like Virginia's, it generally takes at least a year of being exposed to the elements before a body is fully skeletonized, or reduced to disarticulated bones. Muscle tissue, cartilage, and ligaments are tenacious. She was petite, and I recalled the photograph of the lovely young athlete posed on a balance beam. Her shirt, I noted, was some sort of pullover, possibly a sweatshirt, and her jeans were zipped up and snapped. Unfolding the other sheet, I went through the same procedure with her companion. Turning over decomposed bodies is like turning over rocks. You never know what you'll find underneath, except that you can usually count on insects. My flesh crawled as several spiders skittered off, vanishing beneath leaves.

Shifting positions in a fruitless attempt to get more comfortable, I realized Wesley and Marino were gone. Kneeling alone in the rain, I began feeling through leaves and mud, searching for fingernails, small bones, and teeth. I noticed at least two teeth missing from one of the mandibles. Most likely, they were somewhere near the skulls. After fifteen or twenty minutes of this, I had recovered one tooth, a small transparent button, possibly from the male's shirt, and two cigarette butts. Several cigarette butts had been found at each of the scenes, though not all of the victims were known to smoke. What was unusual was that not one of the filters bore a manufacturer's brand mark or name.

When Morrell returned, I pointed this out to him.

"Never been to a scene where there aren't cigarette butts," he replied, and I wondered just how many scenes he could swear he had been to. Not many, I guessed.

"It's as if part of the paper has been peeled away or the end of the filter nearest the tobacco pinched off," I explained, and

when this evoked no response from him I dug in the mud
some more.

Night was falling when we headed back to our cars, a
somber procession of police officers gripping stretchers bearing bright orange body bags. We reached the narrow unpaved
logging road as a sharp wind began to kick in from the north
and the rain began to freeze. My dark blue state station wagon
was equipped as a hearse. Fasteners in the plyboard floor in
back locked stretchers into place so they did not slide around
during transport. I positioned myself behind the wheel and
buckled up as Marino climbed in, Morrell slammed shut the
tailgate, and photographers and television cameramen
recorded us on film. A reporter who wouldn't give up rapped
on my window, and I locked the doors.

"God bless it. I hope like hell I ain't called to another one
of these," Marino exclaimed, turning on the heat full blast.

I drove around several potholes.

"What a bunch of vultures." Eyeing his side mirror, he
watched journalists scurrying into their cars. "Some asshole
must've run his mouth over the radio. Probably Morrell. The
dumb-ass. If he was in my squad, I'd send his ass back to traffic, get him transferred to the uniform room or information
desk."

"You remember how to get back on Sixty-four from here?"
I asked.

"Hang a left at the fork straight ahead. Shit." He cracked
the window and got out his cigarettes. "Nothing like driving
in a closed-up car with decomposed bodies."

Thirty miles later I unlocked the back door to the OCME

and pushed a red button on the wall inside. The bay door made a loud grating noise as it opened, light spilling onto the wet tarmac. Backing in the wagon, I opened the tailgate. We slid out the stretchers and wheeled them inside the morgue as several forensic scientists got off the elevator and smiled at us without giving our cargo more than a glance. Body-shaped mounds on stretchers and gurneys were as common as the cinderblock walls. Blood drips on the floor and foul odors were unpleasantnesses you learned to step around and quietly hurry past.

Producing another key, I opened the padlock on the refrigerator's stainless-steel door, then went to see about toe tags and signing in the bodies before we transferred them to a double-decker gurney and left them for the night.

"You mind if I stop by tomorrow to see what you figure out about these two?" Marino asked.

"That would be fine."

"It's them," he said. "Gotta be."

"I'm afraid that's the way it looks, Marino. What happened to Wesley?"

"On his way back to Quantico, where he can prop his Florsheim shoes on top of his big desk and get the results over the phone."

"I thought you two were friends," I said warily.

"Yeah, well, life's funny like that, Doc. It's like when I'm supposed to go fishing. All the weather reports predict clear skies, and the minute I put the boat in the water it begins to friggin' rain."

"Are you on evening shift this weekend?"

"Not last I heard."

"Sunday night—how about coming over for dinner? Six, six-thirty?"

"Yeah, I could probably manage that," he said, looking away, but not before I caught the pain in his eyes.

I had heard his wife supposedly had moved back to New Jersey before Thanksgiving to take care of her dying mother. Since then I had had dinner with Marino several times, but he had been unwilling to talk about his personal life.

Letting myself into the autopsy suite, I headed for the locker room, where I always kept personal necessities and a change of clothes for what I considered hygienic emergencies. I was filthy, the stench of death clinging to my clothing, skin, and hair. I quickly stuffed my scene clothes inside a plastic garbage bag and taped a note to it instructing the morgue supervisor to drop it by the cleaners first thing in the morning. Then I got into the shower, where I stayed for a very long time.

One of many things Anna had advised me to do after Mark moved to Denver was to make an effort to counteract the damage I routinely inflicted upon my body.

"*Exercise*." She had said that frightful word. "The endorphins relieve depression. You will eat better, sleep better, feel so much better. I think you should take up tennis again."

Following her suggestion had proved a humbling experience. I had scarcely touched a racket since I was a teenager, and though my backhand had never been good, over the decades it ceased to exist at all. Once a week I took a lesson late at night, when I was less likely to be subjected to the curious stares of the cocktail and happy hour crowd lounging in the observation gallery of Westwood Racquet Club's indoor facility.

After leaving the office, I had just enough time to drive to the club, dash into the ladies' locker room, and change into tennis clothes. Retrieving my racket from my locker, I was out on the court with two minutes to spare, muscles straining as I fell into leg stretches and bravely tried to touch my toes. My blood began to move sluggishly.

Ted, the pro, appeared from behind the green curtain shouldering two baskets of balls.

"After hearing the news, I didn't think I'd be seeing you tonight," he said, setting the baskets on the court and slipping out of his warm-up jacket. Ted, perennially tan and a joy to look at, usually greeted me with a smile and a wisecrack. But he was subdued tonight.

"My younger brother knew Fred Cheney. I knew him, too, though not well." Staring off at people playing several courts away, he said, "Fred was one of the nicest guys I've ever met. And I'm not just saying that because he's . . . Well. My brother's really shook up about it." He bent over and picked up a handful of balls. "And it sort of bothers me, if you want to know the truth, that the newspapers can't get past who Fred was dating. It's like the only person who disappeared was Pat Harvey's daughter. And I'm not saying that the girl wasn't terrific and what happened to her isn't just as awful as what happened to him." He paused. "Well. I think you know what I mean."

"I do," I said. "But the other side of that is Deborah Harvey's family is being subjected to intense scrutiny, and they will never be permitted to grieve privately because of who Deborah's mother is. It's unfair and tragic any way you look at it."

Ted thought about this and met my eyes. "You know, I hadn't considered it that way. But you're right. I don't think being famous would be a whole lot of fun. And I don't think you're paying me by the hour to stand out here and talk. What would you like to work on tonight?"

"Ground strokes. I want you to run me corner to corner so I can remind myself how much I hate smoking."

"No more lectures from me on that subject." He moved to the center of the net.

I backed up to the baseline. My first forehand wouldn't have been half bad had I been playing doubles.

Physical pain is a good diversion, and the harsh realities of the day were pushed aside until the phone rang at home later as I was peeling off my wet clothes.

Pat Harvey was frantic. "The bodies they found today. I have to know."

"They have not been identified, and I have not examined them yet," I said, sitting on the edge of the bed and nudging off my tennis shoes.

"A male and a female. That's what I heard."

"So it appears at this point. Yes."

"Please tell me if there's *any* possibility it isn't them," she said.

I hesitated.

"Oh, God," she whispered.

"Mrs. Harvey, I can't confirm—"

She cut me off in a voice that was getting hysterical. "The police told me they found Debbie's purse, her driver's license."

Morrell, I thought. The half-brained bastard.

I said to her, "We can't make identifications solely from personal effects."

"She's my daughter!"

Next would follow threats and profanity. I had been through this before with the other parents who under ordinary circumstances were as civilized as Sunday school. I decided to give Pat Harvey something constructive to do.

"The bodies have not been identified," I repeated.

"I want to see her."

Not in a million years, I thought. "The bodies aren't visually identifiable," I said. "They're almost skeletonized."

Her breath caught.

"And depending on you, we might establish identity with certainty tomorrow or it might take days."

"What do you want me to do?" she asked shakily.

"I need X-rays, dental charts, anything pertaining to Deborah's medical history that you can get your hands on."

Silence.

"Do you think you could track these down for me?"

"Of course," she said. "I'll see to it immediately."

I suspected she would have her daughter's medical records before sunrise, even if she had to drag half of the doctors in Richmond out of bed.

*

The following afternoon, I was removing the plastic cover from the OCME's anatomical skeleton when I heard Marino in the hall.

"I'm in here," I said loudly.

He stepped inside the conference room, a blank expression on his face as he stared at the skeleton, whose bones were wired together, a hook in the vertex of his skull attached to the top of an L-shaped bar. He stood a little taller than I was, feet dangling over a wooden base with wheels.

Gathering paperwork from a table, I said, "How about rolling him out for me?"

"You taking Slim for a stroll?"

"He's going downstairs, and his name's Haresh," I replied.

Bones and small wheels clattered quietly as Marino and his grinning companion followed me to the elevator, attracting amused glances from several members of my staff. Haresh did not get out very often, and as a rule, when he was spirited away from his corner, his abductor was not motivated by serious intent. Last June I had walked into my office on the morning of my birthday to find Haresh sitting in my chair, glasses and lab coat on, a cigarette clamped between his teeth. One of the more preoccupied forensic scientists from upstairs—or so I had been told—had walked past my doorway and said good morning without noticing anything odd.

"You're not going to tell me he talks to you when you're working down here," Marino said as the elevator doors shut.

"In his own way he does," I said. "I've found having him on hand is a lot more useful than referring to diagrams in *Gray's*."

"What's the story on his name?"

"Apparently, when he was purchased years ago, there was an Indian pathologist here named Haresh. The skeleton is also Indian. Male, fortyish, maybe older."

"As in Little Bighorn Indian or the other kind that paint dots on their foreheads?"

"As in the Ganges River in India," I said as we got out on the first floor. "The Hindus cast their dead upon the river, believing they will go straight to heaven."

"I sure as hell hope this joint ain't heaven."

Bones and wheels clattered again as Marino rolled Haresh into the autopsy suite.

On top of a white sheet covering the first stainless-steel table were Deborah Harvey's remains, gray dirty bones, clumps of muddy hair, and ligaments as tan and tough as shoe leather. The stench was relentless but not as overpowering, since I had removed her clothes. Her condition was made all the more pitiful by the presence of Haresh, who bore not so much as a scratch on his bleached white bones.

"I have several things to tell you," I said to Marino. "But first I want your promise that nothing leaves this room."

Lighting a cigarette, he looked curiously at me. "Okay."

"There's no question about their identities," I began, arranging clavicles on either side of the skull. "Pat Harvey brought in dental X-rays and charts this morning—"

"In person?" he interrupted, surprised.

"Unfortunately," I said, for I had not expected Pat Harvey to deliver the records herself—a miscalculation on my part, and one I wasn't likely to forget.

"That must've created quite a stir," he said.

It had.

When she pulled up in her Jaguar, she had left it illegally parked by the curb and appeared full of demands and on the verge of tears. Intimidated by the presence of the famous public official the receptionist let her in, and Mrs. Harvey promptly set off down the hall in search of me. I think she would have come down to the morgue had my administrator not intercepted her at the elevator and ushered her into my office, where I found her moments later. She was sitting rigidly in a chair, her face as white as chalk. On top of my desk were death certificates, case files, autopsy photographs, and an excised stab wound suspended in a small bottle of formalin tinted pink by blood. Hanging on the back of the door were bloodstained clothes I was intending to take upstairs when I made evidence rounds later in the day. Two facial reconstructions of unidentified dead females were perched on top of a filing cabinet like decapitated clay heads.

Pat Harvey had gotten more than she had bargained for. She had run head-on into the hard realities of this place.

"Morrell also brought me Fred Cheney's dental records," I said to Marino.

"Then it's definitely Fred Cheney and Deborah Harvey?"

"Yes," I said, and then I directed his attention to X-rays clipped to a view box on the wall.

"That ain't what I think it is." A look of amazement passed over his face as he fixed on a radiopaque spot within the shadowy outline of lumbar vertebrae.

"Deborah Harvey was shot." I picked up the lumbar in

question. "Caught right in the middle of the back. The bullet fractured the spinous process and the pedicles and lodged in the vertebral body. Right here." I showed him.

"I don't see it." He leaned closer.

"No, you can't see it. But you see the hole?"

"Yeah? I see a lot of holes."

"This is the bullet hole. The others are vascular foramina, holes for the vascular vessels that supply blood to bone and marrow."

"Where are the fractured pedestals you mentioned?"

"Pedicles," I said patiently. "I didn't find them. They would be in pieces and are probably still out there in the woods. An entrance and no exit. She was shot in the back versus the abdomen."

"You find a bullet hole in her clothes?"

"No."

On a nearby table was a white plastic tray in which I had placed Deborah's personal effects, including her clothing, jewelry, and red nylon purse. I carefully lifted up the sweatshirt, tattered, black, and putrid.

"As you can see," I pointed out, "the back of it, in particular, is in terrible shape. Most of the fabric's completely rotted away, torn by predators. The same goes for the waistband of her jeans in back, and that makes sense, since these areas of her clothing would have been bloody. In other words, the area of fabric where I would expect to have found a bullet hole is gone."

"What about distance? You got any idea about that?"

"As I've said, the bullet didn't exit. This would make me

suspect we're not dealing with a contact gunshot wound. But it's hard to say. As for caliber, and again I'm conjecturing, I'm thinking a thirty-eight or better, based on the size of this hole. We won't know with certainty until I crack open the vertebra and take the bullet upstairs to the firearms lab."

"Weird," Marino said. "You haven't looked at Cheney yet?"

"He's been rayed. No bullets. But no, I haven't examined him yet."

"Weird," he said again. "It don't fit. Her being shot in the back don't fit with the other cases."

"No," I agreed. "It doesn't."

"So that's what killed her?"

"I don't know."

"What do you mean, you don't know?" He looked at me.

"This injury isn't immediately fatal Marino. Since the bullet didn't go right on through, it didn't transect the aorta. Had it done so at this lumbar level, she would have hemorrhaged to death within minutes. What's significant is that the bullet had to have transected her cord, instantly paralyzing her from the waist down. And of course, blood vessels were hit. She was bleeding."

"How long could she have survived?"

"Hours."

"What about the possibility of sexual assault?"

"Her panties and brassiere were in place," I answered. "This doesn't mean that she wasn't sexually assaulted. She could have been allowed to put her clothes back on afterward, assuming she was assaulted before she was shot."

"Why bother?"

"If you're raped," I said, "and your assailant tells you to put your clothes back on, you assume you're going to live. A sense of hope serves to control you, make you do as you're told because if you struggle with him, he might change his mind."

"It don't feel right." Marino frowned. "I just don't think that's what happened, Doc."

"It's a scenario. I don't know what happened. All I can tell you with certainty is that I didn't find any articles of her clothing torn, cut, inside out, or unfastened. And as for seminal fluid, after so many months in the woods, forget it." Handing him a clipboard and a pencil, I added, "If you're going to hang around, you might as well scribe for me."

"You plan to tell Benton about this?" he asked.

"Not at the moment."

"What about Morrell?"

"Certainly, I'll tell him she was shot," I said. "If we're talking about an automatic or semiautomatic, the cartridge case may still be at the scene. If the cops want to run their mouths, that's up to them. But nothing's coming from me."

"What about Mrs. Harvey?"

"She and her husband know their daughter and Fred have been positively identified. I called the Harveys and Mr. Cheney as soon as I was sure. I will be releasing nothing further until I've concluded the examinations."

Ribs sounded like Tinker Toys quietly clacking together as I separated left from right.

"Twelve on each side," I began to dictate. "Contrary to legend, women don't have one more rib than men."

"Huh?" Marino looked up from the clipboard.

"Have you never read Genesis?"

He stared blankly at the ribs I had arranged on either side of the thoracic vertebrae.

"Never mind," I said.

Next I began looking for carpals, the small bones of the wrist that look very much like stones you might find in a creek bed or dig up in your garden. It is hard to sort left from right, and this is where the anatomical skeleton was helpful. Moving him closer, I propped his bony hands on the edge of the table and began comparing. I went through the same process with the distal and proximal phalanges, or bones of the fingers.

"Looks like she's missing eleven bones in her right hand and seventeen in her left," I reported.

Marino scribbled this down. "Out of how many?"

"There are twenty-seven bones in the hand," I replied as I worked. "Giving the hand its tremendous flexibility. It's what makes it possible for us to paint, play the violin, love each other through touch."

It is also what makes it possible for us to defend ourselves.

It was not until the following afternoon that I realized Deborah Harvey had attempted to ward off an assailant who had been armed with more than a gun. It had gotten considerably warmer out, the weather had cleared, and the police had been sifting through soil all day. At not quite four P.M., Morrell stopped by my office to deliver a number of small bones recovered from the scene. Five of them belonged to Deborah, and on the dorsal surface of her left proximal phalange—or the top of the shaft, the longest of the index finger bones I found a half-inch cut.

The first question when I find injury to bone or tissue is whether it is pre- or postmortem. If one is not aware of the artifacts that can occur after death, he can make serious mistakes.

People who burn up in fires come in with fractured bones and epidural hemorrhages, looking for all practical purposes as if someone worked them over and then torched the house to disguise a homicide, when the injuries are actually postmortem and caused by extreme heat. Bodies washed up on the beach or recovered from rivers and lakes often look as if a deranged killer mutilated faces, genitals, hands, and feet, when fish, crabs, and turtles are to blame. Skeletal remains get gnawed, chewed on, and torn from limb to limb by rats, buzzards, dogs, and raccoons.

Predators of the four-legged, winged, or finned variety inflict a lot of damage, but blessedly, not until the poor soul is already dead. Then nature simply begins recycling. Ashes to ashes. Dust to dust.

The cut on Deborah Harvey's proximal phalange was too neat and linear to have been caused by tooth or claw, it was my opinion. But this still left much open to speculation and suspicion, including the inevitable suggestion that I might have nicked the bone myself with a scalpel at the morgue.

By Wednesday evening the police had released Deborah's and Fred's identities to the press, and within the next forty-eight hours there were so many calls that the clerks in the front office could not manage their regular duties because all they did was answer the phone. Rose was informing everyone, including Benton Wesley and Pat Harvey, that the cases were pending while I stayed in the morgue.

By Sunday night, there was nothing more I could do. Deborah's and Fred's remains had been defleshed, degreased, photographed from every angle, the inventory of their bones completed. I was packing them in a cardboard box when the buzzer went off in back. I heard the night watchman's footsteps down the hall and the bay door open. Then Marino was walking in.

"You sleeping down here or what?" he asked.

Glancing up at him, I was surprised to note that his overcoat and hair were wet.

"It's snowing." He pulled off his gloves and set his portable radio on the edge of the autopsy table where I was working.

"That's all I need," I said, sighing.

"Coming down like a bitch, Doc. Was driving by and saw your ride in the lot. Figured you'd been in this cave since the crack of dawn and had no idea."

It occurred to me as I tore off a long strip of tape and sealed the box. "I thought you weren't on evening shift this weekend."

"Yeah, and I thought you was having me in for dinner."

Pausing, I stared curiously at him. Then I remembered. "Oh, no," I muttered, glancing up at the clock. It was past eight P.M. "Marino, I'm so sorry."

"Don't matter. Had a couple of things to follow up on, anyway."

I always knew when Marino was lying. He wouldn't look me in the eye and his face got red. It wasn't coincidence that he had seen my car in the lot. He had been looking for me, and not simply because he wanted dinner. Something was on his mind.

Leaning against the table, I gave him my full attention.

"Thought you might want to know that Pat Harvey was in Washington over the weekend, went to see the Director," he said.

"Did Benton inform you of this?"

"Yo. He also said he'd been trying to get hold of you but you ain't returning his calls. The Drug Czar's complaining that you ain't returning her calls either."

"I'm not returning anybody's calls," I replied wearily. "I've been rather preoccupied, to say the least, and I don't have anything to release at this point."

Looking at the box on the table, he said, "You know Deborah was shot, a homicide. What are you waiting for?"

"I don't know what killed Fred Cheney or if there's any possibility drugs might have been involved. I'm waiting for tox reports, and I don't intend to release a thing until those are in and I've had a chance to talk to Vessey."

"The guy at the Smithsonian?"

"I'm seeing him in the morning."

"Hope you got four-wheel drive."

"You haven't explained the purpose of Pat Harvey's going to see the Director."

"She's accusing your office of stonewalling, says the FBI is stonewalling her, too. She's pissed. Wants her daughter's autopsy report, police reports, the whole nine yards, and is threatening to get a court order and raise hell if her demands aren't met right away."

"That's crazy."

"Bingo. But if you don't mind a little advice, Doc, I think you might consider calling Benton before the night's out."

"Why?"

"I don't want you getting burned, that's why."

"What are you talking about, Marino?" I untied my surgical gown.

"The more you avoid everybody right now, the more you're adding fuel to the fire. According to Benton, Mrs. Harvey's convinced there's some sort of cover-up and all of us are involved."

When I did not reply he said, "Are you listening?"

"Yes. I've listened to every word you said."

He picked up the box.

"Incredible to think there's two people inside this thing," he marveled.

It was incredible. The box wasn't much bigger than a microwave oven and weighed ten or twelve pounds. As he placed it in the trunk of my state car, I said under my breath, "Thank you for everything."

"Huh?"

I knew he'd heard me, but he wanted me to say it again.

"I appreciate your concern, Marino. I really do. And I'm so sorry about dinner. Sometimes I really screw up."

The snow was falling fast, and as usual, he wasn't wearing a hat. Cranking the engine and turning on the heat full blast,

I looked up at him and thought how odd it was that I should find him such a comfort. Marino got on my nerves more than anyone I knew, and yet I could not imagine him not being around.

Locking my door, he said, "Yeah, well you owe me."

"*Semifreddo di cioccolato.*"

"I love it when you talk dirty."

"A dessert. My specialty, you big jerk. Chocolate mousse with ladyfingers."

"*Ladyfingers!*" He stared pointedly in the direction of the morgue, feigning horror.

It seemed to take forever to get home. I crept along snow-covered roads, concentrating so fiercely my head was splitting by the time I was in my kitchen pouring myself a drink. Sitting at the table, I lit a cigarette and gave Benton Wesley a call.

"What have you found?" he asked immediately.

"Deborah Harvey was shot in the back."

"Morrell told me. Said the bullet was unusual. Hydra-Shok, nine millimeter."

"That's correct."

"What about her boyfriend?"

"I don't know what killed him. I'm waiting on tox results, and I need to confer with Vessey at the Smithsonian. I'm pending both cases for now."

"The longer you pend them, the better."

"I beg your pardon?"

"I'm saying that I'd like you to pend the cases for as long as possible, Kay. I don't want reports going out to anyone, not even to the parents, and especially not to Pat Harvey. I don't want anyone knowing that Deborah was shot—"

"Are you telling me that the Harveys don't know?"

"When Morrell informed me, I made him promise to keep the information under wraps. So, no, the Harveys haven't been told. Uh, the police haven't told them. They know only that their daughter and Cheney are dead." He paused, adding, "Unless you've released something that I don't know about."

"Mrs. Harvey has tried to get hold of me a number of times, but I haven't talked to her or hardly anybody else during the past few days."

"Keep it that way," Wesley said firmly. "I'm asking you to release information only to me."

"There will come a point, Benton," I said just as firmly, "when I will have to release cause and manner of death. Fred's family, Deborah's family, are entitled to that by Code."

"Hold off as long as possible."

"Would you be so kind as to tell me why?"

Silence.

"Benton?" I was about to wonder if he was still on the line.

"Just don't do anything without conferring with me first." He hesitated again. Then, "I presume you're aware of this book Abby Turnbull is under contract to write."

"I saw something about it in the paper," I answered, getting angry.

"Has she contacted you again? Uh, recently?"

Again! How did Wesley know Abby had come to see me

last fall? Damn you, Mark, I thought. When he had tele-
phoned me, I had mentioned that Abby was with me that
night.

"I haven't heard from her," I replied curtly.

6

Monday morning the road in front of my house was blanketed in deep snow, the sky gray and threatening more bad weather to come. I fixed a cup of coffee and debated the wisdom of my driving to Washington. On the verge of scrapping my plans, I called the state police and learned that I-95 North was clear, the snow tapering off to less than an inch by Fredericksburg. Deciding that my state car wasn't likely to make it out of my driveway, I loaded the cardboard box in my Mercedes.

As I turned off on the Interstate, I realized that if I had a wreck or were pulled over by the police, it wasn't going to be easy explaining why I was heading north in an unofficial car with human skeletons in the trunk. Sometimes flashing my medical examiner shield wasn't enough. I never would forget flying to California carrying a large briefcase packed with sadomasochistic sexual paraphernalia. The briefcase got as far as the X-ray scanner, and the next thing I knew airport security was squiring me away for what was nothing less than an interrogation. No matter what I said, they couldn't seem to get it through their heads that I was a forensic pathologist en route to the National Association of Medical Examiners' annual meeting, where I was to give a presentation on auto-erotic asphyxiation. The handcuffs, studded collars, leather bindings, and other unseemly odds and ends were evidence from old cases and did not *belong* to me.

By ten-thirty I was in D.C. and had managed to find a parking place within a block of Constitution Avenue and Twelfth. I had not been to the Smithsonian's National Museum of Natural History since attending a forensic anthropology course there several years before. When I carried the cardboard box inside a lobby fragrant with potted orchids and noisy with the voices of tourists, I wished I could leisurely peruse dinosaurs and diamonds, mummy cases and mastodons, and never know the bleaker treasures housed within these walls.

Rising from ceiling to floor in every available inch of space not visible to guests were green wooden drawers containing, among other dead things, more than thirty thousand human skeletons. Bones of every description arrived by registered mail every week for Dr. Alex Vessey to examine. Some remains were archaeological, others turned out to be bear or beaver paws or the hydrocephalic skulls of calves, human-looking artifacts found along the wayside or turned up by plows, and feared, at first, to be what was left of a person who had met a violent end. Other parcels truly did contain bad news, the bones of someone murdered. In addition to being a natural scientist and curator, Dr. Vessey worked for the FBI and assisted people like me.

Gaining clearance from the unsmiling security guard, I clipped on my visitor's pass and headed for the brass elevator that took me up to the third floor. As I passed walls of drawers inside a dimly lit, crowded corridor, the sounds of people levels below looking at the great stuffed elephant faded. I began to feel claustrophobic. I remembered being so desperate for sensory input after eight hours of class inside this place that when I finally escaped at the end of the day, crowded sidewalks were welcome, the noise of traffic a relief.

I found Dr. Vessey where I had seen him last, inside a laboratory cluttered with steel carts bearing skeletons of birds and animals, teeth, femurs, mandibles. Shelves were covered with more bones and other unhappy human relics such as skulls and shrunken heads. Dr. Vessey, white haired and wearing thick glasses, was sitting behind his desk talking on the phone. While he concluded his call, I opened the box and got out the plastic envelope containing the bone from Deborah Harvey's left hand.

"The Drug Czar's daughter?" he asked right off, taking the envelope from me.

It seemed a strange question. But, in a way, it was correctly posed, for Deborah had been reduced to a scientific curiosity, a piece of physical evidence.

"Yes," I said as he took the phalange out of the envelope and began gently turning it under the light.

"I can tell you without hesitation, Kay, that this is not a

postmortem cut. Though some old cuts can look fresh, fresh cuts can't look old," he said. "The inside of the cut is discolored from the environment in a manner consistent with the rest of the bone's surface. In addition, the way the lip of the cut is bent back tells me this wasn't inflicted on dead bone. Green bone bends. Dead bone doesn't."

"My conclusion exactly," I replied, pulling up a chair. "But you know the question will be asked, Alex."

"And it should be," he said, peering at me over the rim of his glasses. "You wouldn't believe the things that come through here."

"I suspect I would," I said, unpleasantly reminded that the degree of forensic competence dramatically varied from state to state.

"A coroner sent me a case a couple months ago, a chunk of soft tissue and bone he told me was a newborn child found in the sewer. The question was sex and race. The answer was male beagle, two weeks old. Not long before that, another coroner who didn't know pathology from plants sent in a skeleton found in a shallow grave. He had no idea how the person had died. I counted forty-some cuts, lips bent back, textbook examples of green bone plasticity. Definitely not a natural death." He cleaned his glasses with the hem of his lab coat. "Of course, I get the other, too. Bones cut during autopsy."

"Any chance this was caused by a predator?" I said, even though I didn't see how it could have been.

"Well, cuts aren't always easy to distinguish from marks made by carnivores. But I'm fairly certain we're talking about some sort of blade." Getting up, he added cheerfully, "Let's take a look."

The anthropological minutiae that drove me to distraction gave Dr. Vessey joy, and he was energized and animated as he moved to the dissecting microscope on a countertop and centered the bone on the stage. After a long, silent moment of peering through the lenses and turning the bone in the field of light, he commented, "Now, that's interesting."

I waited.

"And this was the only cut you found?"

"Yes," I said. "Perhaps you'll find something else when you conduct your own examination. But I found nothing else except the bullet hole I mentioned. In her lower lumbar, the tenth dorsal."

"Yes. You said the bullet hit the spinal cord."

"Right. She was shot in the back. I recovered the slug from her vertebra."

"Any idea of the location of the shooting?"

"We don't know where she was in the woods—or if she was even in the woods when she was shot."

"And she has this cut to her hand," Dr. Vessey mused, peering into the scope again. "No way to know which came first. She would have been paralyzed from the waist down after being shot, but she still could have moved her hands."

"A defense injury?" I asked what I suspected.

"A very unusual one, Kay. The cut is dorsal versus palmar." He leaned back in the chair and looked up at me. "Most defense injuries to the hands are palmar." He held up his hands palm out. "But she took this cut to the *top* of her hand."

He turned his hands palm in. "I usually associate cuts on the top of the hand with someone who is aggressive in defending himself."

"Punching," I said.

"Right. If I'm coming at you with a knife and you're punching away, you're likely to get cut on the top of your hand. Certainly, you're not going to receive a cut to your palmar surfaces, unless you unclench your fists at some point. But what's more significant is that most defense injuries are slices. The perpetrator is swinging or stabbing, and the victim raises his hands or forearms to ward off the blade. If the cut goes deep enough to strike bone, I'm usually not going to be able to tell you much about the cutting surface."

"If the cutting surface is serrated," I interpolated, "with a slice, the blade covers its own tracks."

"That's one reason this cut is so interesting," he said. "There's no question it was inflicted by a serrated blade."

"Then she wasn't sliced but *hacked*?" I asked, puzzled.

"Yes." He returned the bone to its envelope. "The pattern of serrations means that at least a half an inch of the blade must have struck the top of her hand." Returning to his desk, he added, "I'm afraid that's as much information as I can give you about the weapon and what might have occurred. As you know, there's so much variability. I can't tell you the size of the blade, for example, whether the injury occurred before or after she was shot, and what position she was in when she received the cut."

Deborah could have been on her back. She could have been kneeling or on her feet, and as I returned to my car, I began to analyze. The cut to her hand was deep and would have bled profusely. This most likely placed her on the logging road or in the woods when she received the injury, because there was no blood inside her Jeep. Did this hundred-pound gymnast struggle with her assailant? Did she try to punch him, was she terrified and fighting for her life because Fred already had been murdered? And where did the gun fit in? Why did the killer use two weapons when it did not seem he had needed a gun to kill Fred?

I was willing to bet that Fred's throat was cut. Quite likely, after Deborah was shot, her throat was cut or else she was strangled. She was not shot and left to die. She did not drag herself, half paralyzed, to Fred's side and slip her arm under his. Their bodies had been positioned this way deliberately.

Turning off Constitution, I finally found Connecticut, which eventually led me to a northwest section of the city that I suspected would have been little better than a slum were it not for the Washington Hilton. Rising from a grassy slope that covered a city block, the hotel was a magnificent white luxury liner surrounded by a troubled sea of dusty liquor stores, laundromats, a nightclub featuring "live dancers," and dilapidated row houses with broken windows boarded up and cement front stoops almost on the street. Leaving my car in the hotel's underground parking deck, I crossed Florida Avenue and climbed the front steps of a dingy tan brick apartment building with a faded blue awning, in front. I pressed the button for Apartment 28, where Abby Turnbull lived.

"Who is it?"

I barely recognized the disembodied voice blaring out of the intercom. When I announced myself, I wasn't sure what Abby muttered, or maybe she simply gasped. The electronic lock clicked open.

I stepped inside a dimly lit landing with soiled tan carpet on the floor and a bank of tarnished brass mailboxes on a wall paneled in Masonite. I remembered Abby's fear about someone tampering with her mail. It certainly did not appear that one could easily get past the apartment building's front door without a key. The mailboxes required keys as well. Everything she had said to me in Richmond last fall rang false. By the time I climbed the five flights to her floor, I was out of breath and angry.

Abby was standing in her doorway.

"What are you doing here?" she whispered, her face ashen.

"You're the only person I know in this building. So what do you think I'm doing here?"

"You didn't come to Washington just to see me." Her eyes were frightened.

"I was here on business."

Through her open doorway I could see arctic white furniture, pastel throw pillows, and abstract monotype Gregg Carbo prints, furnishings I recognized from her former house in Richmond. For an instant I was unsettled by images from that terrible day. I envisioned her sister's decomposing body on the bed upstairs, police and paramedics moving about as Abby sat on a couch, her hands trembling so violently she could barely hold a cigarette. I did not know her then except by reputation, and I had not liked her at all. When her sister was murdered, Abby at least had gotten my sympathy. It wasn't until later that she had earned my trust.

"I know you won't believe me," Abby said in the same hushed tone, "but I was going to come see you next week."

"I have a phone."

"I couldn't," she pleaded, and we were having this conversation in the hall.

"Are you going to ask me in, Abby?"

She shook her head.

Fear tingled up my spine.

Glancing past her, I asked quietly, "Is someone in there?"

"Let's walk," she whispered.

"Abby, for God's sake . . ."

She stared hard at me and raised a finger to her lips.

I was convinced she was losing her mind. Not knowing what else to do, I waited in the hall as she went inside to get her coat. Then I followed her out of the building, and for the better part of half an hour we walked briskly along Connecticut Avenue, neither of us speaking. She led me into the Mayflower Hotel and found a table in the darkest corner of the bar. Ordering espresso, I leaned back in the leather chair and regarded her tensely across the polished table.

"I know you don't understand what's going on," she began, glancing around. At this early hour in the afternoon, the bar was almost empty.

"*Abby! Are you all right?*"

Her lower lip trembled. "I couldn't call you. I can't even talk to you inside my own fucking apartment! It's like I told you in Richmond, only a thousand times worse."

"You need to see someone," I said very calmly.

"I'm not crazy."

"You're an inch away from being completely unglued."

Taking a deep breath, she met my eyes fiercely. "Kay, I'm being followed. I'm positive my phone is being tapped, and I can't even be sure there aren't listening devices planted inside my place—which is why I couldn't ask you in. There, go ahead. Conclude that I'm paranoid, psychotic, whatever you want to think. But I live in my world and you don't. I know what I've been going through. I know what I know about these cases and what's been happening ever since I got involved in them."

"What, exactly, has been happening?"

The waitress returned with our order. After she left, Abby said, "Less than a week after I'd been in Richmond talking to you, my apartment was broken into."

"You were burglarized?"

"Oh, no." Her laugh was hollow. "Not hardly. The person—or persons were much too clever for that. Nothing was stolen."

I looked quizzically at her.

"I have a computer at home for my writing, and on the hard disk is a file about these couples, their strange deaths. I've been keeping notes for a long time, writing them into this file. The word processing package I use has an option that automatically backs up what you're working on, and I have it set to do this every ten minutes. You know, to make sure I don't lose anything should the power go out or something. Especially in my building—"

"Abby," I interrupted. "What in God's name are you talking about?"

"What I'm saying is that if you go into a file on my computer, if you're in there for ten minutes or more, not only is a backup created, but when you save the file, the date and time are recorded. Are you following me?"

"I'm not sure." I reached for my espresso.

"You remember when I came to see you?"

I nodded.

"I took notes when I talked to the clerk at the Seven-Eleven."

"Yes. I remember."

"And I talked to a number of other people, including Pat Harvey. I intended to put the notes from these interviews into the computer after I got home. But things went haywire. As you recall, I saw you on a Tuesday night and drove back here the next morning. Well that day, Wednesday, I talked to my editor around noon, and he was suddenly uninterested, said he wanted to hold off on the Harvey-Cheney story because the paper was going to run a series over the weekend about AIDS.

"It was strange," she went on. "The Harvey-Cheney story was hot, the *Post* was in one big hurry for it. Then I return from Richmond and suddenly have a new assignment?" She paused to light a cigarette. "As it turned out, I didn't have a free moment until Saturday, which was when I finally sat down in front of my computer to pull up this file, and there was a date and time listed after it that I didn't understand. Friday, September twentieth, two-thirteen in the afternoon *when I wasn't even home*. The file had been opened, Kay. Someone went into it, and I know it wasn't me because I didn't touch my computer—not even once—until that Saturday, the twenty-first, when I had some free time."

"Perhaps the clock in your computer was off . . ."

She was already shaking her head. "It wasn't. I checked.'

"How could anybody do that?" I asked. "How could someone break into your apartment without anyone seeing them, without your knowing?"

"The FBI could."

"Abby," I said, exasperated.

"There's a lot you don't know."

"Then fill me in, please," I said.

"Why do you think I took a leave of absence from the *Post*?"

"According to the *New York Times*, you're writing a book."

"And you're assuming I already knew I was going to write this book when I was with you in Richmond."

"It's more than an assumption," I said, feeling angry again.

"I wasn't. I swear." Leaning forward, she added in a voice trembling with emotion, "My beat was changed. Do you understand what that means?"

I was speechless.

"The only thing worse would have been to be fired, but they couldn't do that. There was no cause. Jesus Christ, I won an investigative reporting award last year, and all of a sudden they want to switch me over to features. Do you hear me? *Features*. Now, you tell me what you make of that."

"I don't know, Abby."

"I don't know, either." She blinked back tears. "But I have my self-respect. I know there's something big going on, a story. And I sold it. There. Think what you want, but I'm trying to survive. I have to live and I had to get away from the paper for a while. Features. Oh, God. Kay, I'm so scared."

"Tell me about the FBI," I said firmly.

"I've already told you a lot. About the wrong turn I took, about ending up at Camp Peary, and the FBI agents coming to see me."

"That's not enough."

"The jack of hearts, Kay," she said as if she were telling me something I already knew.

When it dawned on her that I had no idea what she was talking about, her expression changed to astonishment.

"You don't know?" she asked.

"What jack of hearts?"

"In each of these cases, a playing card has been found." Her incredulous eyes were fixed on mine.

I vaguely remembered something from one of the few transcripts of police interviews I had seen. The detective from Gloucester had talked to a friend of Bruce Phillips and Judy Roberts, the first couple. What was it the detective had asked? I recalled it had struck me as rather peculiar. Cards. Did Judy and Bruce ever play cards? Had the friend ever seen any cards inside Bruce's Camaro?

"Tell me about the cards, Abby," I said.

"Are you familiar with the ace of spades, with how it was used in Vietnam?"

I told her I wasn't.

"When a particular outfit of American soldiers wanted to make a point after making a kill, they would leave an ace of spades on the body. In fact, a company that manufactures playing cards supplied this unit with boxes of the cards just for this purpose."

"What does this have to do with Virginia?" I asked, baffled.

"There's a parallel. Only we're not talking about an ace of spades, but a jack of hearts. In each of the first four cases, a jack of hearts was found in the abandoned car."

"Where did you get this information?"

"You know I can't tell you that, Kay. But we're talking about more than one source. That's why I'm so sure of it."

"And did one of your *sources* also tell you that a jack of hearts was found in Deborah Harvey's Jeep?"

"Was one found?" She idly stirred her drink.

"Don't toy with me," I warned.

"I'm not." She met my eyes. "If a jack of hearts was found inside her Jeep or anywhere else, I don't know about it. Obviously, it's an important detail because it would definitely link Deborah Harvey's and Fred Cheney's deaths with those of the first four couples. Believe me, I'm looking hard for that link. I'm not sure it's there. Or if it is, what it means."

"What does this have to do with the FBI?" I asked reluctantly, for I was not sure I wanted to hear her reply.

"They've been preoccupied with these cases almost from the start, Kay. And it goes way beyond VICAP's usual participation. The FBI's known about the cards for a long time. When a jack of hearts was found inside the first couple's Camaro—on the dash—no one paid much attention. Then the second couple disappeared, and there was another card, this one on the passenger seat. When Benton Wesley found out, he immediately started controlling things. He went back to the detective in Gloucester County and told him not to say a word about the jack of hearts found inside the Camaro. He told the investigator in the second case the same thing. Each time another abandoned car turned up, Wesley was on the phone with that investigator."

She paused, studying me as if trying to read my thoughts. "I guess I shouldn't be surprised, you didn't know," she added. "I don't suppose it would be that hard for the police to withhold from you what was discovered inside the cars."

"It wouldn't be hard for them to do that," I replied. "Were the cards found with the bodies, that would be another matter. I don't know how that could be kept from me."

Even as I heard myself say the words, doubt whispered in the back of my mind. The police had waited hours before calling me to the scene. By the time I got there, Wesley had arrived, and Deborah Harvey's and Fred Cheney's bodies had been tampered with, searched for personal effects.

"I would expect the FBI to keep quiet about this," I continued to reason. "The detail could be critical to the investigation."

"I'm so sick of hearing shit like that," Abby said angrily. "The detail about the killer leaving a calling card, so to speak, is critical to the investigation only if the guy comes forward and confesses, says he left a card in each couple's car when there's no way for him to know about that unless he really did it. I don't think that's going to happen. And I don't think the FBI is sitting on this thing just because they want to make sure nothing screws up the investigation."

"Then why?" I asked uneasily.

"Because we're not just talking about serial murders. We're not just talking about some fruitcake out there who's got a thing about couples. This thing's political. It's got to be."

Falling silent, she caught the waitress's eye. Abby did not say another word until a second round of drinks was placed on our table and she had taken several sips.

"Kay," she continued, and she was calmer, "does it surprise you that Pat Harvey talked to me when I was in Richmond?"

"Yes, frankly."

"Have you given any thought as to why she agreed to it?"

"I suppose she would have done anything to bring her daughter back," I said. "And sometimes publicity can help."

Abby shook her head. "When I talked to Pat Harvey she told me a lot of things that I would never have put in the paper. And it's not the first encounter I'd had with her, not by a long shot."

"I don't understand." I was feeling shaky, and it was due to more than the espresso.

"You know about her crusade against illegal charities."

"Vaguely," I replied.

"The tip that alerted her about all that originally came from me."

"From you?"

"Last year I began work on a big investigative piece about drug trafficking. As I was going along, I began to uncover a lot of things I couldn't verify, and this is where the fraudulent charities come in. Pat Harvey has an apartment here, at the Watergate, and one evening I went there to interview her, to get a couple quotes for my story. We got to talking. I ended up telling her about the allegations I'd heard to see if she could corroborate any of them. That's how it began."

"What allegations, exactly?"

"About ACTMAD, for example," Abby said. "Allegations that some of these antidrug charities are really fronts for drug cartels and other illegal activities in Central America. I told her I'd been informed by what I considered to be reliable sources that millions of dollars donated each year were ending up in the pockets of people like Manuel Noriega. Of course, this was before Noriega was arrested. But it's believed that funds from ACTMAD and other so-called charities are being used to buy intelligence from U.S. agents and facilitate the heroin trade through Panamanian airports, customs offices, in the Far East and the Americas."

"And Pat Harvey, prior to your coming to her apartment, had heard nothing about this?"

"No, Kay. I don't think she had a clue, but she was outraged. She started investigating, and then finally went before Congress with a report. A special subcommittee was formed to investigate, and she was invited to serve as a consultant, as you probably know. Apparently, she's uncovered a great deal and a hearing has been set for this April. Some people aren't happy about it, including the Justice Department."

I was beginning to see where this was going.

"There are informants involved," Abby went on, "that the DEA, FBI, and CIA have been after for years. And you know how it works. When Congress gets involved, they have the power to offer special immunity in exchange for information.

Once these informants testify in this congressional hearing, the game's over. No way the Justice Department will be able to prosecute."

"Meaning that Pat Harvey's efforts are not exactly appreciated by the Justice Department."

"Meaning that the Justice Department would be secretly thrilled if her entire investigation fell apart."

"The National Drug Policy Director, or Drug Czar," I said, "is subservient to the Attorney General, who commands the FBI and DEA. If Mrs. Harvey is having a conflict of interests with the Justice Department, why doesn't the AG reign her in?"

"Because it's not the AG she's having a problem with, Kay. What she's doing is going to make him look good, make the White House look good. Their Drug Czar is making a dent in drug crimes. What your average citizen won't understand is that as far as the FBI and DEA are concerned, the consequences of this congressional hearing aren't great enough. All that will occur is a full disclosure, the names of these charities and the truth about what they've been doing. The publicity will put groups like ACTMAD out of business, but the scumbags involved will suffer nothing more than a slap on the wrist. The agents working the cases end up with an empty bag because nobody gets put away. Bad people don't stop doing bad things. It's like closing down a nip joint. Two weeks later, it's reopened on another corner."

"I fail to see how this is connected to what's happened to Mrs. Harvey's daughter," I said again.

"Start with this. If you were at cross-purposes with the

FBI," Abby said, "and maybe even doing battle with them, how would you feel if your daughter disappeared and the FBI was working the case?"

It was not a pleasant thought. "Justified or not, I would feel very vulnerable and paranoid. I suppose it would be hard for me to trust."

"You've just skimmed the surface of Pat Harvey's feelings. I think she really believes that someone used her daughter to get to her, that Deborah's not the victim of a random crime, but a hit. And she's not sure that the FBI isn't involved—"

"Let me get this straight," I said, stopping her. "Are you implying that Pat Harvey is suspicious the *FBI* is behind the deaths of her daughter and Fred?"

"It's entered her mind that the feds are involved."

"Are you going to tell me that you're entertaining this notion yourself?"

"I'm to the point of believing anything."

"Good God," I muttered under my breath.

"I know how off-the-wall it sounds. But if nothing else, I believe the FBI knows what's going on and maybe even knows who's doing it, and that's why I'm a problem. The feds don't want me snooping around. They're worried I might turn over a rock and find out what's really crawling underneath it."

"If that's the case," I reminded her, "then it would seem to me the *Post* would be offering you a raise, not sending you over to features. It's never been my impression that the *Post* is easily intimidated."

"I'm not Bob Woodward," she replied bitterly. "I haven't

been there very long, and the police beat is chicken shit, usually where rookies get their feet wet. If the Director of the FBI or someone in the White House wants to talk lawsuits or diplomacy with the powers that be at the *Post*, I'm not going to be invited in on the meeting or necessarily told what's going on."

She was probably right about that, I thought. If Abby's demeanor in the newsroom was anything like it was now, it was unlikely anyone was eager to deal with her. In fact, I wasn't sure I was surprised she had been relieved of her beat.

"I'm sorry, Abby," I said. "Maybe I could understand politics being a factor in Deborah Harvey's case, but the others? How do the other couples fit? The first couple disappeared two and a half years before Deborah and Fred did."

"Kay," she said fiercely, "I don't know the answers. But I swear to God something is being covered up. Something the FBI, the government, doesn't want the public ever to find out. You mark my words, even if these killings stop, the cases will never be solved if the FBI has its way about it. That's what I'm up against. And that's what you're up against." Finishing her drink, she added, "And maybe that would be all right—as long as the killings stopped. But the problem is, when will they stop? And could they have been stopped before now?"

"Why are you telling me all this?" I asked bluntly.

"We're talking about innocent teenage kids who are turning up dead. Not to mention the obvious—I trust you. And maybe I need a friend."

"You're going to continue with the book?"

"Yes. I just hope there will be a final chapter to write."

"Please be careful Abby."

"Believe me," she said, "I know."

When we left the bar it was dark out and very cold. My mind was in turmoil as we were jostled along crowded sidewalks, and I felt no better as I made the drive back to Richmond. I wanted to talk to Pat Harvey, but I did not dare. I wanted to talk to Wesley, but I knew he would not divulge his secrets to me, were there any, and more than ever I was unsure of our friendship.

The minute I was home, I called Marino.

"Where in South Carolina does Hilda Ozimek live?" I asked.

"Why? What did you find out at the Smithsonian?"

"Just answer my question, please."

"Some little armpit of a town called Six Mile."

"Thank you."

"Hey! Before you hang up, you mind telling me what went down in D.C.?"

"Not tonight, Marino. If I can't find you tomorrow, you get hold of me."

7

At 5:45 A.M., Richmond International Airport was deserted. Restaurants were closed, newspapers were stacked in front of locked-up gift shops, and a janitor was slowly wheeling a trash can around, a somnambulist picking up gum wrappers and cigarette butts.

I found Marino inside the USAir terminal, eyes shut and raincoat wadded behind his head as he napped in an airless, artificially lit room of empty chairs and dotted blue carpet. For a fleeting moment I saw him as if I did not know him, my heart touched in a sad, sweet way. Marino had aged.

I don't think I had been in my new job more than several days when I met him for the first time. I was in the morgue performing an autopsy when a big man with an impassive face walked in and positioned himself on the other side of the table. I remembered feeling his cool scrutiny. I had the uncomfortable sensation he was dissecting me as thoroughly as I was dissecting my patient.

"So you're the new chief." He had posed the comment as a challenge, as if daring me to acknowledge that I believed I could fill a position never before held by a woman.

"I'm Dr. Scarpetta," I had replied. "You're with Richmond City, I assume?"

He had mumbled his name, then waited in silence while I removed several bullets from his homicide case and receipted them to him. He strolled off without so much as a "good-bye" or "nice to meet you," by which point our professional rapport had been established. I perceived he resented me for no cause other than my gender, and in turn I dismissed him as a dolt with a brain pickled by testosterone. In truth, he had secretly intimidated the hell out of me.

It was hard for me to look at Marino now and imagine I had ever found him threatening. He looked old and defeated, shirt straining across his big belly, wisps of graying hair unruly, brow drawn in what was neither a scowl nor a frown but a series of deep creases caused by the erosion of chronic tension and displeasure.

"Good morning." I gently touched his shoulder.

"What's in the bag?" he muttered without opening his eyes.

"I thought you were asleep," I said, surprised.

He sat up and yawned.

Settling next to him, I opened the paper sack and got out Styrofoam cups of coffee and cream cheese bagels I had fixed at home and heated in the microwave oven just before heading out in the dark.

power Marino had to make the world tilt slightly on its axis. He had chosen to sit in an area designated as non-smoking, then had carried an upright ashtray from rows away and placed it by his chair. This served as a subliminal invitation for other semi-awake smokers to settle near us, several of whom carried over additional ashtrays. By the time we were ready to board there was hardly an ashtray to be found in the smoking area and nobody seemed quite sure where to sit. Embarrassed and determined to have no part in this unfriendly takeover, I left my pack in my purse.

Marino, who disliked flying more than I did, slept to Charlotte, where we boarded a commuter prop plane that reminded me unpleasantly of how little there is between fragile human flesh and empty air. I had worked my share of disasters and knew what it was like to see an aircraft and passengers scattered over miles of earth. I noted there was no rest room or beverage service, and when the engines started, the plane shook as if it were having a seizure. For the first part of the trip, I had the rare distinction of watching the pilots chat with each other, stretching and yawning until a stewardess made her way up the aisle and yanked the curtain shut. The air was getting more turbulent, mountains drifting in and out of fog. The second time the plane suddenly lost altitude, sending my stomach into my throat, Marino gripped both armrests so hard his knuckles went white.

"Jesus Christ," he muttered, and I began to regret bringing him breakfast. He looked as if he were about to get sick. "If this bucket ever makes it on the ground in one piece, I'm having a drink. I don't friggin' care what time it is."

"Hey, I'll buy," a man in front of us turned around and said.

Marino was staring at a strange phenomenon occurring in a section of the aisle directly ahead of us. Rolling up from a metal strip at the edge of the carpet was a ghostly condensation that I had never seen on any previous flight. It looked as if clouds were seeping inside the plane, and when Marino pointed this out with a loud "What the hell?" to the stewardess, she completely ignored him.

"Next time I'm going to slip phenobarbital in your coffee," I warned him between clenched teeth.

"Next time you decide to talk to some wild-ass gypsy who lives in the sticks, I ain't coming along for the ride."

For half an hour we circled Spartanburg, bumped and tossed, fits of freezing rain pelting the glass. We could not land because of the fog, and it honestly occurred to me that we might die. I thought about my mother. I thought about Lucy, my niece. I should have gone home for Christmas, but I was so weighted down by my own concerns, and I had not wanted to be asked about Mark. *I'm busy, Mother. I simply can't get away right now.* "But it's Christmas, Kay." I could not remember the last time my mother had cried, but I always knew when she felt like it. Her voice got funny. Words were spaced far apart. "Lucy will be so disappointed," she had said. I had mailed Lucy a generous check and called her Christmas morning. She missed me terribly, but I think I missed her more.

Suddenly, clouds parted and the sun lit up windows. Spontaneously, all of the passengers, including me, gave God and pilots a round of applause. We celebrated our survival by chatting up and down the aisle as if all of us had been friends for years.

"So maybe Broom Hilda's looking out for us," Marino said sarcastically, his face covered with sweat.

"Maybe she is," I said, taking a deep breath as we landed.

"Yeah, well, be sure to thank her for me."

"You can thank her yourself, Marino."

"Yo," he said, yawning and fully recovered.

"She seems very nice. Maybe for once, you might consider having an open mind."

"Yo," he said again.

When I had gotten Hilda Ozimek's number from directory assistance and given her a call, I was expecting a woman shrewd and suspicious who bracketed every comment in dollar signs. Instead, she was unassuming and gentle, and surprisingly trusting. She did not ask questions or want proof of who I was. Her voice sounded worried only once, and this was when she mentioned that she could not meet us at the airport.

Since I was paying and in a mood to be chauffeured, I told Marino to pick out what he wanted. Like a sixteen-year-old on his first test drive to manhood, he selected a brand-new Thunderbird, black, with a sunroof, a tape deck, electric windows, leather bucket seats. He drove west with the sunroof open and the heat turned on as I went into more detail about what Abby had said to me in Washington.

"I know Deborah Harvey's and Fred Cheney's bodies were moved," I was explaining. "And now I suspect I understand why."

"I'm not sure I do," he said. "So why don't you lay it out for me one point at a time."

"You and I got to the rest stop before anyone went through the Jeep," I began. "And we didn't see a jack of hearts on the dash, on a seat, or anywhere else."

"Don't mean the card wasn't in the glove compartment or something, and the cops didn't find it until after the dogs was finished sniffing." Setting the cruise control, he added, "If this card business is true. Like I said, it's the first I've heard of it."

"Let's for the sake of argument assume it is true."

"I'm listening."

"Wesley arrived at the rest stop after we did, so he didn't see a card, either. Later, the Jeep was searched by the police, and you can be sure that Wesley was either on hand or he called Morrell and wanted to know what was found. If there was no sign of a jack of hearts, and I'm willing to bet that's the case, this had to have thrown Wesley a curve. His next thought may have been that either Deborah's and Fred's disappearance was unrelated to the other couples' disappearances and deaths, or else if Deborah and Fred were already dead, then it was possible that this time a card may have been left at the scene, left with the bodies."

"And you're thinking this was why their bodies was moved before you got there. Because the cops was looking for the card."

"Or Benton was. Yes, that's what I'm considering. Otherwise it doesn't make much sense to me. Benton and the police *know* not to touch a body before the medical examiner arrives. But

Benton also wouldn't want to take the chance that a jack of hearts might come into the morgue with the bodies. He wouldn't want me or anyone else to find it or know about it."

"Then it would make more sense for him to just tell us to keep our mouths shut instead of him screwing around with the scene," Marino argued. "It's not like he was out there in the woods alone. There was other cops around. They would have noticed if Benton found a card."

"Obviously," I said. "But he would also realize that the fewer people who know, the better. And if I found a playing card among Deborah's or Fred's personal effects, that would go into my written report. Commonwealth's attorneys, members of my staff, families, insurance companies—other people are going to see the autopsy reports eventually."

"Okay, okay." Marino was getting impatient. "But so what? I mean, what's the big deal?"

"I don't know. But if what Abby's implying is true, these cards turning up must be a very big deal to someone."

"No offense, Doc, but I never liked Abby Turnbull worth a damn. Not when she was working in Richmond, and I sure as hell don't think better of her now that she's at the *Post*."

"I've never known her to lie," I said.

"Yeah. You've never *known* it."

"The detective in Gloucester mentioned playing cards in a transcript I read."

"And maybe that's where Abby picked up the ball. Now

140

she's running around the block with it. Making assumptions. Hoping. All she gives a shit about is writing her book."

"She's not herself right now. She's frightened, angry, but I don't agree with you about her character."

"Right," he said. "She comes to Richmond, acts like your long-lost friend. Says she don't want nothing from you. Next thing, you have to read the *New York Times* to find out she's writing a friggin' book about these cases. Oh, yeah. She's a real friend, Doc."

I shut my eyes and listened to a country-music song playing softly on the radio. Sunlight breaking through the windshield was warm on my lap, and the early hour I had gotten out of bed hit me like a stiff drink. I dozed off. When I came to, we were bumping slowly along an unpaved road out in the middle of nowhere.

"Welcome to the big town of Six Mile," Marino announced.

"What town?"

There was no skyline, not so much as a single convenience store or gas station in sight. Roadsides were dense with trees, the Blue Ridge a haze in the distance, and houses were poor and spread so far apart a cannon could go off without your neighbor hearing it.

Hilda Ozimek, psychic to the FBI and oracle to the Secret Service, lived in a tiny white frame house with white-painted tires in the front yard where pansies and tulips probably grew in the spring. Dead cornstalks leaned against the porch, and in the drive was a rusting Chevrolet Impala with flat tires. A mangy dog began to bark, ugly as sin and big enough to give me pause as I considered getting out of the car. Then he trotted off on three legs, favoring his right front paw, as the front screen door screeched open and a woman squinted at us in the bright, cold morning.

"Be still, Tootie." She patted the dog's neck. "Now go on around back." The dog hung his head, tail wagging, and limped off to the backyard.

"Good morning," Marino said, his feet heavy on the front wooden steps.

At least he intended to be polite, and there had been no guarantee of that.

"It is a fine morning," Hilda Ozimek said.

She was at least sixty and looked as country as corn bread. Black polyester pants were stretched over wide hips, a beige sweater buttoned up to her neck, and she wore thick socks and loafers. Her eyes were light blue, hair covered by a red head rag. She was missing several teeth. I doubted Hilda Ozimek ever looked in a mirror or gave a thought to her physical self unless she was forced to by discomfort or pain.

We were invited into a small living room cluttered with musty furniture and bookcases filled with a variety of unexpected volumes not arranged in any sort of sensible order. There were books on religion and psychology, biographies and histories, and a surprising assortment of novels by some of my favorite authors: Alice Walker, Pat Conroy, and Keri Hulme. The only hint of our hostess's otherworldly inclinations was several works by Edgar Cayce and half a dozen or so crystals placed about on tables and shelves. Marino and I were seated on a couch near a kerosene heater, Hilda across from us in an overstuffed chair, sunlight from the window behind us shining through the open blinds and painting white bars across her face.

"I hope you had no trouble, and I am so sorry I couldn't come get you. But I don't drive anymore."

"Your directions were excellent," I reassured her. "We had no problem finding your house."

"If you don't mind my asking," Marino said, "how do you get around? I didn't see a store or nothing within walking distance."

"Many people come here for readings or just to talk. Somehow, I always have what I need or can get a ride."

A telephone rang in another room, and was instantly silenced by an answering machine.

"How may I help you?" Hilda asked.

"I brought photographs," Marino replied. "The Doc said you wanted to see them. But there's a couple things I want to clear up first. No offense or nothing, Miss Ozimek, but this mind-reading stuff is something I've never put much stock in. Maybe you can help me understand it better."

For Marino to be so forthright without a trace of combativeness in his tone was uncommon, and I glanced over at him, rather startled. He was studying Hilda with the openness of a child, his expression an odd mix of curiosity and melancholy.

"First, let me say that I'm not a mind reader," Hilda replied matter-of-factly. "And I don't even feel comfortable with being called a psychic, but for lack of a better term, I suppose, that is how I am referred to and how I refer to myself. All of us have the capability. Sixth sense, some part of our brain most people choose not to use. I explain it as an enhanced intuition.

I feel energy coming from people and just relay the impressions that come into my mind."

"Which is what you did when Pat Harvey was with you," he said.

She nodded. "She took me into Debbie's bedroom, showed me photographs of her, and then she took me to the rest stop where the Jeep was found."

"What impressions did you get?" I inquired.

Staring off, she thought hard for a moment. "I can't remember all of them. That's the thing. It's the same when I give readings. People come back to me later and tell me about something I said and what's happened since. I don't always remember what I've said until I'm reminded."

"Do you remember anything you said to Mrs. Harvey?" Marino wanted to know, and he sounded disappointed.

"When she showed me Debbie's picture, I knew right away the girl was dead."

"What about the boyfriend?" Marino asked.

"I saw his picture in the newspaper and knew he was dead. I knew both of them were dead."

"So you been reading about these cases in the newspaper," Marino then said.

"No," Hilda answered. "I don't take the newspaper. But I saw the boy's picture because Mrs. Harvey had clipped it out to show me. She didn't have a photograph of him, only of her daughter, you see."

"You mind explaining how you knew they was dead?"

"It was something I felt. An impression I got when I touched their pictures."

Reaching into his back pocket and pulling out his wallet, Marino said, "If I give you a picture of someone, can you do the same thing? Give me your impressions?"

"I'll try," she said as he handed her a snapshot.

Closing her eyes, she rubbed her fingertips over the photograph in slow circles. This went on for at least a minute before she spoke again. "I'm getting guilt. Now, I don't know if it's because this woman was feeling guilty when the picture was taken, or if it's because she's feeling that way now. But that's coming in real strong. Conflict, guilt. Back and forth. She's made up her mind one minute, then doubting herself the next. Back and forth."

"Is she alive?" Marino asked, clearing his throat.

"I feel that she is alive," Hilda replied, still rubbing. "I'm also getting the impression of a hospital. Something medical. Now I don't know if this means that she's sick or if someone close to her is. But something medical is involved, a concern. Or maybe it will be involved at some future point."

"Anything else?" Marino asked.

She shut her eyes again and rubbed the photograph a little longer. "A lot of conflict," she repeated. "It's as if something's past but it's hard for her to let it go. Pain. And yet she feels she has no choice. That's all that's coming to me." She looked up at Marino.

When he retrieved the photograph, his face was red. Returning the wallet to his pocket without saying a word, he unzipped his briefcase and got out a microcassette tape recorder and a manila envelope containing a series of retrospective photographs that began at the logging road in New

Kent County and ended in the woods where Deborah Harvey's and Fred Cheney's bodies had been found. Hilda spread them out on the coffee table and began rubbing her fingers over each one. For a very long time she said nothing, eyes closed as the telephone continued to ring in the other room. Each time the machine intervened, and she did not seem to notice. I was deciding that her skills were in more demand than those of any physician.

"I'm picking up fear," she began talking rapidly. "Now, I don't know if it's because someone was feeling fear when these pictures were taken, or if it's because someone was feeling fear in these places at some earlier time. But fear." She nodded, eyes still shut. "I'm definitely picking it up with each picture. All of them. Very strong fear."

Like the blind, Hilda moved her fingers from photograph to photograph, reading something that seemed as tangible to her as the features of a person's face.

"I feel death here," she went on, touching three different photographs. "I feel that strong." They were photographs of the clearing where the bodies were found. "But I don't feel it here." Her fingers moved back to photographs of the logging road and a section of woods where I had walked when being led to the clearing in the rain.

I glanced over at Marino. He was leaning forward on the couch, elbows on his knees, his eyes fixed on Hilda. So far, she wasn't telling us anything dramatic. Neither Marino nor I had ever assumed that Deborah and Fred had been murdered on the logging road, but in the clearing where their bodies were found.

"I see a man," Hilda went on. "Light-complected. He's not real tall. Not short. Medium height and slender. But not skinny. Now, I don't know who it is, but since nothing is coming to me strongly, I'll have to assume it was someone who had an encounter with the couple. I'm picking up friendliness. I'm hearing laughter. It's like he was, you know, friendly with the couple. Maybe they met him somewhere, and I can't tell you why I'm thinking this, but I'm feeling as if they were laughing with him at some point. Trusted him."

Marino spoke. "Can you see anything else about him? About the way he looked?"

She continued rubbing the photographs. "I'm seeing darkness. It's possible he has a dark beard or something dark over part of his face. Maybe he's dressed in dark clothing. But I'm definitely picking him up in connection with the couple and with the place where the pictures were taken."

Opening her eyes, she stared up at the ceiling. "I'm feeling that the first meeting was a friendly encounter. Nothing to make them worry. But then there's fear. It's so strong in this place, the woods."

"What else?" Marino was so intense, the veins were standing out in his neck. If he leaned forward another inch, he was going to fall off the couch.

"Two things," she said. "They may not mean anything but they're coming to me. I have a sense of another place that's not in these pictures, and I'm feeling this in connection with the girl. She might have been taken somewhere or gone somewhere. Now this place could be close by. Maybe it's not.

I don't know, but I'm getting a sense of crowdedness, of things grabbing. Of panic, a lot of noise and motion. Nothing about these impressions is good. And then there is something lost. I'm seeing this as something metal that has to do with war. I'm not getting anything more about that except I don't feel anything bad—I'm not picking up that the object itself is harmful."

"Who lost whatever this metal thing is?" Marino inquired.

"I have a sense that this is a person who is still alive. I'm not getting an image, but I feel this is a man. He perceives the item as lost versus discarded and is not real worried about it, but there is some concern. As if whatever he has lost enters his mind now and then."

She fell silent as the telephone rang again.

I asked, "Did you mention any of this to Pat Harvey last fall?"

"When she wanted to see me," Hilda replied, "the bodies had not been found. I didn't have these pictures."

"Then you did not get any of these same impressions."

She thought hard. "We went to the rest stop and she led me right over to where the Jeep was found. I stood there for a while. I remember there was a knife."

"What knife?" Marino asked.

"I saw a knife."

"What kind of knife?" he asked, and I recalled that Gail, the dog handler, had borrowed Marino's Swiss army knife when opening the Jeep's doors.

"A long knife," Hilda said. "Like a hunting knife or maybe some kind of military knife. It seems there was something about the handle. Black and rubbery, maybe, with one of those blades I associate with cutting through hard things like wood."

"I'm not sure I understand," I said, even though I had a good idea what she meant. I did not want to lead her.

"With teeth. Like a saw. I guess serrated is what I'm trying to say," she replied.

"This is what came into your mind when you was standing out there at the rest stop?" Marino asked, staring at her in disbelief.

"I did not feel anything that was frightening," she said. "But I saw the knife, and I knew it was not the couple who had been in the Jeep when it was left where it was. I did not feel their presence at that rest stop. They were never there." She paused, closing her eyes again, brow furrowed. "I remember feeling anxiety. I had the impression of someone anxious and in a hurry. I saw darkness. Like it was night. Then someone was walking quickly. I couldn't see who it was."

"Can you see this individual now?" I asked.

"No. I can't see him."

"*Him!*" I said.

She paused again. "I believe my feeling was that it was a man."

It was Marino who spoke. "You told Pat Harvey all this when you was with her at the rest stop?"

"Some of it, yes," Hilda replied. "I don't remember everything I said."

"I need to walk around," Marino muttered, getting up from the couch. Hilda did not seem surprised or concerned as he went out, the screen door slamming shut behind him.

"Hilda," I said, "when you met with Pat Harvey, did you pick up anything about her? Did you get any sense that she knew something, for example, about what might have happened to her daughter?"

"I picked up guilt real strong, like she was feeling responsible. But this would be expected. When I deal with the relatives of someone who has disappeared or been killed, I always pick up guilt. What was a little more unusual was her aura."

"Her aura?"

I knew what an aura was in medicine, a sensation that can precede the onset of a seizure. But I did not think this was what Hilda meant.

"Auras are invisible to most people," she explained. "I see them as colors. An aura surrounding a person. A color. Pat Harvey's aura was gray."

"Does that mean something?"

"Gray is neither death nor life," she said. "I associate it with illness. Someone sick of body, mind, or soul. As if something is draining the color from her life."

"I suppose that makes sense when you consider her emotional state at the time," I pointed out.

"It might. But I remember that it gave me a bad feeling. I picked up that she might be in some sort of danger. Her energy wasn't good, wasn't positive or healthy. I felt she was at risk for opening herself up to harm, or maybe bringing harm upon herself through her own doings."

"Have you ever seen a gray aura before?"

"Not often."

I could not resist asking, "Are you picking up a color from me?"

"Yellow with a little brown mixed in."

"That's interesting," I said, surprised. "I never wear either color. In fact, I don't believe I have anything yellow or brown inside my house. But I love sunlight and chocolate."

"Your aura has nothing to do with colors or foods you like." She smiled. "Yellow can mean spiritual. And brown I associate with good sense, practical. Someone grounded in reality. I see your aura as being very spiritual but also very practical. Now mind you, that is my interpretation. For each person, colors mean a different thing."

"And Marino?"

"A thin margin of red. That's what I see around him," she said. "Red often means anger. But he needs more red, I think."

"You're not serious," I said, for the last thing I would have thought that Marino needed was more anger.

"When someone is low on energy, I tell them they need more red in their life. It gives energy. Makes you get things done, fight against your troubles. Red can be real good if channeled properly. But I get the sense he is afraid of what he is feeling, and this is what is weakening him."

"Hilda, have you seen pictures of the other couples who disappeared?"

She nodded. "Mrs. Harvey had their pictures. From the newspaper."

"And did you touch them, read them?"

"I did."

"What did you perceive?"

"Death," she said. "All of the young people were dead."

"What about the light-complected man who may have a beard or something dark over part of his face?"

She paused. "I don't know. But I do remember picking up this friendliness I mentioned. Their initial encounter was not one of fear. I had the impression that none of the young people were afraid at first."

"I want to ask you about a card now," I said. "You mentioned that you read people's cards. Are you talking about playing cards?"

"You can use most anything. Tarot cards, a crystal ball. It doesn't matter. These things are tools. It's whatever makes it easy for you to concentrate. But yes, I use a deck of playing cards."

"How does that work?"

"I ask the person to cut the cards, then I begin to pick one at a time and tell what impressions come to mind."

"Were you to pick the jack of hearts, would there be any special significance?" I asked.

"It all depends on the person I'm dealing with, what energy I'm picking up from this individual. But the jack of hearts is equal to the knight of cups in tarot cards."

"A good card or a bad card?"

"It depends on who the card represents in relation to the individual whose reading I'm doing," she said. "In tarot cards, cups are love and emotion cards, just as swords and pentacles are business and money cards. The jack of hearts would be a love and emotion card. And this could be very good. It could also be very bad if the love has gone sour or turned vengeful, hateful."

"How would a jack of hearts be different from a ten of hearts or queen of hearts, for example?"

"The jack of hearts is a face card," she said. "I would say this is a card that represents a man. Now a king of hearts is also a face card, but I would associate a king with power, someone who is perceived or perceives himself as in control, in charge, possibly a father or boss, something like that. A jack, like a knight, might represent someone who is perceived or perceives himself as a soldier, a defender, a champion. He might be someone who is out in the world doing battle on the business front. Maybe he's into sports, a competitor. He could be a lot of things, but since hearts are emotion, love cards, that would make me say that whoever this card represents, there is an emotional element versus a money or work element."

Her telephone rang again.

She said to me, "Don't always trust what you hear, Dr. Scarpetta."

"About what?" I asked, startled.

"Something that matters a great deal to you is causing unhappiness, grief. It has to do with a person. A friend, a romantic interest. It could be a member of your family. I don't know. Definitely someone of great importance in your life. But you are hearing and maybe even imagining many things. Be careful what you believe."

Mark, I thought, or maybe Benton Wesley. I couldn't resist asking, "Is this someone currently in my life? Someone I'm having encounters with?"

She paused. "Since I'm sensing confusion, much that is unknown, I'll have to say that it isn't someone you are currently close to. I'm feeling a distance, you know, not necessarily geographical, but emotional. Space that is making it hard for you to trust. My advice is to let it go, don't do anything about this now. A resolution will come, and I can't tell you when this will be, but it will be all right if you relax, don't listen to the confusion, or act impulsively.

"And there's something else," she went on. "Look beyond what is before you, and I don't know what this is about. But there is something you aren't seeing and it has to do with the past, something of importance that happened in the past. It will come to you and lead you to the truth, but you will not recognize its significance unless you open yourself first. Let your faith guide you."

Wondering what had happened to Marino, I got up and looked out the window.

Marino drank two bourbon and waters in the Charlotte airport, then had one more when we were in the air. He had very little to say during the trip back to Richmond. It wasn't until we were walking to our cars in the parking lot that I decided to take initiative.

"We need to talk," I said, getting out my keys.

"I'm beat."

"It's almost five o'clock," I said. "Why don't you come to my house for dinner?"

He stared off across the parking lot, squinting in the sun. I could not tell if he was in a rage or on the verge of tears, and I wasn't sure I'd ever seen him this out of sorts.

"Are you angry with me, Marino?"

"No, Doc. Right now I just want to be alone."

"Right now, I don't think you should be."

Fastening the top button of his coat, he muttered, "See ya later," and walked off.

I drove home, absolutely drained, and was mindlessly puttering in the kitchen when my doorbell rang. Looking through the peephole, I was amazed to see Marino.

"I had this in my pocket," he explained the instant I opened the door. He handed me his canceled plane ticket and inconsequential paperwork from the rental car. "Thought you might need it for your tax records or whatever."

"Thank you," I said, and I knew this was not why he had come. I had charge card receipts. Nothing he had given to me was necessary. "I was just fixing dinner. You might as well stay since you're already here."

"Maybe for a little while." He would not meet my eyes. "Then I got things to do."

Following me into the kitchen, he sat at the table while I resumed slicing sweet red peppers and adding them to chopped onions sautéing in olive oil.

"You know where the bourbon is," I said, stirring.

He got up, heading to the bar.

"While you're at it," I called after him, "would you please fix me a Scotch and soda?"

He did not reply, but when he came back he set my drink on the counter nearby and leaned against the butcher's block. I added the onions and peppers to tomatoes sautéing in another pan, then began browning sausage.

"I don't have a second course," I apologized as I worked.

"Don't look to me like you need one."

"Spring lamb with white wine, breast of veal, or roast pork would be perfect." I filled a pot with water and set it on the stove. "I'm pretty amazing with lamb, but I'll have to give you a rain check."

"Maybe you ought to forget cutting up dead bodies and open a restaurant."

"I'll assume you mean that as a compliment."

"Oh, yeah." His face was expressionless, and he was lighting a cigarette. "So what do you call this?" He nodded at the stove.

"I call it yellow and green broad noodles with sweet peppers and sausage," I replied, adding the sausage to the sauce. "But if I really wanted to impress you, I would call it *le papardelle del Cantunzein*."

"Don't worry. I'm impressed."

"Marino." I glanced over at him. "What happened this morning?"

He replied with a question, "You mention to anyone what Vessey told you about the hack mark's being made with a serrated blade?"

"So far, you're the only person I've told."

"Hard to figure how Hilda Ozimek came up with that, with the hunting knife with a serrated edge she claims popped into her mind when Pat Harvey took her to the rest stop."

"It is hard to understand," I agreed, placing pasta in the boiling water. "There are some things in life that can't be reasoned away or explained, Marino."

Fresh pasta takes only seconds to cook, and I drained it and transferred it to a bowl kept warm in the oven. Adding the sauce, I tossed in butter and grated fresh Parmesan, then told Marino we were ready to eat.

"I've got artichoke hearts in the refrigerator." I served our plates. "But no salad. I do have bread in the freezer."

"This is all I need," he said, his mouth full. "It's good. Real good."

I had barely touched my meal when he was ready for a second helping. It was as though Marino had not eaten in a week. He was not taking care of himself, and it was showing. His tie was in serious need of a dry cleaner, the hem on one leg of his trousers had unraveled, and his shirt was stained yellow under the arms. Everything about him cried out that he was needy and neglected, and I was as repelled by this as I was disturbed. There was no reason why an intelligent grown man should allow himself to fall into poor repair like an abandoned house. Yet I knew his life was out of control, that in a way he could not help himself. Something was terribly wrong.

I got up and retrieved a bottle of Mondavi red wine from the wine rack.

"Marino," I said, pouring each of us a glass, "whose photograph did you show to Hilda? Was it your wife?"

He leaned back in his chair and would not look at me.

"You don't have to talk about it if you don't want to. But you haven't been yourself for quite a while. It's very apparent."

"What she said freaked me out," he replied.

"What Hilda said?"

"Yeah."

"Would you like to tell me about it?"

"I haven't told no one about it." He paused, reaching for his wine. His face was hard, eyes humiliated. "She went back to Jersey last November."

"I'm not sure you've ever told me your wife's name."

"Wow," he muttered bitterly. "Ain't that a comment."

"Yes, it is. You keep an awful lot to yourself."

"I've always been that way. But I guess being a cop has made it worse. I'm so used to hearing the guys bitch and moan about their wives, girlfriends, kids. They cry on your shoulder, you think they're your brothers. Then when it's your turn to have a problem, you make the mistake of spilling your guts and next thing it's all the hell over the police department. I learned a long time ago to keep my mouth shut."

He paused, getting out his wallet. "Her name's Doris." He handed me the snapshot he had shown Hilda Ozimek this morning.

Doris had a good face and a round, comfortable body. She was standing stiffly, dressed for church, her expression self-conscious and reluctant. I had seen her a hundred times, for the world was full of Dorises. They were the sweet young women who sat on porch swings dreaming of love as they stared into nights magic with stars and the smells of summer. They were mirrors, their images of themselves reflections of the significant people in their lives. They derived their importance from the services they rendered, survived by killing off their expectations in inches, and then one day woke up mad as hell.

"We would've been married thirty years this June," Marino

said as I returned the photograph. "Then suddenly she ain't happy. Says I work too much, never around. She don't know me. Things like that. But I wasn't born yesterday. That's not the real story."

"Then what is?"

"It got started last summer when her mother had a stroke. Doris went to look after her. Was up north for almost a month, getting her mother out of the hospital and into a nursing home, taking care of everything. When Doris came home, she was different. It's like she was somebody else."

"What do you think happened?"

"I know she met this guy up there whose wife died a couple years back. He's into real estate, was helping sell her mother's house. Doris mentioned him once or twice like it was no big deal. But something was going on. The phone would ring late, and when I answered it, the person would hang up. Doris would rush out to get the mail before I did. Then in November, she suddenly packs up and leaves, says her mother needs her."

"Has she been home since?" I asked.

He shook his head. "Oh, she calls now and then. She wants a divorce."

"Marino, I'm sorry."

"Her mother's in this home, you see. And Doris is looking after her, seeing this real estate guy, I guess. Upset one minute, happy the next. Like she wants to come back, but don't want to. Guilty, then don't give a damn. It's just like Hilda said when she was looking at her picture. Back and forth."

"Very painful for you."

"Hey." He tossed his napkin on the table. "She can do what she wants. Screw her."

I knew he did not mean that. He was devastated, and my heart ached for him. At the same time, I could not help but feel sympathy for his wife. Marino would not be easy to love.

"Do you want her to come home?"

"I've been with her longer than I was alive before we met. But let's face it, Doc." He glanced at me, his eyes frightened. "My life sucks. Always counting nickels and dimes, called out on the street in the middle of the night. Plan vacations and then something goes down and Doris unpacks and waits at home—like Labor Day weekend when the Harvey girl and her boyfriend disappeared. That was the last straw."

"Do you love Doris?"

"She don't believe I do."

"Maybe you should make sure she understands how you feel," I said. "Maybe you should show that you want her a lot and don't need her so much."

"I don't get it." He looked bewildered.

He would never get it, I thought, depressed.

"Just take care of yourself," I told him. "Don't expect her to do that for you. Maybe it will make a difference."

"I don't earn enough bucks, and that's it, chapter and verse."

"I'll bet your wife doesn't care so much about money. She'd rather feel important and loved."

"He's got a big house and a Chrysler New Yorker. Brand new, with leather seats, the whole nine yards."

I did not reply.

"Last year he went to Hawaii for his vacation." Marino was getting angry.

"Doris spent most of her life with you. That was her choice, Hawaii or not—"

"Hawaii's nothing but a tourist trap," he cut in, lighting a cigarette. "Me, I'd rather go to Buggs Island and fish."

"Has it occurred to you that Doris might have grown weary of being your mother?"

"She ain't my mother," he snapped.

"Then why is it that since she left, you've begun looking like you desperately need a mother, Marino?"

"Because I don't got time to sew buttons on, cook, and clean, do shit like that."

"I'm busy, too. I find time for shit like that."

"Yeah, you also got a maid. You also probably earn a hundred G's a year."

"I would take care of myself if I earned only ten G's a year," I said. "I would do it because I have self-respect and because I *don't want* anyone to take care of me. I simply want to be cared for, and there's a very big difference between the two."

"If you got all the answers, Doc, then how come you're divorced? And how come your friend Mark's in Colorado and you're here? Don't sound to me like you wrote the book on relationships."

I felt a flush creeping up my neck. "Tony did not truly care for me, and when I finally figured that out, I left. As for Mark, he has a problem with commitments."

"And you were committed to him?" Marino almost glared at me.

I did not respond.

"How come you didn't go out west with him? Maybe you're only committed to being a chief."

"We were having problems, and certainly part of it was my fault. Mark was angry, went out west . . . maybe to make a point, maybe just to get away from me," I said, dismayed that I could not keep the emotion out of my voice. "Professionally, my going with him wouldn't have been possible, but it was never an option."

Marino suddenly looked ashamed. "I'm sorry. I didn't know that."

I was silent.

"Sounds like you and me are in the same boat," he offered.

"In some ways," I said, and I did not want to admit to myself what those ways were. "But I'm taking care of myself. If Mark ever reappears, he won't find me looking like hell, my life down the drain. I want him, but I don't *need* him. Maybe you ought to try that with Doris?"

"Yeah." He seemed encouraged. "Maybe I will. I think I'm ready for coffee."

"Do you know how to fix it?"

"You gotta be kidding," he said, surprised.

"Lesson number one, Marino. Fixing coffee. Step this way."

While I showed him the technical wonders of a drip coffee maker that required nothing more than a fifty IQ, he resumed contemplating this day's adventures.

"A part of me don't want to take what Hilda said seriously," he explained. "But another part of me has to. I mean, it sure gave me second thoughts."

"In what way?"

"Deborah Harvey was shot with a nine-millimeter. They never found the shell. Kind of hard to believe the squirrel could collect the shell out there in the dark. Makes me think Morrell and the rest of them wasn't looking in the right place. Remember, Hilda wondered if there wasn't another place, and she mentioned something lost. Something metal that had to do with war. That could be a spent shell."

"She also said this object wasn't harmful," I reminded him.

"A spent shell couldn't hurt a fly. It's the bullet that's harmful and only when it's being fired."

"And the photographs she looked at were taken last fall," I went on. "Whatever this lost item is may have been out there then but isn't there now."

"You thinking the killer came back during daylight to look for it?"

"Hilda said the person who lost this metal object was concerned about it."

"I don't think he went back," Marino said. "He's too careful for that. Be a big damn risk. The area was crawling with cops and bloodhounds right after the kids disappeared. You can bet the killer laid low. He's got to be pretty cool to have gotten away with what he's doing for so long, whether we're talking about a psychopath or a paid hit man."

"Maybe," I said as the coffee began to drip.

"I think we should go back out there and poke around a little. You up for it?"

"Frankly, the idea has crossed my mind."

8

In the light of a clear afternoon, the woods did not seem so ominous until Marino and I drew closer to the small clearing. Then the faint, foul odor of decomposing human flesh was an insidious reminder. Pine tags and leaves had been displaced and piled in small mounds by the scraping of shovels and emptying of sieves. It would take time and hard rains before the tangible remnants of murder were no longer to be found in this place.

Marino had brought a metal detector and I carried a rake. He got out his cigarettes and looked around.

"Don't see any point in scanning right here," he said. "It's been gone over half a dozen times."

"I assume the path's been gone over thoroughly as well," I said, staring back at the trail we had followed from the logging road.

"Not necessarily, because the path didn't exist when the couple was taken out here last fall."

I realized what he was saying. The trail of displaced leaves and hard-packed dirt had been made by police officers and other interested parties going back and forth from the logging road to the scene.

Surveying the woods, he added, "The fact is, we don't even know where they was parked, Doc. It's easy to assume it's close to where we parked, and that they got here pretty much the same way we did. But it depends on whether the killer was actually *heading* here."

"I have a feeling the killer knew where he was going," I replied. "It doesn't make sense to think he randomly turned down the logging road and then ended up out here after haphazardly wandering around in the dark."

Shrugging, Marino switched on the metal detector. "Can't hurt to give it a try."

We began at the perimeter of the scene, scanning the path, sweeping yards of undergrowth and leaves on either side as we slowly made our way back toward the logging road. For almost two hours we probed any opening in trees and brush that looked remotely promising for human passage, the detector's first high-frequency tone rewarding our efforts with an Old Milwaukee beer can, the second with a rusty bottle opener. The third alert did not sound until we were at the edge of the woods, within sight of our car, where we uncovered a shotgun shell, the red plastic faded by the years.

Leaning against the rake, I stared dismally back down the path, thinking. I pondered what Hilda had said about another place being involved, perhaps somewhere that the killer had taken Deborah, and I envisioned the clearing and the bodies.

My first thought had been that if Deborah had broken free of the killer at some point, it may have been when she and Fred were being led in the dark from the logging road to the clearing. But as I looked through the woods, this theory didn't really make sense.

"Let's accept as a given that we're dealing with one killer," I said to Marino.

"Okay, I'm listening." He wiped his damp forehead on his coat sleeve.

"If you were the killer and had abducted two people and then forced them, perhaps at gunpoint, to come out here, who would you kill first?"

"The guy's going to be a bigger problem," he said without pause. "Me, I'm going to take him out first and save the little girl for last."

It was still difficult to imagine. When I tried to envision one person forcing two hostages to walk through these woods after dark, I continued to draw a blank. Did the killer have a flashlight? Did he know this area so well he could find the clearing blindfolded? I voiced these questions aloud to Marino.

"I've been trying to see the same thing," he said. "A couple ideas come to mind. First, he probably restrained them, tied their hands behind their back. Second, if it was me, I'd hold on to the girl, have the gun to her ribs while we're walking through the woods. This would make the boyfriend as gentle as a lamb. One false move, and his girl gets blown away. As for a flashlight? He had to have had some way of seeing out here."

"How are you going to hold a gun, a flashlight, and the girl at the same time?" I asked.

"Easy. Want me to show you?"

"Not particularly." I backed away as he reached toward me.

"The rake. Geez, Doc. Don't be so damn jumpy."

He handed me the metal detector and I gave him the rake.

"Pretend the rake's Deborah, okay? I'm yoking her around the neck with my left arm, the flashlight in my left hand, like this." He demonstrated. "In my right hand I've got the gun, which is stuck against her ribs. No problem. Fred's gonna be a couple feet in front of us, following the beam of the flashlight while I watch him like a hawk." Pausing, Marino stared down the path. "They're not going to be moving very fast."

"Especially if they're barefoot," I pointed out.

"Yeah, and I'm thinking they were. He can't tie up their feet if he's going to walk them out here. But if he makes them take off their shoes, then that's going to slow them down, make it harder for them to run. Maybe after he whacks them, he keeps the shoes as souvenirs."

"Maybe." I was thinking about Deborah's purse again.

I said, "If Deborah's hands were bound behind her back, then how did her purse get out here? It didn't have a strap, no way to loop it over her arm or shoulder. It wasn't attached to a belt, in fact it doesn't appear she was wearing a belt. And if someone were forcing you out into the woods at gunpoint, why would you take your purse with you?"

"Got no idea. That's been bothering me from the start."

"Let's give it one last try," I said.

"Oh, shit."

By the time we got back to the clearing, clouds had passed over the sun and it was getting windy, making it seem that the temperature had dropped ten degrees. Damp beneath my coat from exertion, I was cold, the muscles in my arms trembling from raking. Moving to the perimeter farthest from the path, I studied an area beyond which stretched a terrain so uninviting that I doubted even hunters ventured there. The police had dug and sifted maybe ten feet in this direction before running into an infestation of kudzu that had metastasized over the better part of an acre. Trees covered in the vine's green mail looked like prehistoric dinosaurs rearing up over a solid green sea. Every living bush, pine, and plant was slowly being strangled to death.

"Good God," Marino said as I waded out with my rake. "You're not serious."

"We won't go very far," I promised.

We did not have to.

The metal detector responded almost immediately. The tone got louder and higher pitched as Marino positioned the scanner over an area of kudzu less than fifteen feet from where the bodies had been found. I discovered that raking kudzu was worse than combing snarled hair and finally resorted to dropping to my knees and ripping off leaves and feeling around roots with fingers sheathed in surgical gloves until I felt something cold and hard that I knew wasn't what I was hoping for.

"Save it for the tollbooth," I said dejectedly, tossing Marino a dirty quarter.

Several feet away the metal detector signaled us again, and

this time my rooting around on hands and knees paid off. When I felt the unmistakable hard, cylindrical shape, I gently parted kudzu until I saw the gleam of stainless steel, a cartridge case still as shiny as polished silver. I gingerly plucked it out, touching as little of its surface as possible, while Marino bent over and held open a plastic evidence bag.

"Nine-millimeter, Federal," he said, reading the head stamp through plastic. "I'll be damned."

"He was standing right around here when he shot her," I muttered, a strange sensation running along my nerves as I recalled what Hilda had said about Deborah's being in a place "crowded" with things "grabbing" at her. *Kudzu.*

"If she was shot at close range," Marino said, "then she went down not too far from here."

Wading out a little farther as he followed me with the metal detector, I said, "How the hell did he *see* to shoot her, Marino? Lord. Can you imagine this place at night?"

"The moon was out."

"But it wasn't full," I said.

"Full enough so it wouldn't have been pitch-dark."

The weather had been checked months ago. The Friday night of August thirty-first when the couple had disappeared, the temperature had been in the upper sixties, the moon three-quarters full, the sky clear. Even if the killer had been armed with a powerful flashlight, I still could not understand how he could force two hostages out here at night without being as disoriented and vulnerable as they were. All I could imagine was confusion, a lot of stumbling about.

Why didn't he just kill them on the logging road, drag their bodies several yards into the woods, and then drive away? Why did he want to bring them out here?

And yet the pattern was the same with the other couples. Their bodies also had been found in remote, wooded areas like this.

Looking around at the kudzu, an unpleasant expression on his face, Marino said, "Glad as hell this ain't snake weather."

"That's a lovely thought," I said, unnerved.

"You want to keep going?" he asked in a tone that told me he had no interest in venturing an inch farther into this gothic wasteland.

"I think we've had enough for one day." I waded out of the kudzu as quickly as possible, my flesh crawling. The mention of snakes had done me in. I was on the verge of a full-blown anxiety attack.

It was almost five, the woods gloomy with shadows as we headed back to the car. Every time a twig snapped beneath Marino's feet, my heart jumped. Squirrels scampering up trees and birds flying off branches were startling intrusions upon the eerie silence.

"I'll drop this off at the lab first thing in the morning," he said. "Then I gotta be in court. Great way to spend your day off."

"Which case?"

"The case of Bubba shot by his friend named Bubba, the only witness was another drone named Bubba."

"You're not serious."

"Hey," he said, unlocking the car doors, "I'm as serious as

a sawed-off shotgun." Starting the engine, he muttered, "I'm starting to hate this job, Doc. I swear, I really am."

"At the moment you hate the whole world, Marino."

"No, I don't," he said, and he actually laughed. "I like you all right."

The last day of January began when the morning's mail brought an official communication from Pat Harvey. Brief and to the point, it stated that if copies of her daughter's autopsy and toxicology reports were not received by the end of the following week, she would get a court order. A copy of the letter had been sent to my immediate boss, the Commissioner of Health and Human Services, whose secretary was on the phone within the hour summoning me to his office.

While autopsies awaited me downstairs, I left the building and made the short walk along Franklin to Main Street Station, which had been vacant for years, then converted into a short-lived shopping mall before the state had purchased it. In a sense, the historic red building with its clock tower and red-tile roof had become a train station again, a temporary stop for state employees forced to relocate while the Madison Building was stripped of asbestos and renovated. The Governor had appointed Dr. Paul Sessions commissioner two years before, and though face-to-face meetings with my new boss were infrequent, they were pleasant enough. I had a feeling today might prove a different story. His secretary had sounded apologetic on the phone, as if she knew I were being called in to be gaffed.

The commissioner resided in a suite of offices on the second level, accessible by a marble stairway worn smooth by travelers scuffing up and down steps in an era long past. The spaces the commissioner had appropriated had once been a sporting goods store and a boutique selling colorful kites and wind socks. Walls had been knocked out, plate glass windows filled in with brick, his offices carpeted, paneled, and arranged with handsome furnishings. Dr. Sessions was familiar enough with the sluggish workings of government to have settled into his temporary headquarters as if the relocation were permanent.

His secretary greeted me with a sympathetic smile that made me feel only worse as she swiveled around from her keyboard and reached for the phone.

She announced that I was here, and immediately the solid oak door across from her desk opened and Dr. Sessions invited me in.

An energetic man with thinning brown hair and large-framed glasses that swallowed his narrow face, he was living proof that marathon running was never intended for human beings. His chest was tubercular, body fat so low he rarely took his suit jacket off and frequently wore long sleeves in the summer because he was chronically cold. He still wore a splint on the left arm he had broken several months ago while running a race on the West Coast and getting tangled up in a coathanger that had eluded the feet of runners ahead of him and sent him crashing to the street. He was, perhaps, the only contender not to finish the race and end up in the newspapers anyway.

He seated himself behind his desk, the letter from Pat Harvey centered on the blotter, his face unusually stern.

"I assume you've already seen this?" He tapped the letter with an index finger.

"Yes," I said. "Understandably, Pat Harvey is very interested in the results of her daughter's examination."

"Deborah Harvey's body was found eleven days ago. Am I to conclude you don't yet know what killed her or Fred Cheney?"

"I know what killed her. His cause of death is still undetermined."

He looked puzzled. "Dr. Scarpetta, would you care to explain to me why this information has not been released to the Harveys or to Fred Cheney's father?"

"My explanation is simple," I said. "Their cases are still pending as further special studies are conducted. And the FBI has asked me to withhold releasing anything to anyone."

"I see." He gazed at the wall as if it contained a window to look out of, which it did not.

"If you direct me to release my reports, I will do so, Dr. Sessions. In fact, I would be relieved if you would order me to meet Pat Harvey's request."

"Why?" He knew the answer, but he wanted to hear what I had to say.

"Because Mrs. Harvey and her husband have a right to know what happened to their daughter," I said. "Bruce Cheney has a right to hear what we do or don't know about his son. The wait is anguish for them."

"Have you talked to Mrs. Harvey?"

"Not recently."

"Have you talked to her since the bodies were found, Dr. Scarpetta?" He was fidgeting with his sling.

"I called her when the identifications were confirmed, but I haven't talked with her since."

"Has she tried to reach you?"

"She has."

"And you have refused to talk to her?"

"I've already explained why I'm not talking to her," I said. "And I don't believe it would be polite for me to get on the phone and tell her that the FBI doesn't want me to release information to her."

"You haven't mentioned the FBI's directive to anyone, then."

"I just mentioned it to you."

He recrossed his legs. "And I appreciate that. But it would be inappropriate to mention this business to anybody else. Especially reporters."

"I've been doing my best to avoid reporters."

"The *Washington Post* called me this morning."

"Who from the *Post*?"

He began sorting through message slips as I waited uneasily. I did not want to believe that Abby would go behind my back and over my head.

"Someone named Clifford Ring." He glanced up. "Actually, it's not the first time he's called, nor am I the only person he's attempted to milk for information. He's also been badgering my secretary and other members of my staff, including my deputy and the Secretary of Human Resources. I assume he's called you as well, which was why he finally resorted to administration, because, as he put it, 'the medical examiner won't talk to me.'"

"A lot of reporters have called. I don't remember most of their names."

"Well, Mr. Ring seems to think there's some sort of cover-up going on, something conspiratorial and based on the direction of his questioning, he seems to have information that buttresses this."

Strange, I thought. It didn't sound to me as if the *Post* was holding off on investigating these cases, as Abby had stated so emphatically.

"He's under the impression," the commissioner continued, "that your office is stonewalling, and that it's therefore part of this so-called conspiracy."

"And I suppose we are." I worked hard to keep the annoyance out of my voice. "And that leaves me caught in the middle. Either I defy Pat Harvey or the Justice Department, and frankly, given a choice, I would prefer to accommodate Mrs. Harvey. Eventually, I will have to answer to her. She is Deborah's mother. I don't have to answer to the FBI."

"I'm not interested in antagonizing the Justice Department," Dr. Sessions said.

He did not have to outline why. A substantial portion of the commissioner's departmental budget was supplied by money from federal grants, some of which trickled down to my office to subsidize the collection of data needed by various injury prevention and traffic safety agencies. The Justice Department knew how to play hardball. If antagonizing the feds did not dry up much-needed revenues, we could at least count on our lives being made miserable. The last thing the commissioner wanted was to account for every pencil and sheet of stationery purchased with grant money. I knew how it worked. All of us would be nickel-and-dimed, papered to death.

The commissioner reached for the letter with his good arm and studied it for a moment.

He said, "Actually, the only answer may be for Mrs. Harvey to go through with her threat."

"If she gets a court order, then I will have no choice but to send her what she wants."

"I realize that. And the advantage is the FBI can't hold us accountable. The disadvantage, obviously, will be the negative publicity," he thought aloud. "Certainly, it won't shine a good light on the Department of Health and Human Services if the public knows we were forced by a judge to give Pat Harvey what she is entitled to by law. I suppose it may corroborate our friend Mr. Ring's suspicions."

The average citizen didn't even know that the Medical Examiner's Office was part of Health and Human Services. I was the one who was going to look bad. The commissioner, in good bureaucratic fashion, was setting me up to take it on the nose because he had no intention of aggravating the Justice Department.

"Of course," he considered, "Pat Harvey will come across as rather heavy-handed, as using her office to throw her weight around. She may be bluffing."

"I doubt it," I said tersely.

"We'll see." He got up from his desk and showed me to the door. "I'll write Mrs. Harvey, saying you and I talked."

I'll just bet you will, I thought.

"Let me know if I can be of any assistance." He smiled, avoiding my eyes.

I had just let him know I needed assistance. He might as well have had two broken arms. He wasn't going to lift a finger.

As soon as I got back to the office, I asked the clerks up front and Rose if a reporter from the *Post* had been calling. After searching memories and digging through old message slips, no one could come up with a Clifford Ring. He couldn't exactly accuse me of stonewalling if he'd never tried to reach me, I reasoned. All the same, I was perplexed.

"By the way," Rose added as I headed down the hall, "Linda's been looking for you, says she needs to see you right away."

Linda was a firearms examiner. Marino must have been by with the cartridge case, I thought. Good.

The toolmarks and firearms laboratory was on the third floor and could have passed for a used-gun shop. Revolvers, rifles, shotguns, and pistols covered virtually every inch of counter space, and evidence wrapped in brown paper was stacked chest high on the floor. I was about to decide that everyone was at lunch when I heard the muffled explosions of a gun discharging behind closed doors. Adjoining the lab was a small room used to test-fire weapons into a galvanized steel tank filled with water.

Two rounds later Linda emerged, .38 Special in one hand,

spent bullets and cartridge cases in the other. She was slender and feminine, with long brown hair, good bones, and wide-spaced hazel eyes. A lab coat protected a flowing black skirt and pale yellow silk blouse with a gold circle pin at the throat. Were I sitting next to her on a plane and trying to guess her profession, teaching poetry or running an art gallery would have come to mind.

"Bad news, Kay," she said, setting the revolver and spent ammunition on her desk.

"I hope it doesn't pertain to the cartridge case Marino brought in," I said.

"Afraid it does. I was about to etch my initials and a lab number on it when I got a little surprise." She moved over to the comparison microscope. "Here." She offered me the chair. "A picture's worth a thousand words."

Seating myself, I peered into the lenses. In the field of light to my left was the stainless-steel cartridge case.

"I don't understand," I muttered, adjusting the focus. Etched inside the cartridge case's mouth were the initials "J.M."

"I thought Marino receipted this to you." I looked up at her.

"He did. He came by about an hour ago," Linda said. "I asked him if he etched these initials, and he said he didn't. Not that I really thought he had. Marino's initials are P.M., not J.M., and he's been around long enough to know better."

Though some detectives initialed cartridge cases just as some medical examiners initialed bullets recovered from bodies, the firearms examiners discouraged the practice.

Taking a stylus to metal is risky because there's always the threat one might scratch breech block, firing pin, ejector marks, or other features, such as lands and grooves, suitable for identification. Marino did know better. Like me, he always initialed the plastic bag and left the evidence inside untouched.

"Am I to believe these initials were *already* on this cartridge case when Marino brought it in?" I asked.

"Apparently so."

J.M. *Jay Morrell*, I thought, mystified. Why would a cartridge case left at the scene be marked with his initials?

Linda proposed, "I'm wondering if a police officer working the scene out there had this in his pocket for some reason, and inadvertently lost it. If he had a hole in his pocket, for example?"

"I'd find that hard to believe," I said.

"Well, I've got one other theory I'll toss out. But you aren't going to like it, and I don't like it much, either. The cartridge case could have been reloaded."

"Then why would it be marked with an investigator's initials? Who on earth would reload a cartridge case marked as evidence?"

"It's happened before, Kay, and you didn't hear this from me, all right?"

I just listened.

"The number of weapons and the amount of ammunition and cartridge cases collected by the police and submitted to the courts are astronomical and worth a lot of money. People get greedy, even judges. They take the stuff for themselves or sell it to gun dealers, other enthusiasts. I suppose it's remotely possible this cartridge case was collected by a police officer or submitted to the courts as evidence at some point, and ended up reloaded. It may be that whoever fired it had no idea someone's initials were etched inside it."

"We can't prove that this cartridge case belongs to the bullet I found in Deborah Harvey's lumbar spine, and won't be able to do so unless we recover the pistol," I reminded her. "We can't even say with certainty it's from a Hydra-Shok cartridge. All we know is it's nine-millimeter, Federal.

"True. But Federal holds the patent for Hydra-Shok ammunition, has since the late eighties. For whatever that's worth."

"Does Federal sell Hydra-Shok bullets for reloading?" I asked.

"That's the problem. No. Only the cartridges are available on the market. But that doesn't mean someone couldn't get hold of the bullets in some other way. Steal them from the factory, have a contact who steals them from the factory. I could get them, for example, if I claimed I were working on a special project. Who knows?" She retrieved a can of Diet Coke from her desk, adding, "Nothing much surprises me anymore."

"Is Marino aware of what you found?"

"I called him."

"Thank you, Linda," I said, getting up, and I was formulating my own theory, which was quite different from hers and, unfortunately, more probable. Just the thought of it made me furious. In my office I snatched up the phone and dialed Marino's pager number. He returned my call almost immediately.

"The little fuckhead," he said right off.

"Who? Linda?" I asked, startled.

"Morrell, that's who. The lying son of a bitch. Just got off the phone with him. Said he didn't know what I was talking about until I accused him of stealing evidence for reloads—asked him if he was stealing guns and live ammo, too. Said I'd have his ass investigated by Internal Affairs. Then he started singing."

"He etched his initials in the cartridge case and left it out there deliberately, didn't he, Marino?"

"Oh, yeah. They found the goddam cartridge case last week. The real one. Then the asshole leaves this goddam plant, starts whining that he was just doing what the FBI told him to do."

"Where is the real cartridge case?" I demanded, blood pounding in my temples.

"The FBI lab's got it. You and yours truly spent an entire afternoon in the woods, and guess what, Doc? The whole goddam time we was being watched. The place is under physical surveillance. Just a damn good thing neither one of us wandered behind a bush to take a piss, right?"

"Have you talked to Benton?"

"Hell, no. As far as I'm concerned, he can screw himself." Marino slammed down the receiver.

9

There was something reassuring about the Globe and Laurel that made me feel safe. Brick, with simple lines and not a hint of ostentation, the restaurant occupied a sliver of northern Virginia real estate in Triangle, near the U.S. Marine Corps base. The narrow strip of lawn in front was always tidy, boxwoods neatly pruned, the parking lot orderly, every car within the painted boundaries of its allotted space.

Semper Fidelis was over the door, and stepping inside I was welcomed by the cream of the "always faithful" crop: police chiefs, four-star generals, secretaries of defense, directors of the FBI and CIA, the photographs so familiar to me that the men sternly smiling in them seemed a host of long-lost friends. Maj. Jim Yancey, whose bronzed combat boots from Vietnam were on top of the piano across from the bar, strode across red Highland tartan carpet and intercepted me.

"Dr. Scarpetta," he said, grinning as he shook my hand. "I was afraid you didn't like the food when last you were here, and that's why you waited so long to come back."

The major's casual attire of turtleneck sweater and corduroy trousers could not camouflage his former profession. He was as military as a campaign hat, posture proudly straight, not an ounce of fat, white hair in a buzz cut. Past retirement age, he still looked fit enough for combat, and it wasn't hard for me to imagine him bumping over rugged terrain in a Jeep or eating rations from a can in the jungle while monsoon rains hammered down.

"I've never had a bad meal here, and you know it," I said warmly.

"You're looking for Benton, and he's looking for you. The old boy's around there"—he pointed—"in his usual foxhole."

"Thank you, Jim. I know the way. And it's so good to see you again."

He winked at me and returned to the bar.

It was Mark who had introduced me to Major Yancey's restaurant when I drove to Quantico two weekends every month to see him. As I walked beneath a ceiling covered with police patches and passed displays of old Corps memorabilia, recollections tugged at my heart. I could pick out the tables where Mark and I had sat, and it seemed odd to see strangers there now, engaged in their own private conversations. I had not been to the Globe in almost a year.

Leaving the main dining room, I headed for a more secluded section where Wesley was waiting for me in his "foxhole," a corner table before a window with red draperies. He was sipping a drink and did not smile as we greeted each other formally. A waiter in a black tuxedo appeared to take my drink order.

Wesley looked up at me with eyes as impenetrable as a bank vault, and I responded in kind. He had signaled the first round, and we were going to come out swinging.

"I am very concerned that we're having a problem with communication, Kay," he began.

"My sentiments exactly," I said with the iron-hard calm I had perfected on the witness stand. "I, too, am concerned by our problem with communication. Is the Bureau tapping my phone, tailing me as well? I hope whoever was hiding in the woods got good photographs of Marino and me."

Wesley said just as calmly, "You, personally, are not under surveillance. The wooded area where you and Marino were spotted yesterday afternoon is under surveillance."

"Perhaps if you had kept me informed," I said, holding in my anger, "I might have told you in advance when Marino and I had decided to go back out there."

"It never occurred to me you might."

"I routinely pay retrospective visits to scenes. You've worked with me long enough to be aware of that."

"*My* mistake. But now you know. And I would prefer that you not go back out there again."

"I have no plans to do so," I said testily. "But should the need arise, I will be happy to give you advance warning. Might as well, since you'll find out anyway. And I certainly don't need to waste my time picking up evidence that has been planted by your agents or the police."

"Kay," he said in a softer tone, "I'm not trying to interfere with your job."

"I'm being lied to, Benton. I'm told no cartridge case was recovered from the scene, only to discover it was receipted to the Bureau's laboratory more than a week ago."

"When we decided to set up surveillance, we didn't want word of it to leak," he said. "The fewer people told about what we were up to the better."

"Obviously, you must be assuming the killer might return to the scene."

"It's a possibility."

"Did you entertain this possibility with the first four cases?"

"It's different this time."

"Why?"

"Because he left evidence, and he knows it."

"If he were so worried about the cartridge case, he had plenty of time to go back and look for it last fall," I said.

"He may not know we would figure out Deborah Harvey was shot, that a Hydra-Shok bullet would be recovered from her body."

"I don't believe the individual we're dealing with is stupid," I said.

The waiter returned with my Scotch and soda.

Wesley went on, "The cartridge case you recovered was planted. I won't deny that. And yes, you and Marino walked into an area under physical surveillance. There were two men hiding in the woods. They saw everything the two of you did, including picking up the cartridge case. Had you not called me, I would have called you."

"I'd like to think you would have."

"I would have explained. Would have had no choice, really, because you inadvertently upset the apple cart. And you're right." He reached for his drink. "I should have let you know in advance; then none of this would have happened and we wouldn't have been forced to call things off, or better put, postpone them."

"What have you postponed, exactly?"

"Had you and Marino not stumbled upon what we were doing, tomorrow morning's news would have carried a story targeted at the killer." He paused. "Disinformation to draw him out, make him worry. The story will run, but not until Monday."

"And the point of it?" I asked.

"We want him to think that something turned up during the examination of the bodies. Something to make us believe he left important evidence at the scene. Alleged this, alleged that, with plenty of denials and no comments from the police. All of it intended to imply that whatever this evidence is, we've had no luck finding it yet. The killer knows he left a cartridge case out there. If he gets sufficiently paranoid and returns to look for it, we'll be waiting, watching him pick up the one we planted, get it on film, and then grab him."

"The cartridge case is worthless unless you have him and the gun. Why would he risk returning to the scene, especially if it appears that the police are busy looking around out there for this evidence?" I wanted to know.

"He may be worried about a lot of things, because he lost control of the situation. Had to have, or it would not have been necessary to shoot Deborah in the back. It might not have been necessary to shoot her at all. It appears he murdered Cheney without using a gun. How does he know what we're really looking for, Kay? Maybe it's a cartridge case. Maybe it's something else. He isn't going to be certain about the exact condition of the bodies when they were found. We don't know what he did to the couple, and he doesn't really know what you may have discovered while doing the autopsies. And he might not go back out there the day after the story runs, but he might try it a week or two later if everything seems quiet."

"I doubt your disinformation tactic will work," I said.

"Nothing ventured, nothing gained. The killer left evidence. We'd be foolish not to act on that."

The opening was too wide for me to resist walking through it. "And have you acted on evidence found in the first four cases, Benton? It's my understanding that a jack of hearts was recovered inside each of the vehicles. A detail you apparently have worked very hard to suppress."

"Who told you this?" he asked, the expression on his face unchanged. He did not even look surprised.

"Is it true?"

"Yes."

"And did you find a card in the Harvey-Cheney case?"

Wesley stared off across the room, nodding at the waiter. "I recommend the filet mignon." He opened his menu. "That or the lamb chops."

I placed my order as my heart pounded. I lit a cigarette, unable to relax, my mind frenetically groping for a way to breakthrough.

"You didn't answer my question."

"I don't see how it is relevant to your role in the investigation," he said.

"The police waited hours before calling me to the scene. The bodies had been moved, tampered with, by the time I got there. I'm being stonewalled by investigators, you've asked me to indefinitely pend the cause and manner of Fred's and Deborah's deaths. Meanwhile, Pat Harvey is threatening to get a court order because I won't release my findings." I paused. He remained unflappable.

"Finally," I concluded, my words beginning to bite, "I make a retrospective visit to a scene without knowing it's under surveillance or that the evidence I collected was planted. And you don't think the details of these cases are relevant to my role in the investigation? I'm no longer sure I even have a role in the investigation. Or at least you seem determined to make sure I don't have one."

"I'm not doing anything of the sort."

"Then someone is."

He did not reply.

"If a jack of hearts was found inside Deborah's Jeep or somewhere near their bodies, it's important for me to know. It would link the deaths of all five couples. When there's a serial killer on the loose in Virginia, it is of great concern to me."

Then he caught me off guard. "How much have you been telling Abby Turnbull?"

"I haven't been telling her anything," I said, my heart pounding harder.

"You've met with her, Kay. I'm sure you won't deny that."

"Mark told you, and I'm sure you won't deny that."

"Mark would have no reason to know you saw Abby in Richmond or Washington unless you told him. And in any event, he would have no reason to pass this along to me."

I stared at him. How could Wesley have known I had seen Abby in Washington unless she really was being watched?

"When Abby came to see me in Richmond," I said, "Mark called and I mentioned she was visiting. Are you telling me he said nothing to you?"

"He didn't."

"Then how did you find out?"

"There are some things I can't tell you. And you're just going to have to trust me."

The waiter set down our salads, and we ate in silence. Wesley did not speak again until our main courses arrived.

"I'm under a lot of pressure," he said in a quiet voice.

"I can see that. You look exhausted, run-down."

"Thank you, Doctor," he said ironically.

"You've changed in other ways as well." I pushed the point.

"I'm sure that is your perception."

"You're shutting me out, Benton."

"I suppose I keep my distance because you ask questions that I can't answer; so does Marino. And then I feel even more pressure. Do you understand?"

"I'm trying to understand," I said.

"I can't tell you everything. Can you let it go at that?"

"Not quite. Because that's where we're at cross-purposes. I have information you need. And you have information I need. I'm not going to show you mine unless you show me yours."

He surprised me by laughing.

"Do you think we can strike a deal under these terms?" I persisted.

"It looks like I don't have much of a choice."

"You don't," I said.

"Yes, we did find a jack of hearts in the Harvey-Cheney case. Yes, I did have their bodies moved before you arrived at the scene, and I know that was poor form, but you have no idea why the cards are so significant or the problems that would be precipitated by word of them leaking. If it made the newspapers, for example. I'm not going to say anything further about that right now."

"Where was the card?" I asked.

"We found it inside Deborah Harvey's purse. When a couple of the cops helped me turn her over, we found the purse under her body."

"Are you suggesting that the killer carried her purse out into the woods?"

"Yes. It wouldn't make any sense to think that Deborah carried her purse out there."

"In the other cases," I pointed out, "the card was left in plain sight inside the vehicle."

"Exactly. Where the card was found is just one more inconsistency. Why *wasn't* it left inside the Jeep? Another inconsistency is that the cards left in the other cases are Bicycle playing cards. The one left with Deborah is a different brand. Then there's the matter of fibers."

"What fibers?" I asked.

Though I had collected fibers from all of the decomposed

bodies, most of them were consistent with the victims' own clothing or the upholstery of their vehicles. Unknown fibers—what few I had found—had supplied no link between the cases, had proved useless so far.

"In the four cases preceding Deborah's and Fred's murders," Wesley said, "white cotton fibers were recovered from the driver's seat of each abandoned car."

"That's news to me," I said, irritation flaring again.

"The fiber analysis was done by our labs," he explained.

"And what is your interpretation?" I asked.

"The pattern of fibers recovered is interesting. Since the victims weren't wearing white cotton clothing at the time of their deaths, I have to assume that the fibers were left by the perpetrator, and this places him driving the victims' cars after the crimes. But we've been assuming that all along. One has to consider his clothing. And a possibility is that he was wearing some type of uniform when he encountered the couples. White cotton trousers. I don't know. But no white cotton fibers were recovered from the driver's seat of Deborah Harvey's Jeep."

"What did you find inside her Jeep?" I asked.

"Nothing that tells me anything right now. In fact, the interior was immaculate." He paused, cutting his steak. "The point is, the MO's different enough in this case to worry me a lot, because of the other circumstances."

"Because one of the victims is the Drug Czar's daughter, and you're still considering that what happened to Deborah may have been politically motivated, related to her mother's antidrug endeavors," I said.

He nodded. "We can't rule out that the murders of Deborah and her boyfriend were disguised to resemble the other cases."

"If their deaths aren't related to the others, and were a hit," I asked skeptically, "then how do you explain their killer knowing about the cards, Benton? Even I didn't find out about the jack of hearts until recently. Certainly it hasn't been in the newspapers."

"Pat Harvey knows," he startled me by saying.

Abby, I thought. And I was willing to bet that Abby had divulged the detail to Mrs. Harvey, and that Wesley knew this.

"How long has Mrs. Harvey known about the cards?" I asked.

"When her daughter's Jeep was found, she asked me if we'd recovered a card. And she called me about it again after the bodies turned up."

"I don't understand," I said. "Why would she have known last fall? It sounds to me as if she knew the details of the other cases *before* Deborah and Fred disappeared."

"She knew some of the details. Pat Harvey was interested in these cases long before she had personal motivation."

"Why?"

"You've heard some of the theories," he said. "Drug overdoses. Some new weird designer drug on the street, the kids going out in the woods to party and ending up dead. Or some drug dealer who gets his thrills by selling bad stuff in some remote place, then watching the couples die."

"I've heard the theories, and there is nothing to support

them. Toxicology results were negative for drugs in the first eight deaths."

"I remember that from the reports," he said thoughtfully. "But I also assumed this didn't necessarily mean the kids hadn't been involved in drugs. Their bodies were almost skeletonized. Doesn't seem there was much left to test."

"There was some red tissue left, muscle. That's enough for testing. Cocaine or heroin, for example. We, at least, would have expected to find their metabolites of benzoylecogonine or morphine. As for designer drugs, we tested for analogues of PCP, amphetamines."

"What about China White?" he proposed, referring to a very potent synthetic analgesic popular in California. "From what I understand, it doesn't take much for an overdose and is difficult to detect."

"True. Less than one milligram can be fatal, meaning the concentration is too low to detect without using special analytical procedures such as RLA." Noting the blank expression on his face, I explained, "Radioimmunoassay, a procedure based on specific drug antibody reactions. Unlike conventional screening procedures, RIA can detect small levels of drugs, so it's what we resort to when looking for China White, LSD, THC."

"None of which you found."

"That's correct."

"What about alcohol?"

"Alcohol's a problem when bodies are badly decomposed. Some of those tests were negative, others less than point oh-five, possibly the result of decomposition. Inconclusive, in other words."

"With Harvey and Cheney as well?"

"No trace of drugs so far," I told him. "What is Pat Harvey's interest in the early cases?"

"Don't get me wrong," he replied. "I'm not saying it was a major preoccupation. But she must have gotten tips back when she was a U.S. attorney, inside information, and she asked some questions. Politics, Kay. I suppose if it had turned out that these deaths of couples in Virginia were related to drugs—either accidental deaths or drug homicides—she would have used the information to buttress her antidrug efforts."

That would explain why Mrs. Harvey seemed well informed when I had lunch at her house last fall, I thought. No doubt she had information on file in her office because of her early interest in the cases.

"When her inquiries into this didn't go anywhere," Wesley continued, "I think she pretty much let it go until her daughter and Fred disappeared. Then it all came back to her, as you can imagine."

"Yes, I can imagine. And I can also imagine the bitter irony had it turned out that drugs killed the Drug Czar's daughter."

"Don't think that hasn't crossed Mrs. Harvey's mind," Wesley said grimly.

The reminder made me tense again. "She has a right to know, Benton. I can't pend these cases forever."

He nodded to the waiter that we were ready for coffee.

"I need you to buy me more time, Kay."

"Because of your disinformation tactics?"

"We need to give that a shot, let the stories run without

interference. The minute Mrs. Harvey gets anything from you, all hell's going to break loose. Believe me, I know how she'll react better than you do at this point. She'll go to the press, and in the process screw up everything we've been setting up to lure the killer."

"What happens when she gets her court order?"

"That will take time. It won't happen tomorrow. Will you stall a little longer, Kay?"

"You haven't finished explaining about the jack of hearts," I reminded him. "How could a hit man have known about the cards?"

Wesley replied reluctantly, "Pat Harvey doesn't gather information or investigate situations alone. She has aides, a staff. She talks to other politicians, any number of people, including constituents. It all depends on who she divulged information to, and who out there might have wished to destroy her, assuming that's the case, and I'm not saying it is."

"A paid hit disguised to look like the early cases," I considered. "Only the hit man made a mistake. He didn't know to leave the jack of hearts in the car. He left it with Deborah's body, inside her purse. Someone perhaps involved with the fraudulent charities Pat Harvey is supposed to testify against?"

"We're talking about bad people who know other bad people. Drug dealers. Organized crime." He idly stirred his coffee. "Mrs. Harvey's not faring too well through all this. She's very distracted. This congressional hearing isn't exactly foremost on her mind, at the moment."

"I see. And I suspect she's not exactly on friendly terms with the Justice Department, because of this hearing."

Wesley carefully set his teaspoon on the edge of his saucer. "She's not," he said, looking up at me. "What she's trying to bring about isn't going to help us. It's fine to put ACTMAD and other scams like it out of business. But it's not enough. We want to prosecute. In the past, there's been some friction between her and the DEA, FBI, also the CIA."

"And now?" I continued to probe.

"It's worse, because she's emotionally involved, has to rely on the Bureau to assist in solving her daughter's homicide. She's uncooperative, paranoid. She's trying to work around us, take matters into her own hands." Sighing, he added, "She's a problem, Kay."

"She probably says the same thing about the Bureau."

He smiled wryly. "I'm sure she does."

I wanted to continue the mental poker game to see if Wesley was keeping anything else from me, so I gave him more. "It appears that Deborah received a defensive injury to her left index finger. Not a cut, but a hack, inflicted by a knife with a serrated blade."

"Where on her index finger?" he asked, leaning forward a little.

"Dorsal." I held up my hand to show him. "On top, near her first knuckle."

"Interesting. Atypical."

"Yes. Difficult to reconstruct how she got it."

"So we know he was armed with a knife," he thought out loud. "That makes me all the more suspicious that something went wrong out there. Something happened he wasn't expecting. He may have resorted to a gun to subdue the couple, but intended to kill them with the knife. Possibly by cutting their throats. But then something went haywire. Deborah somehow got away and he shot her in the back, then maybe cut her throat to finish her off."

"And then positioned their bodies to look like the others?" I asked. "Arm in arm, face down, and fully clothed?"

He stared at the wall above my head.

I thought of the cigarette butts left at each scene. I thought of the parallels. The fact that the playing card was a different brand and left in a different place this time proved nothing. Killers are not machines. Their rituals and habits are not an exact science or set in stone. Nothing that Wesley had divulged to me, including the absence of white cotton fibers in Deborah's Jeep, was enough to validate the theory that Fred's and Deborah's homicides were unrelated to the other cases. I was experiencing the same confusion that I felt whenever I visited Quantico, where I was never sure if guns were firing bullets or blanks, if helicopters carried marines on real business or FBI agents simulating maneuvers, or if buildings in the Academy's fictitious town of Hogan's Alley were functional or Hollywood facades.

I could push Wesley no further. He wasn't going to tell me more.

"It's getting late," he commented. "You have a long drive back."

I had one last point to make.

"I don't want friendship to interfere with all this, Benton."

"That goes without saying."

"What happened between Mark and me—"

"That's not a factor," he interrupted, and his voice was firm but not unkind.

"He was your best friend."

"I'd like to think he still is."

"Do you blame me for why he went to Colorado, left Quantico?"

"I know why he left," he said. "I'm sorry he left. He was very good for the Academy."

The FBI's strategy of drawing out the killer by way of disinformation did not materialize the following Monday. Either the Bureau had changed its mind, or it was preempted by Pat Harvey, who held a press conference the same day.

At noon, she faced cameras in her Washington office, adding to the pathos by having Bruce Cheney, Fred's father, by her side. She looked awful. Weight added by the camera and makeup could not hide how thin she had gotten or the dark circles under her eyes.

"When did these threats begin, Mrs. Harvey, and what was the nature of them?" a reporter asked.

"The first one came shortly after I began investigating the charities. And I suppose this was a little over a year ago," she said without emotion. "This was a letter mailed to my home in Richmond. I won't divulge the specific nature of what it said, but the threat was directed at my family."

"And you believe this was connected to your probe into fraudulent charities like ACTMAD?"

"There's no question about that. There were other threats, the last one as recent as two months before my daughter and Fred Cheney disappeared."

Bruce Cheney's face flashed on the screen. He was pale, blinking in the blinding haze of TV lights.

"Ms. Harvey . . ."

"Mrs. Harvey . . ."

Reporters were interrupting each other, and Pat Harvey interrupted them, the camera swinging back her way.

"The FBI was aware of the situation, and it was their opinion that the threats, the letters, were originating from one source," she said.

"Mrs. Harvey . . ."

"Ms. Harvey"—a reporter raised her voice above the commotion—"it's no secret that you and the Justice Department have different agendas, a conflict of interests arising from the investigation of the charities. Are you suggesting the FBI knew that the safety of your family was in jeopardy and *didn't do anything?*"

"It's more than a suggestion," she stated.

"Are you accusing the Justice Department of incompetence?"

"What I'm accusing the Justice Department of is conspiracy," Pat Harvey said.

Groaning, I reached for a cigarette as the din, the interruptions reached a crescendo. You've lost it, I thought, staring in disbelief at the TV inside the small medical library in my downtown office.

It got only worse. And my heart was filled with dread as Mrs. Harvey turned her cool stare to the camera and one by one ran her sword through everyone involved in the investigation, including me. She spared no one, and there was nothing sacred, including the detail of the jack of hearts.

It had been a gross understatement when Wesley had said she was uncooperative and a problem. Beneath her armor of reason was a woman crazed by rage and grief. Numbly I listened as she plainly and without reservation indicted the police, the FBI, and the Medical Examiner's Office for complicity in a "cover-up."

"They are deliberately burying the truth about these cases," she concluded, "when the act of doing so serves only their self-interest at the unconscionable expense of human lives."

"What a lot of shit," muttered Fielding, my deputy chief, sitting nearby.

"*Which* cases?" a reporter demanded loudly. "The deaths of your daughter and her boyfriend or are you referring to the four other couples?"

"All of them," Mrs. Harvey replied. "I'm referring to all of the young men and women hunted down like animals and murdered."

"What is being covered up?"

"The identity or identities of those responsible," she said as if she knew. "There has been no intervention on the part of the Justice Department to stop these killings. The reasons are political. A certain federal agency is protecting its own."

"Could you please be more specific?" a voice shot back.

"When my investigation is concluded, I will make a full disclosure."

"At the hearing?" she was asked. "Are you suggesting that the murder of Deborah and her boyfriend . . ."

"His name is Fred."

It was Bruce Cheney who had spoken, and suddenly his livid face filled the television screen.

The room went silent.

"Fred. His name is *Frederick Wilson Cheney.*" The father's voice trembled with emotion. "He's not just Debbie's *boyfriend.* He's dead, murdered, too. My *son!*" Words caught in his throat, and he hung his head to hide his tears.

I turned off the television, upset and unable to sit still.

Rose had been standing in the doorway, watching. She looked at me and slowly shook her head.

Fielding got up, stretched, tightened the drawstring of his surgical greens.

"She just screwed herself in front of the whole damn world," he announced, walking out of the library.

I realized as I was pouring myself a cup of coffee what Pat Harvey had said. I began to really hear it as it replayed inside my head.

"Hunted down like animals and murdered . . ."

Her words had the sound of something scripted. They did not strike me as glib, off the cuff or a figure of speech. *A federal agency protecting its own?*

Hunt.

A jack of hearts like a knight of cups. Someone who is

perceived or perceives himself as a competitor, a defender. One who does battle, Hilda Ozimek had said to me.

A knight. A soldier.

Hunt.

Their murders were meticulously calculated, methodically planned. Bruce Phillips and Judy Roberts disappeared in June. Their bodies were found in mid-August, when hunting season opened.

Jim Freeman and Bonnie Smyth disappeared in July, their bodies found the opening day of quail and pheasant season.

Ben Anderson and Carolyn Bennett disappeared in March, their bodies found in November during deer season.

Susan Wilcox and Mike Martin disappeared in late February, their bodies discovered in mid-May, during spring gobbler season.

Deborah Harvey and Fred Cheney vanished Labor Day weekend and were not found until months later when the woods were crowded with hunters after rabbit, squirrel, fox, pheasant, and raccoon.

I had not assumed the pattern meant anything because most of the badly decomposed and skeletonized bodies that end up in my office are found by hunters. When someone drops dead or is dumped in the woods, a hunter is the most likely person to stumble upon the remains. But when and where the couples' bodies were discovered could have been planned.

The killer wanted his victims found, but not right away, so

he killed them off season, knowing that it was probable his victims would not be discovered until hunters were out in the woods again. By then the bodies were decomposed. Gone with the tissue were the injuries he had inflicted. If rape was involved, there would be no seminal fluid. Most trace evidence would be dislodged by wind and washed away by rain. It may even be that it was important to him that the bodies be found by hunters because in his fantasies he, too, was a hunter. The greatest hunter of all.

Hunters hunted animals, I thought as I sat at my downtown desk the following afternoon. Guerrillas, military special agents, and soldiers of fortune hunted human beings.

Within the fifty-mile radius where the couples had vanished and turned up dead were Fort Eustis, Langley Field, and a number of other military installations, including the CIA's West Point, operated under the cover of a military base called Camp Peary. "The Farm," as Camp Peary is referred to in spy novels and investigative nonfiction books about intelligence, was where officers were trained in the paramilitary activities of infiltration, exfiltration, demolitions, nighttime parachute jumps, and other clandestine operations.

Abby Turnbull took a wrong turn and ended up at the entrance of Camp Peary, and days later FBI agents came looking for her.

The feds were paranoid, and I had a suspicion I might know why. After reading the newspaper accounts of Pat Harvey's press conference, I had become only more convinced.

A number of papers, including the *Post*, were on my desk, and I had studied the write-ups several times. The byline on the *Post*'s story was Clifford Ring, the reporter who had been pestering the commissioner and other personnel of the Department of Health and Human Services. Mr. Ring mentioned me only in passing when he implied that Pat Harvey was inappropriately using her public office to intimidate and threaten all involved into releasing details about her daughter's death. It was enough to make me wonder if Mr. Ring was Benton Wesley's media source, the FBI's conduit for planted releases, and that would not have been so bad, really. It was the point of the stories that I found disturbing.

What I had assumed would be dished out as the sensational exposé of the month was, instead, being bruited about as the colossal degradation of a woman who, just weeks before, had been talked of by some as a possible Vice President of the United States. I would be the first to say that Pat Harvey's diatribe at the press conference was reckless in the least, premature at best. But I found it odd that there was no evidence of a serious attempt at corroborating her accusations. Reporters in this case did not seem inclined to get the usual incriminating "no comments" and other double-talk evasions from the governmental bureaucrats that journalists typically pursue with enthusiasm.

The media's only quarry, it seemed, was Mrs. Harvey, and she was shown no pity. The headline for one editorial was SLAUGHTERGATE? She was being ridiculed, not only in print but in political cartoons. One of the nation's most respected officials was being dismissed as a hysterical female whose "sources" included a South Carolina psychic. Even her staunchest allies were backing away, shaking their heads, her enemies subtly finishing her off with attacks softly wrapped in sympathy. "Her reaction is certainly understandable in light of her terrible personal loss," said one Democratic detractor, adding, "I think it wise to overlook her imprudence. Consider her accusations the slings and arrows of a deeply troubled mind." Said another, "What's happened to Pat Harvey is a tragic example of self-destruction brought on by personal problems too overwhelming to endure."

Rolling Deborah Harvey's autopsy report into my typewriter, I whited out "pending" in the manner and cause of death spaces. I typed in "homicide" and "exsanguination due to gunshot wound to lower back and cutting injuries." Amending her death certificate and CME-1 report, I went up front and made photocopies. These I enclosed with a cover letter explaining my findings and apologizing for the delay, which I attributed to the long wait for toxicology results, which were still provisional. I would give Benton Wesley that much. Pat Harvey would not hear from me that I had been strong-armed by him to indefinitely pend the results of her daughter's medicolegal examination.

The Harveys were going to get it all—my findings on gross and microscopically, the fact that the first rounds of toxicology tests were negative, the bullet in Deborah's lower lumbar, the defense injury to her hand, and, pathetically, the detailed description of her clothing, or what had been left of it. The police had recovered her earrings, watch, and the friendship ring given to her by Fred for her birthday.

I also mailed copies of Fred Cheney's reports to his father,

10

A frigid wind wreaked havoc with the dark shapes of trees, and in the scant light of the moon the terrain looked foreign and foreboding as I drove to Benton Wesley's house. There were few streetlights, and the rural routes were poorly marked. I finally stopped at a country store with a single island of gas pumps in front. Switching on the overhead lamp, I studied my scribbled directions. I was lost.

I could see the store was closed but spotted a pay phone near the front door. Pulling close, I got out, leaving headlights burning and the engine on. I dialed Wesley's number and his wife, Connie, answered.

"You've really gotten tangled up," she said after I did my best to describe where I was.

"Oh, God," I said, groaning.

"Well, it's really not that far. The problem is it's complicated getting from where you are to here." She paused, then decided, "I think the wise thing would be for you to stay put, Kay. Lock your doors and sit tight. Better if we come and you follow us. Fifteen minutes, all right?"

Backing out, I parked closer to the road, turned on the radio, and waited. Minutes passed like hours. Not a single car went by. My headlights illuminated a white fence girdling a frosty pasture across the road. The moon was a pale sliver floating in the hazy darkness. I smoked several cigarettes, my eyes darting around.

I wondered if it had been like this for the murdered couples, what it would be like to be forced barefoot and bound into the woods. They had to have known they were going to die. They had to have been terrified by what he would do to them first. I thought of my niece, Lucy. I thought of my mother, my sister, my friends. Fearing for the pain and death of one you loved would be worse than fearing for your own life. I watched as headlights grew brighter far down the dark narrow road. A car I did not recognize turned in and stopped not far from mine. When I caught a glimpse of the driver's profile, adrenaline rushed through my blood like electricity.

Mark James climbed out of what I assumed was a rental car. I rolled down the window and stared at him, too shocked to speak.

"Hello, Kay."

Wesley had said this was not a good night, had tried to talk me out of it, and now I understood why. Mark was visiting. Perhaps Connie had asked Mark to meet me, or he had volunteered. I could not imagine my reaction had I walked through Wesley's front door and found Mark sitting in the living room.

"It's a maze to Benton's house from here," Mark said. "I suggest you leave your car. It will be safe. I'll drive you back later so you won't have a problem finding your way."

Wordlessly, I parked closer to the store, then got in his car.

"How are you?" he asked quietly.

"Fine."

"And your family? How's Lucy?"

Lucy still asked about him. I never knew what to say. "Fine," I said again.

As I looked at his face, his strong hands on the wheel, every contour, line, and vein familiar and wonderful to me, my heart ached with emotion. I hated and loved him at the same time.

"Work's all right?"

"Please stop being so goddam polite, Mark."

"Would you rather I be rude like you?"

"I'm not being rude."

"What the hell do you want me to say?"

I replied with silence.

He turned on the radio and we drove deeper into the night.

"I know this is awkward, Kay." He stared straight ahead. "I'm sorry. Benton suggested I meet you."

"That was very thoughtful of him," I said sarcastically.

"I didn't mean it like that. I would have insisted had he not asked. You had no reason to think I might be here."

We rounded a sharp bend and turned into Wesley's subdivision.

As we pulled into Wesley's driveway, Mark said, "I guess I'd better warn you that Benton's not in a very good mood."

"I'm not either," I replied coldly.

A fire burned in the living room, and Wesley was sitting near the hearth, a briefcase open and resting against the leg of his chair, a drink on the table nearby. He did not get up when I walked in, but nodded slightly as Connie invited me to the couch. I sat on one end, Mark the other.

Connie left to get coffee, and I started in. "Mark, I know nothing of your involvement in all this."

"There isn't much to know. I was in Quantico for several days and am spending the night with Benton and Connie before returning to Denver tomorrow. I'm not involved in the investigation, not assigned to the cases."

"All right. But you're aware of the cases." I wondered what Wesley and Mark had discussed in my absence. I wondered what Wesley had said to Mark about me.

"He's aware of them," Wesley answered.

"Then I'll ask both of you," I said. "Did the Bureau set up Pat Harvey? Or was it the CIA?"

Wesley did not move or change the expression on his face. "What leads you to suppose she's been set up?"

"Obviously, the Bureau's disinformation tactics went beyond luring the killer. It was someone's intention to destroy Pat Harvey's credibility, and the press has done this quite successfully."

"Even the President doesn't have that much influence over the media. Not in this country."

"Don't insult my intelligence, Benton," I said.

"What she did was anticipated. Let's put it that way." Wesley recrossed his legs and reached for his drink.

"And you laid the trap," I said.

"No one spoke for her at her press conference."

"It doesn't matter because no one needed to. Someone made sure her accusations would come across in print as the ravings of a lunatic. Who primed the reporters, the politicians, her former allies, Benton? Who leaked that she consulted a psychic? Was it you?"

"No."

"Pat Harvey saw Hilda Ozimek last September," I went on. "It never made the news until now, meaning the press didn't know about it until now. That's pretty low, Benton. You told me yourself that the FBI and Secret Service have resorted to Hilda Ozimek on a number of occasions. That's probably how Mrs. Harvey found out about her, for God's sake."

Connie returned with my coffee, then left again as quickly as she had appeared.

I could feel Mark's eyes on me, the tension. Wesley continued staring into the fire.

"I think I know the truth." I made no effort to disguise my outrage. "I intend to have it out in the open now. And if you can't accommodate me this way, then I don't think it will be possible for me to continue accommodating you."

"What are you implying, Kay?" Wesley looked over at me.

"If it happens again, if another couple dies, I can't guarantee that reporters won't find out what's really going on—"

"Kay." It was Mark who interrupted, and I refused to look

at him. I was doing my best to block him out. "You don't want to trip up like Mrs. Harvey."

"She didn't exactly trip up on her own," I said. "I think she's right. Something is being covered up."

"You sent her your reports, I presume," Wesley said.

"I did. I will no longer play a part in this manipulation."

"That was a mistake."

"My mistake was not sending them to her earlier."

"Do the reports include information about the bullet you recovered from Deborah's body? Specifically, that it was nine-millimeter Hydra-Shok?"

"The caliber and brand would be in the firearms report," I said. "I don't send out copies of firearms reports any more than I send out copies of police reports, neither of which are generated by my office. But I'm interested in why you're so concerned over that detail."

When Wesley did not reply, Mark intervened. "Benton, we need to smooth this out."

Wesley remained silent.

"I think she needs to know," Mark added.

"I think I already know," I said. "I think the FBI has reason to fear the killer is a federal agent gone bad. Quite possibly, someone from Camp Peary."

Wind moaned around the eaves, and Wesley got up to tend to the fire. He put on another log, rearranged it with the poker, and swept ashes off the hearth, taking his time. When he was seated again, he reached for his drink and said, "How did you come to this conclusion?"

"It doesn't matter," I said.

"Did someone say this to you directly?"

"No. Not directly." I got out my cigarettes. "How long has this been your suspicion, Benton?"

Hesitating, he replied, "I believe you are better off not knowing the details. I really do. It's only going to be a burden. A very heavy one."

"I'm already carrying a very heavy burden. And I'm tired of stumbling over disinformation."

"I need your assurance nothing discussed leaves here."

"You know me too well to worry about that."

"Camp Peary entered into it not long after the cases began."

"Because of the close proximity?"

He looked at Mark. "I'll let you elaborate," Wesley said to him.

I turned and confronted this man who once had shared my bed and dominated my dreams. He was dressed in navy blue corduroy trousers and a red-and-white-striped oxford shirt that I had seen him wear in the past. He was long legged and trim. His dark hair was gray at the temples, eyes green, chin strong, features refined, and he still gestured slightly with his hands and leaned forward when he talked.

"In part, the CIA got interested," Mark explained, "because the cases were occurring close to Camp Peary. And I'm sure it comes as no surprise to you that the CIA is privy to most of what goes on around their training facility. They know a lot more than anyone might imagine, and in fact, local settings and citizens are routinely incorporated into maneuvers."

"What sorts of maneuvers?" I asked.

"Surveillance, for example. Officers in training at Camp Peary often practice surveillance, using local citizens as guinea pigs, for lack of a better term. Officers set up surveillance operations in public places, restaurants, bars, shopping centers. They tail people in cars, on foot, take photographs, and so on. No one is ever aware this is going on, of course. And there's no harm done, I suppose, except that local citizens wouldn't be keen on knowing they were being tailed, watched, or captured on film."

"I shouldn't think so," I said uncomfortably.

"These maneuvers," he continued, "also include going through dry runs. An officer might feign car trouble and stop a motorist for assistance, see how far he can go in getting this individual to trust him. He might pose as a law enforcement officer, tow truck operator, any number of things. It's all practice for overseas operations, to train people how to spy and avoid being spied upon."

"And it's an MO that may parallel what's been going on with these couples," I interpolated.

"That's the point," Wesley interjected. "Someone at Camp Peary got worried. We were asked to help monitor the situation. Then when the second couple turned up dead, and the MO was the same as the first case, the pattern had been established. The CIA began to panic. They're a paranoid lot anyway, Kay, and the last thing they needed was to discover that one of their officers at Camp Peary was practicing *killing* people."

"The CIA has never admitted that Camp Peary is its main training facility," I pointed out.

"It's common knowledge," Mark said, meeting my eyes. "But you're right, the CIA has never admitted it publicly. Nor do they wish to."

"Which is all the more reason they wouldn't want these murders connected to Camp Peary," I said, wondering what he was feeling. Maybe he wasn't feeling anything.

"That and a long list of other reasons," Wesley took over. "The publicity would be devastating, and when was the last time you read anything positive about the CIA? Imelda Marcos was accused of theft and fraud, and the defense claimed that every transaction the Marcoses made was with the full knowledge and encouragement of the CIA . . ."

He wouldn't be so tense, so afraid to look at me, if he felt nothing.

". . . Then it came out that Noriega was on the CIA's payroll," Wesley continued making his case. "Not long ago it was publicized that CIA protection of a Syrian drug smuggler made it possible for a bomb to be placed on a Pan Am seven-forty-seven that exploded over Scotland, killing two hundred and seventy people. Not to mention the more recent allegation that the CIA is financing certain drug wars in Asia to destabilize governments over there."

"If it turned out," Mark said, shifting his eyes away from me, "that teenage couples were being murdered by a CIA officer at Camp Peary, you can imagine the public's reaction."

"It's unthinkable," I said, willing myself to concentrate on the discussion. "But why would the CIA be so sure these murders are being committed by one of their own? What hard evidence do they have?"

"Most of it's circumstantial," Mark explained. "The militaristic touch of leaving a playing card. The similarities between the patterns in these cases and the maneuvers that go on both inside the Farm and on streets of nearby cities and towns. For example, the wooded areas where the bodies have been turning up are reminiscent of the 'kill zones' inside Camp Peary, where officers practice with grenades, automatic weapons, utilizing all the trade craft, such as night-vision equipment, allowing them to see in the woods after dark. They also receive training in defense, how to disarm someone, maim and kill with their bare hands."

"When there was no apparent cause of death with these couples," Wesley said, "one had to wonder if they were being murdered without the use of weapons. Strangulation, for example. Or even if their throats were cut, this is associated with guerrilla warfare, taking out an enemy swiftly and in silence. You cut through his airway and he's not going to be making any noise."

"But Deborah Harvey was shot," I said.

"With an automatic or semiautomatic weapon," Wesley replied. "Either a pistol or something like an Uzi. The ammunition uncommon, associated with law enforcement, mercenary soldiers, people whose targets are human beings. You don't associate exploding bullets or Hydra-Shok ammo with deer hunting." Pausing, he added, "I would think this gives you a better idea why we don't want Pat Harvey cognizant of the type of weapon and ammunition that was used on her daughter."

"What about the threats Mrs. Harvey mentioned in her press conference?" I asked.

"That is true," Wesley said. "Not long after she was appointed National Drug Policy Director, someone did send communications threatening her and her family. It isn't true that the Bureau didn't take them seriously. She's been threatened before and we've always taken it seriously. We have an idea who's behind the more recent threats and don't believe they're related to Deborah's homicide."

"Mrs. Harvey also implicated a 'federal agency,'" I said. "Was she referring to the CIA? Is she aware of what you've just told me?"

"That concerns me," Wesley admitted. "She's made comments to suggest she has an idea, and what she said in the press conference only increases my anxiety. She might have been referring to the CIA. Then again, maybe she wasn't. But she has a formidable network. For one thing, she has access to CIA information, providing it's relevant to the drug trade. More worrisome is that she's close friends with an ex-United Nations ambassador who is a member of the President's Foreign Intelligence Advisory Board. Members of the board are entitled to top-secret intelligence briefings on any subject at any time. The board knows what's going on, Kay. It's possible Mrs. Harvey knows everything."

"So she's set up Martha Mitchell-style?" I asked. "To make sure she comes off as irrational unreliable, so that no one takes her seriously, so that if she does blow the lid, no one will believe her?"

Wesley was running his thumb around the rim of his glass. "It's unfortunate. She's been uncontrollable, uncooperative. And the irony is, we want to know who murdered her daughter more than she does, for obvious reasons. We're doing everything within our power, have mobilized everything we can think of to find this individual—or individuals."

"What you're telling me seems patently inconsistent with your earlier suggestion that Deborah Harvey and Fred Cheney may have been a paid hit, Benton," I said angrily. "Or was that just a lot of smoke you were blowing out to hide the Bureau's real fears?"

"I don't know if they were a paid hit," he said grimly. "Frankly, there's so little we really know. Their murders could be political as I've already explained. But if we're dealing with a CIA officer gone haywire, someone like that, the cases of the five couples may, in fact, be connected, may be serial killings."

"It could be an example of escalation," Mark offered. "Pat Harvey's been in the news a lot, especially over the past year. If we're looking for a CIA officer who's practicing homicidal maneuvers, he may have decided to target a presidential appointee's daughter."

"Thus adding to the excitement, the risk," Wesley explained. "And making the kill similar to the sorts of operations you associate with Central America, the Middle East, political neutralizations. Assassinations, in other words."

"It's my understanding that the CIA is not supposed to be in the business of assassinations, not since the Ford administration," I said. "In fact, the CIA's not even supposed to engage in coup attempts in which a foreign leader is in danger of being killed."

"That's correct," Mark replied. "The CIA's not supposed to

be in that business. American soldiers in Vietnam weren't supposed to kill civilians. And cops aren't supposed to use excessive force on suspects and prisoners. When it's all reduced to individuals, sometimes things get out of control. Rules get broken."

I could not help but wonder about Abby Turnbull. How much of this did she know? Had Mrs. Harvey leaked something to her? Was this the true nature of the book Abby was writing? No wonder she suspected her phones were being bugged, that she was being followed. The CIA, the FBI, and even the President's Foreign Intelligence Advisory Board, which had a backdoor entrée straight into the Oval Office, had very good reason to be nervous about what Abby was writing, and she had very good reason to be paranoid. She may have placed herself in real danger.

The wind had died down, a light fog settling over treetops as Wesley closed the door behind us. Following Mark to his car, I felt a sense of resolution and validation because of what had been said, and yet I was more unsettled than before.

I waited to speak until we left the subdivision. "What's happening to Pat Harvey is outrageous. She loses her daughter, now her career and reputation are being destroyed."

"Benton's had nothing to do with leaks to the press, any sort of 'setup,' as you put it." Mark kept his eyes on the dark narrow road.

"It's not a matter of how I *put* it, Mark."

"I'm just referring to what you said," he replied.

"You know what's going on. Don't act naive with me."

"Benton's done everything he can for her, but she's got a vendetta against the Justice Department. To her, Benton's just another federal agent out to get her."

"If I were her, I might feel the same way."

"Knowing you, you probably would."

"And what's that supposed to mean?" I asked, as my anger, which went far deeper than Pat Harvey, surfaced.

"It doesn't mean a thing."

Minutes passed in silence as the tension grew. I did not recognize the road we were on, but I knew our time together was nearing an end. Then he turned into the store's parking lot and pulled up next to my car.

"I'm sorry we had to see each other under these circumstances," he said quietly.

I did not reply, and he added, "But I'm not sorry to see you, not sorry it happened."

"Good night, Mark." I started to get out of the car.

"Don't, Kay." He put his hand on my arm.

I sat still. "What do you want?"

"To talk to you. Please."

"If you're so interested in talking to me, then why haven't you gotten around to it before now?" I replied with emotion, pulling my arm away. "You've made no effort to say a goddam thing to me for months."

"That works both ways. I called you last fall and you never called me back."

"I knew what you were going to say, and I didn't want to hear it," I replied, and I could feel his anger building, too.

"Excuse me. I forgot that you have always had the uncanny

220

ability of reading my mind." He placed both hands on the wheel and stared straight ahead.

"You were going to announce that there was no chance of reconciliation, that it was over. And I wasn't interested in having you put into words what I already assumed."

"Think what you want."

"It has nothing to do with what I *want* to think!" I hated the power he had to make me lose my temper.

"Look." He took a deep breath. "Do you think there's any chance we can declare a truce? Forget the past?"

"Not a chance."

"Great. Thanks for being so reasonable. At least I tried."

"Tried? It's been what? Eight, nine months since you left? What the hell have you tried, Mark? I don't know what it is you're asking, but it's impossible to forget the past. It's impossible for the two of us to run into each other and pretend there was never anything between us. I refuse to act that way."

"I'm not asking that, Kay. I'm asking if we can forget the fights, the anger, what we said back then."

I really could not remember exactly what had been said or explain what had gone wrong. We fought when we weren't sure what we were fighting about until the focus became our injuries and not the differences that had caused them.

"When I called you last September," he went on with feeling, "I wasn't going to tell you there was no hope of reconciliation. In fact, when I dialed your number I knew I was running the risk of hearing you say that. And when you never called me back, I was the one who made assumptions."

"You're not serious."

"The hell I'm not."

"Well, maybe you were wise to make assumptions. After what you did."

"After what I did?" he asked, incredulous. "What about what you did?"

"The only thing I did was to get sick and tired of making concessions. You never really tried to relocate to Richmond. You didn't know what you wanted and expected me to comply, concede, uproot myself whenever you figured everything out. No matter how much I love you, I can't give up what I am and I never asked you to give up what you are."

"Yes, you did. Even if I could have transferred to the field office in Richmond, that's not what I wanted."

"Good. I'm glad you pursued what you wanted."

"Kay, it's fifty-fifty. You're to blame, too."

"I'm not the one who left." My eyes filled with tears, and I whispered, "Oh, shit."

Getting out a handkerchief, he gently placed it on my lap.

Dabbing my eyes, I moved closer to the door, leaning my head against the glass. I did not want to cry.

"I'm sorry," he said.

"Your being sorry doesn't change anything."

"Please don't cry."

"I will if I want," I said, ridiculously.

"I'm sorry," he said again, this time in a whisper, and I thought he was going to touch me. But he didn't. He leaned back in the seat and stared up at the roof.

"Look," he said, "if you want to know the truth, I wish you had been the one who left. Then you could have been the one who screwed up instead of me."

I did not say anything. I did not dare.

"Did you hear me?"

"I'm not sure," I said to the window.

He shifted his position. I could feel his eyes on me.

"Kay, look at me."

Reluctantly, I did.

"Why do you think I've been coming back here?" he asked in a low voice. "I'm trying to get back to Quantico, but it's tough. The timing's bad with the federal budget cuts, the economy, the Bureau's being hit hard. There are a lot of reasons."

"You're telling me you're professionally unhappy?"

"I'm telling you I made a mistake."

"I regret any professional mistakes you've made," I said.

"I'm not referring just to that, and you know it."

"Then what are you referring to?" I was determined to make him say it.

"You know what I'm referring to. Us. Nothing's been the same."

His eyes were shining in the dark. He looked almost fierce.

"Has it been for you?" he pushed.

"I think both of us have made a lot of mistakes."

"I'd like to start undoing some of them, Kay. I don't want it to end this way with us. I've felt that for a long time but . . . well, I just didn't know how to tell you. I didn't know if you wanted to hear from me, if you were seeing someone else."

I did not admit that I had been wondering the same about him and was terrified of the answers.

He reached for me, taking my hand. This time I could not pull away.

"I've been trying to sort through what went wrong with us," he said. "All I know is I'm stubborn, you're stubborn. I wanted my way and you wanted yours. So here we are. I can't say what your life has been like since I left, but I'm willing to bet it hasn't been good."

"How arrogant of you to bet on such a thing."

He smiled. "I'm just trying to live up to your image of me. One of the last things you called me before I left was an arrogant bastard."

"Was that before or after I called you a son of a bitch?"

"Before, I believe."

"As I remember it, you called me a few rather choice names as well. And I thought you just suggested that we forget what was said back then."

"And you just said *no matter how much I love you.*"

"I beg your pardon?"

"'Love,' as in present tense. Don't try to take it back. I heard it."

He pressed my hand to his face, his lips moving over my fingers.

"I've tried to stop thinking about you. I can't." He paused, his face close to mine. "I'm not asking you to say the same thing."

But he was asking that, and I answered him.

I touched his cheek and he touched mine, then we kissed

the places our fingers had been until we found each other's lips. And we said nothing more. We stopped thinking entirely until the windshield suddenly lit up and the night beyond was throbbing red. We frantically rearranged ourselves as a patrol car pulled up and a deputy climbed out, flashlight and portable radio in hand.

Mark was already opening his door.

"Everything all right?" the deputy asked, bending over to peer inside. His eyes wandered disconcertingly over the scene of our passion, his face stern, an unseemly bulge in his right cheek.

"Everything's fine," I said, horrified as I not so subtly probed the floor with my stocking foot. Somehow I had lost a shoe.

He stepped back and spat out a stream of tobacco juice.

"We were having a conversation," Mark offered, and he had the presence of mind not to display his badge. The deputy knew damn well we had been doing a lot of things when he pulled up. Conversing was not one of them.

"Well, now, if y'all intend to continue your *conversation*," he said, "I'd 'preciate it if you'd go someplace else. You know, it ain't safe to be sitting out here late at night in a car, been some problems. And if you're not from around here, maybe you hadn't heard about the couples disappearing."

He went on with his lecture, my blood running cold.

"You're right, and thank you," Mark finally said. "We're leaving now."

Nodding, the deputy spat again, and we watched him climb into his car. He pulled out onto the road and slowly drove away.

"Jesus," Mark muttered under his breath.

"Don't say it," I replied. "Let's not even get into how stupid we are. Lord."

"Do you see how damn easy it is?" He said it anyway. "Two people out at night and someone pulls up. Hell, my damn gun's in the glove compartment. I never even thought about it until he was right in my face, and then it would have been too late—"

"Stop it, Mark. Please."

He startled me by laughing.

"It's not funny!"

"Your blouse is buttoned crooked," he gasped.

Shit!

"You better hope like hell he didn't recognize you, Chief Scarpetta."

"Thank you for the reassuring thought, Mr. FBI. And now I'm going home." I opened the door. "You've gotten me into enough trouble for one night."

"Hey. You started it."

"I most certainly did not."

"Kay?" He got serious. "What do we do now? I mean, I'm going back to Denver tomorrow. I don't know what's going to happen, what I can make happen or if I should try to make anything happen."

There were no easy answers. There never had been with us.

"If you don't try to make anything happen, nothing will."

"What about you?" he asked.

"There's a lot of talking we need to do, Mark."

He turned on the headlights and fastened his seat belt. "What about you?" he asked again. "It takes two to try."

"Funny you should say that."

"Kay, don't. Please don't start in."

"I need to think." I got out my keys. I was suddenly exhausted.

"Don't jerk me around."

"I'm not jerking you around, Mark," I said, touching his cheek.

We kissed one last time. I wanted the kiss to go on for hours, and yet I wanted to get away. Our passion had always been reckless. We had always lived for moments that never seemed to add up to any sort of future.

"I'll call you," he said.

I opened my car door.

"Listen to Benton," he added. "You can trust him. What you're involved in is very bad stuff."

I started the engine.

"I wish you'd stay out of it."

"You always wish that," I said.

Mark did call late the following night and again two nights after that. When he called a third time, on February tenth, what he said sent me out in search of the most recent issue of *Newsweek*.

Pat Harvey's lusterless eyes stared out at America from the magazine's cover. A headline in bold, black letters read, THE MURDER OF THE DRUG CZAR'S DAUGHTER, the "exclusive" inside a rehashing of her press conference, her charges of conspiracy, and the cases of the other teenagers who had vanished and been found decomposed in Virginia woods. Though I had declined to be interviewed for the story, the magazine had found a file photograph of me climbing the steps of Richmond's John Marshall Court House. The caption read, "Chief Medical Examiner releases findings under threat of court order."

"It just goes with the turf. I'm fine," I reassured Mark when I called him back.

Even when my mother rang me up later that same night, I remained calm until she said, "There's someone here who's dying to talk to you, Kay."

My niece, Lucy, had always had a special talent for doing me in.

"How come you got in trouble?" she asked.

"I didn't get in trouble."

"The story says you did, that someone threatened you."

"It's too complicated to explain, Lucy."

"It's really awesome," she said, unfazed. "I'm going to take the magazine to school tomorrow and show it to everybody."

Great, I thought.

"Mrs. Barrows," she went on, referring to her homeroom teacher, "has already asked if you can come for career day in April . . . ?"

I had not seen Lucy in a year. It did not seem possible she was already a sophomore in high school, and though I knew she had contact lenses and a driver's license, I still envisioned her as a pudgy, needy child wanting to be tucked into bed, an *enfant terrible* who, for some strange reason, had bonded to me before she could crawl. I would never forget flying to

Miami the Christmas after she was born and staying with my sister for a week. Lucy's every conscious minute, it seemed, was spent watching me, eyes following my every move like two luminous moons. She would smile when I changed her diapers and howl the instant I walked out of the room.

"Would you like to spend a week with me this summer?" I asked.

Lucy hesitated, then said disappointedly, "I guess that means you can't come for career day."

"We'll see, all right?"

"I don't know if I can come this summer." Her tone had turned petulant. "I've got a job and might not be able to get away."

"It's wonderful you have a job."

"Yeah. In a computer store. I'm going to save enough to get a car. I want a sports car, a convertible, and you can find some of the old ones pretty cheap."

"Those are death traps," I said before I could stop myself. "Please don't get something like that, Lucy. Why don't you come see me in Richmond? We'll go around and shop for cars, something nice and safe."

She had dug a hole, and as usual, I had fallen in it. She was an expert at manipulation, and it didn't require a psychiatrist to figure out why. Lucy was the victim of chronic neglect by her mother, my sister.

"You are a bright young lady with a mind of your own," I said, changing tactics. "I know you'll make a good decision about what to do with your time and money, Lucy. But if you can fit me in this summer, maybe we can go somewhere. The beach or mountains, wherever you'd like. You've never been to England, have you?"

"No."

"Well, then, that's a thought."

"Really?" she asked suspiciously.

"Really. I haven't been in years," I said, warming up to the idea. "I think it's time for you to see Oxford and Cambridge, the museums in London. I'll arrange a tour of Scotland Yard, if you'd like, and if we could manage to get away as early as June, we might be able to get tickets for Wimbledon."

Silence.

Then she said cheerfully, "I was just teasing. I don't really want a sports car, Aunt Kay."

The next morning there were no autopsies, and I sat at my desk trying to diminish piles of paperwork. I had other deaths to investigate, classes to teach, and trials demanding my testimony, yet I could not concentrate. Every time I turned to something else, my attention was drawn back to the couples. There was something important I was overlooking, something right under my nose.

I felt it had to do with Deborah Harvey's murder.

She was a gymnast, an athlete with superb control of her body. She may not have been as strong as Fred, but she would have been quicker and more agile. I believed the killer had underestimated her athletic potential and this was why he momentarily lost control of her in the woods. As I stared blankly at a report I was supposed to be reviewing, Mark's words came back to me. He had mentioned "kill zones," officers at Camp Peary utilizing automatic weapons, grenades, and night vision equipment to hunt each other down in fields and woods. I tried to imagine this. I began toying with a gruesome scenario.

Perhaps when the killer abducted Deborah and Fred and took them to the logging road, he had a terrifying game in store for them. He told them to take off their shoes and socks, and bound their hands behind their backs. He may have been wearing night-vision goggles, which enhanced moonlight, making it possible for him to see quite well as he forced them into the woods, where he intended to track them down, one at a time.

I believed Marino was right. The killer would have gotten Fred out of the way first. Perhaps he told him to run, gave him a chance to get away, and all the while Fred was stumbling through trees and brush, panicking, the killer was watching, able to see and move about with ease, knife in hand. At the opportune moment, it would not have been very difficult for him to ambush his victim from behind, yoke arm under chin and jerk the head back, then slash through the windpipe and carotid arteries. This commando style of attack was silent and swift. If the bodies were not discovered for a while, the medical examiner would have difficulty finding a cause of death because tissue and cartilage would have decomposed.

I took the scenario further. Part of the killer's sadism might have been to force Deborah to witness her boyfriend being tracked and murdered in the dark. I was considering that once they were in the woods, the killer held her captive audience by binding her feet at the ankles, but what he did not anticipate was her flexibility. It was possible that while he was occupied with Fred, she managed to bring her bound hands under her buttocks and work her legs through her arms, thus getting her hands in front of her. This would have allowed her to untie her feet and defend herself.

I held my hands in front of me, as if they were bound at the wrists. Had Deborah locked her fingers together in a double fist and swung, and had the killer's reflex been to defensively raise his hands, in one of which he was holding the knife he had just used to murder Fred, then the hack to Deborah's left index finger made sense. Deborah ran like hell, and the killer, knocked off guard, shot her in the back.

Was I right? I could not know. But the scenario continued to play in my mind without a hitch. What didn't fit were several presuppositions. If Deborah's death was a paid hit carried out by a professional or the work of a psychopathic federal agent who had selected her in advance because she was Pat Harvey's daughter, then did this individual not know that Deborah was an Olympic-caliber gymnast? Would he not have considered that she would be unusually quick and agile and have incorporated this into his premeditations?

Would he have shot her *in the back*?

Was the manner in which she was killed consistent with the cold, calculating profile of a professional killer?

In the back.

When Hilda Ozimek had studied the photographs of the dead teenagers, she continued to pick up fear. Obviously, the victims had felt fear. But it had never occurred to me before this moment that the killer may have felt fear, too. Shooting someone in the back is cowardly. When Deborah resisted her assailant, he was unnerved. He lost control. The more I thought about it, the more I was convinced that Wesley and perhaps everybody else was wrong about this character. To hunt bound, barefoot teenagers in the woods after dark, when you have weapons, are familiar with the terrain, and are perhaps equipped with a night vision scope or goggles would be like shooting fish in a barrel. It's cheating. It's too damn easy. It did not strike me as the modus operandi I would expect were the killer an expert who thrived on taking risks.

And then there was the matter of his weapons.

If I were a CIA officer hunting human prey, what would I use? An Uzi? *Maybe.* More likely I would pick a nine-millimeter pistol, something that would do the job, nothing more, nothing less. I would use commonplace cartridges, something unremarkable. Everyday hollowpoints, for example. What I would not use was anything unusual like Exploder bullets or Hydra-Shoks.

The ammunition. Think hard, Kay! I could not remember the last time I had recovered Hydra-Shok bullets from a body.

The ammunition was originally designed with law enforcement officers in mind, the bullets having greater expansion upon impact than any other round fired from a two-inch barrel. When the lead projectile with its hollowpoint construction and distinctive raised central post enters the body, hydrostatic pressure forces the peripheral rim to flare like the petals of a flower. There's very little recoil, making it easier for one to fire repeat shots. The bullets rarely exit the body; the disruption to soft tissue and organs is devastating.

This killer was into specialized ammunition. He, no doubt, had sighted his gun by his cartridges of choice. To select one of the most lethal types of ammunition probably gave him confidence, made him feel powerful and important. He might even be superstitious about it.

I picked up the phone and told Linda what I needed.

"Come on up," she said.

When I walked into the firearms lab, she was seated before a computer terminal.

"No cases so far this year, except for Deborah Harvey, of course," she said, moving the cursor down the screen. "One for last year. One the year before that. Nothing else for Federal. But I did find two cases involving Scorpions."

"Scorpions?" I puzzled, leaning over her shoulder.

She explained, "An earlier version. Ten years before Federal bought the patent, Hydra-Shok Corporation was manufacturing basically the same cartridges. Specifically, Scorpion thirty-eights and Copperhead three-fifty-sevens." She hit several keys, printing out what she had found. "Eight years ago, we got in one case involving Scorpion thirty-eights. But it wasn't human."

"I beg your pardon?" I asked, baffled.

"Appears this victim was of the canine variety. A dog. Shot, let's see . . . three times."

"Was the shooting of the dog connected with some other case? A suicide, homicide, burglary?"

"Can't tell from what I've got here," Linda replied apologetically. "All I've got is that three Scorpion bullets were recovered from the dead dog. Never matched up with anything. I guess the case was never solved."

She tore off the printout and handed it to me.

The OCME, on rare occasion, did perform autopsies on animals. Deer shot out of season were sometimes sent in by game wardens, and if someone's pet was shot during the commission of a crime or if the pet was found dead along with its owners, we took a look, recovered bullets or tested for drugs. But we did not issue death certificates or autopsy reports for animals. It wasn't likely I was going to find anything on file for this dog shot eight years ago.

I rang up Marino and filled him in.

"You gotta be kidding," he said.

"Can you track it down without making a commotion? I don't want this raising any antennas. It may be nothing, but the jurisdiction is West Point, and that's rather interesting. The bodies of the second couple were found in West Point."

"Yeah, maybe. I'll see what I can do," he said, and he didn't sound thrilled about it.

The next morning Marino appeared while I was finishing work on a fourteen-year-old boy thrown out of the back of a pickup truck the afternoon before.

"That ain't something you got on, I hope." Marino moved closer to the table, sniffing.

"He had a bottle of aftershave in a pocket of his pants. It broke when he hit the pavement, and that's what you're smelling." I nodded at clothing on a nearby gurney.

"Brut?" He sniffed again.

"I believe so," I replied absently.

"Doris used to buy me Brut. One year she got me Obsession, if you can believe that."

"What did you find out?" I continued to work.

"The dog's name was Dammit, and I swear that's the truth," Marino said. "Belonged to some old geezer in West Point, a Mr. Joyce."

"Did you find out why the dog came into this office?"

"No connection to any other cases. A favor, I think."

"The state veterinarian must have been on vacation," I replied, for this had happened before.

On the other side of my building was the Department of Animal Health, complete with a morgue where examinations were conducted on animals. Normally, the carcasses went to the state veterinarian. But there were exceptions. When asked, the forensic pathologists indulged the cops and pitched in when the veterinarian was unavailable. During my career I had autopsied tortured dogs, mutilated cats, a sexually assaulted mare, and a poisoned chicken left in a judge's mailbox. People were just as cruel to animals as they were to each other.

"Mr. Joyce don't got a phone, but a contact of mine says he's still in the same crib," Marino said. "Thought I might run over there, check out his story. You want to come along?"

I snapped in a new scalpel blade as I thought about my cluttered desk, the cases awaiting my dictation, the telephone calls I had yet to return and the others I needed to initiate.

"Might as well," I said hopelessly.

He hesitated, as if waiting for something.

When I looked up at him, I noticed. Marino had gotten his hair cut. He was wearing khaki trousers held up by suspenders and a tweed jacket that looked brand new. His tie was clean, so was his pale yellow shirt. Even his shoes were shined.

"You look downright handsome," I said like a proud mother.

"Yeah." He grinned, his face turning red. "Rose whistled at me when I was getting on the elevator. It was kinda funny. Hadn't had a woman whistle at me in years, except Sugar, and Sugar don't exactly count."

"Sugar?"

"Hangs out on the corner of Adam and Church. Oh yeah, found Sugar, also known as Mad Dog Mama, down in an alleyway, passed out drunk as a skunk, practically ran over her sorry ass. Made the mistake of bringing her to. Fought me like a damn cat and cussed me all the way to lockup. Every time I pass within a block of her, she yells, whistles, hitches up her skirt."

"And you were worrying that you were no longer attractive to women," I said.

11

Dammit's origin was undetermined, though it was patently clear that every genetic marker he had picked up from every dog in his lineage was the worst of the lot.

"Raised him from a pup," said Mr. Joyce as I returned to him a Polaroid photograph of the dog in question. "He was a stray, you know. Just appeared at the back door one morning and I felt sorry for him, threw him some scraps. Couldn't get rid of him to save my life after that."

We were sitting around Mr. Joyce's kitchen table. Sunlight seeped wanly through a dusty window above a rust-stained porcelain sink, the faucet dripping. Ever since we had arrived fifteen minutes ago, Mr. Joyce had not had a kind word to offer about his slain dog, and yet I detected warmth in his old eyes, and the rough hands thoughtfully stroking the rim of his coffee mug looked capable of tender affection.

"How did he get his name?" Marino wanted to know.

"Never did give him a name, you see. But I was always hollering at him. 'Dammit, shut up! Come here, dammit! Dammit, if you don't stop yapping, I'm gonna wire your mouth shut.'" He smiled sheepishly. "Got to where he thought his name was Dammit. So that's what I took to calling him."

Mr. Joyce was a retired dispatcher for a cement company, his tiny house a monument to rural poverty out in the middle of farmland. I suspected the house's original owner had been a tenant farmer, for on either side of the property were vast expanses of fallow fields that Mr. Joyce said were thick with corn in the summer.

And it had been summer, a hot, sultry July night, when Bonnie Smyth and Jim Freeman had been forced to drive along the sparsely populated dirt road out front. Then November had come, and I passed over the same road, passed right by Mr. Joyce's house, the back of my station wagon packed with folded sheets, stretchers, and body pouches. Less than two miles east of where Mr. Joyce lived was the dense wooded area where the couple's bodies had been found some two years before. An eerie coincidence? What if it wasn't?

"So tell me what happened to Dammit," Marino was saying as he lit a cigarette.

"It was a weekend," Mr. Joyce began. "Middle of August, it seems. Had all the windows open and was sitting in the living room watching TV. *Dallas.* Funny I can remember that. Guess it means it was a Friday. Nine o'clock's when it came on."

"Then it was between nine and ten when your dog was shot," Marino said.

"That's my guess. Couldn't have been shot much before that or he'd never made it home. I'm watching TV, and next thing I hear him scratching at the door, whimpering. I knew he was hurt, just figured he'd gotten tangled up with a cat or something until I opened the door and got a good look at him."

He got out a pouch of tobacco and began to roll a cigarette in expert, steady hands.

Marino prodded him. "What did you do after that?"

"Put him in my truck and drove him to Doc Whiteside's house. About five miles northwest."

"A veterinarian?" I asked.

He slowly shook his head. "No, ma'am. Didn't have a vet or even know one. Doc Whiteside took care of my wife before she passed on. A mighty nice fellow. Didn't know where else to go, to tell you the truth. Course, it was too late. Wasn't a thing the doc could do by the time I carried the dog in. He said I ought to call the police. Only thing in season in the middle of August is crow, and no good reason in the world anybody should be out late at night shooting at crow or anything else. I did what he said. Called the police."

"Do you have any idea who might have shot your dog?" I asked.

"Like I said, Dammit was bad about chasing folks, going after cars like he was going to chew the tires off. You want my personal opinion, I've always halfway suspected it might have been a cop who done it."

"Why?" Marino asked.

"After the dog was examined, I was told the bullets came from a revolver. So maybe Dammit chased after a police car and that's how it happened."

"Did you see any police cars on your road that night?" Marino asked.

"Nope. Don't mean there wasn't one, though. And I can't be sure where the shooting happened. I know it wasn't nearby. I would've heard it."

"Maybe not if you had your TV turned up loud," Marino said.

"I would've heard it, all right. Not much sound around here, specially late at night. You live here awhile, you get to where you hear the smallest thing out of the ordinary. Even if your TV's on, the windows shut tight."

"Did you hear any cars on your road that night?" Marino asked.

He thought for a moment. "I know one went by not long before Dammit started scratching on the door. The police asked me that. I got the feeling whoever was in it is the one who shot the dog. The officer who took the report sort of thought that, too. Least, that's what he suggested." He paused, staring out the window. "Probably just some kid."

A clock gonged off-key from the living room, then silence, the passing empty seconds measured by water clinking in the sink. Mr. Joyce had no phone. He had very few neighbors, none of whom were close by. I wondered if he had children. It didn't appear he had gotten another dog or found himself a cat. I saw no sign that anybody or anything lived here except him.

"Old Dammit was worthless as hell, but he sort of grew on

you. Used to give the mailman a fit. I'd stand there in the living room looking out the window, laughing so hard my eyes was streaming. The sight of it. A puny little fellow, looking around, scared to death to get out of his little mail truck. Old Dammit running in circles snapping at the air. I'd give it a minute or two before I'd start hollering, then out I'd go in the yard. All I had to do was point my finger, and off Dammit would go, tail 'tween his legs." He took a deep breath, the cigarette forgotten in the ashtray. "Lot of meanness out there."

"Yes, sir," Marino agreed, leaning back in his chair. "Meanness everywhere, even in a nice, quiet area like this. Last time I was out this way must've been two years ago, a few weeks before Thanksgiving, when that couple was found in the woods. You remember that?"

"Sure do." Mr. Joyce nodded deeply. "Never seen so much commotion. I was out getting firewood when all of a sudden these police cars come thundering past, lights flashing. Must have been a dozen of them and a couple ambulances, too." He paused, eyeing Marino thoughtfully. "Don't recall seeing you out there." Turning his attention to me, he added, "Guess you were out there, too?"

"I was."

"Thought so." He seemed pleased. "Thought you looked familiar and I've been raking my brain the whole time we've been talking, trying to figure out where I might have seen you before."

"Did you go down to the woods where the bodies were?" Marino asked casually.

"With all those police cars going right past my house, wasn't a way in the world I could just sit here. I couldn't imagine what was going on. No neighbors down that way, just woods. And I was thinking, well, if it's a hunter who got shot, then that don't make sense either. Too many cops for that. So I got in my truck and headed down the road. Found an officer standing by his car and asked him what was going on. He told me some hunters had found a couple bodies back there. Then he wanted to know if I lived nearby. Said I did, and next thing there's a detective at my door asking questions."

"Do you remember the detective's name?" Marino asked.

"Can't say I do."

"What sorts of questions did he ask?"

"Mostly wanted to know if I'd seen anybody in the area, specially around the time this young couple was thought to have disappeared. Any strange cars, things like that."

"Had you?"

"Well, I got to thinking about it after he left, and it's entered my mind now and again ever since," Mr. Joyce said. "Now, the night the police think this couple was taken out here and killed, I didn't hear a thing that I remember. Sometimes I turn in early. Could be I was asleep. But there was something that I remembered a couple months back, after this other couple was found the first of the year."

"Deborah Harvey and Fred Cheney?" I asked.

"The girl whose mother's important."

Marino nodded.

Mr. Joyce went on, "Those murders got me to thinking

243

again about the bodies found out here, and it popped into my mind. If you noticed when you drove up, I have a mailbox out front. Well, I had a bad spell maybe a couple weeks before they think that girl and boy was killed out here several years back."

"Jim Freeman and Bonnie Smyth," Marino said.

"Yes, sir. I had the flu, was throwing up, felt like I had a toothache from head to toe. Stayed in bed what must've been two days and didn't even have the strength to go out and fetch the mail. This night I'm talking about, I was finally up and around, made myself some soup and kept it down all right. So I went out to get the mail. Must have been nine, ten o'clock at night. And right as I was walking back toward the house, I heard this car. Black as tar out and the person was creeping along with his headlights off."

"Which direction was the car going?" Marino asked.

"That way." Mr. Joyce pointed west. "In other words, he was heading away from the area down there where the woods are, back toward the highway. Could be nothing, but I remember it crossed my mind that it was strange. For one thing, there's nothing down there but farmland and woods. I just figured it was kids drinking or parking or something."

"Did you get a good look at the car?" I inquired.

"Seems like it was mid-size, dark in color. Black, dark blue, or dark red, maybe."

"New or old?" Marino asked.

"Don't know if it was brand new, but it wasn't old. Wasn't one of these foreign cars, either."

"How could you tell?" Marino asked.

"By the sound," Mr. Joyce replied easily. "These foreign cars don't sound the same as American ones. The engine's louder, chugs more, don't know exactly how to describe it, but I can tell. Just like when you were pulling up earlier. I knew you were in an American car, probably a Ford or Chevy. This car that went by with its headlights off, it was real quiet, smooth sounding. The shape of it reminded me of one of these new Thunderbirds, but I can't swear to it. Might have been a Cougar."

"It was sporty, then," Marino said.

"Depends on how you look at it. To me, a Corvette's sporty. A Thunderbird or Cougar's fancy."

"Could you tell how many people were inside this car?" I asked.

He shook his head. "Now, I got no idea about that. It was mighty dark out, and I didn't stand there staring."

Marino got a notepad out of his pocket and began flipping through it.

"Mr. Joyce," he said, "Jim Freeman and Bonnie Smyth disappeared July twenty-ninth on a Saturday night. You sure when you saw this car it was before then? Sure it wasn't later on?"

"Sure as I'm sitting here. Reason I know's because I got sick, like I told you. Started coming down with whatever it was the second week of July. I remember that because my wife's birthday's July thirteenth. I always go to the cemetery on her birthday and put flowers on her grave. Had just come home from doing that when I started feeling a little funny.

The next day I was too sick to get out of bed." He stared off for a moment. "Must've been the fifteenth or sixteenth I went out to get the mail and saw the car."

Marino got out his sunglasses, ready to leave.

Mr. Joyce, who wasn't born yesterday, asked him, "You thinking there's something about these couples dying that's got to do with my dog being shot?"

"We're looking into a lot of things. And it's best if you don't mention this conversation to anyone."

"Won't breathe a word of it, no, sir."

"I'd appreciate it."

He walked us to the door.

"Drop by again when you can," he said. "Come July the tomatoes will be in. Got a garden out back there, best tomatoes in Virginia. But you don't have to wait till then to visit. Anytime. I'm always here."

He watched us from the porch as we drove off.

Marino gave me his opinion as we followed the dirt road back to the highway.

"I'm suspicious about the car he saw two weeks before Bonnie Smyth and Jim Freeman was killed out here."

"So am I."

"As for the dog, I have my doubts. If the dog had been shot weeks, even months, before Jim and Bonnie disappeared, I'd think we were on to something. But hell, Dammit got whacked a good five years before these couples started dying."

Kill zones, I thought. Maybe we were on to something, anyway.

"Marino, have you considered that we may be dealing with

someone for whom the place of death is more important than victim selection?"

He glanced over at me, listening.

"This individual may spend quite a long time finding just the right spot," I went on. "When that is done, he hunts, brings his quarry to this place he has carefully chosen. The place is what is most important, and the time of year. Mr. Joyce's dog was killed in mid-August. The hottest time of the year, but off season as far as hunting goes, except for crow. Each of these couples has been killed off season. In every instance, the bodies have been found weeks, months later, in season. By hunters. It's a pattern."

"Are you suggesting this killer was out scouting the woods for a place to commit murders when the dog trotted up and spoiled his plan?" He glanced over at me, frowning.

"I'm just throwing out a lot of things."

"No offense, but I think you can throw that idea right out the window. Unless the squirrel was fantasizing about whacking couples for years, then finally got around to it."

"My guess is this individual's got a very active fantasy life."

"Maybe you should take up profiling," he said. "You're beginning to sound like Benton."

"And you're beginning to sound as if you've written Benton off."

"Nope. Just not in a mood to deal with him right now."

"He's still your VICAP partner, Marino. You and I are not the only ones under pressure. Don't be too hard on him."

"You sure are into handing out free advice these days," he said.

"Just be glad it's free, because you need all the advice you can get."

"You want to grab some dinner?"

It was getting close to six P.M.

"Tonight I exercise," I replied dismally.

"Geez. Guess that's what you'll be telling me to do next."

Just the thought of it made both of us reach for our cigarettes.

I was late for my tennis lesson, despite my doing everything short of running red lights to get to Westwood on time. One of my shoelaces broke, my grip was slippery, and there was a Mexican buffet in progress upstairs, meaning the observation gallery was full of people with nothing better to do than eat tacos, drink margaritas, and witness my humiliation. After sending five backhands in a row sailing well beyond the baseline, I started bending my knees and slowing my swing. The next three shots went into the net. Volleys were pathetic, overheads unmentionable. The harder I tried, the worse I got.

"You're opening up too soon and hitting everything late." Ted came around to my side of the net. "Too much backswing, not enough follow-through. And what happens?"

"I consider taking up bridge," I said, my frustration turning to anger.

"Your racket face is open. Take your racket back early, shoulder turned, step, hitting the ball out front. And keep it on your strings as long as you can."

Following me to the baseline, he demonstrated, stroking several balls over the net as I watched jealously. Ted had Michelangelo muscle definition, liquid coordination, and he could, without effort, put enough spin on a ball to make it bounce over your head or die at your feet. I wondered if magnificent athletes had any concept of how they made the rest of us feel.

"Most of your problem's in your head, Dr. Scarpetta," he said. "You walk out here and want to be Martina when you'd be much better off being yourself."

"Well, I sure as hell can't be Martina," I muttered.

"Don't be so determined to win points when you ought to be working at not losing them. Playing smart, setting up, keeping the ball in play until your opponent misses or gives you an easy opening to put the ball away. Out here that's the game. Club-level matches aren't won. They're lost. Someone beats you not because they win more points than you but because you lose more points than them." Looking speculatively at me, he added, "I'll bet you're not this impatient in your work. I'll bet you hit every ball back, so to speak, and can do it all day long."

I wasn't so sure about that, but Ted's coaching did the opposite of what he had intended. It took my mind off tennis. Playing smart. Later, I pondered this at length while soaking in the tub.

We weren't going to beat this killer. Planting bullets and newspaper stories were offensive tactics that had not worked. A little defensive strategy was in order. Criminals who escape apprehension are not perfect but lucky. They make mistakes. All of them do. The problem is recognizing the errors, realizing their significance, and determining what was intentional and what was not.

I thought of the cigarette butts we'd been finding near the bodies. Had the killer intentionally left them? Probably. Were they a mistake? No, because they were worthless as evidence and we could not determine their brand. The jacks of hearts left in the vehicles were intentional, but they were not a mistake either. No fingerprints had been recovered from them, and if anything, their purpose may be to make us think what the person who had left them wanted us to think.

Shooting Deborah Harvey I was sure was a mistake.

Then there was the perpetrator's past, which was what I was considering now. He didn't suddenly go from being a law-abiding citizen to becoming an experienced murderer. What sins had he committed before, what acts of evil?

For one thing, he may have shot an old man's dog eight years ago. If I was right, then he had made another mistake, because the incident suggested he was local, not new to the area. It made me wonder if he had killed before.

Immediately after staff meeting the following morning, I had my computer analyst, Margaret, give me a printout of every homicide that had occurred within a fifty-mile radius of Camp Peary over the past ten years. Though I wasn't necessarily looking for a double homicide, that was exactly what I found.

Numbers C0104233 and C0104234. I had never heard of the related cases, which had occurred several years before I moved to Virginia. Returning to my office, I shut the doors and reviewed the files with growing excitement. Jill Harrington and Elizabeth Mott had been murdered eight years ago in September, a month after Mr. Joyce's dog was shot.

Both women were in their early twenties when they disappeared on the Friday night of September fourteenth, their bodies found the next morning in a church cemetery. It wasn't until the following day that the Volkswagen belonging to Elizabeth was located in a motel parking lot off Route 60 in Lightfoot, just outside of Williamsburg.

I began studying autopsy reports and body diagrams. Elizabeth Mott had been shot once in the neck, after which, it was conjectured, she was stabbed once in the chest, her throat cut. She was fully clothed, with no evidence of sexual assault, no bullet was recovered, and there were ligature marks around her wrists. There were no defense injuries. Jill's records, however, told another story. She bore defense cuts to both forearms and hands, and contusions and lacerations to her face and scalp consistent with being "pistol whipped," and her blouse was torn. Apparently, she had put up one hell of a struggle, ending with her being stabbed eleven times.

According to newspaper clips included in their files, the James City County police said the women were last seen drinking beer in the Anchor Bar and Grill in Williamsburg, where they stayed until approximately ten P.M. It was theorized that it was here they met up with their assailant, a "Mr. Goodbar" situation, in which the two women left with him and followed him to the motel where Elizabeth's car was later found. At some point he abducted them, perhaps in the parking lot, and forced them to drive him to the cemetery where he murdered them.

There was a lot about the scenario that didn't make sense to me. The police had found blood in the backseat of the Volkswagen that could not be explained. The blood type did not match up with either woman's. If the blood was the killer's, then what happened? Did he struggle with one of the women in the backseat? If so, why wasn't her blood found as well? If both women were up front and he was in back, then how did he get injured? If he cut himself while struggling with Jill in the cemetery, then that didn't make sense, either. After the murders, he would have had to drive their car from the cemetery to the motel, and his blood should have been in the driver's area, not in the backseat. Finally, if the man intended to murder the women after engaging in sexual activity, why didn't he just kill them inside the motel room? And why were the women's physical evidence recovery kits negative for sperm? Had they engaged in intercourse with this man and then cleaned up afterward? *Two* women with one man? A ménage à trois? Well, I supposed, there wasn't much I hadn't seen in my line of work.

Buzzing the computer analyst's office, I got Margaret on the line.

"I need you to run something else for me," I said. "A list of all drug-positive homicide cases worked by James City County Detective R. P. Montana. And I need the information right away, if you can manage it."

"No problem." I could hear her fingers clicking over the keyboard.

When I got the printout there were six drug-positive

homicides investigated by Detective Montana. The names of Elizabeth Mott and Jill Harrington were on the list, because their postmortem blood was positive for alcohol. The result in each instance was insignificant, less than .05. In addition, Jill was positive for chlordiazepoxide and clidinium, the active drugs found in Librax.

Reaching for the phone, I dialed the James City County Detective Division and asked to speak to Montana. I was told he was a captain now in Internal Affairs, and my call was transferred to his desk.

I intended to be very careful. If it were perceived I was considering that the murders of the two women might be related to the deaths of the other five couples, I feared Montana would back off, not talk.

"Montana," a deep voice answered.

"This is Dr. Scarpetta," I said.

"How'ya doing, Doc? Everybody in Richmond's still shooting each other, I see."

"It doesn't seem to get much better," I agreed. "I'm surveying for drug-positive homicides," I explained. "And I wonder if I could ask you a question or two about several old cases of yours I came across in our computer."

"Fire away. But it's been a while. I may be a little fuzzy on the details."

"Basically, I'm interested in the scenarios, the details surrounding the deaths. Most of your cases occurred before I came to Richmond."

"Oh, yeah, back in the days of Doc Cagney. Working with him was something." Montana laughed. "Never forget the way he used to sometimes dig around in bodies without gloves. Nothing fazed him except kids. He didn't like doing kids."

I began reviewing the information from the computer printout, and what Montana recalled about each case didn't surprise me. Hard drinking and domestic problems had culminated in husband shooting wife or the other way around—the Smith & Wesson divorce, as it was irreverently referred to by the police. A man tanked to the gills was beaten to death by several drunk companions after a poker game went sour. A father with a .30 blood alcohol level was shot to death by his son. And so on. I saved Jill's and Elizabeth's cases for last.

"I remember them real well," Montana said. "Weird's all I got to say about what happened to those two girls. Wouldn't have thought they were the type to go off to a motel with some guy who picked them up in a bar. Both of them college graduates, had good jobs, smart, attractive. It's my opinion the guy they met up with had to be mighty slick. We're not talking about some redneck type. I've always suspected it was someone just passing through, not from around here."

"Why?"

"Because if it was someone local I think we might have had a little luck developing a suspect. Some serial killer, it's my opinion. Picks up women in bars and murders them. Maybe some guy on the road a lot, hits in different cities and towns, then moves on."

"Was robbery involved?" I asked.

"Didn't appear to be. My first thought when I got the cases was maybe the two girls were into recreational drugs, went off with someone to make a buy, maybe agreed to meet him at the motel to party or exchange cash for coke. But no money or jewelry was missing, and I never found out anything to make me think the girls had a history of snorting or shooting up."

"I notice from the toxicology reports that Jill Harrington tested positive for Librax, in addition to alcohol," I said. "Do you know anything about that?"

He thought for a moment. "Librax. Nope. Doesn't ring a bell."

I asked him nothing else and thanked him.

Librax is a versatile therapeutic drug used as a muscle relaxant and to relieve anxiety and tension. Jill may have suffered from a bad back or soreness due to sports injuries, or she may have had psychosomatic problems such as spasms in her gastrointestinal tract. My next chore was to find her physician. I began by calling one of my medical examiners in Williamsburg and asking him to fax the section in his Yellow Pages that listed pharmacies in his area. Then I dialed Marino's pager number.

"Do you have any police friends in Washington? Anyone you trust?" I said when Marino rang me back.

"I know a couple of guys. Why?"

"It's very important I talk to Abby Turnbull. And I don't think it's a good idea for me to call her."

"Not unless you want to take the risk of someone knowing about it."

"Exactly."

"You ask me," he added, "it's not a good idea for you to talk to her anyway."

"I understand your point of view. But that doesn't change my mind, Marino. Could you contact one of your friends up there and send him to her apartment, have him see if he can locate her?"

"I think you're making a mistake. But yeah. I'll take care of it."

"Just have him tell her I need to talk to her. I want her to contact me immediately." I gave Marino her address.

By this time, the copies of the Yellow Pages I was interested in had come off the fax machine down the hall and Rose placed them on my desk. For the rest of the afternoon, I called every pharmacy that Jill Harrington might have patronized in Williamsburg. I finally located one that had her listed in their records.

"Was she a regular customer?" I asked the pharmacist.

"Sure was. Elizabeth Mott was, too. Both of them didn't live too far from here, in an apartment complex just down the road. Nice young women, never will forget how shocked I was."

"Did they live together?"

"Let me see." A pause. "Wouldn't appear so. Different addresses and phone numbers, but the same apartment complex. Old Towne, about two miles away. Nice enough place. A lot of young people, William and Mary students out there."

He went on to give me Jill's medication history. Over a period of three years, Jill had brought in prescriptions for various antibiotics, cough suppressants, and other medications associated with the mundane flu bugs and respiratory or urinary tract infections that commonly afflict the hoi polloi. As recently as a month before her murder, she had been in to fill a prescription for Septra, which she apparently was no longer on when she died, since trimethoprim and sulfamethoxazole were not detected in her blood.

"Did you ever dispense Librax to her?" I asked.

I waited while he looked.

"No, ma'am. No record of that."

Perhaps the prescription was Elizabeth's, I considered.

"What about her friend Elizabeth Mott?" I asked the pharmacist. "Did she ever come in with a prescription for Librax?"

"No."

"Was there any other pharmacy either woman patronized that you're aware of?"

"Afraid I can't help you on that one. Got no idea."

He gave me the names of other pharmacies close by. I had already called most of them, and calls to the rest confirmed neither woman had brought in a prescription for Librax or any other drug. The Librax itself wasn't necessarily important, I reasoned. But the mystery of who had prescribed it and why bothered me considerably.

12

Abby Turnbull had been a crime reporter in Richmond when Elizabeth Mott and Jill Harrington were murdered. I was willing to bet that Abby not only remembered the cases, but probably knew more about them than Captain Montana did.

The next morning she called from a pay phone and left a number where she told Rose she would wait for fifteen minutes. Abby insisted that I call her back from a "safe place."

"Is everything all right?" Rose asked quietly as I peeled off my surgical gloves.

"God only knows," I said, untying my gown.

The nearest "safe place" I could think of was a pay phone outside the cafeteria in my building. Breathless and somewhat frantic to meet Abby's deadline, I dialed the number my secretary had given me.

"What's going on?" Abby asked immediately. "Some Metro cop came by my apartment, said you'd sent him."

"That's correct," I reassured her. "Based on what you've told me, I didn't think it a good idea to call you at home. Are you all right?"

"Is that why you wanted me to call?" She sounded disappointed.

"One of the reasons. We need to talk."

There was a long silence on the line.

"I'll be in Williamsburg on Saturday," she then said. "Dinner, The Trellis at seven?"

I did not ask her why she was going to be in Williamsburg. I wasn't sure I wanted to know, but when I parked my car in Merchant's Square Saturday, I found my apprehensions diminishing with each step I took. It was hard to be preoccupied with murder and other acts of incivility while sipping hot apple cider in the sharp wintry air of one of my favorite places in America.

It was a low season for tourists, and there were still plenty of people about, strolling, browsing inside the restored shops, and riding past in horse-drawn carriages driven by liverymen in knee breeches and three-cornered hats. Mark and I had talked about spending a weekend in Williamsburg. We would rent one of the nineteenth-century carriage houses inside the Historic District, follow cobblestone sidewalks beneath the glow of gaslights and dine in one of the taverns, then drink wine before the fire until falling asleep in each other's arms.

Of course, none of it had come to pass, the history of our

relationship more wishes than memories. Would it ever be different from this? Recently, he had promised me on the phone that it would. But he had promised before, and so had I. He was still in Denver and I was still here.

Inside the Silversmith's Shop, I bought a handwrought sterling silver pineapple charm and a handsome chain. Lucy would get a late Valentine's Day present from her negligent aunt. A forage inside the Apothecary Shop brought forth soaps for my guest room, spicy shaving cream for Fielding and Marino, and potpourri for Bertha and Rose. At five minutes before seven, I was inside The Trellis looking for Abby. When she arrived half an hour later, I was impatiently waiting at a table nestled against a planter of wandering jew.

"I'm sorry," she said with feeling, slipping out of her coat. "I got delayed. Got here as fast as I could."

She looked keyed up and exhausted, her eyes nervously darting about. The Trellis was doing a brisk business, people talking in low voices in the wavering shadows of candlelight. I wondered if Abby felt she had been followed.

"Have you been in Williamsburg all day?" I asked.

She nodded.

"I don't suppose I dare ask what you've been doing."

"Research," was all she said.

"Nowhere near Camp Peary, I hope." I looked her in the eye.

She got my meaning very well. "You know," she said.

The waitress arrived and then went off to the bar to get Abby a Bloody Mary.

"How did you find out?" Abby asked, lighting a cigarette.

"A better question is how did you find out?"

"I can't tell you that, Kay."

Of course she couldn't. But I knew. Pat Harvey.

"You have a source," I said carefully. "Let me just ask you this. Why would this source want you to know? Information wasn't passed on to you without there being motive on the source's part."

"I'm well aware of that."

"Then why?"

"The truth is important." Abby stared off. "I'm also a source."

"I see. In exchange for information, you pass on what you dig up."

She did not respond.

"Does this include me?" I asked.

"I'm not going to screw you, Kay. Have I ever?" She looked hard at me.

"No," I said sincerely. "So far, you never have."

Her Bloody Mary was set before her, and she absently stirred it with the stalk of celery.

"All I can tell you," I went on, "is you're walking on dangerous ground. I don't need to elaborate. You should realize this better than anyone. Is it worth the stress? Is your book worth the price, Abby?"

When she made no comment, I added with a sigh, "I don't guess I'm going to change your mind, am I?"

"Have you ever gotten into something you can't get out of?"

"I do it all the time." I smiled wryly. "That's where I am now."

"That's where I am, too."

"I see. And what if you're wrong, Abby?"

"I'm not the one who can be wrong," she replied. "Whatever the truth is about who's committing these murders, the fact remains that the FBI and other interested agencies are acting on certain suspicions and making decisions based on them. That's reportable. If the feds, the police, are wrong, it just adds another chapter."

"That sounds awfully cold," I said uneasily.

"I'm being professional, Kay. When you talk professionally, sometimes you sound cold, too."

I had talked to Abby directly after the body of her murdered sister was discovered. If I hadn't sounded cold on that horrible occasion, at best I had come across as clinical.

"I need your help with something," I said. "Eight years ago, two women were murdered very close to here. Elizabeth Mott and Jill Harrington."

She looked curiously at me. "You don't think—"

"I'm not sure what I'm thinking," I interrupted. "But I need to know the details of the cases. There's very little in my office reports. I wasn't in Virginia then. But there are news clips in the files. Several of them have your byline."

"It's hard for me to imagine that what happened to Jill and Elizabeth is connected to the other cases."

"So you remember them," I said, relieved.

"I will never forget them. It was one of the few times working on something actually gave me nightmares."

"Why is it hard for you to imagine a connection?"

"A number of reasons. There was no jack of hearts found. The car wasn't found abandoned on a roadside, but in a motel parking lot, and the bodies didn't turn up weeks or months after the fact decomposing in the woods. They were found within twenty-four hours. Both victims were women, and they were in their twenties, not teenagers. And why would the killer strike and then not do it again until some five years later?"

"I agree," I said. "The timing doesn't fit with the profile of your typical serial killer. And the MO seems inconsistent with the others. The victim selection seems inconsistent as well."

"Then why are you so interested?" She sipped her drink.

"I'm groping, and I'm troubled by their cases, which were never solved," I admitted. "It's unusual for two people to be abducted and murdered. There was no evidence of sexual assault. The women were killed around here, in the same area where the other murders have occurred."

"And a gun and a knife were used," Abby mused.

She knew about Deborah Harvey, then.

"There are some parallels," I said evasively.

Abby looked unconvinced but interested.

"What do you want to know, Kay?"

"Anything you might remember about them. Anything at all."

She thought for a long moment, toying with her drink.

"Elizabeth was working in sales for a local computer company and doing extremely well," she said. "Jill had just

263

finished law school at William and Mary and had gone to work with a small firm in Williamsburg. I never did buy the notion that they went off to a motel to have sex with some creep they met in a bar. Neither of the women struck me as the type. And two of them with one man? I always thought it was strange. Also, there was blood in the backseat of their car. It didn't match either Jill's or Elizabeth's blood types."

Abby's resourcefulness never ceased to amaze me. Somehow she had gotten hold of the serology results.

"I assume the blood belonged to the killer. There was a lot of it, Kay. I saw the car. It looked as if someone had been stabbed or cut in the backseat. Possibly, this would place the killer there, but it was hard to come up with a good interpretation of what might have occurred. The police were of the opinion the women met up with this animal in the Anchor Bar and Grill. But if he rode off with them in their car and was planning to kill them, then how was he going to get back to his car later on?"

"Depends on how far the motel is from the bar. He could have walked back to his car after the murders."

"The motel is a good four or five miles from the Anchor Bar, which isn't around anymore, by the way. The women were last seen inside the bar at around ten P.M. If the killer had left his car there, it probably would have been the only one in the lot by the time he got back to it, and that wouldn't have been very bright. A cop might have noticed the car, or at least the night manager would have as he was locking up to go home."

"This doesn't preclude the killer leaving his car at the motel and abducting them in Elizabeth's, then returning later, getting into his car, and driving off," I pointed out.

"No, it doesn't. But if he drove his own car to the motel, then when did he get inside hers? The scenario of the three of them being inside a motel room together, and then forcing them to drive him to the cemetery, has never set well with me. Why go to all the trouble, the risk? They could have started screaming in the parking lot, could have resisted. Why not just murder them inside the room?"

"Was it verified that the three of them were ever inside one of the rooms?"

"That's the other thing," she said. "I questioned the clerk who was on duty that night. The Palm Leaf, a low-rent motel off Route Sixty in Lightfoot. Doesn't exactly do a thriving business. But the clerk didn't remember either woman. Nor did he remember some guy coming in and renting a room near where the Volkswagen was found. In fact, most of the rooms in that section of the motel were vacant at the time. More important, no one checked in and then left without turning in the key. Hard to believe this guy would have had opportunity or inclination to check out. Certainly not after committing the crimes. He would have been bloody."

"What was your theory when you were working on your stories?" I asked.

"The same as it is now. I don't think they met up with their killer inside the bar. I think something happened shortly after Elizabeth and Jill left."

"Such as?"

Frowning, Abby was stirring her drink again. "I don't know. They definitely weren't the type to pick up a hitch-hiker, certainly not at that late hour. And I never believed there was a drug connection. Neither Jill nor Elizabeth was found to have used coke, heroin, or anything like that, and no paraphernalia was found inside their apartments. They didn't smoke, weren't heavy drinkers. Both of them jogged, were health nuts."

"Do you know where they were heading after they left the bar? Were they going straight home? Might they have stopped somewhere?"

"No evidence if they did."

"And they left the bar alone?"

"Nobody I talked to remembered seeing them with another person while they were in the bar drinking. As I remember it, they had a couple of beers, were at a corner table talking. Nobody recalled seeing them leave with anyone."

"They might have met someone in the parking lot when they left," I said. "This individual might even have been waiting in Elizabeth's car."

"I doubt they would have left the car unlocked, but I suppose it's possible."

"Did the women frequent this bar?"

"As I remember it, they didn't frequent it, but they'd gone there before."

"A rough place?"

"That was my expectation since it was a favorite watering hole for military guys," she replied. "But it reminded me of an English pub. Civilized. People talking, playing darts. It was the sort of place I could have gone with a friend and felt quite comfortable and private. The theory was that the killer was either someone passing through town or else a military person temporarily stationed in the area. It wasn't someone they knew."

Perhaps not, I thought. But it must have been someone they felt they could trust, at least initially, and I recalled what Hilda Ozimek had said about the encounters being "friendly" at first. I wondered what would come to her if I showed her photographs of Elizabeth and Jill.

"Did Jill have any medical problems you're aware of?" I asked.

She thought about this, her face perplexed. "I don't recall."

"Where was she from?"

"Kentucky comes to mind."

"Did she go home often?"

"I didn't get that impression. I think she made it home for holidays and that was about it."

Then it wasn't likely she had a prescription for Librax filled in Kentucky where her family lived, I thought.

"You mentioned she had just begun practicing law," I went on. "Did she travel much, have reason to be in and out of town?"

She waited as our chef's salads were served, then said, "She had a close friend from law school. I can't remember his name, but I talked to him, asked him about her habits, activities. He said he was suspicious Jill was having an affair."

"What made him suspect that?"

"Because during their third year of law school she drove to

Richmond almost every week, supposedly because she was job hunting, liked Richmond a lot, and wanted to find an opening in a firm there. He told me she often needed to borrow his notes because her out-of-town excursions caused her to miss classes. He thought it was strange, especially since she ended up going with a firm here in Williamsburg right after graduation. He went on and on about it because he was afraid her trips might be related to her murder, if she were seeing a married man in Richmond, for example, and perhaps threatened to expose their affair to his wife. Maybe she was having an affair with someone prominent, a successful lawyer or judge, who couldn't afford the scandal so he silenced Jill forever. Or got someone else to, and it just so happened Elizabeth had the misfortune of being around at the time."

"What do you think?"

"The lead went nowhere, like ninety percent of the tips I get."

"Was Jill romantically involved with the student who told you this?"

"I think he would have liked for her to have been," she said. "But no, they weren't involved. I got the impression this was, in part, the reason for his suspicions. He was pretty sure of himself and figured the only reason Jill never succumbed to his charms was because she had somebody else nobody knew about. A secret lover."

"Was he ever a suspect, this student?" I asked.

"Not at all. He was out of town when the murders occurred, and that was verified beyond a doubt."

"Did you talk to any of the other lawyers in the firm where Jill worked?"

"I didn't get very far with that," Abby answered. "You know how lawyers are. In any event, she'd been with the firm only a few months before she was murdered. I don't think her colleagues knew her very well."

"Doesn't sound as if Jill was an extrovert," I remarked.

"She was described as charismatic, witty, but self-contained."

"And Elizabeth?" I asked.

"More outgoing, I think," she said. "Which I suppose she had to have been to be good in sales."

The glow of gaslight lamps pushed the darkness back from cobblestone sidewalks as we walked to the Merchant's Square parking lot. A heavy layer of cloud obscured the moon, the damp, cold air penetrating.

"I wonder what these couples would be doing now, if they'd still be with each other, what difference they might have made," Abby said, chin tucked into her collar, hands in her pockets.

"What do you think Henna would be doing?" I gently asked about her sister.

"She'd probably still be in Richmond. I guess both of us would be."

"Are you sorry you moved?"

"Some days I'm sorry about everything. Ever since Henna died, it's as if I've had no options, no free will. It's as if I've been propelled along by things out of my control."

"I don't see it that way. You chose to take the job at the *Post*, move to D.C. And now you've chosen to write a book."

"Just as Pat Harvey chose to hold that press conference and do all the other things she's done that have burned her so badly," she said.

"Yes, she has made choices, too."

"When you're going through something like this, you don't know what you're doing, even if you think you do," she went on. "And no one can really understand what it's like unless they've suffered the same thing. You feel isolated. You go places and people avoid you, are afraid to meet your eyes and make conversation because they don't know what to say. So they whisper to each other. 'See her over there? Her sister was the one murdered by the strangler.' Or 'That's Pat Harvey. Her daughter was the one.' You feel as if you're living inside a cave. You're afraid to be alone, afraid to be with others, afraid to be awake, and afraid to go to sleep because of how awful it feels when morning comes. You run like hell and wear yourself out. As I look back, I can see that everything I've done since Henna died was half crazy."

"I think you've done remarkably well," I said sincerely.

"You don't know the things I've done. The mistakes I've made."

"Come on. I'll drive you to your car," I said, for we had reached Merchant's Square.

I heard a car engine start in the dark lot as I got out my keys. We were inside my Mercedes, doors locked and seat belts on when a new Lincoln pulled up beside us and the driver's window hummed down.

I opened my window just enough to hear what the man

wanted. He was young, clean cut, folding a map and struggling with it.

"Excuse me." He smiled helplessly. "Can you tell me how to get back on Sixty-four East from here?"

I could feel Abby's tension as I gave him quick directions.

"Get his plate number," she said urgently as he drove away. She dug in her pocketbook for a pen and notepad.

"E-N-T-eight-nine-nine," I read quickly.

She wrote it down.

"What's going on?" I asked, unnerved.

Abby looked left and right for any sign of his car as I pulled out of the lot.

"Did you notice his car when we got to the parking lot?" she asked.

I had to think. The parking lot was nearly empty when we had gotten there. I had been vaguely aware of a car that might have been the Lincoln parked in a poorly lit corner.

I told Abby this, adding, "But I assumed no one was in it."

"Right. Because the car's interior light wasn't on."

"I guess not."

"Reading a map in the dark, Kay?"

"Good point," I said, startled.

"And if he's from out of town, then how do you explain the parking sticker on his rear bumper?"

"Parking sticker?" I repeated.

"It had the Colonial Williamsburg seal on it. The same sticker I was given years ago when the skeletal remains were discovered at that archaeology dig, Martin's Hundred. I did a series, was out here a lot, and the sticker permitted me to park inside the Historic District and at Carter's Grove."

"The guy works here and needed directions to Sixty-four?" I muttered.

"You got a good look at him?" she asked.

"Pretty good. Do you think it was the man who followed you that night in Washington?"

"I don't know. But maybe . . . Damn it, Kay! This is making me crazy!"

"Well, enough is enough," I said firmly. "Give me that license number. I intend to do something about it."

The next morning Marino called with the cryptic message, "If you haven't read the *Post*, better go out and get a copy."

"Since when do you read the *Post*?"

"Since never, if I can help it. Benton alerted me about an hour ago. Call me later. I'm downtown."

Putting on a warm-up suit and ski jacket, I drove through a downpour to a nearby drugstore. For the better part of half an hour I sat inside my car, heater blasting, windshield wipers a monotonous metronome in the hard, cold rain. I was appalled by what I read. Several times it entered my mind that if the Harveys didn't sue Clifford Ring, I should.

The front page carried the first in a three-part series about Deborah Harvey, Fred Cheney, and the other couples who had died. Nothing sacred was spared, Ring's reporting so comprehensive it included details even I did not know.

Not long before Deborah Harvey was murdered, she had confided to a friend her suspicions that her father was an alcoholic and having an affair with an airline flight attendant half his age. Apparently, Deborah had eavesdropped on a number of telephone conversations between her father and his alleged mistress. The flight attendant lived in Charlotte, and according to the story, Harvey was with her the night his daughter and Fred Cheney disappeared, which was why the police and Mrs. Harvey were unable to reach him. Ironically, Deborah's suspicions did not make her bitter toward her father but her mother, who, consumed with her career, was never home, and therefore, in Deborah's eyes, to blame for her father's infidelity and alcohol abuse.

Column after column of vitriolic print added up to paint a pathetic portrait of a powerful woman bent on saving the world while her own family disintegrated from neglect. Pat Harvey had married into money, her home in Richmond was palatial, her quarters at the Watergate filled with antiques and valuable art, including a Picasso and a Remington. She wore the right clothes, went to the right parties, her decorum impeccable, her policies and knowledge of world affairs brilliant.

Yet lurking behind this plutocratic, flawless facade, Ring concluded, was "a driven woman born in a blue-collar section of Baltimore, someone described by her colleagues as tormented by insecurity that perpetually propelled her into proving herself." Pat Harvey, he said, was a megalomaniac. She was irrational—if not rabid—when threatened or put to the test.

His treatment of the homicides that had occurred in Virginia over the past three years was just as relentless. He disclosed the fears of the CIA and FBI that the killer might be someone at Camp Peary, and served up this revelation with such a wild spin that it made everyone involved look bad.

The CIA and the Justice Department were involved in a cover-up, their paranoia so extreme they had encouraged investigators in Virginia to withhold information from each other. False evidence had been planted at a scene. Disinformation had been "leaked" to reporters, and it was even suspected that some reporters were under surveillance. Pat Harvey, meanwhile, was supposedly privy to all this, and her indignation was not exactly depicted as righteous, as evidenced by her demeanor during her infamous press conference. Engaged in a turf battle with the Justice Department, Mrs. Harvey had exploited sensitive information to incriminate and harass those federal agencies with which she had become increasingly at odds due to her campaign against fraudulent charities such as ACTMAD.

The final ingredient in this poisonous stew was me. I had stonewalled and withheld case information at the request of the FBI until forced by threat of a court order to release my reports to the families. I had refused to talk to the press. Though I had no formal obligation to answer to the FBI, it was suggested by Clifford Ring that it was possible my professional behavior was influenced by my personal life. "According to a source close to Virginia's Chief Medical Examiner," the article read, "Dr. Scarpetta has been romantically involved with an FBI Special

Agent for the past two years, has frequently visited Quantico and is on friendly terms with the Academy's personnel, including Benton Wesley, the profiler involved in these cases."

I wondered how many readers would conclude from this that I was having an affair with Wesley.

Impeached along with my integrity and morals was my competence as a forensic pathologist. In the ten cases in question, I had been unable to determine a cause of death in all of them but one, and when I discovered a cut on one of Deborah Harvey's bones, I was so worried that I had inflicted this myself with a scalpel, claimed Ring, that I "drove to Washington in the snow, Harvey's and Cheney's skeletons in the trunk of her Mercedes, and sought the advice of a forensic anthropologist at the Smithsonian's National Museum of Natural History."

Like Pat Harvey, I had "consulted a psychic." I had accused investigators of tampering with Fred Cheney's and Deborah Harvey's remains at the scene, and then returned to the wooded area to search for a cartridge case myself because I did not trust the police to find it. I had also taken it upon myself to question witnesses, including a clerk at a 7-Eleven, where Fred and Deborah were last seen alive. I smoked, drank, had a license to carry my .38 concealed, had "almost been killed" on several occasions, was divorced and "from Miami." The latter somehow seemed an explanation for all of the above.

The way Clifford Ring made it sound, I was an arrogant, gunslinging wild woman who, when it came to forensic medicine, didn't know her ass from a hole in the ground.

Abby, I thought, as I sped home over rain-slick streets. Was this what she meant last night when she referred to mistakes she had made? Had she fed information to her colleague Clifford Ring?

"That wouldn't add up," Marino pointed out later as we sat in my kitchen drinking coffee. "Not that my opinion about her's changed. I think she'd sell her grandmother for a story. But she's working on this big book, right? Don't make sense that she'd share information with the competition, especially since she's pissed off at the *Post*."

"Some of the information had to have come from her." It was hard for me to admit. "The bit about the Seven-Eleven clerk, for example. Abby and I were together that night. And she knows about Mark."

"How?" Marino looked curiously at me.

"I told her."

He just shook his head.

Sipping my coffee, I stared out at the rain. Abby had tried to call twice since I'd gotten home from the drugstore. I had stood by my machine listening to her tense voice. I wasn't ready to talk to her yet. I was afraid of what I might say.

"How's Mark going to react?" Marino asked.

"Fortunately, the story didn't mention his name."

I felt another wave of anxiety. Typical of FBI agents, especially those who had spent years under deep cover, Mark was secretive about his personal life to the point of paranoia. The paper's allusion to our relationship would upset him considerably, I feared. I had to call him. Or maybe I shouldn't. I didn't know what to do.

"Some of the information, I suspect, came from Morrell," I went on, thinking aloud.

Marino was silent.

"Vessey must have talked, too. Or at least someone at the Smithsonian did," I said. "And I don't know how the hell Ring found out that we went to see Hilda Ozimek."

Setting down his cup and saucer, Marino leaned forward and met my eyes.

"My turn to give advice."

I felt like a child about to be scolded.

"It's like a cement truck with no brakes going down a hill. You ain't going to stop it, Doc. All you can do is get out of the way."

"Would you care to translate?" I said impatiently.

"Just do your work and forget it. If you get questioned, and I'm sure you will, just say you never talked to Clifford Ring, don't know nothing about it. Brush it off, in other words. You get into a pissing match with the press and you're going to end up like Pat Harvey. Looking like an idiot."

He was right.

"And if you got any sense, don't talk to Abby anytime soon."

I nodded.

He stood up. "Meanwhile, I got a few things to run down. If they pan out, I'll let you know."

That reminded me. Fetching my pocketbook, I got out the slip of paper with the plate number Abby had taken down.

"Wonder if you could check NCIC. A Lincoln Mark Seven, dark gray. See what comes back."

"Someone tailing you?" He tucked the slip of paper in his pocket.

"I don't know. The driver stopped to ask directions. I don't think he was really lost."

"Where?" he asked as I walked him to the door.

"Williamsburg. He was sitting in the car in an empty parking lot. This was around ten-thirty, eleven last night at Merchant's Square. I was getting into my car when his headlights suddenly went on and he drove over, asked me how to get to Sixty-four."

"Huh," Marino said shortly. "Probably some dumbshit detective working under cover, bored, waiting for someone to run a red light or make a U-turn. Might have been trying to hit on you, too. A decent-looking woman out at night alone, climbing into a Mercedes."

I didn't offer that Abby had been with me. I didn't want another lecture.

"I wasn't aware that many detectives drive new Lincolns," I said.

"Would you look at the rain. Shit," he complained as he ran to his car.

Fielding, my deputy chief, was never too preoccupied or busy to glance at any reflective object he happened to pass. This included plate-glass windows, computer screens, and the bulletproof security partitions separating the lobby from our inner offices. When I got off the elevator on the first floor, I spotted him pausing before the morgue's stainless-steel refrigerator door, smoothing back his hair.

"It's getting a little long over your ears," I said.

"And yours is getting a little gray." He grinned.

"Ash. Blondes go ash, never gray."

"Right." He absently tightened the drawstring of his surgical greens, biceps bulging like grapefruits. Fielding couldn't blink without flexing something formidable. Whenever I saw him hunched over his microscope, I was reminded of a steroid version of Rodin's *The Thinker*.

"Jackson was released about twenty minutes ago," he said, referring to one of the morning's cases. "That's it, but we've already got one for tomorrow. The guy they had on life support from the shoot-out over the weekend."

"What's on your schedule for the rest of the afternoon?" I asked. "And that reminds me, I thought you had court in Petersburg."

"The defendant pleaded." He glanced at his watch. "About an hour ago."

"He must have heard you were coming."

"Micros are stacked up to the ceiling in the cinder-block cell the state calls my office. That's my agenda for the afternoon. Or at least it was." He looked speculatively at me.

"I've got a problem I'm hoping you can help me with. I need to track down a prescription that may have been filled in Richmond eight or so years ago."

"Which pharmacy?"

"If I knew that," I said as we took the elevator to the

second floor, "then I wouldn't have a problem. What it amounts to is we need to organize a telethon, so to speak. As many people as possible on the lines calling every pharmacy in Richmond."

Fielding winced. "Jesus, Kay, there's got to be at least a hundred."

"A hundred and thirty-three. I've already counted. Six of us with a list of twenty-two, twenty-three, each. That's fairly manageable. Can you help me out?"

"Sure." He looked depressed.

In addition to Fielding, I drafted my administrator, Rose, another secretary, and the computer analyst. We assembled in the conference room with lists of the pharmacies. My instructions were quite clear. Discretion. Not a word about what we were doing to family, friends, or the police. Since the prescription had to be at least eight years old and Jill was deceased, there was a good chance the records were no longer in the active files. I told them to ask the pharmacist to check the drugstore's archives. If he was uncooperative or reluctant to release the information, roll that call over to me.

Then we disappeared into our respective offices. Two hours later, Rose appeared at my desk, tenderly massaging her right ear.

She handed me a call sheet and could not suppress a triumphant smile. "Boulevard Drug Store at Boulevard and Broad. Jill Harrington had two prescriptions for Librax filled." She gave me the dates.

"Her physician?"

"Dr. Anna Zenner," she answered.

Good God.

Hiding my surprise, I congratulated her. "You're wonderful, Rose. Take the rest of the day off."

"I leave at four-thirty anyway. I'm late."

"Then take a three-hour lunch tomorrow." I felt like hugging her. "And tell the others mission accomplished. They can put down the phones."

"Wasn't Dr. Zenner the president of the Richmond Academy of Medicine not so long ago?" Rose asked, pausing thoughtfully in my doorway. "Seems I read something about her. Oh! She's the musician."

"She was the president of the Academy year before last. And yes, she plays the violin for the Richmond Symphony."

"Then you know her." My secretary looked impressed.

All too well, I thought, reaching for the phone.

That evening, when I was home, Anna Zenner returned my call.

"I see from the papers you have been very busy lately, Kay," she said. "Are you holding up?"

I wondered if she had read the *Post*. This morning's installment had included an interview with Hilda Ozimek and a photograph of her with the caption: "Psychic Knew All of Them Were Dead." Relatives and friends of the slain couples were quoted, and half of a page was filled with a color diagram showing where the couples' cars and bodies had been found. Camp Peary was ominously positioned in the center of this cluster like a skull and crossbones on a pirate's map.

"I'm doing all right," I told her. "And I'll be doing even better if you can assist me with something." I explained what I needed, adding, "Tomorrow I will fax you the form citing the Code giving me statutory rights to Jill Harrington's records."

It was pro forma. Yet it seemed awkward reminding her of my legal authority.

"You can bring the form in person. Dinner at seven on Wednesday?"

"It's not necessary for you to go to any trouble—"

"No trouble, Kay," she interrupted warmly. "I have missed seeing you."

13

The art deco pastels of uptown reminded me of Miami Beach. Buildings were pink, yellow, and Wedgwood blue with polished brass door knockers and brilliant handmade flags fluttering over entrances, a sight that seemed even more incongruous because of the weather. Rain had turned to snow.

Traffic was rush-hour awful and I had to drive around the block twice before spotting a parking place within a reasonable walk of my favorite wine shop. I picked out four good bottles, two red, two white.

I drove along Monument Avenue, where statues of Confederate generals on horses loomed over traffic circles, ghostly in the milky swirl of snow. Last summer I had traveled this route once a week on my way to see Anna, the visits tapering off by fall and ending completely this winter.

Her office was in her house, a lovely old white frame where

the street was blacktopped cobblestone and gas carriage lamps glowed after dark. Ringing the bell to announce my arrival just as her patients did, I let myself into a foyer that led into what was Anna's waiting room. Leather furniture surrounded a coffee table stacked with magazines, and an old Oriental rug covered the hardwood floor. There were toys in a box in a corner for her younger patients, a receptionist's desk, a coffee maker, and a fireplace. Down a long hallway was the kitchen, where something was cooking that reminded me I had skipped lunch.

"Kay? Is that you?"

The unmistakable voice with its strong German accent was punctuated by brisk footsteps, and then Anna was wiping her hands on her apron and giving me a hug.

"You locked the door after you?"

"I did, and you know to lock up after your last patient leaves, Anna." I used to say this every time.

"You are my last patient."

I followed her to the kitchen. "Do all of your patients bring you wine?"

"I wouldn't permit it. And I don't cook for or socialize with them. For you I break all the rules."

"Yes." I sighed. "How will I ever repay you?"

"Certainly not with your services, I hope." She set the shopping bag on a countertop.

"I promise I would be very gentle."

"And I would be very naked and very dead, and I wouldn't give a damn how gentle you were. Are you hoping to get me drunk or did you run into a sale?"

"I neglected to ask what you were cooking," I explained. "I didn't know whether to bring red or white. To be on the safe side, I got two of each."

"Remind me to never tell you what I'm cooking, then. Goodness, Kay!" She set the bottles on the counter. "This looks marvelous. Do you want a glass now, or would you rather have something stronger?"

"Definitely something stronger."

"The usual?"

"Please." Looking at the large pot simmering on the stove, I added, "I hope that's what I think it is." Anna made fabulous chili.

"Should warm us up. I threw in a can of the green chilies and tomatoes you brought back last time you were in Miami. I've been hoarding them. There's sourdough bread in the oven, and coleslaw. How's your family, by the way?"

"Lucy has suddenly gotten interested in boys and cars but I won't take it seriously until she's more interested in them than in her computer," I said. "My sister has another children's book coming out next month, and she's still clueless about the child she's supposedly raising. As for my mother, other than her usual fussing and fuming about what's become of Miami, where no one speaks English anymore, she's fine."

"Did you make it down there for Christmas?"

"No."

"Has your mother forgiven you?"

"Not yet," I said.

"I can't say that I blame her. Families should be together at Christmas."

I did not reply.

"But this is good," she surprised me by saying. "You did not feel like going to Miami, so you didn't. I have told you all along that women need to learn to be selfish. So perhaps you are learning to be selfish?"

"I think selfishness has always come pretty easily to me, Anna."

"When you no longer feel guilty about it, I will know you are cured."

"I still feel guilty, so I suppose I'm not cured. You're right."

"Yes. I can tell."

I watched her uncork a bottle to let it breathe, the sleeves of a white cotton blouse rolled up to her elbows, forearms as firm and strong as those of a woman half her age. I did not know what Anna had looked like when she was young, but at almost seventy, she was an eye-catcher with strong Teutonic features, short white hair, and light blue eyes. Opening a cupboard, she reached for bottles and in no time was handing me a Scotch and soda and fixing herself a manhattan.

"What has happened since I saw you last, Kay?" We carried our drinks to the kitchen table. "That would have been before Thanksgiving? Of course, we have talked on the phone. Your worries about the book?"

"Yes, you know about Abby's book, at least know as much as I do. And you know about these cases. About Pat Harvey. All of it." I got out my cigarettes.

"I've been following it in the news. You're looking well. A little tired, though. Perhaps a little too thin?"

"One can never be too thin," I said.

"I've seen you look worse, that's my point. So you are handling the stress from your work."

"Some days better than others."

Anna sipped her manhattan and stared thoughtfully at the stove. "And Mark?"

"I've seen him," I said. "And we've been talking on the phone. He's still confused, uncertain. I suppose I am, too. So maybe nothing's new."

"You have seen him. That is new."

"I still love him."

"That isn't new."

"It's so difficult, Anna. Always has been. I don't know why I can't seem to let it go."

"Because the feelings are intense, but both of you are afraid of commitment. Both of you want excitement and want your own way. I noticed he was alluded to in the newspaper."

"I know."

"And?"

"I haven't told him."

"I shouldn't think you would need to. If he didn't see the paper himself, certainly someone from the Bureau has called him. If he's upset, you would hear, no?"

"You're right," I said, relieved. "I would hear."

"You at least have contact, then. You are happier?"

I was.

"You are hopeful?"

"I'm willing to see what will happen," I replied. "But I'm not sure it can work."

"No one can ever be sure of anything."

"That is a very sad truth," I said. "I can't be sure of anything. I know only what I feel."

"Then you are ahead of the pack."

"Whatever the pack is, if I am ahead of it, then that's another sad truth," I admitted.

She got up to take the bread out of the oven. I watched her fill earthenware bowls with chili, toss coleslaw, and pour the wine. Remembering the form I had brought, I got it out of my pocketbook and placed it on the table.

Anna did not even glance at it as she served us and sat down. She said, "Would you like to review her chart?"

I knew Anna well enough to be sure she would not record details of her counseling sessions. People like me have statutory rights to medical records, and these documents can also end up in court. People like Anna are too shrewd to put confidences in print.

"Why don't you summarize," I suggested.

"I diagnosed her as having an adjustment disorder," she said.

It was the equivalent of my saying that Jill's death was due to respiratory or cardiac arrest. Whether you are shot or run over by a train, you die because you stop breathing and your heart quits. The diagnosis of adjustment disorder was a catchall straight out of the *Diagnostic and Statistical Manual of Mental Disorders*. It qualified a patient for insurance coverage without divulging one scrap of useful information about his history or problems.

"The entire human race has an adjustment disorder," I said to Anna.

She smiled.

"I respect your professional ethics," I said. "And I have no intention of amending my own records by adding information that you consider confidential. But it's important for me to know anything about Jill that might give me insight into her murder. If there was something about her lifestyle, for example, that might have placed her at risk."

"I respect your professional ethics as well."

"Thank you. Now that we've established our mutual admiration for each other's fairness and integrity, might we push formalities aside and hold a conversation?"

"Of course, Kay," she said gently. "I remember Jill vividly. It is hard not to remember an unusual patient, especially one who is murdered."

"How was she special?"

"Special?" She smiled sadly. "A very bright, endearing young woman. So much in her favor. I used to look forward to her appointments. Had she not been my patient, I would have liked to know her as a friend."

"How long had she been seeing you?"

"Three to four times a month for more than a year."

"Why you, Anna?" I asked. "Why not someone in Williamsburg, someone closer to where she lived?"

"I have quite a number of patients from out of town. Some come from as far away as Philadelphia."

"Because they don't want anyone to know they are seeing a psychiatrist."

She nodded. "Unfortunately, many people are terrified by the prospect of others knowing. You would be surprised at the number of people who have been in this office and left by way of the back door."

I had never told a soul I was seeing a psychiatrist, and had Anna not refused to charge me, I would have paid for the sessions in cash. The last thing I needed was for someone in Employee Benefits to get hold of my insurance claims and spread gossip throughout the Department of Health and Human Services.

"Obviously, then, Jill did not want anyone to know she was seeing a psychiatrist," I said. "And this might also explain why she had her prescriptions for Librax filled in Richmond."

"Before you called, I did not know she filled the prescriptions in Richmond. But I'm not surprised." She reached for her wine.

The chili was spicy enough to bring tears to my eyes. But it was outstanding, Anna's best effort, and I told her so. Then I explained to her what she probably already suspected.

"It's possible Jill and her friend, Elizabeth Mott, were murdered by the same individual killing these couples," I said. "Or at least, there are some parallels between their homicides and the others that cause me concern."

"I'm not interested in what you know about the cases you are involved in now; unless you feel it necessary to tell me. So I'll let you ask me questions and I'll do my best to recall what I can about Jill's life."

"Why was she so worried about anyone knowing she was seeing a psychiatrist? What was she hiding?" I asked.

"Jill was from a prominent family in Kentucky, and their

approval and acceptance were very important to her. She went to the right schools, did well and was going to be a successful lawyer. Her family was very proud of her. They did not know."

"Know what? That she was seeing a psychiatrist?"

"They did not know that," Anna said. "More importantly, they did not know she was involved in a homosexual relationship."

"Elizabeth?" I knew the answer before I asked. The possibility had crossed my mind.

"Yes. Jill and Elizabeth became friends during Jill's first year in law school. Then they became lovers. The relationship was very intense, very difficult, rife with conflict. It was a first for both of them, or at least this was how it was presented to me by Jill. You must remember that I never met Elizabeth, never heard her side. Jill came to see me, initially, because she wanted to change. She did not want to be homosexual, was hoping therapy might redeem her heterosexuality."

"Did you see any hope for that?" I asked.

"I don't know what would have happened eventually," Anna said. "All I can tell you is that based on what Jill said to me, her bond with Elizabeth was quite strong. I got the impression that Elizabeth was more at peace with the relationship than Jill, who intellectually could not accept it but emotionally could not let it go."

"She must have been in agony."

"The last few times I saw Jill it had become more acute. She had just finished law school. Her future was before her. It was time to make decisions. She began suffering psycho-somatic problems. Spastic colitis. I prescribed Librax."

"Did Jill ever mention anything to you that might have given you a hint as to who might have done this to them?"

"I thought about that, studied the matter closely after it happened. When I read about it in the papers, I could not believe it. I had just seen Jill three days before. I can't tell you how hard I concentrated on everything she had ever said to me. I hoped I would recall something, any detail that might help. But I never have."

"Both of them hid their relationship from the world?"

"Yes."

"What about a boyfriend, someone Jill or Elizabeth dated from time to time? For appearances?"

"Neither dated, I was told. Not a jealousy situation, there-fore, unless there was something I did not know." She glanced at my empty bowl. "More chili?"

"I couldn't."

She got up to load the dishwasher. For a while we did not speak. Anna untied her apron and hung it on a hook inside the broom closet. Then we carried our glasses and the bottle of wine into her den.

It was my favorite room. Shelves of books filled two walls, a third centered by a bay window through which she could monitor from her cluttered desk flowers budding or snow falling over her small backyard. From that window I had watched magnolias bloom in a fanfare of lemony white, I had watched the last bright sparks of autumn fade. We had talked about my family, my divorce, and Mark. We had talked about suffering and we had talked about death. From the worn leather wing chair where I sat, I had awkwardly led Anna through my life, just as Jill Harrington had done.

They had been lovers. This linked them to the other murdered couples and made the "Mr. Goodbar" theory that much more implausible, and I pointed this out to Anna.

"I agree with you," she said.

"They were last seen in the Anchor Bar and Grill. Did Jill ever mention this place to you?"

"Not by name. But she mentioned a bar they occasionally went to, a place where they talked. Sometimes they went to out-of-the-way restaurants where people would not know them. Sometimes they went on drives. Generally, these excursions occurred when they were in the midst of emotionally charged discussions about their relationship."

"If they were having one of these discussions that Friday night at the Anchor, they were probably upset, one or the other possibly feeling rejected, angry," I said. "Is it possible either Jill or Elizabeth might have gone through the motions of picking up a man, flirting, to jerk the other around?"

"I can't say that's impossible," Anna said. "But it would surprise me a great deal. I never got the impression that Jill or Elizabeth played games with each other. I'm more inclined to suspect that when they were talking that night, the conversation was very intense and they were probably unaware of their surroundings, focused only on each other."

"Anyone observing them might have overheard."

"That is the risk if one has personal discussions in public, and I had mentioned this to Jill."

"If she were so paranoid about anyone suspecting, then why did she take the risk?"

"Her resolve was not strong, Kay." Anna reached for her wine. "When she and Elizabeth were alone, it was too easy to slip back into intimacy. Hugging, comforting, crying, and no decisions were made."

That sounded familiar. When Mark and I had discussions either at his place or mine, inevitably we ended up in bed. Afterward, one of us would leave, and the problems were still there.

"Anna, did you ever consider that their relationship might have been connected to what happened to them?" I asked.

"If anything, their relationship made it seem all the more unusual. I should think that a woman alone in a bar looking to be picked up is in much greater danger than two women together who are not interested in drawing attention to themselves."

"Let's return to the subject of their habits and routines," I said.

"They lived in the same apartment complex but did not live together, and again, this was for the sake of appearances. But it was convenient. They could lead their separate lives, and then get together late at night at Jill's apartment. Jill preferred to be in her own place. I remember her telling me that if her family or other people repeatedly tried to call her late at night and she was never home, there would have been questions." She paused, thinking. "Jill and Elizabeth also exercised, were very fit. Running, I think, but they didn't always do this together."

"Where did they run?"

"I believe there was a park near where they lived."

"Anything else? Theaters, shops, malls they may have frequented?"

"Nothing comes to mind."

"What does your intuition tell you? What did it tell you at the time?"

"I felt that Jill and Elizabeth were having a stressful conversation in the bar. They probably wanted to be left alone and would have resented an intrusion."

"Then what?"

"Clearly they encountered their killer at some point that evening."

"Can you imagine how that might have happened?"

"It has always been my opinion it was someone they knew, or at least were well enough acquainted with so that they had no reason not to trust him. Unless they were abducted at gunpoint by one or more persons, either in the bar's parking lot or somewhere else they might have gone."

"What if a stranger had approached them in the bar's parking lot, asked them for a lift somewhere, claimed to have car trouble . . . ?"

She was already shaking her head. "It is inconsistent with my impressions of them. Again, unless it was someone with whom they were acquainted."

"And if the killer was impersonating a police officer, perhaps pulled them over for a routine traffic stop?"

"That's another matter. I suppose even you and I might be vulnerable to that."

Anna was looking tired, so I thanked her for dinner and her time. I knew our conversation was difficult for her. I wondered how I would feel were I in her position.

Minutes after I walked through my front door, the phone rang.

"One last thing that I remember but probably does not matter," Anna said. "Jill mentioned something about the two of them working crossword puzzles when they wanted to stay in, just the two of them, on Sunday mornings, for example. Insignificant, perhaps. But a routine, something they did together."

"A book of puzzles? Or the ones in the newspapers?"

"I don't know. But Jill did read a variety of newspapers, Kay. She usually had something with her to read while waiting for her appointment. The *Wall Street Journal*, the *Washington Post*."

I thanked her again and said next time it was my turn to cook. Then I called Marino.

"Two women were murdered in James City County eight years ago," I went straight to the point. "It's possible there's a connection. Do you know Detective Montana out there?"

"Yeah. I've met him."

"We need to get with him, review the cases. Can he keep his mouth shut?"

"Hell if I know," Marino said.

Montana looked like his name, big, rawboned, with hazy blue eyes set in a rugged, honest face topped by thick gray hair. His accent was that of a native Virginian, his conversation peppered with "yes, ma'am"s. The following afternoon he, Marino, and I met at my home, where we were ensured privacy and no interruptions.

Montana must have depleted his annual film budget on Jill and Elizabeth's case, for covering my kitchen table were photographs of their bodies at the scene, the Volkswagen abandoned at the Palm Leaf Motel, the Anchor Bar and Grill, and, remarkably, of every room inside the women's apartments, including pantries and closets. He had a brief-case bulging with notes, maps, interview transcriptions, diagrams, evidence inventories, logs of telephone tips. There is something to be said for detectives who rarely have homicides in their jurisdictions. Cases like these come along once or twice in their careers, and they work them meticulously.

"The cemetery is right next to the church." He moved a photograph closer to me.

"It looks quite old," I said, admiring weathered brick and slate.

"It is and it isn't. Was built in the seventeen-hundreds, did all right until maybe twenty years ago, when bad wiring did it in. I remember seeing the smoke, was on patrol, thought one of my neighbor's farmhouses was burning. Some historical society took an interest. It's supposed to look just like it used to inside and out.

"You get to it by this secondary road right here"—he tapped another photograph—"which is less than two miles west of Route Sixty and about four miles west of the

Anchor Bar, where the girls were last seen alive the night before."

"Who discovered the bodies?" Marino asked, eyes roaming the photograph spread.

"A custodian who worked for the church. He came in Saturday morning to clean up, get things ready for Sunday. Says he had just pulled in when he spotted what looked like two people sleeping in the grass about twenty feet inside the cemetery's front gate. The bodies were visible from the church parking lot. Doesn't seem whoever did it was concerned about anybody finding them."

"Am I to assume there was no activity at the church that Friday night?" I asked.

"No, ma'am. It was locked up tight, nothing going on."

"Does the church ever have activities scheduled for Friday nights?"

"They do on occasion. Sometimes the youth groups get together on Friday nights. Sometimes there's choir practice, things like that. The point is, if you selected this cemetery in advance to kill someone, it wouldn't make a whole lot of sense. There's no guarantee the church would be deserted, not on any night of the week. That's one of the reasons I figured from the start that the murders were random, the girls just met up with someone, maybe in the bar. There isn't much about these cases to make me think the homicides were carefully planned."

"The killer was armed," I reminded Montana. "He had a knife and a handgun."

"The world's full of folks carrying knives, guns in their cars or even on their person," he said matter-of-factly.

I collected the photographs of the bodies in situ and began to study them carefully.

The women were less than a yard from each other, lying in the grass between two tilting granite headstones. Elizabeth was face down, legs slightly spread, left arm under her stomach, right arm straight and by her side. Slender, with short brown hair, she was dressed in jeans and a white pullover sweater stained dark red around the neck. In another photograph, her body had been turned over, the front of her sweater soaked with blood, eyes the dull stare of the dead. The cut to her throat was shallow, the gunshot wound to her neck not immediately incapacitating, I recalled from her autopsy report. It was the stab wound to her chest that had been lethal.

Jill's injuries had been much more mutilating. She was on her back, face so streaked by dried blood that I could not tell what she had looked like in life, except that she had short black hair and a straight, pretty nose. Like her companion, she was slender. She was dressed in jeans and a pale yellow cotton shirt, bloody, untucked, and ripped open to her waist, exposing multiple stab wounds, several of which had gone through her brassiere. There were deep cuts to her forearms and hands. The cut to her neck was shallow and probably inflicted when she was already dead or almost dead.

The photographs were invaluable for one critical reason. They revealed something that I had not been able to determine from any of the newspaper clippings or reports I had reviewed in their cases on file in my office.

I glanced at Marino and our eyes met.

I turned to Montana. "What happened to their shoes?"

14

"You know, it's interesting you should mention that," Montana replied. "I never have come up with a good explanation for why the girls took their shoes off, unless they were inside the motel, got dressed when it was time to leave, and didn't bother. We found their shoes and socks inside the Volkswagen."

"Was it warm that night?" Marino asked.

"It was. All the same, I would have expected them to put their shoes back on when they got dressed."

"We don't know for a fact they ever went inside a motel room," I reminded Montana.

"You're right about that," he agreed.

I wondered if Montana had read the series in the *Post*, which had mentioned that shoes and socks were missing in the other murder cases. If he had, it did not seem he had made the connection yet.

"Did you have much contact with the reporter Abby

Turnbull when she was covering Jill's and Elizabeth's murders?" I asked him.

"The woman followed me like tin cans tied to a dog's tail. Everywhere I went, there she was."

"Do you recall if you told her that Jill and Elizabeth were barefoot? Did you ever show Abby the scene photographs?" I asked, for Abby was too smart to have forgotten a detail like that, especially since it was so important now.

Montana said without pause, "I talked to her, but no, ma'am. I never did show her these pictures. Was right careful what I said, too. You read what was in the papers, didn't you?"

"I've seen some of the articles."

"Nothing in there about the way the girls were dressed, about Jill's shirt being torn, their shoes and socks off."

So Abby didn't know, I thought, relieved.

"I notice from the autopsy photographs that both women had ligature marks around their wrists," I said. "Did you recover whatever might have been used to bind them?"

"No, ma'am."

"Then apparently he removed the ligatures after killing them," I said.

"He was right careful. We didn't find any cartridge cases, no weapon, nothing he might have used to tie them up. No seminal fluid. So it doesn't appear he got around to raping them, or if he did, no way to tell. And both were fully clothed. Now, as far as this girl's blouse being ripped"—he reached for a photograph of Jill—"that might have happened when he was struggling with her."

"Did you recover any buttons at the scene?"

"Several. In the grass near her body."

"What about cigarette butts?"

Montana began calmly looking through his paperwork. "No cigarette butts." He paused, pulling out a report. "Tell you what we did find, though. A lighter, a nice silver one."

"Where?" Marino asked.

"Maybe fifteen feet from where the bodies were. As you can see, an iron fence surrounds the cemetery. You enter through this gate." He was showing us another photograph. "The lighter was in the grass, five, six feet inside the gate. One of these expensive, slim lighters shaped like an ink pen, the kind people use to light pipes."

"Was it in working order?" Marino asked.

"Worked just fine, polished up real nice," Montana recalled. "I'm pretty sure it didn't belong to either of the girls. They didn't smoke, and no one I talked to remembered seeing either one of them with a lighter like that. Maybe it fell out of the killer's pocket, no way to know. Could have been anybody who lost it, maybe someone out there a day or two earlier sightseeing. You know how folks like to wander in old cemeteries looking at the graves."

"Was this lighter checked for prints?" Marino asked.

"The surface wasn't good for that. The silver's engraved with these crisscrosses, like you see with some of these fancy silver fountain pens." He stared off thoughtfully. "The thing probably cost a hundred bucks."

"Do you still have the lighter and the buttons you found out there?" I asked.

"I've got all the evidence from these cases. Always hoped we might solve them someday."

Montana didn't hope it half as much as I did, and it wasn't until after he left some time later that Marino and I began to discuss what was really on our minds.

"It's the same damn bastard," Marino said, his expression incredulous. "The damn squirrel made them take their shoes off just like he done with the other couples. To slow them down when he led them off to wherever it was he planned to kill them."

"Which wasn't the cemetery," I said. "I don't believe that was the spot he had selected."

"Yo. I think he took on more than he could handle with those two. They weren't cooperating or something went down that freaked him out—maybe having to do with the blood in the back of the Volkswagen. So he made them pull over at the earliest opportunity, which just happened to be a dark, deserted church with a cemetery. You got a map of Virginia handy?"

I went back to my office and found one. Marino spread it open on the kitchen table and studied it for a long moment.

"Take a look," he said, his face intense. "The turnoff for the church is right here on Route Sixty, about two miles before you get to the road leading to the wooded area where Jim Freeman and Bonnie Smyth were killed five, six years later. I'm saying we drove right past the damn road leading to the church where the two women was whacked when we went to see Mr. Joyce the other day."

"Good God," I muttered. "I wonder—"

"Yeah, I'm wondering, too," Marino interrupted. "Maybe the squirrel *was* out there casing the woods, selecting the right spot when Dammit surprised him. He shoots the dog. About a month later, he's abducted his first set of victims, Jill and Elizabeth. He intends to force them to drive him to this wooded area, but things get out of control. He ends the trip early. Or maybe he's confused, rattled, and tells Jill or Elizabeth the wrong road to turn off on. Next thing, he sees this church and now he's really freaked, realizes they didn't turn where they were supposed to. He may not have even known where the hell they were."

I tried to envision it. One of the women was driving and the other was in the front passenger's seat, the killer in the back holding a gun on them. What had happened to cause him to lose so much blood? Had he accidentally shot himself? That was highly unlikely. Had he cut himself with his knife? Maybe, but again, it was hard for me to imagine. The blood inside the car, I had noted from Montana's photographs, seemed to begin with drips on the back of the passenger's headrest. There were also drips on the back of the seat with a lot of blood on the floor mat. This placed the killer directly behind the passenger's seat, leaning forward. Was his head or face bleeding?

A *nosebleed*?

I proposed this to Marino.

"Must've been one hell of a one. There was a lot of blood." He thought for a moment. "So maybe one of the women threw back an elbow and hit him in the nose."

"How would you have responded if one of the women had done that to you?" I said. "Provided you were a killer."

"She wouldn't have done it again. I probably wouldn't have shot her inside the car, but I might have punched her, hit her in the head with the gun."

"There was no blood in the front seat," I reminded him. "Absolutely no evidence that either of the women was injured inside the car."

"Hmmmm."

"Perplexing, isn't it?"

"Yeah." He frowned. "He's in the backseat, leaning forward, and suddenly starts bleeding? Perplexing as shit."

I put on a fresh pot of coffee while we began to toss around more ideas. For starters, there continued to be the problem of how one individual subdues two people.

"The car belonged to Elizabeth," I said. "Let's assume she was driving. Obviously, her hands were not tied at this point."

"But Jill's might have been. He might have tied her hands during the drive, made her hold them up behind her head so he could tie them from the backseat."

"Or he could have forced her to turn around and place her arms over the headrest," I proposed. "This might have been when she struck him in the face, if that's what happened."

"Maybe."

"In any event," I went on, "we'll assume that by the time they stopped the car, Jill was already bound and barefoot. Next he orders Elizabeth to remove her shoes and binds her. Then he forces them at gunpoint into the cemetery."

"Jill had a lot of cuts on her hands and forearms," Marino said. "Are they consistent with her warding off a knife with her hands tied?"

305

"As long as her hands were tied in front of her and not behind her back."

"It would have been smarter to tie their hands behind their backs."

"He probably found that out the hard way and improved his techniques," I said.

"Elizabeth didn't have any defense injuries?"

"None."

"The squirrel killed Elizabeth first," Marino decided.

"How would you have done it? Remember, you've got two hostages to handle."

"I would have made both of them lie face down in the grass. I would have put the gun to the back of Elizabeth's head to make her behave as I get ready to use the knife on her. If she surprised me by resisting, I might have pulled the trigger, shot her when I wasn't really intending to."

"That might explain why she was shot in the neck," I said. "If he had the gun to the back of her head and she resisted, the muzzle may have slipped. The scenario is reminiscent of what happened to Deborah Harvey, except that I seriously doubt she was lying down when she was shot."

"This guy likes to use a blade," Marino replied. "He uses his gun when things don't go down the way he planned. And so far, that's only happened twice that we know of. With Elizabeth and Deborah."

"Elizabeth was shot, then what, Marino?"

"He finishes her off and takes care of Jill."

"He fought with Jill," I reminded him.

"You can bet she struggled. Her friend's just been killed.

Jill knows she don't got a chance, may as well fight like hell."

"Or else she was already fighting with him," I ventured.

Marino's eyes narrowed the way they did when he was skeptical.

Jill was a lawyer. I doubted she was naive about the cruel deeds people perpetrate upon one another. When she and her friend were being forced into the cemetery late at night, I suspected Jill knew both of them were going to die. One or both women may have begun resisting as he opened the iron gate. If the silver lighter did belong to the killer, it may have fallen out of his pocket at this point. Then, and perhaps Marino was right, the killer forced both women to lie face down, but when he started on Elizabeth, Jill panicked, tried to protect her friend. The gun discharged, shooting Elizabeth in the neck.

"The pattern of Jill's injuries sends a message of frenzy, someone who is angry, frightened, because he's lost control," I said. "He may have hit her in the head with the gun, gotten on top of her and ripped open her shirt and started stabbing. As a parting gesture, he cuts their throats. Then he leaves in the Volkswagen, ditches it at the motel, and heads out on foot, perhaps back to wherever his car was."

"He should have blood on him," Marino considered. "Interesting there wasn't any blood found in the driver's area, only in the backseat."

"There hasn't been any blood found in the driver's areas of any of the couples' vehicles," I said. "This killer is very careful. He may bring a change of clothing, towels, who knows what, when he's planning to commit his murders."

Marino dug into his pocket and produced his Swiss army knife. He began to trim his fingernails over a napkin. Lord knows what Doris had put up with all these years, I thought. Marino probably never bothered to empty an ashtray, place a dish in the sink, or pick his dirty clothes off the floor. I hated to think what the bathroom looked like after he had been in it.

"Abby *Turncoat* still trying to get hold of you?" he asked without looking up.

"I wish you wouldn't call her that."

He didn't respond.

"She hasn't tried in the last few days, at least not that I'm aware of."

"Thought you might be interested in knowing that she and Clifford Ring have more than a professional relationship, Doc."

"What do you mean?" I asked uneasily.

"I mean that this story about the couples Abby's been working on has nothing to do with why she was taken off the police beat." He was working on his left thumb, fingernail shavings falling on the napkin. "Apparently, she was getting so squirrelly no one in the newsroom could deal with her anymore. Things reached a head last fall, right before she came to Richmond and saw you."

"What happened?" I asked, staring hard at him.

"Way I heard it, she made a little scene right in the middle of the newsroom. Dumped a cup of coffee in Ring's lap and then stormed out, didn't tell her editors where the hell she was going or when she'd be back. That's when she got reassigned to features."

"Who told you this?"

"Benton."

"How would Benton know what goes on in the *Post*'s newsroom? "

"I didn't ask." Marino folded the knife and slipped it back into his pocket. Getting up, he wadded the napkin and put it in the trash.

"One last thing," he said, standing in the middle of my kitchen. "That Lincoln you was interested in?"

"Yes?"

"A 1990 Mark Seven. Registered to a Barry Aranoff, thirty-eight-year-old white male from Roanoke. Works for a medical supply company, a salesman. On the road a lot."

"Then you talked to him," I said.

"Talked to his wife. He's out of town and has been for the past two weeks."

"Where was he supposed to have been when I saw the car in Williamsburg?"

"His wife said she wasn't sure of his schedule. Seems he sometimes hits a different city every day, buzzes all over the place, including out of state. His territory goes as far north as Boston. As best she could remember, around the time you're talking about, he was in Tidewater, then was flying out of Newport News, heading to Massachusetts."

I fell silent, and Marino interpreted this as embarrassment, which it wasn't. I was thinking.

"Hey, what you done was good detective work. Nothing wrong with writing down a plate number and checking it out. Should make you happy you wasn't being followed by some spook."

I did not respond.

He added, "Only thing you missed was the color. You said the Lincoln was dark gray. Aranoff's ride is brown."

Later that night lightning flashed high over thrashing trees as a storm worthy of summer unloaded its violent arsenal. I sat up in bed, browsing through several journals as I waited for Captain Montana's telephone line to clear.

Either his phone was out of order or someone had been on it for the past two hours. After he and Marino had left, I had recalled a detail from one of the photographs that reminded me of what Anna had said to me last. Inside Jill's apartment, on the carpet beside a La-Z-Boy chair in the living room, was a stack of legal briefs, several out-of-town newspapers, and a copy of the *New York Times Magazine*. I have never bothered with crossword puzzles. God knows I have too many other things to figure out. But I knew the *Times* crossword puzzle was as popular as manufacturers' coupons.

Reaching for the phone, I tried Montana's home number again. This time I was rewarded.

"Have you ever considered getting Call Waiting?" I asked good-naturedly.

"I've considered getting my teenage daughter her own switchboard," he said.

"I've got a question."

"Ask away."

"When you went through Jill's and Elizabeth's apartments, I'm assuming you went through their mail."

"Yes, ma'am. Checked out their mail for quite a while, seeing what all came in, seeing who wrote them letters, went through their charge card bills, that sort of thing."

"What can you tell me about Jill's subscriptions to newspapers that were delivered by mail?"

He paused.

It occurred to me. "I'm sorry. Their cases would be in your office . . ."

"No, ma'am. I came straight home, have 'em right here. I was just trying to think, it's been a long day. Can you hold on?"

I heard pages turning.

"Well, there were a couple of bills, junk mail. But no newspapers."

Surprised, I explained Jill had several out-of-town newspapers in her apartment. "She had to have gotten them from somewhere."

"Maybe vending machines," he offered. "Lots of them around the college. That would be my guess."

The *Washington Post* or the *Wall Street Journal*, maybe, I thought. But not the Sunday *New York Times*. Most likely that had come from a drugstore or a newsstand where Jill and Elizabeth may routinely have stopped when they went out for breakfast on Sunday mornings. I thanked him and hung up.

Switching off the lamp, I got in bed, listening as rain drummed the roof in a relentless rhythm. I pulled the covers more tightly around me. Thoughts and images drifted, and I envisioned Deborah Harvey's red purse, damp and covered with dirt.

Vander, in the fingerprints lab, had finished examining it and I had looked over the report the other day.

"What are you going to do?" Rose was asking me. Oddly, the purse was in a plastic tray on Rose's desk. "You can't send it back to her family like that."

"Of course not."

"Maybe we could just take out the charge cards and things, wash them off and send those?" Rose's face twisted in anger. She shoved the tray across her desk and screamed, "Get it out of here! I can't stand it!"

Suddenly I was in my kitchen. Through the window I saw Mark drive up, only the car was unfamiliar, but I recognized it somehow. Rummaging in my pocketbook for a brush, I frantically fixed my hair. I started to run to the bathroom to brush my teeth, but there wasn't time. The doorbell rang, just once.

He took me in his arms, whispering my name, like a small cry of pain. I wondered why he was here, why he was not in Denver.

He kissed me as he pushed the door with his foot. It slammed shut with a tremendous bang.

My eyelids flew open. Thunder cracked. Lightning lit up my bedroom again and then again as my heart pounded.

The next morning I performed two autopsies, then went upstairs to see Neils Vander, section chief of the fingerprints examination lab. I found him inside the Automated Fingerprint Identification System computer room, deep in thought in front of a monitor. In hand was my copy of the report detailing the examination of Deborah Harvey's purse, and I placed it on top of his keyboard.

"I need to ask you something." I raised my voice over the computer's pervasive hum.

He glanced down at the report with preoccupied eyes, unruly gray hair wisping over his ears.

"How did you find anything after the purse had been in the woods so long? I'm amazed."

He returned his gaze to the monitor. "The purse is nylon, waterproof, and the credit cards were protected inside plastic windows, which were inside a zipped-up compartment. When I put the cards in the superglue tank, a lot of smudges and partials popped up. I didn't even need the laser."

"Pretty impressive."

He smiled a little.

"But nothing identifiable," I pointed out.

"Sorry about that."

"What interests me is the driver's license. Nothing popped up on it."

"Not even a smudge," he said.

"Clean?"

"As a hound's tooth."

"Thank you, Neils."

He was off somewhere again, gone in his land of loops and whorls.

I went back downstairs and looked up the number for the 7-Eleven Abby and I had visited last fall. I was told that Ellen Jordan, the clerk we had talked to, would not be in until nine P.M. I mowed through the rest of the day without stopping for lunch, unaware of the passing hours. I wasn't the slightest bit tired when I got home.

I was loading the dishwasher when the doorbell rang at eight P.M. Drying my hands on a towel, I walked anxiously to the front door.

Abby Turnbull was standing on the porch, coat collar turned up around her ears, face wan, eyes miserable. A cold wind rocked dark trees in my yard and lifted strands of her hair.

"You didn't answer my calls. I hope you won't refuse me entrance into your house," she said.

"Of course not, Abby. Please." I opened the door wide and stepped back.

She did not take off her coat until I invited her to do so, and when I offered to hang it up, she shook her head and draped it over the back of a chair, as if to reassure me that she did not intend to stay very long. She was dressed in faded denim jeans and a heavy-knit maroon sweater flecked with lint. Brushing past her to clear paperwork and newspapers off the kitchen table, I detected the stale odor of cigarette smoke and a pungent hint of sweat.

"Something to drink?" I asked, and for some reason I could not feel angry with her.

"Whatever you're having would be fine." She got out her cigarettes while I fixed both of us a drink.

"It's hard to start," she said when I was seated. "The articles were unfair to you, to say the least. And I know what you must be thinking."

314

"It's irrelevant what I'm thinking. I'd rather hear what's on your mind."

"I told you I've made mistakes." Her voice trembled slightly. "Cliff Ring was one of them."

I sat quietly.

"He's an investigative reporter, one of the first people I got to know after moving to Washington. Very successful exciting. Bright and sure of himself. I was vulnerable, having just moved to a new city, having been through . . . well, what happened to Henna." She glanced away from me.

"We started out as friends, then everything went too fast. I didn't see what he was like because I didn't want to see it." Her voice caught and I waited in silence while she steadied herself.

"I trusted him with my life, Kay."

"From which I am to conclude that the details in his story came from you," I said.

"No. They came from my reporting."

"What does that mean?"

"I don't talk to anybody about what I'm writing," Abby said. "Cliff was aware of my involvement in these cases, but I never went into detail about them. He never seemed all that interested." She was beginning to sound angry. "But he was, more than a little. That's the way he operates."

"If you didn't go into detail with him," I said, "then how did he get the information from you?"

"I used to give him keys to my building, my apartment, when I'd go out of town so he could water my plants, bring the mail in. He could have had copies made."

Our conversation at the Mayflower came back to me. When Abby had talked about someone breaking into her computer and had gone on to accuse the FBI or CIA, I had been skeptical. Would an experienced agent open a word-processing file and not realize that the time and date might be changed? Not likely.

"Cliff Ring went into your computer?"

"I can't prove it, but I know he did," Abby said. "I can't prove he's been going through my mail but I know he has. It's no big deal to steam open a letter, reseal it, and then place it back in the box. Not if you've made a copy of the mailbox key."

"Were you aware he was writing the story?"

"Of course not. I didn't know a damn thing about it until I opened the Sunday paper! He'd let himself into my apartment when he knew I wouldn't be there. He was going through my computer, anything he could find. Then he followed up by calling people, getting quotes and information, which was pretty easy, since he knew exactly where to look and what he was looking for."

"Easy because you had been relieved of your police beat. When you thought the *Post* had backed off from the story, what your editors had really backed away from was you."

Abby nodded angrily. "The story was passed into what they viewed as more reliable hands. Clifford Ring's hands," she said.

I realized why Clifford Ring had made no effort to contact me. He would know that Abby and I were friends. Had he asked me for details about the cases, I might have said something to Abby, and he had wanted to keep Abby in the dark about what he was doing for as long as possible. So Ring had avoided me, gone around me.

"I'm sure he . . ." Abby cleared her throat and reached for her drink. Her hand shook. "He can be very convincing. He'll probably win a prize. For the series."

"I'm sorry, Abby."

"It's nobody's fault but my own. I was stupid."

"We take risks when we allow ourselves to love—"

"I'll never take a risk like that again," she cut me off. "It was always a problem with him, one problem after another. I was always the one making concessions, giving him a second chance, then a third and a fourth."

"Did the people you work with know about you and Cliff?"

"We were careful," She got evasive.

"Why?"

"The newsroom is a very incestuous, gossipy place."

"Certainly your colleagues must have seen the two of you together."

"We were very careful," she repeated.

"People must have sensed something between you. Tension, if nothing else."

"Competition. Guarding my turf. That's what he would say if asked."

And jealousy, I thought. Abby never had been good at hiding her emotions. I could imagine her jealous rages. I could imagine those observing her in the newsroom misconstruing, assuming she was ambitious and jealous of Clifford Ring, when that was not the case. She was jealous of his other commitments.

"He's married, isn't he, Abby?"

She could not stop the tears this time.

I got up to refresh our drinks. She would tell me he was unhappy with his wife, contemplating divorce, and Abby had believed he would leave it all for her. The story was as threadbare and predictable as something in Ann Landers. I had heard it a hundred times before. Abby had been used.

I set her drink on the table and gently squeezed her shoulder before I moved back to my chair.

She told me what I expected to hear, and I just looked at her sadly.

"I don't deserve your sympathy," she cried.

"You've been hurt much more than I have."

"Everybody has been hurt. You. Pat Harvey. The parents, friends of these kids. If the cases hadn't happened, I'd still be working cops. At least I'd be all right professionally. No one person should have the power to cause such destruction."

I realized she was no longer thinking about Clifford Ring. She was thinking of the killer.

"You're right. No one should have the power. And no one will if we don't allow it."

"Deborah and Fred didn't allow it. Jill, Elizabeth, Jim, Bonnie. All of them." She looked defeated. "They didn't want to be murdered."

"What will Cliff do next?" I asked.

"Whatever it is, it won't involve me. I've changed all my locks."

"And your fears that your phones are bugged, that you're being followed?"

"Cliff's not the only one who wants to know what I'm

doing. I can't trust anyone anymore!" Her eyes filled with angry tears. "You were the last person I wanted to hurt, Kay."

"Stop it, Abby. You can cry all year and it won't do me any good."

"I'm sorry . . ."

"No more apologies." I was very firm but gentle.

She bit her bottom lip and stared at her drink.

"Are you ready to help me now?"

She looked up at me.

"First, what color was the Lincoln we saw in Williamsburg last week?"

"Dark gray, the interior leather dark, maybe black," she said, her eyes coming alive.

"Thank you. That's what I thought."

"What's going on?"

"I'm not sure. But there's more."

"More what?"

"I've got an *assignment* for you," I said, smiling. "But first, when are you returning to D.C.? Tonight?"

"I don't know, Kay." She stared off. "I can't be there now."

Abby felt like a fugitive, and in a sense she was. Clifford Ring had run her out of Washington. It probably wasn't a bad idea for her to disappear for a while.

She explained, "There's a bed and breakfast in the Northern Neck, and—"

"And I have a guest room," I interrupted. "You can stay with me for a while."

She looked uncertain, then confessed, "Kay, do you have any idea how that would look?"

"Frankly, I don't care at the moment."

"Why not?" She studied me closely.

"Your paper has already fried me in deep fat. I'm going for broke. Things will either get worse or better, but they won't stay the same."

"At least you haven't been fired."

"Neither have you, Abby. You had an affair and acted inappropriately in front of your colleagues when you dumped coffee in your lover's lap."

"He deserved it."

"I'm quite sure he did. But I wouldn't advise your doing battle with the *Post*. Your book is your chance to redeem yourself."

"What about you?"

"My concern is these cases. You can help because you can do things I can't do."

"Such as?"

"I can't lie, hoodwink, finagle, cheat, badger, sneak, snipe, snoop, and pretend to be something or somebody I'm not because I'm an officer of the Commonwealth. But you have great range of motion. You're a reporter."

"Thanks a lot," she protested as she walked out of the kitchen. "I'll get my things from the car."

It was not very often I had houseguests, and the bedroom downstairs was usually reserved for Lucy's visits. Covering the hardwood floor was an Iranian Dergezine rug with a brightly colored floral design that turned the entire room into a garden, in the midst of which my niece had been a rosebud or a stinkweed, depending on her behavior.

"I guess you like flowers," Abby said absently, laying the suit bag on top of the bed.

"The rug is a little overpowering in here," I apologized. "But when I saw it I had to buy it, and there was no place else to put it. Not to mention, it's virtually indestructible, and since this is where Lucy stays, that point is important."

"Or at least it used to be." Abby went to the closet and opened the door. "Lucy's not ten years old anymore."

"There should be plenty of hangers in there." I moved closer to inspect. "If you need more . . ."

"This is fine."

"There are towels, toothpaste, soap in the bath." I started to show her.

She had begun unpacking and wasn't paying any attention. I sat down on the edge of the bed.

Abby carried suits and blouses into the closet. Coat hangers screeched along the metal bar. I watched her in silence, experiencing a prick of impatience.

This went on for several minutes, drawers sliding, more coat hangers screeching, the medicine cabinet in the bathroom wheezing open and clicking shut. She pushed her suit bag inside the closet and glanced around, as if trying to figure out what to do next. Opening her briefcase, she pulled out a novel and a notebook, which she placed on the table by the bed. I watched uneasily as she then tucked a .38 and boxes of cartridges into the drawer.

*

It was midnight when I finally went upstairs. Before settling into bed, I dialed the number for the 7-Eleven again.

"Ellen Jordan?"

"Yeah? That's me. Who's this?"

I told her, explaining, "You mentioned to me last fall that when Fred Cheney and Deborah Harvey came in, Deborah tried to buy beer, and you carded her."

"Yeah, that's right."

"Can you tell me exactly what you did when you carded her?"

"I just said I needed to see her driver's license," Ellen said, and she sounded puzzled. "You know, I asked to see it."

"Did she get it out of her purse?"

"Sure. She had to get it out so I could look at it."

"She handed it to you, then," I said.

"Uh-huh."

"Was it inside anything? Inside a plastic window?"

"It wasn't in nothing," she said. "She just handed it over and I looked at it, then I gave it back to her." A pause. "Why?"

"I'm trying to determine if you touched Deborah Harvey's driver's license."

"Sure I did. I had to touch it to look at it." She sounded frightened. "I'm not in trouble or anything, am I?"

"No, Ellen," I replied reassuringly. "You're not in any trouble at all."

15

Abby's assignment was to see what she could find out about Barry Aranoff, and she left for Roanoke in the morning. The following evening, she returned just minutes before Marino appeared at my front door. I had invited him to dinner.

When he discovered Abby in the kitchen, his pupils contracted. His face turned red.

"Jack Black?" I inquired.

I returned from the bar to find Abby smoking at the table while Marino stood before the window. He had cracked the blinds and was staring sullenly out at the feeder.

"You won't see any birds at this hour, unless you're interested in bats," I said.

He did not reply or turn around.

I began to serve the salad. It wasn't until I was pouring Chianti that Marino finally took his chair.

"You didn't tell me you had company," he said.

"If I had told you, you wouldn't have come," I replied just as bluntly.

"She didn't tell me either," Abby said, testily. "So now that it's been established that we're all happy to be together, let's enjoy dinner."

If I had learned nothing else from my failed marriage to Tony, it was never to engage in confrontations if it's late at night or time to eat. I did the best I could to fill the silence with light conversation. I waited until coffee was served before speaking my mind.

"Abby's going to be staying with me for a while," I said to Marino.

"It's your business." He reached for the sugar.

"It's your business, too. We're all in this together."

"Maybe you ought to explain what it is we're all into, Doc. But first"—he looked at Abby—"I'd like to know where this little dinner scene is going to show up in your book. Then I won't have to read the whole damn thing. I can just turn to the right page."

"You know, Marino, you really can be a jerk," Abby said.

"I can be an asshole, too. You ain't had that pleasure yet."

"Thank you for giving me something to look forward to."

Snatching a pen out of his breast pocket, he tossed it across the table. "Better start writing. Wouldn't want you to quote me wrong."

Abby glared at him.

"Stop it," I said angrily.

They looked at me.

"You're acting no better than the rest of them," I added.

"Who?" Marino's face was blank.

"Everybody," I said. "I'm sick to death of lies, jealousy, power plays. I expect more of my friends. I thought you were my friends."

I pushed back my chair.

"If the two of you wish to continue taking potshots at each other, go ahead. But I've had enough."

Without looking at either of them, I carried my coffee into the living room, turned on the stereo, and closed my eyes. Music was my therapy, and I had been listening to Bach last. His Sinfonia Two, Cantata No. 29 began mid-flight, and I began to relax. For weeks after Mark left, I would come downstairs when I couldn't sleep, put the headphones on, and surround myself with Beethoven, Mozart, Pachelbel.

Abby and Marino had the sheepish expressions of a squabbling couple that have just made up when they joined me fifteen minutes later.

"Uh, we've been talking," Abby said as I turned off the stereo. "I explained things as best I could. We've begun to reach a level of understanding."

I was delighted to hear it.

"May as well pitch in, the three of us," Marino said. "What the hell. Abby ain't really a reporter right now, anyway."

The remark stung her a little, I could tell, but they were going to cooperate, miracle of miracles.

"By the time her book comes out, this will probably be

over with. That's what matters, that it's over with. It's been almost three years now, ten kids. You include Jill and Elizabeth, we're talking twelve." He shook his head, his eyes getting hard. "Whoever's whacking these kids ain't going to retire, Doc. He'll keep on until he gets nailed. And in investigations like this, that usually happens because someone gets lucky."

"We may already have gotten lucky," Abby said to him. "Aranoff's not the man who was driving the Lincoln."

"You sure?" Marino asked.

"Positive. Aranoff's got gray hair, what little hair he has left. He's maybe five-foot-eight and must weigh two hundred pounds."

"You telling me you met him?"

"No," she said. "He was still out of town. I knocked on the door and his wife let me in. I was wearing work pants, boots. I told her I was with the power company and needed to check their meter. We got to chatting. She offered me a Coke. While I was inside, I looked around, saw a family photograph, asked her about the photo to be sure. That's how I found out what Aranoff looks like. It wasn't him, the man we saw. Not the man tailing me in Washington, either."

"I don't guess there's any possibility you read the plate number wrong," Marino asked me.

"No. Even if I had," I said, "the coincidence would be incredible. Both cars 1990 Lincoln Mark Sevens? Aranoff just happens to be traveling in the Williamsburg-Tidewater area around the same time I *erroneously* record a plate number that just happens to be his?"

"Looks like Aranoff and me are going to have to have a little discussion," Marino said.

Marino called my office later that week and said right off, "You sitting down?"

"You talked with Aranoff."

"Bingo. He left Roanoke Monday, February tenth, and hit Danville, Petersburg, and Richmond. On Wednesday the twelfth, he was in the Tidewater area, and this is where it gets real interesting. He was due in Boston on Thursday the thirteenth, which is the night you and Abby was in Williamsburg. The day before that, Wednesday the twelfth, Aranoff left his car in long-term parking at the Newport News airport. From there he flew to Boston, was up in that area buzzing around in a rental car for the better part of a week. Returned to Newport News yesterday morning, got into his car, and headed home."

"Are you suggesting someone may have stolen the tags off his car while it was in long-term parking, then returned them?" I asked.

"Unless Aranoff's lying, and I don't see any reason for that, there's no other explanation, Doc."

"When he retrieved his car, did he notice anything that might have made him think it had been tampered with?"

"Nope. We went into his garage and took a look at it. Both tags were there, screwed on nice and tight. The tags were dirty like the rest of the car and they were smudged, which may or may not mean anything. I didn't lift any prints, but whoever borrowed the tags was probably wearing gloves, which could account for the smudges. No tool or pry marks that I could see."

"Was the car in a conspicuous place in the parking lot?"

"Aranoff said he left it in pretty much in the middle of the lot, which was almost full."

"You would think if his car had been sitting out there for several days without license plates, Security or someone would have noticed," I said.

"Not necessarily. People aren't all that observant. When they leave their ride at the airport or are returning from a trip, the only thing on their mind is hauling their bags, catching their plane, or getting the hell home. Even if some-one noticed, it's not likely he's going to report it to Security. Security couldn't do nothing anyway until the owner returned, then it would be up to him to report the stolen plates. As for the actual theft of the plates, that wouldn't be very hard. You go to the airport after midnight and there's not going to be anybody around. If it was me, I'd just walk into the lot like I was looking for my car, then five minutes later I'd be heading out of there with a set of plates in my briefcase."

"And that's what you think happened?"

"My theory is this," he said. "The guy who asked you direc-tions last week wasn't no detective, FBI agent, or spook out spying. He was somebody up to no good. Could be a drug dealer, could be almost anything. I think the dark gray Mark Seven he was in is his personal car, and to be on the safe side, when he goes out to do whatever he's into, he switches plates in the event his ride is spotted in the area, maybe by cops out on patrol, whatever."

"Rather risky if he gets pulled for running a red light," I pointed out. "The license number would come back to someone else."

"True. But I don't think he plans on getting pulled. I think he's more worried about his car being spotted because he's out to break the law, something's going to go down and he don't want to take the chance his own tag number's going to be on the street when it does."

"Why doesn't he just use a rental car, then?"

"That's just as bad as having his own plate number out there. Any cop knows a rental car when he sees it. All tag numbers in Virginia begin with R. And if you track it down, its going to come back to whoever rented it. Switching tags is a better idea if you're smart enough to figure out a safe routine. It's what I'd do, and I'd probably resort to a longterm parking lot. I'd use the tags, then take them off my car and put my tags back on. I'd drive to the airport, walk out into the lot after dark, make sure no one's looking, and put the tags back on the car I'd stolen them from."

"What if the owner's already returned and found his tags stolen?"

"If the ride's no longer in the lot, I'd just pitch the tags in the nearest Dumpster. Either way I can't lose."

"Good Lord. The man Abby and I saw that night might be the killer, Marino."

"The squirrel you saw wasn't no businessman who was lost

or fruitcake tailing you," he said. "He was up to something illegal. That don't mean he's a killer."

"The parking sticker . . ."

"I'm gonna track that down. See if Colonial Williamsburg can supply me with a list of everybody who's been issued one."

"The car Mr. Joyce saw going down his road with the headlights off could have been a Lincoln Mark Seven," I said.

"Could have been. Mark Sevens came out in 1990. Jim and Bonnie was murdered in the summer of 1990. And in the dark, a Mark Seven wouldn't look all that different from a Thunderbird, which was what Mr. Joyce said the car he saw looked like."

"Wesley will have a field day with this," I muttered, incredulous.

"Yeah," Marino said. "I got to call him."

March came in with a whispered promise that winter would not last forever. The sun was warm on my back as I cleaned the windshield of my Mercedes while Abby pumped gas. The breeze was gentle, freshly scrubbed from days of rain. People were out washing cars and riding bikes, the earth stirring but not quite awake.

Like a lot of service stations these days, the one I frequented doubled as a convenience store, and I bought cups of coffee to go when I went inside to pay. Then Abby and I drove off to Williamsburg, windows cracked, Bruce Hornsby singing "Harbor Lights" on the radio.

"I called my answering machine before we left," Abby said.

"And?"

"Five hang-ups."

"Cliff?"

"I'm willing to make a bet," she said. "Not that he wants to talk to me. I suspect he's just trying to figure out if I'm home, has probably cruised past my parking lot a number of times, too, looking for my car."

"Why would he do that if he's not interested in talking to you?"

"Maybe he doesn't know that I've changed my locks."

"Then he must be stupid. One would think he would realize you would put two and two together when his series ran."

"He's not stupid," Abby said, staring out the side window.

I opened the sunroof.

"He knows I know. But he's not stupid," she said again. "Cliff's fooled everyone. They don't know he's crazy."

"Hard to believe he could have gotten as far as he has if he's crazy," I said.

"That's the beauty of Washington," she replied cynically. "The most successful, powerful people in the world are there and half of them are crazy, the other half neurotic. Most of them are immoral. Power does it. I don't know why Watergate surprised anyone."

"What has power done to you?" I asked.

"I know how it tastes, but I wasn't there long enough to get addicted."

"Maybe you're lucky."

She was silent.

I thought of Pat Harvey. What was she doing these days? What was going through her mind?

"Have you talked to Pat Harvey?" I asked Abby.

"Yes."

"Since the articles ran in the *Post*?"

She nodded.

"How is she?"

"I once read something written by a missionary to what was then the Congo. He recalled encountering a tribesman in the jungle who looked perfectly normal until he smiled. His teeth were filed to points. He was a cannibal."

Her voice was flat with anger, her mood suddenly dark. I had no idea what she was talking about.

"That's Pat Harvey," she went on. "I dropped by to see her before heading out to Roanoke the other day. We talked briefly about the stories in the *Post*, and I thought she was taking it all in stride until she smiled. Her smile made my blood run cold."

I didn't know what to say.

"That's when I knew Cliff's stories had pushed her over the edge. Deborah's murder pushed Pat as far as I thought she could go. But the stories pushed her further. I remember when I talked to her I had this sense that something wasn't there anymore. After a while I figured out what's not there is Pat Harvey."

"Did she know her husband was having an affair?"

"She does now."

"If it's true," I added.

"Cliff wouldn't write something that he couldn't back up, attribute to a credible source."

I wondered what it would take to push me to the edge. Lucy, Mark? If I had an accident and could no longer use my hands or went blind? I did not know what it would take to make me snap. Maybe it was like dying. Once you were gone you didn't know the difference.

We were at Old Towne shortly after noon. The apartment complex where Jill and Elizabeth had lived was unremarkable, a honeycomb of buildings that all looked the same. They were brick with red awnings announcing block numbers over the main entrances; the landscaping was a patchwork of winter-brown grass and narrow margins of flower beds covered in woodchips. There were areas for cookouts with swing sets, picnic tables, and grills.

We stopped in the parking lot and stared up at what had been Jill's balcony. Through wide spaces in the railing two blue-and-white-webbed chairs rocked gently in the breeze. A chain dangled from a hook in the ceiling, lonely for a potted plant. Elizabeth had lived on the other side of the parking lot. From their respective residences the two friends would have been able to check on each other. They could watch lights turn on and off, know when the other got up and went to bed, when one was home or not.

For a moment, Abby and I shared a depressed silence.

Then she said, "They were more than friends, weren't they, Kay?"

"To answer that would be hearsay."

She smiled a little. "To tell you the truth, I wondered about it when I was working on the stories. It crossed my mind, at any rate. But no one ever suggested it or even hinted." She paused, staring out. "I think I know what they felt like."

I looked at her.

"It must have been the way I felt with Cliff. Sneaking, hiding, spending half your energy worrying about what people think, fearing they somehow suspect."

"The irony is," I said, putting the car in gear, "that people don't really give a damn. They're too preoccupied with themselves."

"I wonder if Jill and Elizabeth would ever have figured that out."

"If their love was greater than their fear, they would have figured it out eventually."

"Where are we going, by the way?" She looked out her window at the roadside streaming past.

"Just cruising," I said. "In the general direction of downtown."

I had never given her an itinerary. All I had said was that I wanted to "look around."

"You're looking for that damn car, aren't you?"

"It can't hurt to look."

"And just what are you going to do if you find it, Kay?"

"Write the plate number down, see who it comes back to this time."

"Well"—she started to laugh—"if you find a 1990 charcoal Lincoln Mark Seven with a Colonial Williamsburg sticker on the rear bumper, I'll pay you a hundred dollars."

"Better get your checkbook out. If it's here, I'm going to find it."

And I did, not half an hour later, by following the age-old rule of how you find something lost. I retraced my steps. When I returned to Merchant's Square the car was sitting there big as life in the parking lot, not far from where we had spotted it the first time when its driver had stopped to ask directions.

"Jesus Christ," Abby whispered. "I don't believe it."

The car was unoccupied, sunshine glinting off the glass. It looked as if it had just been washed and waxed. There was a parking sticker on the left side of the rear bumper, the plate number ITU-144. Abby wrote it down.

"This is too easy, Kay. It can't be right."

"We don't know that it's the same car." I was being scientific now. "It looks the same, but we can't be sure."

I parked some twenty spaces away, tucking my Mercedes between a station wagon and a Pontiac, and sat behind the wheel scanning the storefronts. A gift shop, a picture-framing shop, a restaurant. Between a tobacco shop and a bakery was a bookstore, small, inconspicuous books displayed in the window. A wooden sign hung over the door, with the name "The Dealer's Room" painted on it in Colonial-style calligraphy.

"Crossword puzzles," I said under my breath, and a chill ran up my spine.

"What?" Abby was still watching the Lincoln.

"Jill and Elizabeth liked crossword puzzles. They often went out to breakfast on Sunday mornings and picked up the *New York Times*." I was opening my door.

Abby put a hand on my arm, restraining me. "No, Kay. Wait a minute. We've got to think about this."

I settled back into the seat.

"You can't just walk in there," she said, and it sounded like an order.

"I want to buy a paper."

"What if he's in there? Then what are you going to do?"

"I want to see if it's him, the man who was driving. I think I'd recognize him."

"And he might recognize you."

"'Dealer' could refer to cards," I thought out loud as a young woman with short curly black hair walked up to the bookstore, opened the door, and disappeared inside.

"The person who deals cards, deals the jack of hearts," I added, my voice trailing off.

"You talked to him when he asked directions. Your picture's been in the news." Abby was taking charge. "You're not going in there. I will."

"We both will."

"That's crazy!"

"You're right." My mind was made up. "You're staying put. I'm going in."

I was out of the car before she could argue. She got out, too, and just stood there, looking lost, as I walked with purpose in that direction. She did not come after me. She had too much sense to make a scene.

When I put my hand on the cold brass handle of the door, my heart was hammering. When I walked inside, I felt weak in the knees.

He was standing behind the counter, smiling and filling out a charge card receipt while a middle-aged woman in an

Ultrasuede suit prattled on, ". . . That's what birthdays are for. You buy your husband a book you want to read . . ."

"As long as you both enjoy the same books, that's all right." His voice was very soft, soothing, a voice you could trust.

Now that I was inside the shop, I was desperate to leave. I wanted to run. There were stacks of newspapers to one side of the counter, including the *New York Times*. I could pick one up, quickly pay for it, and be gone. But I did not want to look him in the eye.

It was him.

I turned around and walked out without glancing back.

Abby was sitting in the car smoking.

"He couldn't work here and not know his way to Sixty-four," I said, starting the engine.

She got my meaning precisely. "Do you want to call Marino now or wait until we get back to Richmond?"

"We're going to call him now." I found a pay phone and was told Marino was on the street. I left him the message, "ITU-144. Call me."

Abby asked me a lot of questions, and I did my best to answer them. Then there were long stretches of silence as I drove. My stomach was sour. I considered pulling off somewhere. I thought I might throw up.

She was staring at me. I could feel her concern.

"My God, Kay. You're white as a sheet."

"I'm all right."

"You want me to drive?"

"I'm fine. Really."

When we got home, I went straight up to my bedroom. My hands trembled as I dialed the number. Mark's machine answered after the second ring, and I started to hang up but found myself mesmerized by his voice.

"I'm sorry, there's no one to answer your call right now . . ."

At the beep I hesitated, then quietly returned the receiver to its cradle. When I looked up, I found Abby in my doorway. I could tell by the look on her face that she knew what I had just done.

I stared at her, my eyes filling with tears, and then she was sitting next to me on the edge of the bed.

"Why didn't you leave him a message?" she whispered.

"How could you possibly know who I was calling?" I fought to steady my voice.

"Because it's the same impulse that overwhelms me when I'm terribly upset. I want to reach for the phone. Even now, after all of it. I still want to call Cliff."

"Have you?"

She slowly shook her head.

"Don't. Don't ever, Abby."

She studied me closely. "Was it walking into the bookstore and seeing him?"

"I'm not sure."

"I think you know."

I glanced away from her. "When I get too close, I know it. I've gotten too close before. I ask myself why it happens."

"People like us can't help it. We have a compulsion, something drives us. That's why it happens," she said.

I could not admit to her my fear. Had Mark answered the

phone, I didn't know if I could have admitted it to him, either.

Abby was staring off, her voice distant when she asked, "As much as you know about death, do you ever think about your own?"

I got off the bed. "Where the hell is Marino?" I picked up the phone to try him again.

16

Days turned into weeks while I waited anxiously. I had not heard from Marino since giving him the information about The Dealer's Room. I had not heard from anyone. With each hour that passed the silence grew louder and more ominous.

On the first day of spring, I emerged from the conference room after being deposed for three hours by two lawyers. Rose told me I had a call.

Kay? It's Benton."

"Good afternoon," I said, adrenaline surging.

"Can you come up to Quantico tomorrow?"

I reached for my calendar. Rose had penciled in a conference call. It could be rescheduled.

"What time?"

"Ten, if that's convenient. I've already talked to Marino."

Before I could ask questions, he said he couldn't talk and would fill me in when we met. It was six o'clock before I left my office. The sun had gone down and the air felt cold. When I turned into my driveway, I noticed the lights were on. Abby was home.

We had seen little of each other of late, both of us in and out, rarely speaking. She never went to the grocery store, but would leave a fifty-dollar bill taped to the refrigerator every now and then, which more than covered what little she ate. When wine or Scotch got low, I would find a twenty-dollar bill under the bottle. Several days ago, I had discovered a five-dollar bill on top of a depleted box of laundry soap. Wandering through the rooms of my house had turned into a peculiar scavenger hunt.

When I unlocked the front door, Abby suddenly stepped into the doorway, startling me.

"I'm sorry," she said. "I heard you drive in. Didn't mean to scare you."

I felt foolish. Ever since she had moved in, I had become increasingly jumpy. I supposed I wasn't adjusting well to my loss of privacy.

"Can I fix you a drink?" she asked. Abby looked tired.

"Thanks," I said, unbuttoning my coat. My eyes wandered into the living room. On the coffee table, beside an ashtray filled with cigarette butts, were a wineglass and several reporter's notepads.

Taking off my coat and gloves, I went upstairs and tossed them on my bed, pausing long enough to play back the messages on the answering machine. My mother had tried to reach me. I was eligible to win a prize if I dialed a certain number by eight P.M., and Marino had called to tell me what time he would pick me up in the morning. Mark and I continued missing each other, talking to each other's machines.

"I've got to go to Quantico tomorrow," I told Abby when I entered the living room.

She pointed to my drink on the coffee table.

"Marino and I have a meeting with Benton," I said.

She reached for her cigarettes.

"I don't know what it's about," I continued. "Maybe you do."

"Why would I know?"

"You haven't been here much. I don't know what you've been doing."

"When you're at your office, I don't know what you're doing either."

"I haven't been doing anything remarkable. What would you like to know?" I offered lightly, trying to dispel the tension.

"I don't ask because I know how private you are about your work. I don't want to pry."

I assumed she was implying that if I asked about what she was doing I would be prying.

"Abby, you seem distant these days."

"Preoccupied. Please don't take it personally."

Certainly she had plenty to think about, with the book she was writing, what she was going to do with her life. But I had never seen Abby this withdrawn.

"I'm concerned, that's all," I said.

"You don't understand what I'm like, Kay. When I get into something, I'm consumed by it. Can't get my mind off it." She paused. "You were right when you said this book was my chance to redeem myself. It is."

"I'm glad to hear it, Abby. Knowing you, it will be a best-seller."

"Maybe. I'm not the only one interested in writing a book about these cases. My agent's already hearing rumors about other deals out there. I've got a head start, will be all right if I work fast."

"It's not your book I care about, it's you."

"I care about you, too, Kay," she said. "I appreciate what you've done for me by letting me stay here. And that won't go on much longer, I promise."

"You can stay as long as you like."

She collected her notepads and drink. "I've got to start writing soon, and I can't do that until I have my own space, my computer."

"Then you're simply doing research these days."

"Yes. I'm finding a lot of things I didn't know I was look-ing for," she said enigmatically as she headed for her bedroom.

When the Quantico exit came into view the following morn-ing, traffic suddenly stopped. Apparently there had been an accident somewhere north of us on I-95, and cars weren't moving. Marino flipped on his grille lights and veered off onto the shoulder, where we bumped along, rocks pelting the undercarriage of the car, for a good hundred yards.

For the past two hours he had been giving me a complete account of his latest domestic accomplishments, while I wondered what Wesley had to tell us and worried about Abby.

"Never had any idea venetian blinds was such a bitch," Marino complained as we sped past Marine Corps barracks and a firing range. "I'm spraying them with 409, right?" He glanced over at me. "And it's taking me a minute per slat, paper towels shredding the hell all over the place. Finally I get an idea, just take the damn things out of the windows and dump them in the tub. Fill it with hot water and laundry soap. Worked like a charm."

"That's great," I muttered.

"I'm also in the process of tearing down the wallpaper in the kitchen. It came with the house. Doris never liked it."

"The question is whether you like it. You're the one who lives there now."

He shrugged. "Never paid it much mind, you want to know the truth. But I figure if Doris says it's ugly, it probably is. We used to talk about selling the camper and putting in an above-the-ground pool. So I'm finally getting around to that, too. Ought to have it in time for summer."

"Marino, be careful," I said gently. "Make sure what you're doing is for you."

He did not answer me.

"Don't hang your future on a hope that may not be there."

"It can't hurt nothing," he finally said. "Even if she never comes back, it can't hurt nothing for things to look nice."

"Well, you're going to have to show me your place sometime," I said.

"Yeah. All the times I've been to your crib and you've never seen mine."

He parked the car and we got out. The FBI Academy had continued to metastasize over the outer fringes of the U.S. Marine Corps base. The main building with its fountain and flags had been turned into administrative offices, and the center of activity had been moved into a new tan brick building next door. What looked like another dormitory had gone up since I had visited last. Gunfire in the distance sounded like firecrackers popping.

Marino checked his .38 at the desk. We signed in and clipped on visitor passes, then he took me on another series of shortcuts, avoiding the enclosed brick-and-glass breezeways, or gerbil tubes. I followed him through a door that led outside the building, and we walked over a loading dock, through a kitchen. We finally emerged from the back of the gift shop, which Marino strolled right through without a glance in the direction of the young female clerk holding a stack of sweatshirts. Her lips parted in unspoken protest as she viewed our unorthodox passage. Out of the store and around a corner, we entered the bar and grill called The Boardroom, where Wesley was waiting for us at a corner table.

He wasted no time getting down to business.

The owner of The Dealer's Room was Steven Spurrier.

Wesley described him as "thirty-four years old, white, with black hair, brown eyes. Five-eleven, one hundred and sixty pounds." Spurrier had not yet been picked up or questioned, but he had been under constant surveillance. What had been observed so far was not exactly normal.

On several occasions he had left his two-story brick home at a late hour and driven to two bars and one rest stop. He never seemed to stay in one place very long. He was always alone. The previous week he had approached a young couple emerging from a bar called Tom-Toms. It appeared he asked for directions again. Nothing happened. The couple got in their car and left. Spurrier got into his Lincoln and eventually meandered back home. His license tags remained unchanged.

"We've got a problem with the evidence," Wesley reported, looking at me through rimless glasses, his face stern. "We've got a cartridge case in our lab. You've got the bullet from Deborah Harvey in Richmond."

"I don't have the bullet," I replied. "The Forensic Science Bureau does. I presume you've started the DNA analysis on the blood recovered from Elizabeth Mott's car."

"It will be another week or two."

I nodded. The FBI DNA lab used five polymorphic probes. Each probe had to stay in the X-ray developer for about a week, which was why I had written Wesley a letter some time ago suggesting that he get the bloody swatch from Montana and begin its analysis immediately.

"DNA's not worth a damn without a suspect's blood," Marino reminded us.

"We're working on that," Wesley said stoically.

"Yeah, well, seems like we could pop Spurrier because of the license plate. Ask his sorry ass to explain why he was driving around with Aranoff's tags several weeks back."

"We can't prove he was driving around with them. It's Kay and Abby's word against his."

"All we need is a magistrate who will sign a warrant. Then we start digging. Maybe we turn up ten pairs of shoes," Marino said. "Maybe an Uzi some Hydra-Shok ammo, who knows what we'll find?"

"We're planning to do so," Wesley continued. "But one thing at a time."

He got up for more coffee, and Marino took my cup and his and followed him. At this early hour The Boardroom was deserted. I looked around at empty tables, the television in a corner, and tried to envision what must go on here late at night. Agents in training lived like priests. Members of the opposite sex, booze, and cigarettes were not allowed inside the dormitory rooms, which also could not be locked. But The Boardroom served beer and wine. When there were blowouts, confrontations, indiscretions, this was where it happened. I remembered Mark telling me he had broken up a free-for-all in here one night when a new FBI agent went too far with his homework and decided to "arrest" a table of veteran DEA agents. Tables had crashed to the floor, beer and baskets of popcorn everywhere.

Wesley and Marino returned to the table, and setting down his coffee, Wesley slipped out of his pearl-gray suit jacket and hung it neatly on the back of his chair. His white shirt scarcely had a wrinkle, I noticed, his silk tie was peacock blue with tiny white fleur-de-lis, and he was wearing peacock blue suspenders. Marino served as the perfect foil to this Fortune 500 partner of his. With his big belly, Marino couldn't possibly do justice to even the most elegant suit, but I had to give him credit. These days he was trying.

"What do you know about Spurrier's background?" I asked. Wesley was writing notes to himself while Marino reviewed a file, both men seeming to have forgotten there was a third person at the table.

"He doesn't have a record," Wesley replied, looking up. "Never been arrested, hasn't gotten so much as a speeding ticket in the past ten years. He bought the Lincoln in February of 1990 from a dealer in Virginia Beach, traded in an '86 Town Car, paid the rest in cash."

"He must have some bucks," Marino commented. "Drives high-dollar cars, lives in a nice crib. Hard to believe he makes that much from his bookstore."

"He doesn't make that much," Wesley said. "According to what he filed last year, he cleared less than thirty thousand dollars. But he's got assets of over half a million, a money market account, waterfront real estate, stocks."

"Jeez." Marino shook his head.

"Any dependents?" I asked.

"No," Wesley said. "Never married, both parents dead. His father was very successful in real estate in the Northern Neck. He died when Steven was in his early twenties. I suspect this is where the money comes from."

"What about his mother?" I asked.

"She died about a year after the father did. Cancer. Steven came along late in life. His mother had him when she was forty-two. The only other sibling is a brother named Gordon. He lives in Texas, is fifteen years older than Steven, married, with four kids."

Skimming his notes again, Wesley brought forth more information. Spurrier was born in Gloucester, attended the University of Virginia, where he received a bachelor's degree in English. Afterward he joined the navy, where he lasted less than four months. The next eleven months were spent working at a printing press, where his primary responsibility was to maintain the machinery.

"I'd like to know more about his months in the navy," Marino said.

"There's not much to know," Wesley answered. "After enlisting, he was sent to boot camp in the Great Lakes area. He chose journalism as his speciality and was assigned to the Defense Information School at Fort Benjamin Harrison in Indianapolis. Later he was assigned his duty station, working for the Commander-in-Chief of the Atlantic Fleet in Norfolk." He looked up from his notes. "About a month later his father died, and Steven received a hardship discharge so he could return to Gloucester to take care of his mother, who was already ill with cancer."

"What about the brother?" Marino asked.

"Apparently he couldn't get away from his job and family responsibilities in Texas." He paused, glancing at us. "Maybe there are other reasons. Obviously, Steven's relationship with

349

his family is of interest to me, but I'm not going to know a whole lot more about it for a while."

"Why not?" I asked.

"It's too risky for me to confront the brother directly at this point. I don't want him calling Steven, tipping my hand. It's unlikely Gordon would cooperate, anyway. Family members tend to stick together in matters like this, even if they don't get along."

"Well, you've been talking to someone," Marino said.

"A couple of people from the navy, UVA, his former employer at the printing press."

"What else did they have to say about this squirrel?"

"A loner," Wesley said. "Not much of a journalist. Was more interested in reading than interviewing anyone or writing stories. Apparently, the printing press suited him rather well. He stayed in the back, had his nose in a book when things were slow. His boss said Steven loved to tinker with the presses, various machines, and kept them spotless. Sometimes he would go for days without talking to anyone. His boss described Steven as peculiar."

"His boss offer any examples?"

"Several things," Wesley said. "A woman employed by the press took off her fingertip with a paper cutter one morning. Steven got angry because she bled all over a piece of equipment he had just cleaned. His response to his mother's death was abnormal as well. Steven was reading during a lunch break when the call came from the hospital. He showed no emotion, just returned to his chair and resumed reading his book."

"A real warmhearted guy," Marino said.

"No one has described him as warmhearted."

"What happened after his mother died?" I asked.

"Then, I would assume, Steven got his inheritance. He moved to Williamsburg, leased the space at Merchant's Square, and opened The Dealer's Room. This was nine years ago."

"A year before Jill Harrington and Elizabeth Mott were murdered," I said.

Wesley nodded. "He was in the area, then. He's been in the area during all of these murders. He's been working in his bookstore since it opened, except for a period of about five months back, uh, seven years ago. The store was closed during that time. We don't know why or know where Spurrier was."

"He runs his bookstore by himself?" Marino asked.

"It's a small operation. No other employees. The store is closed on Mondays. It's been noted that when there isn't much business he just sits behind the counter and reads, and if he leaves the store before closing time he either closes early or puts a sign on the door that says he'll be back at such and such an hour. He also has an answering machine. If you're looking for a certain book or want him to search for something out of print, you can leave your request on his machine."

"It's interesting that someone so antisocial would open a business that requires him to have contact with customers, even if the contact is rather limited," I said.

"It's actually very appropriate," Wesley said. "The bookstore would serve as a perfect lair for a voyeur, someone intensely interested in observing people without having to personally interact with them. It has been noted that William and Mary students frequent his store, primarily because Spurrier carries unusual out-of-print books in addition to popular fiction and nonfiction. He also carries a wide selection of spy novels and military magazines, which attract business from the nearby military bases. If he's the killer, then watching young, attractive couples and military personnel who come into his store would fascinate him in a voyeuristic fashion and at the same time stir up feelings of inadequacy, frustration, rage. He would hate what he envies, envy what he hates."

"I wonder if he suffered ridicule during his time in the navy," I conjectured.

"Based on what I've been told, he did, at least to a degree. Spurrier's peers considered him a wimp, a loser while his superiors found him arrogant and aloof, even though he was never a disciplinary problem. Spurrier had no success with women and kept to himself, partly by choice and because others did not find his personality particularly attractive."

"Maybe being in the navy was the closest he ever got to being a real man," Marino said, "being what he wanted to be. His father dies and Spurrier has to take care of his sick mother. In his mind, he gets screwed."

"That's quite possible," Wesley agreed. "In any event, the killer we're dealing with would believe that his troubles are the fault of others. He would take no responsibility. He would feel his life was controlled by others, and therefore, controlling others and his environment became an obsession for him."

"Sounds like he's paying back the world," Marino said.

"The killer is showing he has power," Wesley said. "If the military aspects enter into his fantasies, and I think they do, then he believes he's the ultimate soldier. He kills without being caught. He outsmarts the enemy, plays games with them, and wins. It may be possible that he has deliberately set things up in such a way as to make those investigating the murders suspect that the perpetrator is a professional soldier, even someone from Camp Peary."

"His own disinformation campaign," I considered.

"He can't destroy the military," Wesley added, "but he could try to tarnish the image, degrade and defame it."

"Yeah, and all the while he's laughing up his sleeve," Marino said.

"I think the main point is that the killer's activities are the product of violent, sexualized fantasies that existed early on in the context of his social isolation. He believes he lives in an unjust world, and fantasy provides an important escape. In his fantasies he can express his emotions and control other human beings, he can be and get anything he wants. He can control life and death. He has the power to decide whether to injure or kill."

"Too bad Spurrier don't just *fantasize* about whacking couples," Marino said. "Then the three of us wouldn't have to be sitting here having this conversation."

"I'm afraid it doesn't work that way," Wesley said. "If violent, aggressive behavior dominates your thinking, your imagination, you're going to start acting out in ways that move you closer to the actual expression of these emotions.

Violence fuels more violent thoughts, and more violent thoughts fuel more violence. After a while, violence and killing are a natural part of your adult life, and you see nothing wrong with it. I've had serial murderers tell me emphatically that when they killed, they were just doing what everybody else thinks of doing."

"Evil to him who evil thinks," I said.

It was then that I offered my theory about Deborah Harvey's purse.

"I think it's possible the killer knew who Deborah was," I said. "Perhaps not when the couple was first abducted, but he may have known by the time he killed them."

"Please explain," Wesley said, studying me with interest.

"Have either of you seen the fingerprints report?"

"Yeah, I've seen it," Marino replied.

"As you know, when Vander examined Deborah's purse he found partials, smudges on her credit cards, but nothing on her driver's license."

"So?" Marino looked perplexed.

"The contents of her purse were well preserved because the nylon purse was waterproof. And the credit cards and her driver's license were inside plastic windows and zipped inside a compartment, thus protected from the elements and the body fluids of decomposition. Had Vander not picked up anything that would be one thing. But I find it interesting that he picked up something on the credit cards but not on her driver's license, when we know that Deborah got out her license when she went inside the Seven-Eleven and tried to buy beer. So she handled the license, and Ellen Jordan, the clerk, also handled it. What I'm wondering is if the killer didn't touch Deborah's driver's license, too, and then wipe it clean afterward."

"Why would he do that?" Marino asked.

"Maybe when he was inside the car with the couple, had the gun out and was abducting them, Deborah told him who she was," I answered.

"Interesting," Wesley said.

"Deborah may have been a modest young woman, but she was well aware of her family's prominence, of her mother's power," I went on. "She may have informed the killer in hopes that he would change his mind, think that in harming them there would be hell to pay. This may have startled the killer considerably, and he may have demanded proof of her identity, at which point he may have gotten hold of her purse to see the name on her driver's license."

"Then how did the purse end up out in the woods, and why did he leave the jack of hearts in it?" Marino asked.

"Maybe to buy himself a little time," I said. "He would have known that the Jeep would be found quickly, and if he realized who Deborah was, then he was also going to know that half the law enforcement world was going to be out looking for them. Maybe he decided to play it safe by not having the jack of hearts found immediately, so he left it with the bodies instead of inside the Jeep. By placing the card inside the purse and putting the purse under Deborah's body, he ensured that the card would be found, but probably not for a long time. He changes the rules a little but still wins the game."

"Not half bad. What do you think?" Marino looked at Wesley.

"I think we may never know exactly what happened," he said. "But it wouldn't surprise me if Deborah did exactly what Kay has proposed. One thing is certain—no matter what Deborah may have said or threatened, it would have been too risky for the killer to free her and Fred because they probably would have been able to identify him. So he went through with the murders, but the unforeseen turn of events could have thrown him off. Yes," he said to me. "This could have caused him to alter his ritual. It may also be that leaving the card in Deborah's purse was his way of showing contempt toward her and who she was."

"Sort of an 'up yours,'" Marino said.

"Possibly," Wesley replied.

Steven Spurrier was arrested the following Friday when two FBI agents and a local detective who had been tailing him all day followed him to the long-term parking lot of the Newport News airport.

When Marino's call woke me before dawn, my first thought was that another couple had disappeared. It took a moment for me to comprehend what he was saying over the phone.

"They popped him while he was lifting another set of tags," he was saying. "Charged him with petit larceny. The best they could do, but at least we got our probable cause to turn him inside out."

"Another Lincoln?" I asked.

"This time a 1991, silver-gray. He's in lockup waiting to see the magistrate, no way they're going to be able to hold him on a nickel-and-dime class one misdemeanor. Best they can do is stall, take their sweet time processing him. Then he's out of there."

"What about a search warrant?"

"His crib's crawling with cops and the feds even as we speak. Looking for everything from *Soldier of Fortune* magazines to Tinker Toys."

"You're heading out there, I guess," I said.

"Yeah. I'll let you know."

It was not possible for me to go back to sleep. Throwing a robe over my shoulders, I went downstairs and switched on a lamp in Abby's room.

"It's just me," I said as she sat straight up in bed. She groaned, covering her eyes.

I told her what had happened. Then we went into the kitchen and put on a pot of coffee.

"I'd pay to be present when they search his house." She was so wired I was surprised she didn't bolt out the door.

But she stayed inside all day, suddenly industrious. She cleaned up her room, helped me in the kitchen, and even swept the patio. She wanted to know what the police had found and was smart enough to realize that driving to Williamsburg would get her nowhere, because she would not be allowed entrance into Spurrier's residence or bookstore.

Marino stopped by early that evening as Abby and I were loading the dishwasher. I knew instantly by the look on his face that his news wasn't good.

"First I'll tell you what we didn't find," he began. "We didn't find a friggin' thing that will convince a jury Spurrier's ever killed a housefly. No knives except the ones in his kitchen. No guns or cartridges. No souvenirs such as shoes, jewelry, locks of hair, whatever, that might have belonged to the victims."

"Was his bookstore searched as well?" I asked.

"Oh, yeah."

"And his car of course."

"Nothing."

"Then tell us what you did find," I asked, depressed.

"Enough weirdo stuff to make me know it's him, Doc," Marino said. "I mean, this drone ain't no Eagle Scout. He's into skin magazines, violent pornography. Plus, he's got books about the military, especially the CIA, and files filled with newspaper clippings about the CIA. All of it cataloged, labeled. The guy's neater than an old lady librarian."

"Did you find any newspaper clips about these cases?" Abby asked.

"We did, including old stories about Jill Harrington and Elizabeth Mott. We also found catalogs to a number of what I call spy shops, these outfits that sell security-survival shit, everything from bulletproof cars to bomb detectors and night-vision goggles. The FBI's going to check it out, see what all he's ordered over the years. Spurrier's clothes are interesting, too. He must have half a dozen nylon warm-up suits in his bedroom, all of them black or navy blue and never worn, labels cut out of them, like maybe they were intended to be disposable, worn over his clothes and pitched somewhere after the fact."

"Nylon sheds very little," I said. "Windbreakers, nylon warm-ups aren't going to leave many fibers."

"Right. Let's see. What else?" Marino paused, finishing his drink. "Oh, yeah. Two boxes of surgical gloves and a supply of those disposable shoe-covers you wear downstairs."

"Booties?"

"Right. Like you wear in the morgue so you don't get blood on your shoes. And guess what? They found cards, four decks of them, never been opened, still in the cellophane."

"I don't suppose you found an opened deck missing a jack of hearts?" I asked, hopefully.

"No. But that don't surprise me. He probably removes the jack of hearts and then throws the rest of the cards away."

"All the same brand?"

"No. A couple different brands."

Abby was sitting silently in her chair, fingers laced tightly in her lap.

"It doesn't make sense that you didn't find any weapons," I said.

"This guy's slick, Doc. He's careful."

"Not careful enough. He kept the clippings about the murders, the warm-up suits, gloves. And he was caught red-handed stealing license tags, which makes me wonder if he wasn't getting ready to strike again."

"He had stolen tags on his car when he stopped you to ask directions," Marino pointed out. "No couple disappeared that weekend that we've heard about."

"That's true," I mused. "And he wasn't wearing a warm-up suit, either."

"He may save putting that on for last. May even keep it in a gym bag in his trunk. My guess is he has a kit."

"Did you find a gym bag?" Abby asked bluntly.

"No," Marino said. "No murder kit."

"Well, if you ever find a gym bag, or murder kit," Abby added, "then maybe you'll find his knife, gun, goggles, and all the rest of it."

"We'll be looking until the cows come home."

"Where is he now?" I asked.

"Was sitting in his kitchen drinking coffee when I left," Marino replied. "Friggin' unbelievable. Here we are tearing up his house and he's not even sweating. When he was asked about the warm-up suits, the gloves, decks of cards, and so on, he said he wasn't talking to us without his attorney present. Then he took a sip of his coffee and lit a cigarette like we wasn't there. Oh, yeah, I left that out. The squirrel smokes."

"What brand?" I asked.

"Dunhills. Probably buys them in that fancy tobacco shop next to his bookstore. And he uses a fancy lighter, too. An expensive one."

"That would certainly explain his peeling the paper off the butts before depositing them at the scenes, if that's what he did," I said. "Dunhills are distinctive."

"I know," Marino said. "They've got a gold band around the filter."

"You got a suspect's kit?"

"Oh, yeah." He smiled. "That's our little trump card that will beat his jack of hearts hands down. If we can't make these other cases, at least we got the murders of Jill Harrington and Elizabeth Mott to hang him with. DNA ought to nail his ass. Wish the damn tests didn't take so long."

After Marino left, Abby stared coolly at me.

"What do you think?" I asked.

"It's all circumstantial."

"Right now it is."

"Spurrier's got money," she said. "He's going to get the best trial lawyer money can buy. I can tell you exactly how it's going to go. The lawyer's going to suggest that his client was railroaded by the cops and the feds because of the pressure to solve these homicides. It's going to come out that a lot of people are looking for a scapegoat, especially in light of the accusations Pat Harvey has made."

"Abby . . ."

"Maybe the killer *is* someone from Camp Peary."

"You don't really believe that," I protested.

She glanced at her watch. "Maybe the feds already know who it is and have already taken care of the problem. Privately, which would explain why no other couples since Fred and Deborah have disappeared. Someone's got to pay in order to remove the cloud of suspicion, end the matter to the public's satisfaction . . ."

Leaning back in my chair, I turned my face up to the ceiling and shut my eyes while she went on and on.

"No question Spurrier's into something or he wouldn't be stealing license plates. But he could be selling drugs. Maybe he's a cat burglar or gets his jollies from driving around with borrowed tags for a day? He's weird enough to fit the profile, but the world is full of weirdos who don't ever kill anyone. Who's to say the stuff in his house wasn't planted?"

"Please stop," I said quietly.

But she wouldn't. "It's just so goddam neat. The warm-up suits, gloves, decks of cards, pornography, and newspaper clips. And it doesn't make sense that no weapons or ammunition were found. Spurrier was caught by surprise, didn't have any idea he was under surveillance. In fact, it not only doesn't make sense, it's very convenient. One thing the feds couldn't plant was the pistol that fired the bullet you recovered from Deborah Harvey."

"You're right. They couldn't plant that." I got up from the table and began wiping the counters because I couldn't sit still.

"Interesting that the one item of evidence they couldn't plant didn't show up."

There had been stories before about the police, federal agents, planting evidence in order to frame someone. The ACLU probably had a file room full of such accusations.

"You're not listening," Abby said.

"I'm going up to take a bath," I replied wearily.

She walked over to the sink where I was wringing out the dishrag.

"Kay?"

I stopped what I was doing and looked at her.

"You want it to be easy," she admonished.

"I've always wanted things to be easy. They almost never are."

"You want it to be easy," she repeated. "You don't want to think that the people you trust could send an innocent man to the electric chair in order to cover their asses."

"No question about that. I wouldn't want to think it. I refuse to think it unless there is proof. And Marino was at Spurrier's house. He would never have gone along with it."

"He was there." She walked away from me. "But he wasn't the first one there. By the time he arrived, he would have seen what they wanted him to see."

17

The first person I saw when I reached the office on Monday was Fielding.

I had come in through the bay, and he was already dressed in scrubs, waiting to get on the elevator. When I noticed the plasticized blue paper booties over his running shoes, I thought of what the police had found inside Steven Spurrier's house. Our medical supplies were on state contract. But there were any number of businesses in any city that sold booties and surgical gloves. One did not need to be a physician to purchase such items any more than one needed to be a police officer to buy a uniform, badge, or gun.

"Hope you got a good night's rest," Fielding warned as the elevator doors parted. We stepped inside.

"Give me the bad news. What have we got this morning?" I said.

"Six posts, every one of them a homicide."

"Great," I said irritably.

"Yeah, the Knife and Gun Club had a busy weekend. Four shootings, two stabbings. Spring has sprung."

We got off on the second floor and I was already taking off my suit jacket and rolling up my sleeves when I walked into my office. Marino was sitting in a chair, his briefcase on his lap, a cigarette lit. I assumed one of the morning's cases was his until he handed me two lab reports.

"Thought you'd want to see it for yourself," he said.

Typed at the top of one report was the name Steven Spurrier. The serology lab had already completed a workup on his blood. The other report was eight years old, the results of the workup done on the blood found inside Elizabeth Mott's car.

"Of course, it's going to be a while before the DNA results are in," Marino began to explain, "but so far so good."

Settling behind my desk, I took a moment to study the reports. The blood from the Volkswagen was type O, PGM type 1, EAP type B, ADA type 1, and EsD type 1. This particular combination could be found in approximately eight percent of the population. The results were consistent with those of the tests conducted on the blood from Spurrier's suspect kit. He also was type O, types in other blood groups the same, but since more enzymes had been tested for, the combination had been narrowed to approximately one percent of the population.

"It's not enough to charge him with murder," I said to Marino. "You'd have to have more than the fact that his blood type includes him in a group of thousands of people.

"A damn shame the report from the old blood isn't more complete."

"They didn't routinely test for as many enzymes back then," I replied.

"Maybe they could do it now?" he suggested. "If we could narrow it down, that would be a big help. The damn DNA for Spurrier's blood is going to take weeks."

"They're not going to be able to do it," I told him. "The blood from Elizabeth's car is too old. After this many years the enzymes would have degraded, so the results this time would be less specific than what's on this eight-year-old report. The best you could get now is the ABO grouping, and almost half of the population is type O. We have no choice but to wait for the DNA results. Besides," I added, "even if you could lock him up this minute you know he'd make bail. He's still under surveillance, I hope."

"Being watched like a hawk, and you can bet he knows it. The good news is he's not likely to try whacking anyone. The bad news is he's got time to destroy any evidence we missed. Like the murder weapons."

"The alleged missing gym bag."

"Don't add up that we couldn't find it. We did everything short of tearing up his floorboards."

"Maybe you should have torn up his floorboards.

"Yeah, maybe."

I was trying to think where else Spurrier might have hidden a gym bag when it occurred to me. I don't know why I didn't think of it earlier.

"How is Spurrier built?" I asked.

"He ain't very big, but he looks pretty strong. Not an ounce of fat."

"Then he probably works out, exercises."

"Probably. Why?"

"If he belongs to some place, the YMCA, a fitness club, he might have a locker. I do at Westwood. If I wanted to hide something, that would be a good place to do it. No one would think twice when he walked out of the club with his gym bag in hand or when he returned the bag to his locker."

"Interesting idea, " Marino said thoughtfully. "I'll ask around, see what I can find out."

He lit another cigarette and unzipped his briefcase. "I got pictures of his crib, if you're interested."

I glanced up at the clock. "I've got a houseful downstairs. We'll have to make it quick."

He handed me a thick manila envelope of eight-by-tens. They were in order, and going through them was like seeing Spurrier's house through Marino's eyes, beginning with the Colonial brick front lined with boxwoods and a brick walk leading to the black front door. In back was a paved drive leading to a garage that was attached to the house.

I spread out several more photographs and found myself inside his living room. On the bare hardwood floor was a gray leather couch near a glass coffee table. Centered on the table was a jagged brass plant growing out of a chunk of coral. A recent copy of the *Smithsonian* was perfectly aligned with the table's edges. Centered on the magazine was a remote control that I suspected operated the overhead television projector suspended like a spaceship from the whitewashed ceiling. An eighty-inch television screen was retracted into an inconspicuous vertical bar above the bookcase lined with VCR tapes, neatly labeled, and scores of hardbound volumes, the titles of which I could not make out. To one side of the bookcase was a bank of sophisticated electronic equipment.

"The squirrel's got his own movie theater," Marino said. "Got surround sound, speakers in every room. The whole setup probably cost more than your Mercedes, and he wasn't sitting back at night watching *Sound of Music*, either. Those tapes there in the bookcase"—he reached across my desk to point them out. "They're all *Lethal Weapon*-type shit, flicks about Vietnam, vigilantes. Now on the shelf right above is the good stuff. The tapes look like your everyday box office hits, but you pop one of them in the VCR and get a little surprise. The one labeled *On Golden Pond*, for example, should be called *On the Cesspool*. Hardcore violent pornography. Benton and I were together all of yesterday viewing the crap. Friggin' unbelievable. About every other minute, I felt like taking a bath."

"Did you find any home movies?"

"No. Not any photography equipment, either."

I looked at more photographs. In the dining room was another glass table, this one surrounded by transparent acrylic chairs. I noticed that the hardwood floor was bare. I had yet to see a rug or carpet in any room.

The kitchen was immaculate and modern. Windows were

shrouded with gray miniblinds. There were no curtains, no draperies in any room I had seen, not even upstairs where this creature slept. The brass bed was king-size, neatly made, sheets white, but no spread. Dresser drawers pulled open revealed the warm-up suits Marino had told me about, and in boxes on the closet floor were packets of surgical gloves and booties.

"There's nothing fabric," I marveled, returning the photographs to their envelope. "I've never before seen a house that didn't have at least one rug."

"No curtains, either. Not even in the shower," Marino said. "It's enclosed in glass doors. Of course, there are towels, sheets, his clothes."

"Which he probably washes constantly."

"The upholstery in his Lincoln is leather," Marino said. "And the carpet's covered with plastic mats."

"He doesn't have any pets?"

"No."

"The way he has furnished his house may have to do with more than his personality."

Marino met my eyes. "Yeah, I'm thinking that."

"Fibers, pet hairs," I said. "He doesn't have to worry about transferring them."

"You ever thought it interesting that all of the abandoned vehicles in these cases was so clean?"

I had.

"Maybe he vacuums them after the crimes," he said.

"At a car wash?"

"A filling station, apartment complex, any place that has a

coin-operated car vacuum. The murders were committed late at night. By the time he stopped somewhere to vacuum the car afterward, there wouldn't be many people out to see what he was doing."

"Maybe. Who knows what he did?" I said. "But the picture we're getting is of someone who is obsessively neat and careful. Someone very paranoid and familiar with the types of evidence that are important in forensic examinations."

Leaning back in the chair, Marino said, "The Seven-Eleven where Deborah and Fred stopped the night they disappeared, I dropped by there over the weekend and talked to the clerk."

"Ellen Jordan?"

He nodded. "I showed her a photo lineup, asked her if anybody in it looked like the man who was buying coffee in the Seven-Eleven the night Fred and Deborah was in there. She picked out Spurrier."

"She was certain?"

"Yes. Said he was wearing a jacket of some sort, dark. All she really recalled was that the guy was in dark clothes, and I'm thinking Spurrier already had on a warm-up suit when he went inside the Seven-Eleven. I've been running a lot of things through my mind. We'll start with two things we do know for a fact. The interiors of the abandoned cars were very clean, and in the four cases before Deborah and Fred, white cotton fibers were recovered from the driver's seat, right?"

"Yes," I agreed.

"Okay. I think this squirrel was out cruising for victims and spotted Fred and Deborah on the road, maybe saw them sitting real close to each other, her head on Fred's shoulder, that sort of thing. It sets him off. He tails them, pulls into the Seven-Eleven right after they do. Maybe he slips into the warm-up suit at this time, changes in his car. Maybe he already has it on. But he goes inside, hangs around looking through magazines, buying coffee and listening to what they're saying to the clerk. He overhears the clerk giving Fred and Deborah directions to the nearest rest stop where there's a bathroom. Then he leaves, speeds east on Sixty-four, turns into the rest stop and parks. He gets his bag that's got his weapons, ligatures, gloves, and so on, and makes himself scarce until Deborah and Fred pull in. He probably waits until she's gone to use the ladies' room, then he approaches Fred, feeds him some story about his car breaking down or whatever. Maybe Spurrier says he was working out at the gym, on his way home, thus explaining why he's dressed the way he is."

"Fred wouldn't recognize him from the Seven-Eleven?"

"I doubt it," Marino said. "But it don't matter. Spurrier might have been bold enough to mention that, say he was just buying coffee at the Seven-Eleven, and his car conked out right after he left. He says he's just called a wrecker and wonders if Fred could give him a lift back to his car so he can wait for the wrecker, promises that his car isn't very far down the road, et cetera. Fred agrees, then Deborah reappears. Once Spurrier's inside the Cherokee, Fred and Deborah are his."

I remembered Fred described as helpful, generous. He

probably would have helped a stranger in distress, especially one as smooth and clean-cut as Steven Spurrier.

"When the Cherokee's back on the Interstate, Spurrier leans over and unzips his bag, puts on gloves, booties, and slips out his gun, points it at the back of Deborah's head . . ."

I thought of the bloodhound's reaction when he had sniffed the seat where it was believed Deborah had been sitting. What the dog had detected was her terror.

". . . He orders Fred to drive to the spot Spurrier's already picked in advance. By the time they stop on the logging road, Deborah's hands have probably already been tied behind her back. Her shoes and socks are off. Spurrier orders Fred to take off his shoes and socks, then binds his hands. Spurrier orders them out of the Cherokee and walks them into the woods. Maybe he's wearing night-vision goggles so he can see. He might have had those in his bag, too.

"Then he starts his game with them," Marino went on in a detached voice. "He takes out Fred first, then goes after Deborah. She resists, gets cut, and he shoots her. He drags their bodies to the clearing, positioning them side by side, her arm under his, like they was holding hands, holding on to each other. Spurrier smokes a few cigarettes, maybe sits out there in the dark by the bodies, enjoying the afterglow. Then he heads back to the Cherokee, takes off his warm-up, gloves, booties, puts them in a plastic bag he's got inside his gym bag. Maybe puts the kids' shoes and socks in the bag, too. He drives away, finds some deserted place with a coin-operated vacuum and cleans out the inside of the Cherokee, especially the driver's area where he's been sitting. All done, and he disposes of the trash bag, maybe in a Dumpster. I'm guessing he put something over the driver's seat at this point. Maybe a folded white sheet, a white towel in the first four cases—"

"Most athletic clubs," I interrupted, "have a linen service. They keep a supply of white towels in the locker rooms. If Spurrier does keep his murder kit in a locker somewhere—"

Marino cut me off. "Yeah, I'm reading you loud and clear. Damn. Maybe I'd better start working on that one pronto."

"A white towel would explain the white cotton fibers found," I added.

"Except he must have used something different with Deborah and Fred. Hell, who knows? Maybe he sat on a plastic trash bag this time. The point is, I'm thinking he sat on something so he didn't leave fibers from his clothes on the seat. Remember, he's not wearing the warm-up suit anymore, no way he would because it would be bloody. He drives off, dumps the Cherokee where we found it, and trots across the Interstate to the eastbound rest stop where his Lincoln's parked. He's out of there. Mission accomplished."

"There were probably a lot of cars in and out of the rest stop that night," I said. "No one was going to notice his Lincoln parked out there. But even if someone had, the tags wouldn't have come back to him because they were 'borrowed.'"

"Right. That's his last task, either returning the tags to the ride he stole them from or, if that isn't possible, just pitching them somewhere." He paused, rubbing his face in his hands.

"I've got a feeling Spurrier picked an MO early on and has pretty much stuck to it in all of the cases. He cruises, spots his victims, tails them, and knows he's hit pay dirt if they pull of at some place, a bar, a rest stop, where they're going to be long enough for him to get set up. Then he makes his approach, pulls something to make them trust him. Maybe he strikes only once for every fifty times he goes out cruising. But he's still getting off on it."

"The scenario seems plausible for the five recent cases," I said. "But I don't think it works quite as well for Jill and Elizabeth. If the Palm Leaf Motel was where he'd left his car, that was some five miles from the Anchor Bar and Grill."

"We don't know that Spurrier hooked up with them at the Anchor."

"I have a feeling he did."

Marino looked surprised. "Why?"

"Because the women had been in his bookstore before," I explained. "They were familiar with Spurrier, though I doubt they knew him very well. I'm guessing that he watched them when they came in to buy newspapers, books whatever. I suspect he sensed immediately that the two women were more than friends, and this pushed his button. He's obsessed with couples. Maybe he'd been contemplating his first killings, and he thought that two women would be easier than a man and a woman. He planned the crime long in advance, his fantasies fed every time Jill and Elizabeth came into his bookstore. He might have followed them, stalked them after hours, gone through a lot of dry runs.

practicing. He had already selected the wooded area out near where Mr. Joyce lives and probably was the person who shot the dog. Then one night he follows Jill and Elizabeth to the Anchor, and this is when he decides to do it. He leaves his car somewhere, heads to the bar on foot, his gym bag in hand."

"Are you thinking he went inside the bar and watched them while they drank beer?"

"No," I said. "I think he was too careful for that. I think he hung back, waited until they came out to get into the Volkswagen. Then I think Spurrier approached them and put on the same act. His car had broken down. He was the owner of the bookstore they frequented. They had no reason to fear him. He gets inside, and very soon after his plan begins to unravel. They don't end up in the wooded area, but at the cemetery. The women, Jill, in particular, aren't very cooperative."

"And he bleeds inside the Volkswagen," Marino said. "A nosebleed, maybe. Ain't no vacuum cleaner gonna get blood out of a seat or floor mat."

"I doubt he bothered to vacuum. Spurrier probably was panicking. He probably ditched the car as quickly as he could in the most convenient spot, which turned out to be the motel. As for where his car was parked, who knows? But I'm betting he was in for a little hike."

"Maybe the episode with the two women spooked him so bad he didn't try again for five years."

"I don't think that's it," I said. "Something's missing."

*

The telephone rang several weeks later when I was home alone working in my study. My recorded message had barely begun when the person hung up. The phone rang again half an hour later, and this time I answered before my machine. I said hello, and the line was disconnected again.

Perhaps someone was trying to reach Abby and did not want to talk to me? Perhaps Clifford Ring had discovered where she was? Distracted, I went to the refrigerator for a snack and settled on several slices of cheese.

I was back in my study paying bills when I heard a car pull in, gravel crunching beneath tires. I assumed it was Abby until the doorbell rang.

I looked through the peephole at Pat Harvey zipped up in a red windbreaker. The hang-ups, I thought. She had made certain I was home because she wanted to speak to me face-to-face.

She greeted me with "I'm sorry to impose," but I could tell she wasn't.

"Please come in," I said reluctantly.

She followed me to the kitchen, where I poured her a cup of coffee. She sat stiffly at the table, coffee mug cradled in her hands.

"I'm going to be very direct with you," she began. "It has come to my attention that this man they arrested in Williamsburg, Steven Spurrier, is believed to have murdered two women eight years ago."

"Where did you hear this?"

"That's not important. The cases were never solved and have now been linked to the murders of the five couples. The two women were Steven Spurrier's first victims."

I noticed that the lower lid of her left eye was twitching. Pat Harvey's physical deterioration since I had seen her last was shocking. Her auburn hair was lifeless; her eyes were dull; her skin was pale and drawn. She looked even thinner than she had been during her televised press conference.

"I'm not sure I'm following you," I said tensely.

"He inspired their trust and they made themselves vulnerable. Which is exactly what he did with the others, with my daughter, with Fred."

She said all this as if she knew it for a fact. Pat Harvey had convicted Spurrier in her mind.

"But he will never be punished for Debbie's murder," she said. "I know that now."

"It is too early to know anything," I replied calmly.

"They have no proof. What was found inside his house is not enough. It will not hold up in any court, if the cases ever go to court. You can't convict someone of capital murder just because you found newspaper clippings and surgical gloves inside his house, especially if the defense claims the evidence was planted to frame his client."

She had been talking to Abby, I thought with a sick feeling.

"The only evidence," she went on coldly, "is the blood found inside the women's car. It will all depend on DNA, and there will be questions because the cases occurred so long ago. The chain of custody, for example. Even if the prints match and the courts accept the evidence, there is no certainty that a jury will, especially since the police have yet to find the murder weapons."

"They're still looking."

"He's had plenty of time to dispose of those by now," she replied, and she was right.

Marino had discovered that Spurrier worked out at a gym not far from where he lived. The police had searched his rented locker, which not only locked with a key but had had a padlock on it. The locker was empty. The blue athletic bag Spurrier had been seen carrying around the gym had never been found, and never would be, I felt sure.

"What do you need from me, Mrs. Harvey?"

"I want you to answer my questions."

"Which questions?"

"If there is evidence I don't know about, I think you'd be wise to tell me."

"The investigation is not over. The police, the FBI are working very hard on your daughter's case."

She stared across the kitchen. "Are they talking to you?"

Instantly, I understood. No one directly involved in the investigation was giving Pat Harvey the time of day. She had become a pariah, perhaps even a joke. She was not going to admit this to me, but that's why she had appeared at my door.

"Do you believe Steven Spurrier murdered my daughter?"

"Why does my opinion matter?" I asked.

"It matters a great deal."

"Why?" I asked again.

"You don't form opinions lightly. I don't think you jump to conclusions or believe something just because you wish to. You're familiar with the evidence"—her voice trembled—"and you took care of Debbie."

I could not think of what to say.

"So I'll ask you again. Do you believe Steven Spurrier murdered them, murdered her?"

I hesitated, just for an instant, but it was enough. When I told her that I could not possibly answer such a question, and indeed, did not know the answer, she did not listen.

She got up from the table.

I watched her dissolve in the night, her profile briefly illuminated by the interior light of her Jaguar as she got in and drove away.

Abby did not come in until after I had given up waiting for her and had gone to bed. I slept fitfully and opened my eyes when I heard water running downstairs. I squinted at the clock. It was almost midnight. I got up and slipped into my robe.

She must have heard me in the hall, for when I reached her bedroom she was standing in the doorway, her pajamas a sweat suit, feet bare.

"You're up late," she said.

"So are you."

"Well, I . . ." She didn't finish her sentence as I walked inside her room and sat on the edge of the bed.

"What's up?" she asked uneasily.

"Pat Harvey came to see me earlier this evening, that's what's up. You've been talking to her."

"I've been talking to a lot of people."

"I know you want to help her," I said. "I know you've been

outraged by the way her daughter's death has been used to hurt her. Mrs. Harvey's a fine woman, and I think you genuinely care about her. But she needs to stay out of the investigation, Abby."

She looked at me without speaking.

"For her own good," I added empathically.

Abby sat down on the rug, crossing her legs Indian style, and leaned against the wall.

"What did she say to you?" she asked.

"She's convinced Spurrier murdered her daughter and will never be punished for it."

"I certainly had nothing to do with her reaching such a conclusion," she said. "Pat has a mind of her own."

"Spurrier's arraignment is Friday. Does she plan to be there?"

"It's just a petit larceny charge. But if you're asking if I'm worried Pat might appear and make a scene . . ." She shook her head. "No way. It would serve no purpose for her to show up. She's not an idiot, Kay."

"And you?"

"What? Am I an idiot?" She evaded me again.

"Will you be at the arraignment?"

"Sure. And I'll tell you exactly how it will go. He'll be in and out, will plead guilty to petit larceny and get slapped with a fifteen-hundred-dollar fine. And he's going to spend a little time in jail, maybe a month at most. The cops want him to sweat behind bars for a while, break him down so he'll talk."

"How do you know that?"

"He's not going to talk," she went on. "They're going to lead him out of the courthouse in front of everyone and shove him in the back of a patrol car. It's all meant to scare and humiliate him, but it won't work. He knows they don't have enough on him. He'll bide his time in jail, then be out. A month isn't forever."

"You sound as if you feel sorry for him."

"I don't feel anything for him," she said. "Spurrier was into recreational cocaine, according to his attorney, and the night the cops caught him stealing the license tags, he was planning to make a buy. Spurrier was afraid some drug dealer would turn out to be a snitch, record his plate number, maybe give it to the cops. That's the explanation for the stolen tags."

"You can't believe that," I said heatedly.

Abby straightened out her legs, wincing a little. Without saying a word, she stood up and walked out of the room. I followed her to the kitchen, my frustration mounting. As she began to fill a glass with ice, I placed my hands on her shoulders and turned her around until we were face-to-face.

"Are you listening to me?"

Her eyes softened. "Please don't be angry with me. What I'm doing has nothing to do with you, with our friendship."

"What *friendship*? I feel as if I don't even know you anymore. You leave money around my house as if I'm nothing more than the damn maid. I don't remember the last time we ate a meal together. You never talk to me. You're so obsessed with this damn book. You see what's happened to

Pat Harvey. Can't you see that the same thing is happening to you?"

Abby just stared at me.

"It's as if you've made up your mind about something," I continued to plead with her. "Why won't you tell me what it is?"

"There's nothing to make up my mind about," she said quietly, pulling away from me. "Everything's already been decided."

Fielding called early Saturday morning to say there were no autopsies, and exhausted, I went back to bed. It was mid-morning when I got up. After a long, hot shower I was ready to deal with Abby and see if we could somehow repair our damaged relationship.

But when I went downstairs and knocked on her door, there was no answer, and when I went out to get the paper I saw her car was gone. Irritated that she had managed to avoid me again, I put on a pot of coffee.

I was sipping my second cup when a small headline caught my attention:

WILLIAMSBURG MAN GIVEN
SUSPENDED SENTENCE

Steven Spurrier had not been cuffed and hauled off to jail following his arraignment the day before as Abby had predicted, I read, horrified. He pleaded guilty to petit larceny, and because he had no prior record and had always been a law-abiding citizen of Williamsburg, he was fined one thousand dollars and had walked out of the courthouse a free man.

Everything's already been decided, Abby had said.

Is this what she had been referring to? If she knew Spurrier would be released, why would she deliberately mislead me?

I left the kitchen and opened the door to her room. The bed was made, curtains drawn. Inside the bath, I noticed drops of water in the sink and the faint scent of perfume. She had not been gone long. I looked for her briefcase and tape recorder, but could not find them. Her .38 was not in its drawer. I went through dressers until I found her notepads, hidden beneath clothes.

Sitting on the edge of the bed, I frantically flipped through them. I streaked through her days and weeks as the meaning became clearer.

What had begun as Abby's crusade to discover the truth about the couples' murders had turned into her own ambitious obsession. She seemed fascinated by Spurrier. If he was guilty, she was determined to make his story the focus of her book, to explore his psychopathic mind. If he was innocent, it would be "another Gainesville," she wrote, referring to the spree murders of university students in which a suspect became a household name and later turned out to be innocent. "Only it would be worse than Gainesville," she added. "Because of what the card implies."

Initially, Spurrier had repeatedly denied Abby's requests for interviews. Then late last week, she had tried again and he had picked up the phone. He had suggested they meet after the arraignment, telling her his attorney had "made a deal."

"He said he had read my stories in the *Post* over the years," Abby had scribbled, "and had recalled my byline from when I was in Richmond. He remembered what I had written about Jill and Elizabeth, too, and remarked that they were 'nice girls' and he'd always hoped the cops would get the 'psycho.' He also knew about my sister, said he'd read about her murder. That's the reason he finally agreed to talk to me, he said. He 'felt' for me, said he realized I understood what it was like to 'be a victim,' because what happened to my sister made me a victim, too.

"'I am a victim,' he said. 'We can talk about that. Maybe you can help me better understand what that's all about.'

"He suggested I come to his house Saturday morning at eleven, and I agreed, providing all interviews are exclusive. He said that was fine, he had no intention of talking to anybody else as long as I told his side. 'The truth,' as he put it. Thank you, Lord! Screw you and your book, Cliff. You lose."

Cliff Ring was writing a book about these cases, too. Dear Lord. No wonder Abby had been acting so odd.

She had lied when she had told me what was going to happen at Spurrier's arraignment. She did not want me to suspect that she planned to go to his house, and she knew such a thought would never occur to me if I assumed he would be in jail. I remembered her saying that she no longer trusted anyone. She didn't, not even me.

I glanced at my watch. It was eleven-fifteen.

Marino wasn't in, so I left a message on his pager. Then I called the Williamsburg police, and the phone rang forever before a secretary answered. I told her I needed to speak to one of the detectives immediately.

"They're all out on the street right now."

"Then let me speak to whoever's in."

She transferred me to a sergeant.

Identifying myself, I said, "You know who Steven Spurrier is."

"Can't work around here and not know that."

"A reporter is interviewing him at his house. I'm alerting you so you can make sure your surveillance teams know she's there, make sure everything's all right."

There was a long pause. Paper crinkled. It sounded as if the sergeant was eating something. Then, "Spurrier's not under surveillance anymore."

"I beg your pardon?"

"I said our guys have been pulled off."

"Why?" I demanded.

"Now, that I don't know, Doc, been on vacation for the past—"

"Look, all I'm asking is you send a car by his house, make sure everything's all right." It was all I could do not to scream at him.

"Don't you worry about a thing." His voice was as calm as a mill pond. "I'll pass it along."

I hung up as I heard a car pull in.

Abby, thank God.

But when I looked out the window, it was Marino.

I opened the front door before he could ring the bell.

"Was in the area when I got your message on the beeper, so I—"

"Spurrier's house!" I grabbed his arm. "Abby's there! She's got her gun!"

The sky had turned dark and it was raining as Marino and I sped east on 64. Every muscle in my body was rigid. My heart would not slow down.

"Hey, relax," Marino said as we turned off at the Colonial Williamsburg exit. "Whether the cops are watching him or not, he ain't stupid enough to touch her. Really, you know that. He ain't going to do that."

There was only one vehicle in sight when we turned onto Spurrier's quiet street.

"Shit," Marino muttered under his breath.

Parked on the street in front of Spurrier's house was a black Jaguar.

"Pat Harvey," I said. "Oh, God."

He slammed on the brakes.

"Stay here." He was out of the car as if he had been ejected, running up the driveway in the pouring rain. My heart was pounding as he pushed the front door open with his foot, revolver in hand, and disappeared inside.

The doorway was empty when suddenly he filled it again. He stared in my direction, yelling something I could not hear.

I got out of the car, rain soaking my clothes as I ran.

I smelled the burnt gunpowder the instant I entered the foyer.

"I've called for help," Marino said, eyes darting around. "Two of them are in there."

The living room was to the left.

He was hurrying up the stairs leading to the second story as photographs of Spurrier's house crazily flashed in my mind. I recognized the glass coffee table and saw the revolver on top of it. Blood was pooled on the bare wood floor beneath Spurrier's body, a second revolver several feet away. He was face down, inches from the gray leather couch where Abby lay on her side. She stared at the cushion beneath her cheek through drowsy, dull eyes, the front of her pale blue blouse soaked bright red.

For an instant I didn't know what to do, the roaring inside my head as loud as a windstorm. I squatted beside Spurrier, blood spilling and seeping around my shoes as I rolled him over. He was dead, shot through the abdomen and chest.

I hurried to the couch and felt Abby's neck. There was no pulse. I turned her on her back and started CPR, but her heart and lungs had given up too long ago to remember what they were supposed to do. Holding her face in my hands, I felt her warmth and smelled her perfume as sobs welled up and shook me uncontrollably.

Footsteps on the hardwood floor did not register until I realized they were too light to be Marino's. I looked up as Pat Harvey lifted the revolver off the coffee table.

I stared wide-eyed at her, my lips parting.

"I'm sorry." The revolver shook as she pointed it in my direction.

"Mrs. Harvey." My voice stuck in my throat, hands frozen in front of me, stained with Abby's blood. "Please . . ."

"Just stay there." She backed up several steps, lowering the gun a little. For some bizarre reason it occurred to me she was wearing the same red windbreaker she had worn to my house.

"Abby's dead," I said.

Pat Harvey didn't react, her face ashen, eyes so dark they looked black. "I tried to find a phone. He doesn't have any phones."

"Please put the gun down."

"He did it. He killed my Debbie. He killed Abby."

Marino, I thought. *Oh, God, hurry!*

"Mrs. Harvey, it's over. They're dead. Please put the gun down. Don't make it worse."

"It can't be worse."

"That's not true. Please listen to me."

"I can't be here anymore," she said in the same flat tone.

"I can help you. Put the gun down. Please," I said, getting up from the couch as she raised the gun again.

"No," I begged, realizing what she was going to do.

She pointed the muzzle at her chest as I lunged toward her.

"*Mrs. Harvey! No!*"

The explosion knocked her back and she staggered, dropping the revolver. I kicked it away and it spun slowly, heavily, across the smooth wood floor as her legs buckled. She reached for something to hold on to, but nothing was there. Marino was suddenly in the room, exclaiming, "Holy shit!" He held his revolver in both hands, muzzle pointed at the ceiling. Ears ringing, I was trembling all over as I knelt beside Pat Harvey. She lay on her side, knees drawn, clutching her chest.

"Get towels!" I moved her hands out of the way and fumbled with her clothing. Untucking her blouse and pushing up her brassiere, I pressed bunched cloth against the wound below her left breast. I could hear Marino cursing as he rushed out of the room.

"Hold on," I whispered, applying pressure so the small hole would not suck in air and collapse the lung.

She was squirming and began to groan.

'Hold on," I repeated as sirens wailed from the street.

Red light pulsed through blinds covering the living-room windows, as if the world outside Steven Spurrier's house were on fire.

18

Marino drove me home and did not leave. I sat in my kitchen staring out at the rain, only vaguely aware of what was going on around me. The doorbell rang, and I heard footsteps and male voices.

Later, Marino came into the kitchen and pulled out a chair across from me. He perched on the edge of it as if he wasn't planning to sit long.

"Any other places in the house Abby might have put her things, beside her bedroom?" he asked.

"I don't think so," I murmured.

"Well, we've got to look. I'm sorry, Doc."

"I understand."

He followed my gaze out the window.

"I'll make coffee." He got up. "We'll see if I remember what you taught me. My first quiz, huh?"

He moved about in the kitchen, cabinet doors opening and

shutting, water running as he filled the pot. He walked out while coffee dripped, and moments later was back with another detective.

"This won't take very long, Dr. Scarpetta," the detective said. "Appreciate your cooperation."

He said something in a low voice to Marino. Then he left and Marino returned to the table, setting a cup of coffee in front of me.

"What are they looking for?" I tried to concentrate.

"We're going through the notebooks you told me about. Looking for tapes, anything that might tell us what led up to Mrs. Harvey shooting Spurrier.

"You're sure she did it."

"Oh, yeah. Mrs. Harvey did it. Damn miracle she's alive. She missed her heart. She was lucky, but maybe she won't think so if she pulls through."

"I called the Williamsburg police. I told them—"

"I know you did." He cut me off gently. "You did the right thing. You did all you could."

"They couldn't be bothered." I closed my eyes, fighting the tears.

"That wasn't it." He paused. "Listen to me, Doc."

I took a deep breath.

Marino cleared his throat and lit a cigarette. "While I was back there in your office, I talked to Benton. The FBI completed the DNA analysis of Spurrier's blood and compared it with the blood found in Elizabeth Mott's car. The DNA don't match."

"What?"

"The DNA don't match," he said again. "The detectives in Williamsburg who had been tailing Spurrier were just told yesterday. Benton had been trying to get hold of me and we kept missing each other, so I didn't know. You understand what I'm saying?"

I stared numbly at him.

"Legally, Spurrier was no longer a suspect. A pervert, yeah. We're talking the land of fruits and nuts. But he didn't murder Elizabeth and Jill. He didn't leave the blood in the car, couldn't have. If he killed these other couples, we've got no proof. To keep tailing him all the hell over the place, watching his house or banging on his door because they see he's got company, was harassment. Well, I mean there comes a point when there aren't enough cops to keep that up, and Spurrier could sue. And the FBI had backed off. So that's the way it went."

"He killed Abby."

Marino looked away from me. "Yeah, it appears so. She had her tape recorder running, we got the whole thing on tape. But that don't prove he killed the couples, Doc. It's looking like Mrs. Harvey gunned down an innocent man."

"I want to hear the tape."

"You don't want to hear it. Take my word for it."

"If Spurrier was *innocent*, then why did he shoot Abby?"

"I got an idea, based on what I heard on the tape and saw at the scene," he said. "Abby and Spurrier was talking in the living room. Abby was sitting on the couch where we found her. Spurrier heard someone at the door and got up to answer it. I don't know why he let Pat Harvey in. You

would think he would have recognized her, but maybe he
didn't. She had on a windbreaker with a hood, and jeans.
Might have been hard to tell who she was. No way to know
how she identified herself, what she said to him. We won't
know until we can talk to her, and even then we might not
know."

"But he let her in."

"He opened the door," Marino said. "Then she had her
revolver out, a Charter Arms, the one she later shot herself
with. Mrs. Harvey forced him back inside the house, into
the living room. Abby's still sitting there, and the tape
recorder's still running. Since Abby's Saab was out back in
the drive, Mrs. Harvey wouldn't have seen it when she
parked in front. She had no idea Abby was there, and this
diverted her attention long enough for Spurrier to go for
Abby, probably to use her as a shield. Hard to know exactly
what went down, but we know Abby had her revolver with
her, probably in her purse, which was probably next to her
on the couch. She tries to get out her gun, she and Spurrier
struggle and she gets shot. Then, before he can shoot Mrs.
Harvey, she shoots him. Twice. We checked her revolver.
Three spent shells, two live."

"She said something about looking for a phone," I said
dully.

"Spurrier's only got two phones. One in his bedroom
upstairs, the other in the kitchen, same color as the wall and
between two cabinets, hard as shit to see. I almost didn't find
it either. It looks like we rolled up to the house maybe minutes after the shootings, Doc. I think Mrs. Harvey set her gun

on the coffee table when she went over to Abby, saw how bad
it was and tried to find a phone to call for help. Mrs. Harvey
must have been in another room when I walked in, maybe
heard me and ducked out of sight. All I know is when I went
in, I scanned the immediate area. All I saw was the bodies in
the living room, checked their carotids and thought Abby had
a faint pulse, but I wasn't sure. I had a choice, had to make a
split-second decision. I could start searching Spurrier's crib for
Mrs. Harvey, or get you and then look. I mean, I didn't see her
when I first came in. I thought she might have gone out the
back door or upstairs," he said, obviously distressed he'd put
me in jeopardy.

"I want to hear the tape," I said again.

Marino rubbed his face in his hands, his eyes bleary and
bloodshot when he looked back at me. "Don't put yourself
through it."

"I have to."

Reluctantly, he got up from the table and left. When he
returned, he opened a plastic evidence bag that contained a
microcassette recorder. He set it upright on the table, briefly
rewound a portion of the tape, and depressed the Play button.

The sound of Abby's voice filled the kitchen.

". . . I'm just trying to see your side of it, but that doesn't
really explain why you drive around at night, stop and ask
people things that you don't really need to know. Such as
directions."

"Look, I already told you about the coke. You ever snorted
coke?"

"No."

"Try it some time. You do a lot of off-the-wall things when you're high. You get confused and think you know where you're going. Then suddenly you're lost and have to ask directions."

"You said you're not doing coke anymore."

"Not anymore. No way. My big mistake. Never again."

"What about the items the police found in your house . . . ? Uh . . ." There was the faint chime of a doorbell.

"Yeah. Hold on." Spurrier sounded tense.

Footsteps receded. Voices were indistinguishable in the background. I could hear Abby shifting on the couch. Then Spurrier's disbelieving voice: "Wait. You don't know what you're—"

"I know exactly what I'm doing, you bastard." It was Pat Harvey's voice, increasing in volume. "That was my daughter you took out into the woods."

"I don't know what you're—"

"Pat. Don't!"

A pause.

"Abby? Oh my God."

"Pat. Don't do it, Pat." Abby's voice was tight with fear. She gasped as something hit the couch. "Get away from me!" A commotion, rapid breathing, and Abby screaming, "Stop! Stop!" then what sounded like a cap gun going off.

Again and again.

Silence.

Footsteps clicked across the floor and got louder. They stopped.

"Abby?"

395

A pause.

"Please don't die. *Abby* . . ." Pat Harvey's voice was quavering so badly I could barely hear it.

Marino reached for the recorder, turned if off, and slipped it back inside the plastic bag as I stared at him in shock.

On the Saturday morning of Abby's graveside service, I waited until the crowd had thinned, then walked along a footpath beneath the shade of magnolias and oaks, dogwoods blazing fuchsia and white in the gentle spring sun.

The turnout for Abby's funeral had been small. I met several of her former Richmond colleagues and tried to comfort her parents. Marino came. So did Mark, who hugged me tight, then left with the promise he would come by my house later in the day. I needed to talk with Benton Wesley, but first I wanted a few moments alone.

Hollywood Cemetery was Richmond's most formidable city for the dead, some forty acres of rolling hills, streams, and stands of hardwood trees north of the James River. Curving streets were paved and named, with speed limits posted, the sloping grass crowded with granite obelisks, headstones, and angels of grief, many of them more than a century old. Buried here were Presidents James Monroe and John Tyler, and Jefferson Davis, and tobacco magnate Lewis Ginter. There was a soldiers' section for the Gettysburg dead, and a family plot of low-lying lawn where Abby had been buried beside her sister, Henna.

I drew upon a break in the trees, the river below

glimmering like tarnished copper, muddy from recent rains. It did not seem possible that Abby was now part of this population, a granite marker weathering passing time. I wondered if she had ever gone back to her former house, to Henna's room upstairs as she had told me she intended to do when she could find the courage.

When I heard footsteps behind me, I turned to find Wesley walking slowly in my direction.

"You wanted to talk to me, Kay?"

I nodded.

He slipped off his dark suit jacket and loosened his tie. Staring out at the river, he waited to hear what was on my mind.

"There are some new developments," I began. "I called Gordon Spurrier on Thursday."

"The brother?" Wesley replied, looking at me curiously.

"Steven Spurrier's brother, yes. I didn't want to tell you about it until I'd looked into several other things."

"I haven't talked to him yet," he stated. "But he's on my list. Just a damn shame about the DNA results, that's still a major problem."

"That's my point. There isn't a problem with the DNA, Benton."

"I don't understand."

"During Spurrier's autopsy, I discovered a lot of old therapeutic scars, one of them from a small incision made above the middle of the collarbone that I associate with someone having trouble getting in a subclavian line," I said.

"Meaning?"

"You don't run a subclavian line unless the patient has a serious problem, trauma requiring the dumping of fluids very quickly, an infusion of drugs or blood. In other words, I knew Spurrier had a significant medical problem at some point in the past, and I began contemplating that this might have something to do with the five months he was absent from his bookstore not long after Elizabeth and Jill were murdered. There were other scars, too, over his hip and lateral buttock. Minute scars that made me suspect he'd had samples of bone marrow taken before. So I called his brother to find out about Steven's medical history."

"What did you learn?"

"Around the time he disappeared from his bookstore, Steven was treated for aplastic anemia at UVA," I said. "I've talked with his hematologist. Steven received total lymphoid irradiation, chemotherapy. Gordon's marrow was infused into Steven, and Steven then spent time in a laminar flow room, or a bubble, as most people call it. You may recall Steven's house was like a bubble, in a sense. Very sterile."

"Are you saying that the bone-marrow transplant changed his DNA?" Wesley asked, his face intense.

"For blood, yes. His blood cells had been totally wiped out by his aplastic anemia. He was HLA-typed for a suitable match, which turned out to be his brother, whose ABO type and even types in other blood group systems are the same."

"But Steven's and Gordon's DNA wouldn't be the same."

"No, not unless the brothers are identical twins, which, of

course, they aren't," I said. "So Steven's blood type was consistent with the blood recovered from Elizabeth Mott's car. But at the level of DNA a discernible difference would have been noticed because Steven left the blood in the Volkswagen before his marrow transplant. When Steven's blood was recently taken for the suspect kit, what we were getting, in a sense, was Gordon's blood. What was actually compared with the DNA print of the old blood from the Volkswagen was not Steven's DNA, but Gordon's."

"Incredible," he said.

"I want the test run again on tissue from his brain because Steven's DNA in other cells will be the same as it was before the transplant. Marrow produces blood cells, so if you've had a marrow transplant you take on the blood cells of the donor. But brain, spleen, sperm cells don't change."

"Explain aplastic anemia to me," he said as we started walking.

"Your marrow is no longer making anything. It's as if you've already been irradiated, all blood cells wiped out."

"What causes it?"

"It's felt to be idiopathic; nobody really knows. But possibilities are exposure to pesticides, chemicals, radiation, organic phosphates. Significantly, benzene has been associated with aplastic anemia. Steven had worked at a printing press. Benzene is a solvent used to clean printing presses and other machinery. He was exposed to it, so his hematologist said, on a daily basis for almost a year."

"And the symptoms?"

"Fatigue, shortness of breath, fever, possibly infections, and bleeding from the gums and nose. Spurrier was already suffering from aplastic anemia when Jill and Elizabeth were murdered. He may have been having nosebleeds, which would have occurred with very little provocation. Stress always makes everything worse, and he would have been under a great deal of stress while abducting Elizabeth and Jill. If his nose had started bleeding, that would explain the blood in the back of Elizabeth's car."

"When did he finally go to the doctor?" Wesley asked.

"A month after the women were murdered. During his examination, it was discovered that his white count was low, his platelets and hemoglobin low. When your platelets are low you bleed a lot."

"He committed murders while he was that sick?"

"You can have aplastic anemia for a while before it becomes severe," I said. "Some people simply find out during a routine physical."

"Poor health and losing control of his first victims were enough to make him retreat," he thought out loud. "Years went by as he recovered and fantasized, reliving the murders and improving his techniques. Eventually, he was confident enough to start killing again."

"That could explain the long interval. But who knows what went through his mind."

"We'll never really know that," Wesley said grimly.

He paused to study an ancient grave marker before speaking again. "I have some news, too. There's a company in New York, a spy shop whose catalogs were found in Spurrier's house. After some tracking we've ascertained that four years ago he ordered a pair of night-vision goggles from them. In addition, we've located a gun store in Portsmouth where he purchased two boxes of Hydra-Shok cartridges less than a month before Deborah and Fred disappeared."

"Why did he do it, Benton?" I asked. "Why did he kill?"

"I can never answer that satisfactorily, Kay. But I've talked with his former roommate at WA, who indicated that Spurrier's relationship with his mother was unhealthy. She was very critical and controlling, belittled him constantly. He was dependent on her and at the same time probably hated her."

"What about the victimology?"

"I think he spotted young women who reminded him of what he couldn't have, the girls who had never given him the time of day. When he saw an attractive couple, it set him off because he was incapable of relationships. He took possession through murder, fused himself with and overpowered what he envied." Pausing, he added, "If you and Abby hadn't encountered him when you did, I'm not sure we would have gotten him. Scary how it works. Bundy gets pulled because a tail-light's out. Son of Sam gets nailed because of a parking ticket. Luck. We were lucky."

I didn't feel lucky. Abby hadn't been lucky.

"You might find it interesting to know that since all of this has been in the news we've received a lot of phone calls from people claiming someone who fits Spurrier's description approached them outside bars, at service stations, convenience stores. It's been reported that on one occasion he actually got a ride with a couple. He claimed his car had broken down. The kids dropped him off. No problem."

"Did he approach only young male-female couples during these dry runs?" I asked.

"Not always. Thus explaining how you and Abby fit that night he stopped to ask directions. Spurrier loved the risk, the fantasy, Kay. The killing was, in a sense, incidental to the game he was playing."

"I still don't completely understand why the CIA was so worried the killer might be from Camp Peary," I told him.

He paused, draping his suit jacket over his other arm.

"It was more than the MO, the jack of hearts," he said. "The police recovered a plastic computerized gas card in the back of Jim and Bonnie's car, on the floor under the seat. It was assumed the card had inadvertently fallen out of the killer's pocket, a jacket pocket, maybe a shirt pocket, while he was abducting the couple."

"And?"

"The company name on the gas card was Syn-Tron. After some tracking the account came back to Viking Exports. Viking Exports is a cover for Camp Peary. The gas card is issued to Camp Peary personnel for their use at the pumps on base."

"Interesting," I said. "Abby referred to a card in one of her notepads. I assumed she was referring to the jack of hearts. She knew about the gas card, didn't she, Benton?"

"I suspect Pat Harvey told her. Mrs. Harvey had known about the card for quite a while, thus explaining her accusations during the press conference that something was being covered up by the feds."

"Obviously, she no longer believed that when she decided to kill Spurrier."

"The Director briefed her after the press conference, Kay. Had no choice but to inform her that we were suspicious the gas card was left deliberately. We were suspicious from the beginning but that didn't mean we couldn't take it seriously. Obviously, the CIA took it very seriously."

"And this silenced her."

"If nothing else it made her think twice. Certainly, after Spurrier was arrested, what the Director had said to her made a lot of sense."

"How could Spurrier have gotten hold of a Camp Peary gas card?" I puzzled.

"Camp Peary agents frequented his bookstore."

"You're saying that he somehow stole this card from a Camp Peary customer?"

"Yes. Suppose someone from Camp Peary walked out of the bookstore leaving his wallet on the counter. By the time he came back looking for it, Spurrier could have tucked it away, said he hadn't seen it. Then he left the gas card in Jim and Bonnie's car so we would link the killings to the CIA."

"No identification number on the card?"

"The ID numbers are on stickers that had been peeled off, so we couldn't trace the card back to an individual."

I was getting tired and my feet were beginning to hurt when the parking area where we had left our cars came into view. Those who had come to mourn Abby's death were gone.

Wesley waited until I was unlocking my car before touching my arm and saying, "I'm sorry for those times . . ."

"So am I." I didn't let him finish. "We go on from here,

Benton. Do whatever you can to make sure Pat Harvey isn't punished further."

"I don't think a grand jury will have a problem under-standing how she's suffered."

"Did she know about the DNA results, Benton?"

"She's had a way of finding out details critical to the inves-tigation, despite our efforts to keep them from her, Kay. I suspect she knew. Certainly, it would help explain why she did what she did. She would have believed Spurrier was never going to be punished."

I got in and put the key in the ignition.

"I'm sorriest about Abby," he added.

I nodded as I shut the door, my eyes filling with tears.

I followed the narrow road to the cemetery's entrance, pass-ing through elaborate wrought-iron gates. The sun shone on downtown office buildings and steeples in the distance, light caught in the trees. I opened the windows and drove west toward home.

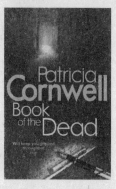

The 'book of the dead' is the morgue log, the ledger in which all cases are entered by hand. For Kay Scarpetta, however, it is about to have a new meaning.

Fresh from her bruising battle with a psychopath in Florida, Scarpetta decides it's time for a change of pace. Moving to the historic city of Charleston, South Carolina, she opens a unique private forensic pathology practice, one in which she and her colleagues offer expert crime scene investigation and autopsies to communities lacking local access to competent death investigation and modern technology. It seems like an ideal situation, until the murders and other violent deaths begin.

A woman is ritualistically murdered in her multi-million-dollar beach home. The body of an abused young boy is found dumped in a desolate marsh. A sixteen-year-old tennis star is found nude and mutilated near Piazza Navona in Rome.

Scarpetta has dealt with many brutal and unusual crimes before, but never a string of them as baffling, or as terrifying, as the ones before her now. Before she is through, that book of the dead will contain many names — and the pen may be poised to write her own.

'Patricia Cornwell is the queen of gritty, grisly, crime fiction writing and her latest offering doesn't disappoint. *Book of the Dead* will keep you gripped throughout' *Heat*

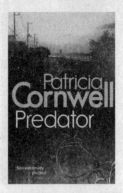

Florida is full of human predators from the animals who thrive in its humid heat to the humans that stalk the air-conditioned malls, and they all give Dr Kay Scarpetta the opportunity and the means to do what she does best – persuading the dead to speak to her.

In the icy chill of Boston, Benton Wesley is working on a secret project involving convicted killers. It is a project which gives Scarpetta deep disquiet, as does the behaviour of her niece, Lucy, who is spending too much time in cheap bars looking for casual pick-ups.

The Academy is called when a woman's body is found in Boston. She has been tortured, sexually abused, her body tattooed with handprints. The same sort of handprints Lucy had seen on the flesh of her latest pick-up . . .

'Sensationally plotted, with a twist at the end that will leave you gasping for breath'
Daily Express

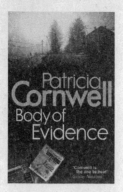

A reclusive writer is dead. And her final manuscript has disappeared ...

Someone is stalking Beryl Madison. Spying on her and making threatening, obscene phone calls. Terrified, Beryl flees to Key West – but on the very night she returns to her Richmond home, Beryl inexplicably invites her killer in.

Now Dr Kay Scarpetta must take on a case that is as convoluted as it is bizarre. Why would Beryl open the door to someone who brutally slashed and then nearly decapitated her? Did she know her killer? Adding to the intrigue is Beryl's enigmatic relationship with a prize-winning author and the disappearance of her own manuscript.

As Scarpetta retraces Beryl's footsteps, an investigation that begins in the laboratory with microscopes and lasers leads her deep into a nightmare that soon becomes her own.

'A great writer ... read these books only in broad daylight'
Daily Mail

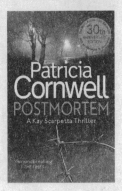

A serial killer is on the loose in Richmond, Virginia. Three women have died, brutalised and strangled in their own bedroom. There is no pattern: the killer appears to strike at random – but always early on Saturday mornings.

So when Dr Kay Scarpetta, chief medical officer, is awakened at 2.33 am, she knows the news is bad: there is a fourth victim. And she fears now for those that will follow unless she can dig up new forensic evidence to aid the police.

But not everyone is pleased to see a woman in this powerful job. Someone may even want to ruin her career and reputation . . .

'Terrific first novel, full of suspense, in which even the scientific bits grip' *The Times*

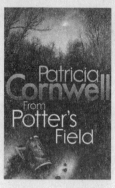

It's Christmas and a naked body is discovered in Central Park ...

Although a holiday for most, the festivities always seem to heighten the alienation felt by society's criminals; and that usually means more work for Dr Kay Scarpetta, Virginia's Chief Medical Examiner and consulting forensic pathologist for the FBI.

The body is found propped against a fountain in a bleak area of New York's Central Park. The unknown female's apparent manner of death points to a modus operandi that is chillingly familiar: the gunshot wound to the head, the sections of skin excised from the body, the displayed corpse – all suggest that Temple Brooks Gault, Scarpetta's nemesis, is back at work.

Calling on all her reserves of courage and skill, and the able assistance of colleagues Marino and Wesley, Scarpetta must track this most dangerous of killers, in pursuit of survival as well as justice – heading inexorably to an electrifying climax amid the dark, menacing labyrinths of the New York subway.

'Cornwell is on magnificent form' *Evening Standard*